Niki Hill is a journalist and broadcaster who was born and brought up in Northern Ireland. She is editor of the Women's News Letter, Belfast, won the Glenfiddich Award for Excellence in Food Writing. This is her first novel.

Niki Hill

DEATH GROWS ON YOU

Paladin

An Imprint of HarperCollins*Publishers*

Paladin
An Imprint of HarperCollins*Publishers*
77–85 Fulham Palace Road,
Hammersmith, London W6 8JB

Published by Paladin 1992
9 8 7 6 5 4 3 2 1

First published in Great Britain by
Michael Joseph Ltd 1990

ISBN 0-586-09133-5

Printed in Great Britain by
HarperCollinsManufacturing Glasgow

Set in Electra

For Pom, chocolate bars and thrillers

Chapter 1

REPORT FROM PATROL CAR Tango India delta one four zero four for Sergeant McEvoy Donegall Pass Station Belfast timed at twenty two thirty November twenty one.

Subject Mrs Annabelle Johnston not available for questioning. Whereabouts unknown by other occupant of house Miss Anne Rooney. Ends.

It had been that last bit of road which had made her realise what she had done, what she had given up, what she had succumbed to, that last stretch of road on the long hill up to the beginning of the rectory wall, the banks on either side topped with fir trees which had grown together over the road linking branches in an embrace of darkness even in high summer sunshine, which now by the lights of her car loomed darker and deeper than ever before. Childhood fears were of no substance now, yet she was glad when she was out on the road beyond, between wiry hedges, straggled bare trees. Now the sky was an open space above her.

She passed the rectory wall, the wrought-iron gates, a shorter piece of wall, then more hedgerow, and still the road wound downwards ahead of her. Another corner, maybe two, she couldn't quite remember, for she blinked, her eyes filling with tears. I'm just tired, she told herself, peering through the windscreen.

Then the gateposts came up in the headlights as the road

swung away on another bend. They were round, grey and fat, only the urns were missing off the tops, but then they always had been, even in her grandfather's time. Tonight she saw how the rhododendrons had clothed them thickly all about, and how the elegant railings on either side were rusted.

The gates stood open and hardly slowing she drove in, feeling the unevenness of the surface. She followed the drive in her mind, past the long line of sentinel pines that started on the left, just by the gates, past the single chestnut tree now bare, its branches nearly touching the ground, one branch where she and her brother had always slung their swing, past the gate to the orchard and the vegetable garden high-hedged about with laurel. To her right was the lawn that spread across the front of the house. A hundred days of childhood fell into place as she passed, of discovery, sorrow and momentary happiness.

She drove into the yard at the back hardly realising that she had not looked at the house at all. Its bulk loomed up reassuringly, but as with an old friend, once remembered and met again, she was half afraid to look, to see how time had passed on its features.

The garage doors were open ahead of her, the garage which was the last in a solid row of outhouses and stables that ran along the back of the house, the yard a strip in between. She drove the car up the slight slope, in a rush, and jammed on the brakes at the last moment. The whitewashed walls at the end flared up in the headlights. She pulled the handbrake on with a jerk.

She sighed. The boys were curled up behind her in the back seat. Rory had striven to stay awake, sitting up straight in the front seat beside her for almost all the way, straining in the dark, reading off the signposts as they passed, asking where they were, how much further there was to go, serious for his eleven years. But the road had proved too long, and he had scrambled into the back seat with Conor, three years younger, his arms about him, the younger boy's face sticky and flushed with sleep, Rory's tight with tiredness.

The last ten miles, once she had left Armagh, had been easy, though the road twisted and turned through the countryside. She had picked off the childhood signs one by one as they had showed up in the headlights: the red barn, corrugated, curved, still red after all her daily travelling on the school bus to and from

Armagh; Larch Hill with its long drive of chestnuts that flamed in autumn; Logue's Corner, the bus stop for the station; the bank under three beech trees where they found white violets in spring; and the long pull up through the pine hollow to the top of the rectory hill. That was all behind her now.

'Are we here?' Rory asked, opening his eyes instantly as if he had not been asleep at all.

'Yes, we're here,' she answered, her voice not quite steady.

She opened the car door and stepped out, feeling the cobblestones under her feet. The back door of the house loomed up in the reflected light of the headlamps. And beside it there was a square chequerboard of brightness through the kitchen window, a square too on the cobbles. The key to the door would be under the quern stone beside it, she knew instinctively, and when she walked stiffly across the yard to the door and stooped to the round flat stone, lifting the edge, feeling the damp stones underneath, the key was there.

It was then, looking back across the yard to the pools of the car's lights that the first doubts, black fears, crept up on her. She slotted the key into the lock, turned it and felt the door open, the rush of warm musty air, the light. She stepped briskly to the car, opening the driver's door wide and pushing the front seat forward so that she could gather Conor into her arms. His breath was hot on her cheeks, the Connemara rug hairy and warm underneath and around him. He seemed as if made of rubber, softened in his sleep.

'Mama,' he murmured, his eyes half opening.

'Yes,' was all she said.

Inside the door she set him down and he staggered on his feet, blinking, staring at this unfamiliar room, the kitchen, sparsely furnished, red-tiled, with a range monumental in an alcove.

Rory was behind her, pushing suddenly with a suitcase which he had lumbered out of the boot of the car. 'Come on, Ma,' he said, 'there's more!'

As if she didn't know, had not packed all those possessions of another life, another place, into the small space allotted in the car. It was only a Mini. A roof-rack thrust on at the last moment held three battered suitcases, their handles threaded with string, string which now resisted her attempts to untie it, fingers whitened at the tips and numb.

Rory was pulling bags and boxes out from the boot as she struggled and groaned to herself. He did not offer to help, but stood for a moment looking on silently, willing her to succeed. By the time she had got the first case down with a thump on to the ground he had disappeared towards the lighted doorway, a hunched figure stumbling with the weight of a cardboard box. She dragged down the other cases.

When she returned to the kitchen with a suitcase in either hand Conor was still standing where she had left him, rubbing his eyes, still half asleep.

'I'm cold,' he said.

She put down the cases and went over to the range. As she undid the iron hooks and let down the front of the grate, the fire glowed and the heat spread out.

'Here's a chair, here,' she guided Conor over, 'sit here, look at the warm fire.' Conor was already pulling the chair a bit closer. 'Careful, not too close,' she reminded him.

He looked up and nodded wisely. 'Yes, I know.'

'Ma!' Rory was at her elbow. 'There's only the big box of books left and the television set. Do you want me to help shift those?'

She realised that she stood surrounded by four suitcases and five oddly assorted cardboard boxes, surrounded so much that she had to step over them to get free. Rory had been quietly emptying the car while she stood, was it only for moments, seeing to Conor.

But had she stood that extra moment to think about other things, other times, her own self at his age, her grandmother at the range stirring soup, bringing out freshly baked wheaten bread from the oven, cloth in hand, tapping it underneath and nodding in that practised way, standing it on edge at the back of the range to cool? Had she seen in an instant her mother making griddle cakes, sodas, ready for her when she came in from school, hot and dripping with butter?

'Leave the rest until morning, I'll lock the car.' Her voice was husky. 'You see if you can find out about the beds upstairs, Rory. It looks as if Mrs D has been to get everything ready for us. She must have got my letter . . .': the letter hastily written and hastily posted, decisions made, acted upon.

Out in the yard the cold damp air caught her and made her draw breath sharply. As she leaned in to the driving seat to make sure that she had left the handbrake on securely, to switch off the headlights, to lift the keys out of the ignition and slam the door shut, the darkness closed about her. It was cold, even for late November she told herself, and stepped out towards the light of the kitchen, hearing the wind in the orchard trees that grew up and around the back of the outhouses, and the house, a dry wind amongst the many bare branches, muffled.

She dropped the car keys, bent to find them on the ground, holding her breath to listen for something; she knew not what. Then the sound of voices through the open door caught her, stopped her fears, voices laughing, then feet on bare boards running, and as she stood there, lights shone out one after another as windows in the rooms above were illuminated.

'Right, Belle, that's it,' she told herself, speaking aloud, 'you always were a fool. Now you know that you are – a child really – it's only the dark.'

The sky is black tonight. There's frost on the air and the stars are so clear that I could try to identify them, if I could remember what John taught me.

I am standing at the bottom of the garden by the dustbin. It's not really a garden, just a patch of rough grass, for I haven't the heart to make a garden. I have been here for seven years, but it doesn't seem so. The house is in the middle of one of those long terraces, with another row backing on to it, and the gardens lie secretly in the canyon between, and a narrow lane slips between them. It's very quiet. The city seems to be holding its breath for the next onslaught, the next bomb, the next fire blazing into the sky.

The phone rings. I rush indoors and lift the receiver. 'Hallo?'

'Hallo.' A pause. 'Mrs Johnston?'

'Yes?' I am a little breathless. I don't recognise the man's voice. The accent is Belfast, but not all Belfast in its tones.

'We just thought that we would give you a call. It's about the girl . . . in the coffee shop . . .'

'What girl?'

'Now, don't pretend . . . not to us! The coffee shop that was bombed. Remember?'

'Are you the police?' I ask.

He laughs. 'The police? Oh aye, the police! We know about you!'

'You know about me?'

'Yes, we know. And if you know what's good for you . . .'

'What do you want?'

'You're asking me?' He laughs again. 'We're keeping an eye on you.'

'Why?'

'Don't pretend to me you don't know!'

'Why?' I repeat like a child.

There's a click. He's gone. A bus rumbles down the road outside. Silence descends heavily. The house seems empty but I know the boys are upstairs asleep. Safe. What have I done?

When she finally got the kitchen door shut, pushing it hard on stiffened hinges into place, Belle found that her fingers were trembling. She tried hard to push the bolt across but her fingers were numb, as if she had gripped the steering wheel of the car too hard on those last few miles before she had found the gateposts. The bolt would not go into its hasp. She sighed. The door was shut, wasn't it? For the moment it would do. She would see to it in a while. And the sound of the boys running overhead diverted her fears.

Rory had got as far as the attics on the second floor, the top floor. She could hear the stairboards creaking as he went up the last flight. Still creaking. She shook her head wryly.

His voice echoed down to her. 'Ma! The light doesn't go on in the big room at the back, I can't find a switch.'

'It doesn't. There isn't one.' Belle stood in the hallway still wearing her jacket, looking upwards, calling to him, a slight figure, copper-red curly hair unruly on her forehead, large green eyes, a wide generous mouth. 'There isn't a light in that attic, there never was one, I don't know why. That is where the water storage tank is. I suppose you don't need a light in there really. There are lights in the other attics though.' There was an attic on each side of the house, stretching from front to back, with another room tucked behind the well of the stairs, a third square room, without windows, without lights.

'The attic next door is as big . . . as big . . . could we put our toys here . . . a railway . . . we could have a railway . . . it could go round and round and round . . . we could have a railway . . . couldn't we?'

Rory was standing in the attic in the gloom of a small-wattage bulb, turning round and round, arms outstretched, Conor with him, dancing first on one foot, and then on the other, when she reached the doorway.

'It's great! It's great! It's going to be our place! We could have a railway here . . . at last . . . you said there was no room in the other house because Anne had the spare room! Look! There's lots of room here. I could put the rails round and round. It's just right, Ma? Ma, we can have this room, can't we?'

Belle shut her eyes. She had said that.

Mother is sweeping the boards, brushing up the dust slowly, methodically, towards the door where I stand, her head down, unspeaking, unanswering my entreaty.

I say it all again. 'I want to build a railway. Why can't I have a railway of my very own?'

'Girls don't play with railways. Anyway, ask your brother John if you must, you could play with his. You don't need one.' She keeps on sweeping as she speaks.

'John's railway is broken. The engine doesn't work and he stood on some of the rails and they're bent . . .'

She stops sweeping, looks hard at me. 'Waste of money, wasn't it?' Sweeps again.

'I want one of my own. I'll look after it, I promise . . .'

She has reached the door where I stand, the pile of dust approaches my feet inexorably, dust hangs and glistens in the air about her, catches in my nostrils.

'Mind your feet! You can't have a railway here . . . anyway . . . not here. This attic is for apples, remember? Isn't it?'

I move on to one foot, unbalanced as the brush goes past me. 'But there isn't room in the other attic, there isn't room. It's full of bits . . . and things . . . and . . .' My voice dies in disappointment. 'There isn't room . . .'

'You could clear a space, mend your brother's train set!' She is right beside me, challenging.

'It wouldn't be the same. I want a place of my own . . . not a space . . .'

She shakes her head. Is it still denial? Or simply that she doesn't understand me?

The apples will be laid out in rows, I know. First layers of newspaper, after the sweeping, then each apple will be carefully laid, an inch from its fellow, row upon row, row upon row, Mother and I and Mrs D together, bending and stooping. Spiders' webs curtain the windows that look out over the bare apple orchard.

The best fruits are laid here, big green Bramleys, not a spot allowed, perfect specimens. Autumn will fade. There will be the first frosts up in the orchard. Then rain and more rain. Up here is warm, scented, shut the door quickly, don't let the air escape, come in quickly, keep them quiet, perfect, for just a week, a day longer. Then once a week, maybe on Saturday, the ritual selection, choosing apples which have given in to time, brown-spotted, softening. Maybe with luck a few will last past Christmas. The flawless survivors will be selected for the feast. Downstairs carols are sung. Outside a cold congregation waits silently for spring, for the first chorus of blossom.

'Your Uncle John had a railway, I remember. Maybe it's still around. Have you looked in the other attic?' Belle asked slowly.

'Yes,' Rory said eagerly, 'but it's full of stuff . . . bits of furniture . . . would there be a railway hidden in it?'

'Possibly,' she replied. 'We'll look in the morning maybe. Not now. It's too late. In the morning.'

'Promise?' He stood beside her looking disappointed.

'Promise,' she agreed. With a bit of luck he would forget. She was not in the mood for digging up memories.

'Can we put it out in the attic, this big empty one?'

'Yes. It will need to be swept out, of course. . . yes, why not?' She put a hand on the shoulder of each as they stood there, she between them, and gathered the boys tightly to her for an instant.

'Let's see about the beds. Now, Rory, you can choose which room you want.'

They went down the two flights of stairs to the first floor where two rooms on one side opened from another.

'Can I have the far one, the one at the back?' Rory asked.

'Yes. That used to be your Uncle John's. Do you remember him? My room was the outer one when I was a child, the one Conor will have. You used to sleep in it . . . before . . . you'll be able to see the orchard from the window . . . in spring you can see the blossom . . .' Her voice faltered, died.

'Uncle John?' Conor asked. 'He died, didn't he?'

'Yes.'

The phone rings. Can no one in this house answer it except me?

I am trying to clear the table in the kitchen after tea. Sam has just come in, late as usual. He is in one of his funny moods. His boots are thick with mud, there's a smell of dung about him for he has been muck-spreading up at his father's. I am trying to heat through some stew for him. He is standing beside me.

'Agh! Get off! You stink, Sam!' He steps back.

Why does my voice have to sound like that, brittle, cold? I don't mean it really. Why does he have to take me so seriously?

And there goes the phone. Still it rings. I'll have to go. Sam is standing in the middle of the kitchen taking off one wellington boot.

'I'll get it! I'll get it!' he says shortly. He hops out towards the hallway where the phone is. Mud. Mud. Mud.

I can hear his voice, monosyllables.

'Oh! I see. Yes. Now. You're sure. Yes. Where was it? Yes. I see.'

There's been an attack, a bomb, something, I know it! He's going to have to go out on patrol again. This was supposed to be his day off. His day off from the UDR. But he spent it up at his father's farm, muck-spreading . . . not with me. Why could he not have stayed with me? At least he did spend the day with Rory, took him away from under my feet. Rory is so good. He is sitting in his high chair beside me eating a biscuit . . . watching . . . why do I feel this way? It must be this child which I am carrying that makes me feel so . . . oh, makes me say these things.

Sam is standing in the doorway. 'It's John!' is all he says.

'What does he want? Did he meet someone? Is he staying late? He said he was only borrowing your car for a couple of hours, for a quick drink, he said.'

'He's dead. Somebody boobytrapped his car while he was in the pub –'

'His car!' I am screaming. 'Your car! Yours! They meant it for you!'

John. Drinking in the wrong pub at the wrong time. In Sam's car. Sam was the soldier. John only ever wanted to look after the orchard. Who was to know that it was the wrong man? It was fate. He never did notice the apple blossom, ever again.

'Do I need to clean my teeth?'

Belle looked down. Rory had unpacked his pyjamas from a suitcase which he had dragged up the stairs. And found Conor's pyjamas too. Conor was standing at the end of his bed beside the neat pile of his pyjamas rather like a soldier at attention, waiting for the next barrack-room order from his brother. The sponge bag dangled from Rory's hand.

'Yes, of course,' she said, hearing her voice as if it were in an empty room.

In the bathroom it was Rory who spread the toothpaste on Conor's brush and ordered the brushing. They stood side by side, the water trickling from the tap; the sound of brushing, rinsing, seemed as if in another place, another dimension, to Belle who stood resting her head against the doorpost of the bathroom. Suddenly she was weary.

Rory pushed Conor impatiently. 'Into bed with you!' he said roughly. 'It's long past your bedtime.'

The smaller boy moved automatically and climbed into bed.

'Do you boys not want hot water bottles?' Belle asked gently.

'No. Those are only for softies,' scoffed Rory, giving Conor a fierce look.

'You're sure?' She looked doubtful.

'No. We're all right,' said Rory, slipping into his own room, kicking aside the bedclothes and pushing his feet under the blankets. 'Are you all right, Ma?'

'Yes. I'm fine. Just a wee bit tired. That's all.'

'Make yourself a cup of tea,' he said, putting a hand up to touch her cheek as she leaned over him. 'This is quite a nice room. I remember Uncle John. Just a little bit. He was sort of fat . . . wasn't he?'

'Yes,' she laughed, 'a little bit fat.'

'When I was small, before . . .' He stopped, waited. 'And you don't want to talk about that ever!' he added as she echoed the words parrot fashion in her mind.

No, she said to herself. That part is over. 'Do you want me to leave the light on?' she asked, walking to the door of his room.

'No!' Rory said firmly.

'Yes!' cried Conor in a small voice from the other room.

'Feardy cat! Feardy cat!' called Rory.

'All right. I'll leave the light on, on the landing outside.' She stood for a moment hesitating, memories crowding in on her. She turned and went out on to the landing.

They'll think we have gone mad in the village, she thought as she went downstairs. Every room must have a light shining out as if the house was some steamer travelling through the waves of the countryside.

In the kitchen she half caught a reflection of herself in the window-panes and wondered if it was herself, or a movement outside. She shifted uneasily from one foot to the other. 'It is me,' she breathed.

Belle drew the curtains over the kitchen window firmly shut and thought about that cup of tea. A blackened kettle was sitting sighing at the back of the range. She moved it forward, leaning towards the heat gratefully, and put it on the hotplate of the range, spreading her fingers to the heat, listening to the changing sound of a slow hiss as the water warmed. All the comforts of home, she reflected, all thanks to Mrs D. She must have been here for hours, cleaning, airing and making up the beds, lighting the range, hours it must have been. The tea was good. She savoured every sip.

No sound came from overhead. The boys must have been so exhausted that they had fallen asleep at once. The pile of luggage sat in the middle of the floor awaiting her attention. Yet again she had committed herself. Yet again she had made the move. Why did it always have to be she? Belle blinked furiously, telling herself that she should get upstairs to bed, pulling her body straight as if she were in the front row of Miss Robinson's mathematics class, once again, and not paying attention, once again. Could try harder, the reports had said. She had, but not succeeded somehow.

You're tired, you're tired, she repeated, that's why you feel like this. 'But it isn't only that,' she said out loud.

The sound of her voice checked her. She stiffened and stood up, walking out to the scullery with the empty mug in her hand. She could not find the light switch for a moment, and stood there, sensing the cold of the stone-flagged floor, the mould of rising damp.

This place could do with a coat of paint to get it right, she told herself, wondering what colour she might do it. In her mother's day it had been painted sporadically, a useless battle, for there was always a sweet grey mould which grew out of the walls by these three steps, flaking the paint in time, as if some corruption of the dead years must seep out.

Belle found the light switch and went down the steps, forgetting about them, staggering out of balance. She caught her reflection again, in the window of the sink, and once more it was disconcerting.

'Don't be silly! You're daft! They couldn't find you here! Not yet!' Her voice steadied her, though it echoed in the small stone-flagged room. She hurried from the scullery, switching off the light from around the corner in the kitchen where the curtains were drawn and those outside could not see her. She shut the scullery door determinedly. She was stupid, they might find her, eventually, they might. But in the mean time . . .

Then she heard the sound of a car engine. Only it wasn't a car. It was a Landrover. She knew the sound of those engines, the definitive noise of the patrol cars. It was coming up the drive, slowing to come into the yard, right by the door. Lock it!

Across to the door in a flash she raged and raged at herself. She had left the key on the outside when she let herself in. The bolt! The hasp had slipped half an inch lower and her fingers fumbled as she tried uselessly to pull the bolt across.

When the door opened, almost casually, she was still behind it, against the wall, stiff, eyes not seeing.

The man who came round the door without knocking was tall, thickset, handsome in his uniform, with dark curly hair.

'Good evening!' he said cheerfully.

Belle did not reply.

'I have just had word over the radio of a lot of lights on here. This house has been empty for a long time, a very long time.

This is most suspicious.' He laughed, a false, jovial sound. She stayed silent. 'So you're in residence again,' he continued. 'Will you be staying long . . . this time, or is this just a flying visit?'

She did not nod her head, or speak, or give any sign of having heard what he said.

He tried again. 'Well, I see you haven't unpacked yet. Do you want those bags carrying upstairs to the bedroom? I suppose you will be putting yourself in the big room?'

Belle still said nothing. She seemed embalmed, her pallor waxen.

His eyes narrowed. 'Ah, come on now! Have you nothing at all to say for yourself, Miss High and Mighty? Is there nothing at all I could do for you?'

She was standing very straight, conscious of the roughness of the wall behind her, the hardness of it, the cold that blew in from the door now just ajar. She shivered. It was her first movement in a long time.

The soldier shut the door and leaned his back against it, putting his hands on his hips, large capable hands.

'Ah, come on now,' he said softly, 'have you nothing at all to say for yourself, nothing at all, even to me?'

A second later he had her pinned to the wall, his mouth hard on hers, lips clenched fiercely, then he muttered to himself and to her, sounds first, then words. 'Come on now . . . don't be like that . . . you're great . . . you look good . . . not a day older . . . and you're dying for me . . . I know you are!'

She stood obdurate as he gathered her to him, feeling the constriction of his arms about her. Her eye caught a patch of plaster peeling on the corner by the doorpost and she sighed, reminding herself yet again of the rising damp. She would go to the shop in the morning, to Crawford's in the square by the church, buy some paint, cover up that awful peeling wall that reminded her of all those long years of childhood and adolescence . . .

He held her very tightly. She could feel the hardness of his bullet-proof vest, and yet another hardness rising against her. He ran his firm hands impatiently down her back, then up again, then down, rounding her buttocks, then upwards, slipping under the edge of her sweater, skin on skin, fingers seeking, his breath coming quick, sharp. Her arms were straight by her sides, her face set. He drew his head back from hers, his lips from her lips and waited, staring. Then he bent his head again and brushed her lips very gently with his own, looking into her eyes intently. Suddenly he let her go and stood back from her. She was only aware that he no longer breathed at her neck, caressed with his hands.

The Landrover engine was revved loudly, the driver turning it in the narrow confines of the yard.

The soldier did not speak. He tugged his parka straight. She could smell his freshly shaved face, soap, and another smell. Was it of the uniform?

'Are you a real soldier, Daddy?'

My father is standing impatiently in the kitchen while my mother fusses at the range. Why does she have to cook at this moment? He is going away!

'No,' he tells me, standing very erect. 'No, I'm not a real soldier, there isn't a war.'

My father, only son of the Neills of Tannaghmore, Margaret and James, gentleman farmer, keeper of the orchard.

'What are you going to do at this camp you're going to? Is it like the Girl Guides?'

'It's only the Territorial Army summer camp. Practising to be soldiers. Don't worry. There isn't going to be a war. It's great fun really, playing soldiers.'

'But you're going . . .'

'For only three weeks,' he chides. 'Not long. I'll be back soon, my little one, I'll be back. Then we can take a look at the Bramleys. Your mother could make us a tart, with the first ones, they're special, aren't they? You could made a wish . . .'

'Don't be long.'

'Don't look so sorrowful. I won't be fighting. There's no danger. I'll be back before you know I'm gone,' he says, picking me up in his arms. He crushes me to him for the last time but I don't know this. He crushes me to his chest, to his uniform, harsh, khaki, unyielding. He has just shaved, and this morning he has been to have his hair cut. I can see now the thinning bit on the top, the grey at the temples. It's very short.

The man in front of her ran a quick hand through his unruly hair.

'You don't have much to say to me,' he said, looking at her with his head on one side, and a sardonic smile now. 'I don't think you feel anything. Did you ever?' He put out his hand tentatively and touched a strand of her hair that fell on her forehead, smoothing it almost nervously. 'Why didn't you tell me you were coming home?' he asked softly.

'I didn't want –' she started to say.

'Come on now, you bugger, we haven't all night to wait while you fool around!'

The hoarse cry came from outside the door, there were snatches of words as the engine was revved again. 'Come on, man, sure you can get a wee drop of tea another night. We have to get away on down the road!'

'I must go,' he said, dropping his hand, turning and walking to the door. He did not turn his head to look at her as he opened it, he simply went out, shutting the door firmly behind him. Belle did not move. She listened for the sound of the vehicle leaving.

When the door opened once more, still she did not move. She felt her hand being taken, the key being pressed cold into it.

'There now, it wouldn't do for you to go to bed with the door unlocked . . . you never know who might call, do you?' He raised his eyebrows and smiled at her. 'Don't forget to lock the door now, don't forget.'

As the door shut once again she heard voices again, a little excited joking.

'Well, that took you long enough, boy, was she pleased to see you?'

She could not hear a reply, but there was a burst of laughter, the engine was revved yet again, the wheels spun on the icy cobbles and there was a final burst of laughter as the Landrover went round the side of the house, speeding off into the dark.

It was quiet for a long time.

Belle moved at last. The key warm in her hand reminded her to lock the door. She thrust it into the lock but did not turn it. She opened the door and felt the cold strike her face, standing there, listening.

There was no sound. The wind had died and up in the orchard the frozen boughs held their breath too, as if listening with her. She shut the door and turned the key.

She walked over to the middle of the floor to the pile of suitcases, searching in one of them until she found a hot water bottle. She filled it slowly, using the last of the hot water in the kettle. Then she refilled the kettle with cold water out of sheer habit, sliding into the gloom of the scullery to do so, not putting on the light, moving resolutely now.

'I feel nothing,' she said aloud, 'I cannot feel anything now.'

She squeezed the suitcase shut, fastened the locks and picked it up, shoving the hot water bottle under her arm. Then she went out into the hallway, snapping off the light in the kitchen. She stood for a moment there, then switched off the light above her head so that she stood adjusting her eyes to the dark. The lawn outside lay bathed in the lights of the house, the lights of the attics far above, and the landings. She drew a quick breath. She was a fool! She was mad! Anyone passing down the road would know, he had known, hadn't he, that she was back at the House. She had no sense, no sense at all!

She sped up the stairs, high up on to the top floor, switching off the lights one by one until at last she stood in complete darkness by the window of the big bedroom, listening again, looking out. Clouds glanced off the moon and the lawn spread out before her, whitish, bleached. At its edge the row of pines that bordered the road were still, and through their branches she could see the lights of the village up ahead.

Nothing moved, no car, not even a patrol car.

She drew the curtains shut determinedly and stripped off her clothes. Moments later she slid between the cold sheets and pressed the too hot water bottle to her breasts, thinking hard.

Would they find her here? Would they look? Fortunately the kitchen was at the back of the house so that if she used it most of the time there would be no lights showing when darkness came. She must warn the boys about leaving lights on in the rest of the house, she could persuade them about the cost of electricity, that was the answer. Yes, being constructive, that was the answer. She held her breath once again to listen. The silence and the dark crowded in on her, suffocating. She must not be afraid. She must think of other things.

'Now what about that paint for the kitchen?' she asked herself out loud. 'Yes, what about a nice yellow? I'd like that.'

Chapter 2

VOICES DOWNSTAIRS. Muffled laughter. A clinking of china plates. Doors shutting and footsteps on the tiled floor in the kitchen.

Belle opened one eye at the greyness about her and felt the cold bite at her shoulders which stuck out of the bedclothes. The morning light was filtering faintly through the curtains of the large window that looked out on to the front of the house, and, as she twisted her head, the window that overlooked the orchard at the side. Four chestnut leaves wide, twelve chestnut leaves deep, red-brown print faded, still the same.

My mother's body is rounded, soft, warm in a blue winceyette nightgown that has a yoke and a neat collar. It's cold this morning, but warm under the blankets, warm where my mother's arms go around me. I have counted the chestnut leaves once again. Mother has her eyes closed but I think she is not asleep.

This bed is very large. It's painted black, made of iron, with ends that are made up of lots of bits put together with little screw knobs. If I put out one hand above my head I can reach one which always works loose and rattles when I move in bed.

'Stay still!'

'I'm only . . .'

'Leave the bed alone! Stay still! We'll get up in a minute.' Still her eyes are closed.

This used to be my granny's bed. Granny Neill. That's my father's mother. She's dead now. This is the Neill house. We have lived here always. We have quite a bit of land. There's the orchard behind the house, running all the way up to Top Hill, and all the fields that go down the other side, to the lake and the railway beyond. My father doesn't bother with those fields. He lets them out to the Johnstons who have a lot of land beyond the railway line. They keep cattle there most of the time. I'm not allowed to go over the railway line, it's dangerous, Mother says, a train might come along. But that's silly, they always whistle when they start going over the big bridge, the viaduct round the corner, you can hear them always . . .

'Stay still! Why must you always fidget?' My mother frowns. Her eyes are still shut.

My father only looks after the orchard. He says anybody can be a farmer, but an orchard is something special. It's a big orchard. There are a lot of apples, mostly cookers, Bramleys. I like climbing the trees. Some are more difficult than others. John – that's my brother – is quite good at it, but I think I'm better . . .

'Time to get up!' My mother is already out of bed, standing on the mat, pulling on her red dressing-gown. She looks very wide awake. But she was asleep a moment ago. 'Come on with you! Out of bed!'

'Let me stay another five minutes?'

'No! Out! Now!' she scolds.

I can't bear the cold, Belle thought. I can't get up, I'll stay for a minute more. She dissuaded herself from getting out of bed, and stuck a tentative toe out, to see how it felt, to see how blue her toe might go. It was the unconscious gesture of a child, not a woman of her years, but it was habit once again, and she sensed it. She sensed the room closing in around her, enveloping her, bringing back moments of another part of her life, a part she thought was dead.

Bare feet on the bare boards of the stairs brought her to the present. Rory charged into her room waving a piece of buttered toast in enthusiastic greeting.

'Mrs D is here. Did you hear her knocking on the back door and calling? I heard her and I went down to let her in. Do you remember her, Ma? She remembers me when I was just,' he gestured, 'just so high. Imagine. I think I remember her. Doesn't she live up the road somewhere? She is making tea, she says, and will you come down and get it while it's hot? Conor is up already. He fell down outside. Did you not hear him? He's all right. He cried a bit. But Mrs D made him better. She's a funny old lady, isn't she? She says that she helped Conor being born. Here. In this house. I was born in hospital, wasn't I? Mrs D says she remembers when you were born. You were only a thin miserable baby –'

'I'll come, in a minute,' Belle interrupted quickly, cursing herself. How could she have slept through all that noise, Mrs D banging on the door, Conor falling down . . . she had been tired, dead tired. 'I'll come.'

'Now, she says, it'll get cold.'

Mrs D – really Mrs Donnelly, but simply called Mrs D because Donnelly was hard to get a child's tongue round – had already slipped back into the role that she knew best. Motherhood. Both her babies had been born dead. Her husband Willy had buried himself alive under the weight of unemployment. He had been a plumber, but in time the journey hardly seemed worth the effort, the journey to town. He was no good with cows or pigs. He had met Ina, wanted her for his wife, wanted to stay in the country. Together they seemed to have given up on life, maybe on love-making. So there were no more pregnancies, no more love. Unemployment had grown on him, long days spent idling between the house in Mill Row and the pubs in Armagh, or down the road in the next village, Corey. He was there, if needed, if a pipe burst in the first winter frost, or a ballcock stuck, sitting by a big coal fire in the small living-room of the two-up, two-down house, even in the heat of summer. A good fire was the foundation of a home. Mrs D found another home, down the road, with the Neills, bearing daily news from one to the other, the village to the House.

Mill Row was four redbrick houses in a terrace, transposed from a town, huddled at the bottom of the hill. Samuel Neill, Belle's great-uncle, built them as a hedge against the 1920s poverty that grew in the countryside. He planned a scutch mill for flax by the small river. Mill Row was the start. It could have been plucked from Belfast's Sandy Row, not dumped in a sleepy

County Armagh village instead. The mill was built, there was the great day it opened, jobs for the men around. It should have prospered, but it sickened, Uncle Samuel lost heart. Some people were like that. One moment bursting with ideas, the next dashed by a cursory word, a challenge by officialdom. There was always the ultimate escape to the colonies. Uncle Samuel slid off one night on a ferry boat to Liverpool with only one suitcase full of clothes, a brand-new suitcase, a present from the family. He had gone to join a long-departed cousin in Australia. If they heard from him it would be because he had been a success. There had been no letters. The mill, Belle reflected, must now be a mere ruin. How much had she been like Uncle Samuel, did she leave because she had failed? She had returned, but she hadn't been successful. She closed her eyes.

'Shall I bring your tea up to you?' Rory was still standing looking at her questioningly.

She would have to get up now, there was no escape. 'I'll come down.'

'Well, don't be long,' he scolded, going towards the door. He stopped in the doorway. 'Is this the room where the lady was kept chained up by her husband for years and years until she died?'

'Yes,' she laughed suddenly, 'do you see the mark on the wall beside the fireplace? That's where the iron ring was that the chain was attached to.'

'Did she really die here?' He stepped back towards her, pointing to the fireplace.

No, not her, Belle smiled grimly to herself, only me. 'Go and ask Mrs D about it. It was she who told me the story when I was a child. Ask her. I'm coming down right now. Go on with you.'

She waited until he was out of the room and the door shut before she got out of bed. Naked, she stood on the patch of old Numdah rug beside the bed, grabbing at the suitcase that stood by the bed, opening the stiff lock with a decisive click, hunting for her dressing-gown. It was not on the top of course, and she felt the cold creep on her back and thighs as she stood there tossing out clothes. She found the dressing-gown and thrust her arms into the sleeves quickly, tying the belt, her teeth beginning to chatter. Beyond the rug lay an acre of cold wooden floor, polished for generations to a smooth finish with here and there the signs of wandering tracks of woodworm. And she couldn't find her slippers. She went towards the door, her toes curling on the bare boards.

Outside on the landing she felt the warmth from down below on the air rather as she had done on her honeymoon with Sam, travelling by ferry in the Aegean, on a velvet night, approaching Crete. This time the heat from the kitchen told her to hasten down but yet she lingered.

Out of the landing window she could see the wide lawn, more like a hayfield with the scythe marks on the stubble grass. In the boys' rooms their possessions were already scattered about. The dingy wallpaper was patterned with secret marks made on the walls by children, once by John and herself and then her own children, whiling away the early hours of the morning when the rest of the house was asleep, marks that made boats and planes and people in gardens outside houses with winding paths and smoke curling out of the chimney.

She retraced her steps back to the landing and looked out once more. Over the tops of the pine trees she could see the village on the hill ahead, the church spire at the square on the top, then the long street with houses straggling down towards her. To the right a line of poplars indicated Mill Row and where the river ran. To the left at the bottom, the main road to Armagh ran upwards and out of sight.

Movement caught her idle eye. Two Landrovers appeared along the main road. They passed her. Could they see her at the window, she wondered, and who else might see her?

She gathered her dressing-gown tightly about her and hurried downstairs, stepping into the kitchen, breathing quickly, then shutting the door, leaning against it, folding her arms defensively.

The boys were sitting on chairs drawn up to the range and Mrs D was on a third chair sitting between them. Conor and Rory were alike in a way, stringy, not thin precisely. Rory had a mop of dark curly hair. Conor who was small for his eight years had what was called 'dirty fair' hair – like her father's had been. The front of the stove was let down so that the coals glowed, and both boys were eating buttered toast, wiping their hands on their dressing-gowns, smiling up at Mrs D as she told them some story or other. Belle paused, trying to think which tale it was that Mrs D had been telling, wanting to put her fears behind her and become part of the enchantment.

'You're after your tea,' Mrs D said unnecessarily, reaching up for the teapot at the back of the range, standing up from her chair. 'Get a cup there, girl. Do you want some toast? Young Conor here is a great man for making toast. He's been trying out the toasting fork for me. Would you like some toast now, it would be made beautifully, this boy is good at it . . .' She was standing with the teapot in one hand, a little greyer, dumpy, full-bosomed, the same crossover apron.

Belle put out a hand to touch her, but the moment somehow had passed. She held a cup out to the proffered teapot. 'It's good to see you,' she began a little formally, 'how's Willy?'

'Grand. Grand,' said Mrs D, looking her up and down critically, 'grand, and you don't look a day older yourself.'

'Is there an army station nearby?' Belle asked the question more abruptly than she had intended. She had meant to be casual, unhurried, but then she never could disguise or dissemble when something was uppermost in her mind.

'Yes. Yes. Sit down there, girl. Bring up a chair for your mother, Rory, by the fire here, it's cold up those stairs you know, and your mother's looking a bit thrawn this morning. Now . . .' She paused as Belle sat down on the chair. 'They are up at the old school.'

'The old school?'

'Yes, you know, on the far side of the hill . . . the school there, don't you remember?'

'Yes. Sure I went there when I was wee, before I went to school in Armagh. Rory went there too, before we left. I didn't know it was closed.' She had never checked, she had just assumed that it would be still there, fine and handy for the boys. Things changed. Times changed. Schools were being closed up and down the country. 'Rationalisation' it was called. If it could happen in Belfast, it could happen here. But this place never changes! she thought desperately. It did and it had.

'The kids all go down to Corey, you know, about two miles down the south road. The main teacher is great there I hear. Called Quinn. It's only a primary school, till the time they do the eleven-plus exam. If they get that they can go to the grammar school in Armagh, or else the intermediate . . . if they fail it.'

'To Corey? But that building was falling down years ago. Rory used to go to the one in the village . . .' Belle could not hide the dismay in her voice. Having wrenched the boys out of school in Belfast, she realised that she had to get them into a nearby school, if only on a temporary basis. She had not imagined the boys having to travel to school, away from the comparative safety of the village.

'Well,' Mrs D shook her head, 'the army wanted the school. It was after the bridge business. They moved in temporarily.'

'The bridge?' Belle was puzzled.

'Did you not see it in the papers? The IRA put a bomb under the railway bridge, you know, the viaduct. It wasn't much of a bomb, maybe twenty pounds or so . . . you must have heard about it?'

Belle shook her head. 'No. You lose track after a while . . . there's bombs . . . and bombs.'

'Well, anyway, it was in the school holidays. The army moved in, for a while, then they stayed. The school was moved down to join the one at Corey. Sure there were only twenty kids there anyway and Corey is not that much further really. They have done up the school at Corey, it's grand, you know . . .'

'When was this?'

'Och, it must have three years ago. You must have seen it in the papers, even,' Mrs D insisted.

'I don't read the papers, not much.'

'Well, there's a whole platoon up there. Regular soldiers from across the water. And the UDR, Ulster people, but you know there's a few English officers come in and out too. I don't understand the half of it, only there's some of the local boys in it. I recognise them, you would too, there's –'

Belle broke in hurriedly. 'Did they get the men who planted the bomb?'

'Och, they lifted a few fellows, you know the way they do. They probably know rightly who's doing it, they're just waiting for them to try something else, catch them at it. It's only a handful of fellows doing it, really . . . and then there was one of those culvert bombs a wee while ago, down near the Border . . . nearly got a patrol car . . .'

'I saw the army patrol cars just now,' Belle said, thinking hard.

'And there's a helicopter that comes in too. They have room for it to land . . . in the playground . . . you know,' Mrs D nodded at her.

Belle stood up, walked to the kitchen door. 'I won't be a moment.'

She climbed to the first floor and looked out of the landing window. The top of the hill in the grey of morning was a blur. She could see Crawford's shop, beyond it the police station surrounded by wire fencing, the church spire above a clump of yew trees that grew in the churchyard around it. She sighed and started up the stairs again until she stood on the top landing by the attics. The window was dusty, shrouded with spiders' webs which she brushed aside, looking out, stooping, for the windows here were low. A spider rushed along the window frame diverting her momentarily.

From here she could see. Just beyond the church a square dark tower showed up. She could see the wire festooning it, the camouflage colouring. The army. She sighed in relief. There was not only the police up there, but also the army. Total protection, it must be.

She straightened and stepped to the door of the tank room. Inside was dark and warm, throbbing. She clapped her hands laughing, and ducked in the doorway. There was a whirring sound inside, a flurry of movement in the shadows. They were still there. Two black forms sped overhead and flew into one of the other attics so fast that she hardly saw them, squeaking as they went.

You're bats, she told herself, smiling at the old joke.

'Now your Uncle John was the man for birds' nests . . .' Mrs D was saying confidentially when Belle came back into the kitchen.

The three of them were still by the stove savouring the heat, and the smell of toast lingered in the air.

'What's all this about birds' nests?' Belle asked.

'I was just telling your boys about how you and your brother were always off looking for nests. You remember? You would be away all day and your mother used to wonder what you were up to.'

'I remember how we were always climbing the apple trees,' Belle said.

'Och, the pair of you were like two wild things.' Mrs D smiled, turning to the boys. 'They would go off in the morning, when they were older they had bikes and then they would go further –'

'Can I have a bike, Ma?' Rory interrupted, looking at her, appealing.

'We'll see. I don't know how safe . . .' she replied.

Mrs D's eyes caught Belle's searchingly.

'Well, if you had one . . .' Rory went on.

'Well, I was telling you this now, wasn't I?' demanded Mrs D, breaking into the conversation, 'I was telling you about nests . . .'

'Did you collect the eggs, Ma, blow them and all . . . like the ones we saw in the museum?' Conor was getting interested now.

'No. If we found a nest we couldn't disturb it. Only look. That was the rule. But we could keep watch, come back the odd day and see what was happening. One day they would be gone and there would just be the empty nest full of downy feathers. Some birds come back . . . to the same nests . . . year after year . . .' Her voice died and she swallowed hard.

Mrs D turned conspiratorially to the boys. 'Let me tell you . . . I know where there's a blackbird's nest. I noticed it yesterday when I came up the drive. Just by the house it is. Where the trees are bare.'

'Where? Where?' asked Conor, waving his arms.

'Well now, if you obey the rules . . . I'll tell you,' said Mrs D, ending up on a triumphant note.

She has the boys spellbound, Belle thought, just like John and me. She hasn't changed. Not one little bit.

'Well, your mother and I have jobs to do in the house. But if we were to hap you boys up you could go out and take a look, couldn't you? It's not far. We'll find the gloves and all, and the wee drop of fresh air will be good for you.' She nodded at Belle who nodded back.

Rory and Conor rushed out into the hall and pounded upstairs to find their bomber jackets, scarves and gloves where they had been dumped the night before, pushing back into the kitchen together.

'Now, I'll just give you the general direction, and you have to creep up quietly . . .' Mrs D started to explain.

'Like terrorists, about to attack,' Rory said excitedly.

'Och, away with you!' Mrs D said, opening the back door. The boys followed her out into the yard.

Belle gathered the cups and plates off the table and was putting them by the sink in the scullery when Mrs D returned.

'Well, that will do them good,' Mrs D said wisely, 'do them good. They're a fine pair of boys. Your Sam would be proud of them.'

Belle turned on her heel, afraid to show her expression.

'You, my girl, and I, are going up those stairs to make the beds. We have some talking to do!'

Belle followed her reluctantly upstairs feeling as if the past had intruded and that she had been guilty of some misdemeanour . . .

'Come on now,' said Mrs D, pointing to Conor's bed, 'you get to the far side,' she was breathing heavily, 'and tuck in and I'll do this side. Just like in the old days,' she added. Belle bent to straighten the bedclothes. 'Well now. I want to know the whole thing!'

'The whole thing?' Belle asked, head bent.

'Yes. Everything.'

Oh, how the past intrudes, Belle told herself. 'You mean . . . why I came back?' she asked carefully.

'Yes. Just that. You took yourself off without talking to me . . . without a word . . . though mind you, I knew you weren't happy . . . but I thought you would talk to me . . . but you didn't . . . it hurt me when you went off like that. I couldn't work it out, why you had to, do you see?'

'You know why,' Belle said tiredly, not wanting to discuss the subject which she had rolled round in her mind for so long, so many years.

'I thought you were happy here with Sam . . . and John . . . I thought you all got on well. Mind you, it was not like you were on your own, husband and wife, but all the same your brother hadn't any harm in him. He and your Sam wouldn't have argued much . . .'

'When John died . . .'

'Sure I know you were desperate . . . anybody would have been. And you with the baby and all. I know,' Mrs D interrupted again.

'John didn't have to die,' Belle cried.

'Och, it just happened . . .'

'If Sam hadn't joined the UDR . . . he didn't have to.'

'Well, he did. He thought it was his duty to join. Sure John could have joined too, but he wouldn't have made much of a soldier. Your Sam, now . . .'

'I never forget the day Sam told me he was going to join. He didn't ask me. Just told me. And sometimes when he was going out, sometimes . . . those nights . . . I was afraid for him . . .'

'Of course,' Mrs D said matter-of-factly, 'every wife and mother feels like that. There could be a boobytrap, a mine in one of those culverts under the road . . . anything.'

'I just couldn't take any more,' Belle said quietly. She had gathered up a pillow and was clasping it tightly to her breasts with both hands. 'Something happened inside me.'

'So off you went to Belfast and took the boys away, away from their father. What did you mean to do there? Hide? And wasn't there the chance that they might get hurt in a bomb there, there's bombs in Belfast . . .'

'Yes, I know. But it's a big city, it's different here in the country. They can pick you off here.' As she said it, she realised the implication of what she said. Why had she come back? It was madness. All her resolution seemed to be fading. But the army and the police were up the hill, weren't they?

'Your Sam . . .' Mrs D went on.

'Don't call him that!' Belle cried, throwing the pillow down on the bed.

Mrs D picked it up and deliberately placed it at the head of the bed, smoothing it fiercely with her fingers. 'Your Sam . . .'

'I tried to explain to him. I couldn't talk to him any more. I couldn't bear him even to touch me.'

'Ah . . . and what sort of life have you been living up there?' Mrs D asked crossly. 'I suppose you've been having a fine old time.'

'What do you think! You know me! I'm not like that! I only wanted the best for the boys, that's all.'

'And now, you're back. Why all of a sudden, just like that? Have you got yourself into trouble? With a man maybe?' Mrs D leaned over the bed shaking one finger.

'How can you say that to me? How can you? You know me!'

'Yes. I just wanted to be sure, that's all. If you came back I thought it was because you had got yourself into trouble. Is it money then?'

'No. No. Not money.'

'Well then?' Mrs D paused, waiting. 'Well then?'

How can I explain? I have to handle this myself. I cannot burden her with this, Belle thought wildly. 'I'm afraid . . .' she started.

'There is something,' Mrs D nodded wisely. 'I know you, girl.'

For a moment Belle wanted to put her arms round her, weep on to that apron, explain it all. But she couldn't. She was half afraid to put it into words, as if to do so would invite disaster.

'I can't . . .' Belle started, then she swallowed and bit back the words. 'I wanted to thank you before now, long before this moment, for opening up the house, making everything ready for us, it was so good to get here yesterday. I felt . . .'

'Safe?' asked Mrs D, looking at her hard.

'I can't talk,' Belle said, turning away from the bed and walking over to the window. 'I'm afraid, for you, for everyone. If you don't know, you won't be involved. But don't tell anyone I'm here. Oh I know the people in the village will see me, bound to, but don't mention me . . . to anyone, even in just conversation. You never know who might be listening. If anyone asks, just tell them I lost my job.' She noted idly that two army Landrovers were cruising up the road.

'Is there somebody after you?' Mrs D came to stand beside her. She grasped Belle's arm and shook it. 'What in God's name have you been up to? Who's after you? What for? What have you done? Tell me!'

'I got involved,' Belle said quietly. 'I got involved.'

'In what? In God's name, what?'

Belle shrugged her shoulders. 'It's not what you think. I was a witness. The police know about it. It seemed better to come here, until things quieten down. Maybe they'll forget about me.'

'Who, in God's name?'

'Who do you think? The IRA of course! Why should they bother to look for me? Not here!

'But you came back here.'

'I came home!' Belle shouted. 'I had to! They threatened us.'

'So you've given up hiding from Sam. Now you're hiding from them.' Mrs D shook her head in disbelief. 'I thought that you didn't want to be involved, that was what it was all about, you and Sam, and John?'

'Yes, yes,' Belle cried, 'but I . . . suddenly . . . wanted to get back at them for what they did to John. Maybe I had all that hate bottled up inside me too long. I got involved.'

'And what about the boys? Where are they in all this?' Mrs D gripped Belle's arm so hard that she could feel each finger pressing in.

'They will be safe here,' Belle said, 'they will, safer, anyway . . .'

'And if someone comes looking for you?' Mrs D went on.

'It's only me they're after. Only me. If I keep quiet, they'll forget about me, they must do!'

'And what are we supposed to do if they do come?'

'Sure look!' Belle waved her arm at the village ahead. 'There's the police, and the UDR. They won't try to get me here. And this house is like a fortress, once I get the doors locked and the windows barred. There are even the old shutters I could put across. I didn't have those in Belfast. I must be safe here!'

'Well, don't be taking any chances. Don't be going back up to Belfast for anything.'

'No. I'm not going back there. That past is over. Finished. I ran away. From here too. I know it wasn't the answer then. I should have stayed here, faced it.'

'Well, I know certain people have missed those boys growing up, and it's only you who is to blame for that. Did you not love your Sam at all?'

Belle turned to face her, furious now. 'Of course I loved him. He was my life. But I loved John too!'

'You had a funny way of showing it.'

'I was afraid, for him, of everything, I told you!'

'And you're afraid now, aren't you? Whatever you got up to, and you won't tell me the half of it, you're afraid now.'

'Yes. I have to face it. I thought I could do it better here.'

'What are you going to do now you're back? Have you contacted . . . ?'

'No! I will get a job. But first I must get the boys settled in school, if that's possible, just for the mean time. I could go down to Corey this morning if you don't mind keeping an eye on the boys. I'll go and see this teacher you talked about. Maybe he'll understand.'

'I wouldn't be telling him too much,' Mrs D warned.

'No. I won't be telling him anything,' Belle said firmly, 'no, not anything more than is necessary.'

'Those are some boys you have got there,' Mrs D said, not hiding the admiration in her voice.

'I know,' Belle said quietly. 'I know.'

'Och, you're just my wee girl, I wiped your nose often enough, put plasters on your knees when you fell off the bike. You were hard on Sam. He was a proud man once. He's been a different man, kept himself to himself. You hurt him more than you know.'

'He knows how I feel. I have to be on my own. I have done all these years. I must start today, go down to school now.'

'Yes. I see. Well, you know what you want.'

The two women stood side by side at the window for some moments without speaking. Down below they could see the boys pointing, ducking out of sight now and again, merging into the landscape, exploring a world far from city streets and lumbering buses. Belle turned to Mrs D and they smiled at each other a slow smile of understanding. She put an arm around the older woman.

'They're grand boys, grand boys,' Mrs D whispered.

Chapter 3

AN HOUR LATER Belle left the house and walked up the yard, pulling her coat collar up against the wind that caught her at the corner. She needed to think. She stopped suddenly in her tracks, and looked back at the car sitting in the garage end of the stable block. Can it be seen from the road? she asked herself, trying not to feel panic rise inside her. And what am I doing, going for a walk? If anybody sees me . . . if I take the car I can be reasonably unobtrusive, if I walk it will take time, too much time out in the open! I could be a sitting duck. I shall have to be very careful where I go. She retraced her steps to the car.

Once inside it, the smell of last night's chips bought to keep the boys from starvation caught her nostrils as she settled herself into the driving seat. She took off the handbrake and let the car run backwards into the yard. Would it start? Probably not in this cold weather.

It did start. She breathed thankfully, put the car into first gear, and set off down the drive. The pines on one side had grown dishevelled, the rhododendrons encroached on the driveway, and in places there was a thick layer of pine needles. In the old days it had been carefully raked gravel. Her mother had said, after her father's fatal coronary, that she had no fear of being attacked in bed at night, for she could hear every footfall. No one, even an animal, could be completely silent over the stones. There had been a rumour too that she kept a pearl-handled revolver under her pillow, which must have helped. Maybe it might do to revive a rumour or two, if she was going to stay. And was she? As she paused before going out on to the road she looked in the driving mirror. No, the garage could not be seen from here, so that her car, in the open garage, would be invisible to passers-by.

The road was empty. There was not even a patrol car. Down the hill to the end of the demesne wall, she reminded herself, then turn right at the bottom, then straight ahead.

The demesne was on her left. Behind it, buried in parkland, was the Lodge. The demesne wall was broken by a small stone gate-lodge. Boarded windows, slates missing, it hadn't changed much. She wondered if the O'Briens were still living at the Lodge. Why should they move?

It took less time to get to Corey than she expected. It is really only a short distance, she told herself, but it was better not to walk it, not today.

She found the school quickly. Single-storey redbrick, one new classroom tacked on the side with big windows. A home-made weathervane moved slowly on one solitary chimney pot. The wind was from the east.

She parked the car on the road outside and walked briskly to the gate. The schoolyard was empty but she could see dim outlines of figures in the classrooms. As she opened the front door and walked into the corridor, past the cloakroom with its row of pegs, coats hanging neatly, and a low bench under which there were shoes and wellington boots, she heard a hum of sound, voices in the classrooms, there could be only two of them and a gymnasium which would serve as a dining-room, and caught a smell, definitive, of the powder which the janitor would shake over the floor then sweep up to gather the dirt and dust for another day.

A small boy spun out of a classroom door, stopping abruptly in front of her. 'Missus?'

'I'm looking for . . . Mr Quinn, is it? The headteacher.'

'In there.' He nodded his head in the direction of the classroom close by.

Better wait until the end of the class, Belle thought, a kind of subservience, fearing what the teacher might say if interrupted between the Wars of the Roses and the Rise of the Plantagenets. Old English history. That was important. She went over to a notice-board and started reading the assortment of bits of paper pinned to it.

'Pupils will not wear their wellingtons in class.' 'Sick notes must be produced before time off is given to attend the dentist.' 'Christmas holidays start on December 17th. Term starts on January 4th at 9 a.m. sharp.' She must remember that last one.

She stood with her hands clasped behind her and read them all over again, slowly. She walked to the front door and looked out. The yard was empty. The road outside was empty.

There was a buzz of noise, the classroom door opened and several children stormed out, shouting, laughing and pushing, immediately silenced by her presence. She hesitated at the doorway and then looked in.

Pat Quinn was taller than she had expected, maybe six feet two, and surprisingly iron-grey-haired for a man, who she reckoned, trying not to look at him too critically, to be around thirty-five years old.

'Excuse me . . .' she began tentatively, 'my name is Johnston . . .'

He nodded. 'From the House,' he finished for her.

'Yes.' For a moment words failed her. Even he knew. Already. She took a deep breath and plunged on. 'Yes, I have two boys . . . Rory, he's the elder, he's eleven, and Conor who is eight. Rory used to go to the school up in the village,' she jerked her head, 'until we went to Belfast some years ago.' She cleared her throat.

'You're back and you're going to be staying . . . is that what you mean?'

'Yes. That's right. I'll be staying for a while . . . I don't know how long. It all depends . . .'

'Depends?' he asked.

Belle looked at him, wondering what to say.

'And you want them to start here?' he continued, raising his eyebrows.

'Yes. Is it possible? I wasn't quite sure . . . I mean, I had to leave my job in Belfast . . . they were moving out of town . . . I didn't want to start in a new job there . . .' Lies. Lies. Lies. You had to go! And you didn't bother to check about the school, did you? she admonished herself. She felt the colour rise in her face. 'Could do well', 'Must try harder', her school reports loomed up in her mind.

'So you came back here?'

'Yes, my family –'

He interrupted, 'Where were the boys at school?'

'They were at Inchmarlo. You could ring the headmaster, if you like, find out how they were doing . . . academically that is . . . I . . .' Her voice died away. She was suddenly thinking what a mess her hair was, standing on end with the wind and the cold, that she hadn't bothered with lipstick as she would have done in Belfast, that he was staring at her in a rather disturbing way which she was resisting hard. I am a mother. A person attached to a family, surrounded and protected from assaults like this, she thought. But his eyes were raking her face and he was waiting for her to say more. Was he waiting for a further explanation about why she had left Belfast, more about the boys? Or was he just waiting for her to react to him? He smiled a slow, very charming smile. Raised his eyebrows again. But his eyes were cold, grey, waiting. She was aware of his broad shoulders, slender hips, the corduroy trousers, the well-worn Aran sweater.

'If Rory is eleven, has he done the transfer procedure exam – the eleven-plus?' he pursued.

'Yes. He did the second paper last week.'

'You timed your move neatly, didn't you?'

'I didn't . . .' she faltered. You didn't think about that, she reminded herself.

'Well, you're here now. I'm sure you're glad to get back here, it's not like the city. I'm sure you will feel much safer. Now the exam results will be out in February. I don't know how bright your boy is, but it would be a good idea to get in touch with the headmaster of the grammar school in Armagh, to see if you can get a place for him there if he passes.'

'Yes, you're right. When could I start the boys?' she whispered.

'Ah . . .' He paused, looking directly at her.

'Will it be all right? Can they come here?' she asked anxiously.

'Bring them over for a chat. Next week if you like, yes, next week. Why not? Make it early in the week.'

'What about – ?' she started, then went on, feeling surer of herself. 'Will you ring the headmaster of their old school?'

'Yes, I'll ring him. There'll be some paperwork but I don't see much of a problem. They could probably start in a matter of days. Better for them.'

'That would be great. Great.' Belle was instantly at ease, relieved.

'Are you going to be living on your own up there?' he asked.

'On my own,' she replied firmly, hearing for a moment a touch of pride in her voice. Then she hastily added, 'The boys are good, very self-reliant.' Then she paused, thinking, Why should I feel threatened by this man? Back in Belfast I did not have this problem, but then they knew me, the few men of my acquaintance, they knew how I felt. Here I shall have to re-establish myself, set new boundaries, find out the old friends and how they feel about me. Pat Quinn is an interloper, new to the district. I don't know him. He doesn't know anything about me . . . or does he? I don't want to know any more of him than I need to for the boys' sake.

'You'll be busy settling in at the moment. Sure you only got in last night, didn't you, and late too?'

Belle blinked. He knew her every move. Even here two miles down the road. But then, it was her own fault, she had put all those lights on last night, hadn't she? What bigger advertisement for a home-coming could she have made? She had lit up the old town last night, certainly. If only she had noticed the lights being on. It was too late, the damage was done.

Pat Quinn stood waiting for her to respond.

'Well, it's Wednesday today,' she said unnecessarily. 'Is next Monday suitable? I shall have to find myself a job, here if possible, or maybe Armagh. And the sooner that I can get the boys settled the sooner I can start looking.' She was tired of explanations, especially when she didn't want to give them.

But he continued to probe. 'What kind of job are you looking for?'

'Oh, I was a secretary, for a firm of accountants. I'll have to find a job, I need the money. I have my own car, that helps. But I don't want to travel far. Mrs D will help me out with the boys.'

He nodded. 'Mrs Donnelly. Husband used to be a plumber.'

'Yes. She's great. She's like a second mother really. She looked after me when I was small.' She paused and swallowed hard. 'After my father died . . . my mother had to find a job. She had been a teacher like yourself, so she went back to it, history and geography.' Why is all this coming out? Is it because he is a teacher and he may be sympathetic because my mother was a teacher? Once a teacher, always a teacher.

'Sure. Sure. I understand.'

Belle realised that she recognised something in his accent, slow, drawling, transatlantic. Something that had been puzzling her about Pat Quinn now seemed clear. There were Armagh tones heavily there, he was obviously local, but in four words she had picked out an angle on the man.

'I know a bit about the problems here, unemployment and the rest, even though I went to the States as a child. I thought that I knew you. But you don't remember me. My father kept the pub down the road . . .'

'Quinn's?'

He nodded.

'Quinn's. Of course. The pub was one end, the grocer's at the other. I remember your mother, she looked after the groceries. But we didn't come down this way to shop, not on down to Corey. We always went to the village, to Crawford's, it was nearer and there was always that big cycle down the main street. It was incredible. My brother and I used to stop here for ice-creams. Yes, I remember. But I'm afraid I don't remember you, I don't think so, I'm sorry . . .'

'Well, we're not quite the same age, I am older than you,' he smiled.

'Did you go to school here? You didn't go to the grammar school in town?'

'No. I went to school in Monaghan, over the Border for a while. I lived with my oldest brother there, Liam. I only came home the odd time at weekends, but then I used to stay with my aunt in England.' He looked keenly at her.

Yes, now she remembered the tall black-haired gangling boy who had been there sometimes. The father had been interned or something and he was always 'putting it around', getting some girl or other in trouble. There had been six or seven children in the Quinn family, not two like John and herself. You could always tell a Catholic, that's what Sam's mother, Mrs Johnston had observed once, they have big families . . . he must be a Mick while I'm a Prod, Belle decided without thinking twice. She shook her head and smiled at him. 'I remember you.'

'My father was a bit of a lad,' Pat Quinn said carefully, choosing his words.

That's an understatement, he was an active Republican, Belle thought, the old prejudices creeping up, fast and furiously.

'He did have a reputation,' Pat Quinn continued, 'for the ladies around these parts.'

She looked up at him, incredulous, and thought quickly. 'Yes, I heard. Of course.' A man's sexual proclivities meant more than his politics? Maybe she had lost touch, maybe that was how people saw things now in the country. After the years of the Troubles she thought differently. Maybe city life was different? Maybe out here politics, bombs and bullets were not so important? He must be joking. She frowned at him.

Pat Quinn laughed. 'He was a bit of a lad for politics too. I don't recall much, but then I must have been twelve or thirteen when we went out to the States. I do recall you though.'

Yes, the stuck-up Prod that lived up the road, she thought with a tinge of regret. Time and events and fate had taken a hand. Where had he been all this time? He could perhaps have been in her life instead of Sam. But that was impossible. The Neills and the Quinns could not mix, like oil and water, it was impossible.

'You have the car, I see.'

They had walked to the front door and were standing side by side on the step, looking out over the schoolyard. The clutch of pupils that had rushed past them from the other classroom as they talked had joined their fellows, scattered about like dead leaves in the wind. Clouds were backing up over Carrigatuke in the far distance and it seemed colder than ever. The wind, Belle noted, looking up at the weathervane, was still in the east. A few hard flakes of snow fell between them as they stood together not speaking.

For an instant Belle felt content, and at peace. She had not looked forward to this part of her new life, though it was only a small key to fit into the lock that would open the door on it, like opening a door on a new home. The boys would be settled soon. It had been so uncomplicated. She must not get over-confident. Somehow this man beside her no longer threatened, he seemed a friend, sent to help her where she least expected it.

'You'll bring the boys over on Monday then? Wait until about half past nine, then I can talk to them once I have the other kids started at work. There is only one other teacher here, a young fellow called Alan. We could start the boys on Tuesday perhaps,' Pat Quinn said eventually.

Belle nodded. A strand of her curly hair fell over one eye and she flicked it back with a practised gesture.

He thought, looking down on her as she looked ahead of her, not staring, not focusing on the washed-out landscape round them, the cluster of two-storeyed houses that made up the single street that was Corey, the green door of the pub that had been Quinn's and now bore the name McGuigan, the twist of smoke from one chimney stack, how little she seemed to have been changed by the years, by marriage and motherhood. He recalled her brother and her cycling by, trying not to notice him, but betraying it by their slightly raised voices coming in snatches as they passed. She seemed ill at ease, as if she had something to hide, something she had not chosen to tell him. Why had she come back? It would do no harm to try to find out. He knew just whom to ask.

Belle gathered the car keys out of her pocket, fumbling with cold fingers, and unlocked the door.

Pat Quinn bent down and opened the car door for her, slipping the keys out of the lock and passing them to her as he gestured in a half mocking, half gallant way for her to get inside. He closed the car door. She did not open the window, and regretted it instantly. She waved shyly and mouthed 'Monday' at him. He nodded, took a couple of steps backwards, stuck his hands into his pockets and nodded again at her.

As she drove up the road again and reached the bend by the gate-lodge she slowed and thought about digressing in the direction of the Lodge and the O'Briens. She changed her mind at once. She needed to go up to the village, to Mrs Crawford's shop, to make sure there was a plausible answer for curious customers who might enquire about her.

Then as she drove past her home she looked at it through the curtains of pines, seeing the grey stone façade, the faded woodwork, the bleached wood of the front door, the bare branches of the creeper now straggled about the front in an untidy fashion. By spring young green leaves would be out, by summer the greyness would be clothed in a rich coating of leaf that would change to rich copper in autumn, glowing from the top of the village street ahead. The house was like some old man sitting on a bench in the park, sitting on the same bench day after day, watching passers-by, watching the village at whose feet it sat. And the village. How much would they notice?

She decided not to drive up the wide street ahead, but to take the less obvious route to the top of the village. But moments later she realised she would be passing by the old school, the army post. Was it the faceless people that looked out from the guardhouse that worried her, or was it another more disturbing memory from another place? To retreat now, to turn the car, would be to excite attention. Her car was strange. They would notice it.

There was a ramp across the road, a slab of concrete moulded into a hummock over which she gingerly eased the car. There was no sign of life behind the high security fence or indeed in the darkened slits of the guardhouse at the gates. It was as if there was nobody there.

She eased the car over a second ramp. She caught sight of movement in her mirror. Two Landrovers were coming up behind her. They were approaching in a leisurely fashion, their dead green shapes skulking amid the flurries of sleet which were skittering across the road surface, whipped into eddies by the wind. She parked the car outside Crawford's shop in the square, and looked in the mirror. The Landrovers had stopped fifty yards behind her. They just sat there. Nobody got out. It seemed as if they were waiting for her to make the first move.

And she did. Getting out of the car quickly. They were watching her, she knew, the army down the road, the police in the shrouded station next door to Crawford's. She was the only figure in the landscape.

She walked briskly to the shop door, lifted the latch and went in. The shop was low-ceilinged, long and narrow. The counter top was littered with bars of chocolate, half a dozen copies of the morning paper, the *News Letter*, a cardboard box full of razors. She stood there in a gloom scented with detergent and bacon, cigarettes and the musty smell of vegetables thick with soil. A small bell at the door had tinkled when she closed it. Nobody came for a moment or two. That was usual.

A rusting refrigerator whirred halfway down the shop, filled with haphazard piles of sausages, bacon rashers, cooked ham ready sliced and curling at the edges, bars of butter and margarine battered at the corners. She wandered down the shop, checking items on the shelves, wondering what she might need. She could get beans, bacon and sausages for the boys, and there must be bread already for they had been toasting it this morning.

'Well, you're back then.' The voice behind her gave her a start.

Mrs Crawford had appeared noiselessly behind the counter, a large woman with a massive bosom encased in a tight nylon overall which through weeks, years of wear was permanently stained at the front where she leaned against the bacon slicer. She hadn't changed either. Not a hint of make-up, her skin had taken on a smooth patina with the years, and her eyes were black and shining in her face. Eyes that missed nothing. While the shop window was small and filled with ageing tins and packets yellowing in the light, she managed to keep a tight visual control on the village. Who came and went, when the electricity man came to read the meters, when the rector walked up the church path opposite, who came to the police station next door, when there was a new car, a new baby, who was dead, dying, sick, injured. Her shop had one of the few telephones in the village, so it was she who entered and stayed in people's lives, carrying messages large and small.

Her husband Cecil would appear only fitfully, sleepily during the long day. They had no children, no small boy to run to the back of the shop for the potatoes, fill a can with lamp oil, roll out a new cylinder of gas. Each customer learned to take life at their pace, to stand and take time to think about whether they needed matches, soap, dog meal. The Crawfords in their world padded up and down like some elderly animals in a zoo cage, knowing the boundaries.

'How are the boys then?' Mrs Crawford questioned.

'Oh grand, grand.'

'Getting bigger, I suppose. Young Rory would be nearly eleven now. And the wee one . . .' her voice softened and she looked downwards, spreading one hand as if a small child was standing there, 'the wee one must be getting big too like his father. Did you see . . . ?'

'Yes, he's not a baby any more,' Belle said quickly.

'You got in last night. I saw . . .' Mrs Crawford parried.

'Yes. The boys were very excited. Did you see all the lights? They were in every room. It makes a change for them, to be back . . .'

'You're back to stay, then?' Mrs Crawford asked.

'It looks like it. I had a good job, but the firm decided to move out of town. I didn't fancy starting from the beginning in another job. It seemed sensible to come home.' There now, that second time the lie sounded plausible, didn't it? Belle drew a deep breath and waited for Mrs Crawford to respond.

'They'll be going down to the school at Corey, I suppose.'

'Yes, Mrs Crawford,' Belle had to stop her somehow, 'I'll take half a pound of sausages, and some bacon, and those beans. How is Mr Crawford?'

'Ah well, you know, as always, never strong, never strong.' Mrs Crawford moved into action. 'Did you see we had an army post here now?' There was a note of pride in her voice, as if, Belle thought wryly, she was announcing a new branch of Marks & Spencer's.

'You can't help feeling safe now they are here, but there's others in the village don't like it. They say the post might be attacked. We're not all that far from the Border. I suppose they could come in with a bomb in a van, and park it outside . . . but then you know I keep an eye out . . . all the time. I know I would see it, wouldn't I?'

'Yes, you would.'

'We're safe here, all of us watching, even you down the hill . . .'

'Yes.'

Mrs Crawford had assembled Belle's small cache of food on the counter, and she added up the cost laboriously on the back of a paper bag.

'You didn't bring a basket?' she said, frowning at Belle.

'Sorry, I was in a rush, I forgot to bring one.' Belle realised that she was already apologising, slipping into that old role from childhood.

'Well, I'm sure you will have a lot to settle, a lot . . .' Mrs Crawford smiled her best benevolent smile.

Belle was backing to the door, taking from Mrs Crawford the plastic bag into which she had pointedly put the purchases, fingers on the latch, her smile a fixed grimace. No more questions, no more statements, no more instructions . . . please! She was glad to reach the car.

Outside the sleet had died away, and only a few traces lay on the wide roadway, devoid of traffic and people, silent sleeping doors shut against the cold. The patrol cars were still in position.

She started down the hill, past the terraced houses fitting side by side like steps and stairs, with here and there a fitful plume of smoke issuing from a chimney, towards the House at the bottom, in the hollow. A movement caught her eye. A flag flickered on the building on the bottom corner of the street, on the right. It was on the Orange Hall, a Union Jack.

This is my first real dance, the New Year's dance. Mrs D helped make my dress. She says I look more than fourteen, but I'm actually fourteen and a half.

John is with me, but when we get inside he gives me a shove and tells me to 'go over there' – that's where the girls are. The boys are on the other side.

The band is starting to play. Nobody seems to want to dance with me. Where's John? He's over there and he has a partner, Elizabeth . . . ugh! I don't like her. I'll just have to go and stand and wait.

There's Sam Johnston. I don't like him. He thinks that he is God's gift to girls. All the girls are mad about him. He hardly speaks to me and when he does he just teases and teases.

There's Marcus O'Brien. He must be on holiday still. We went back last week after the Christmas holidays but he goes to a boarding-school in England. Their holidays are different to ours. He's a bit of a joke the way he combs his hair and all. He's coming over!

'Hallo, Annabelle. How are you?' I don't answer. 'Do you want this dance?'

'Yes, if you like.'

'I'm not much of a dancer. Anyway this one is nearly over. Shall we wait for the next?'

I nod. We stand watching the dancers go round and round. 'Did you hear the news?' he asks.

'What news?'

'There's been a fight somewhere, a riot, up near Londonderry.

I was listening to it on the radio, before I came out. We have no television. Have you?'

'Yes, but I didn't see it, I was washing my hair . . .'

'Well, it was about civil rights, you know there has been trouble before. They had a march to a place called Burntollet, and they got ambushed.'

'I don't understand about civil rights.'

'It's the Catholics. They want jobs . . . something about voting too.'

'Did anyone get hurt?'

'Oh yes, they were attacked with stones and all. A lot of people.'

'What's going to happen?'

'I don't know . . . they say there's going to be more trouble . . . but the police will handle it . . . look, the music has stopped now,' he says, he now has tight hold of my hand. 'I want the next dance.'

'Yes.' Where's John? I can't see him. I can see Sam Johnston and he's with that Elizabeth.

'Annabelle?' Marcus is looking awfully serious. I wish that he did not wear glasses. 'Annabelle?' I wish that he did not call me Annabelle.

'Yes?'

'Can I leave you home after the dance?'

'I'll be going home with John.' There, I have decided. 'It's only a few yards down the hill anyway.'

All those years ago, Belle thought, the start of it all, the Troubles. We never noticed it then, we were too busy with each other. And now I am part of it. Something made her look in her mirror again. The two patrol cars were coming over the top of the village street behind her, side by side in the wide street. They stopped and watched as she went. Yes, I certainly have protection.

Chapter 4

BELLE SHUT THE KITCHEN door with a bang, reflecting how the house looked bare and empty as she had observed it from the village. The windows with their scant curtains drawn back looked desolate. But at the back, in the kitchen, she could do something to make it more lived in. Suddenly she felt galvanised into action, as if some primitive home-making instinct had risen in her, making her want to build a nest and line it for her young. She felt invigorated, stirred in some strange way, as if coming home had not been enough, as if she wished at long last to make her mark on the house, whereas in the past she had felt like a tenant. The feeling was short-lived.

'Mummy! Mummy!'

Why was it when Conor was upset he slipped from the more formal 'Mama' of his babyhood to this insistent hurt tone? Belle knew instantly as the small body clutched its arms around her knees that the face upturned to hers would be wet with tears.

'Rory! Rory!' he said between gulping sobs.

She knew the signs. Rory had been asserting his authority again. In these dark moments Rory would push Conor aside both physically and mentally, in a moment that was pure rejection. Often Conor would get hurt, not seriously, and Belle had learned to accept it as part of growing up, of peer behaviour between brothers and sisters. Oh John! she thought. And stopped herself. She must not think about John. But John had been so different, five years older, not three as with her boys. He had listened to her, listened to her on those days when she had not been able to get close to her mother. Her mother had not always been cold, surely, it was only in adolescence that the indifference came.

'Belle! Belle! Will you stop this instant?'

I can hear it again. It sounds so afraid. Crying out.

The moonlight is shining through the thin curtains of my mother's room. I have crept here from one pool of shadow to another, from my own bed. I'm still shivering even though my mother pulled me in under her bedclothes some time ago.

'I can hear him. I can hear him.'

'It's only a fox. In the orchard,' she says, pulling the sheet and blanket up by my neck. 'Put your arms inside, you'll be cold.'

'What's he doing in the orchard? He sounds so sad. Is he hurt?'

'He's probably baying to the moon. They do that sometimes. He's singing in a way, he's happy. He's calling out to his mate.'

'He's not happy, he's not. He doesn't sound happy.'

'Well, if you were another fox you probably wouldn't think so.'

I put my arms round her. She is very warm but I cannot stop shivering.

'It's only a fox,' she repeats, turning away from me in this big wide empty bed. 'You're just being childish, silly . . .'

I withdraw my arms, fold them on my chest tightly. Outside there is silence, or is there? If I hold my breath for . . . for . . . I count ten, twenty, thirty, forty, fifty in to myself, holding my breath . . . I cannot hear the fox at all, only the wind, a little wind, in the apple tree branches. I let out the air from my lungs slowly. And listen again. Only the trees, I can hear only the trees.

'What do you think he is – ?'

'Oh be quiet! Let's get to sleep. This is silly. At your age you should not be afraid of foxes. You're twelve now. This is enough.'

There is a wide space between us now in the bed. She is lying on her back like me, arms folded. Are we like two crusaders lying on the top of a tomb? Like the pictures in my history book? How many people have slept in this room? My grandmother and grandfather, their mother and father? In this bed, on this hard mattress. It is a very big bed, room enough for two very fat people and more. My mother is quite fat, Father was quite fat too. Now there is only my mother in the bed, and me, on nights like these. Does she miss him? Does she feel alone? Is she alone like the fox? He's stopped crying out now . . .

Belle stooped and gathered Conor into her arms, his wet face and hot sticky hair spread on his forehead pressed into her neck. He sobbed convulsively. Rory came racing into the kitchen, stopping when he saw her, his face fierce.

'I don't want to know what you have been up to this time, Rory, but it seems to me that you never learn. Conor is only small, he doesn't understand your games.' As soon as she spoke she realised how unfeeling her voice was.

Conor had to explain through his gulping sobs. 'We found a box upstairs in the attic. Full of toy soldiers. There's a tank, and a jeep, and the soldiers all have guns. They are just like the real ones. The tank is broken. Maybe we could mend it? Rory said they were for him to play with, I am the baby, I am too young, I don't understand about soldiers. But I do! I do! Mummy, that's not fair!'

John's soldiers. Of course they would be there. Belle stood Conor on his feet and brushed his hair out of his eyes.

Mrs D came in from the scullery with the kettle which she had been filling. 'What a lot of fuss about nothing! They are only soldiers and your Uncle John used to play with them for hours. I am not surprised that the tank is broken. Your Uncle John was very good at breaking things. Your mother was the one that tried to mend things for him. Your uncle had too many toys to play with. I'm surprised you haven't found his old train set.' Mrs D was trying to smooth over the situation.

'I did! I did!' Rory shouted indignantly. 'But it was broken, the rails were all bent too. It's just a dead loss. Broken. Ma, will you buy me a proper train set?' His voice was rising.

They're hungry and they need diverting, Belle realised. There's no point trying to heal the rift now directly. 'I have brought home, guess what,' she paused, 'for lunch?'

Rory gave Conor a shove. Released from the safety of his mother's arms he was vulnerable again.

'Sausages!' Conor was instantly interested. 'And beans, Mama? Great!' he shouted. 'Can I help cook them? Can I?'

'Yes.'

Rory caught her arm. 'Could we go for a walk afterwards?'

'Yes, why not? Up Top Hill?' The moment she said it she realised the implication. There was no going back now, looking at the boys' faces she knew they wanted to go, but she hated the prospect of leaving the safety of the house once again, she had been out in the open too much already today. But the feeling was useless. She couldn't hide for ever. She would just have to rely on the army and the police and hope that those in Belfast would lose interest in her.

Soon the kitchen was full of the smell and sizzling of the sausages and the bacon. Warfare was forgotten as the two boys tucked in at the scrubbed kitchen table. Belle and Mrs D sat over a long cup of tea.

When the boys had finished, Belle stood up. 'Don't worry about the dishes, Mrs D, I'll do them when we get back again. I will be glad of something to do. Away you go, we'll manage.' Regretting instantly, she gave her a quick squeeze. 'Thank you for your help. I don't know what I'd do without you.' Mrs D sniffed and pulled her coat off the peg on the kitchen door.

'It's best we get off now,' Belle explained, 'it gets dark so early these nights. I want us to get back before it does.'

Mrs D lingered only long enough to help Belle wrap the boys up snugly. They left the house together, Belle locking the door. She slipped the key into her pocket, not under the quern stone. That was where anybody would leave a key. They could get in, be waiting for her when she came back. With the key in her pocket she felt safer. She curled her fingers round it, comforted.

At the end of the yard they parted, Belle and the boys going to the garden gate and past it along the laurel hedge to another larger gate, large enough for lorries to pass through on the days when they pulled the apples. There was a carpet of leaves and spent beechnut husks underfoot. The long rows of apple trees planted some forty years before were spread out in front of them, sloping up the hill. The grass was long and lank and wet and a thin mist seemed to hang about the boughs. Belle was glad, it made her feel less conspicuous. She had forgotten how steeply the orchard rose up behind the house on this side of the hill. Now and again she would stop by a tree and remember, feeling the texture of the thin bark with her hand, looking up into the branches and how they grew one from another, reminding the boys which apples grew sweet or which were Bramleys, how hard it was to climb. As they climbed up further she stopped to look back at the house.

'Oohee!' My mother. It must be her.

'Sounds like Mum,' John says. He is just below me in this apple tree. We have spotted a cluster of really red ripe eaters near the top. The question is can we reach them? I have longer arms than John, he says, and I'm lighter, so I should be able to reach the apples without bending the branches too much. The ground is far below.

'Put your left hand just there,' he points, 'that should do it.'

'Oohee!'

'Put your left hand there. No! There!' John sighs, points again.

'Do you mean here?'

'No. There.' He points again. 'Stupid,' he mutters.

'Oohee!'

Mother. Again. I am near the top now. My arm is stretched out, my fingers shaking . . .

'Oohee!'

I look down to the house, to the kitchen door which is open. Mother is standing on the step waving. She has gathered her apron with her other hand into a tight ball on her chest. Is she angry? Or afraid? For me?

'Oohee! You'll fall! I know you will!' Her voice is very shrill.

I am stretching out my hands again, holding on tightly with one to a very thin branch, reaching out . . . maybe if I let go this hand . . .

'Oohee!'

Oh shut up! I lose my balance, swaying, holding on with both hands.

'Whoops!' says John below me. 'Mind out!'

There is a soft series of thuds. The apples have fallen off the tree into the long grass below.

'Now they will be bruised, they are ruined, ruined . . .' mutters John, climbing down.

I follow him. 'I'm sorry, John, I'm sorry.'

'You're useless! Useless!' he fumes.

Belle wondered how good her boys would be at climbing apple trees. They would soon learn. Would she stand at the kitchen door? She brushed these thoughts aside, striding to catch up with the boys who now were some distance ahead.

'Ugh!' said Conor, standing still beside Rory and looking down into the grass.

'What is it?' she asked, coming up beside them.

'Ugh!' they said in chorus, looking at her, then at the ground again.

Amongst the tumbled stems lay lean bare bones, the skeleton of an animal bleached white by frost and rain. A fox.

'It's a fox. Or it was a fox,' Belle said sadly, 'some farmers have to put down snares to catch them. You can get too many foxes and then they will go after anything . . . not just chickens and ducks, but young lambs too if they get a chance,' she explained.

'Its skull is very interesting,' said Conor, picking it out of the grass and holding it up to his face for closer inspection.

'Aah! Put it down, Conor! Put it down!' Rory cried.

'No! I want to keep it, bring it home, keep it,' Conor protested, clasping the skull to his chest.

Belle took it away from him gently. 'Leave it, Conor. Look, let's cover the fox with grass, cover him up.' She leaned down and gathered up some clumps of long grass and laid them over the bones until they were almost out of sight.

Conor sighed loudly, shrugged his shoulders, disappointed.

Rory was already leading the way again, up through the trees.

There was the sound of the wind in the trees at the top of the hill, the thick copse of sycamore, lime, crab-apple and beech had few leaves left on the branches. The wind licked around noisily, blasting in their faces as they stood underneath, looking out ahead over the open countryside spread below. In summer the sound would be soft, muted, the wind murmuring through the thick leaves, cool and shady after the long climb to the top. In late spring the hillside below would be full of meadowsweet, milkmaids, buttercups, with, if you knew how to look, the soft rounded indentation of the form of a hare where it had crouched and waited the hours through. In the steep hedgerows Belle knew there would be violets, purple vetches, blackberries for jam. On the days when cattle grazed there, you could lie in wait like some combat soldier in the long grasses, stalking the cows in a kind of primitive battle. A dozen dog-days, holidays spent in idle dissolution with her brother, sprang to mind as she looked down the hill to the marshy swamp at its foot, the small lake spread out, and the railway line beyond it. She held her breath, waiting for the sound of the train rattling over the viaduct in the distance, but out of sight behind the slight rise of another hill. Only the wind in the trees could be heard. Tears were wetting her cheeks and she shook her head.

'Ma, you're crying. Ma?' Rory said, grasping one of her hands.

'No. It's the wind, just the wind.'

A bunch of crows flew out of one tree with a clatter, flapping. She brushed the tears away and shaded her eyes. 'You can see quite far from here, though it's misty today. Down there, away to the left, can you see? That's Corey. Can you see the school? Mr Quinn is very nice. You'll see him on Monday. Maybe you will be able to start there.'

'Och, Ma! Do I have to go to Corey? Could I not just stay with you, take care of you, and help you in the house?'

'No. Don't be silly. It's only for a short while. And anyway I shall have to find a job. I won't be at home then. What would you do in the house all day long without me?'

'Is it a nice school?' Conor asked, in the long silence that followed.

'Yes. I used to know Mr Quinn; he's a bit older than me. He used to live down at Corey, but then he moved to live in America.'

'America?' Rory asked, his eyes widening. Belle could see that he was impressed.

There was another long silence as that piece of information sank in.

'I can see a man with a gun,' said Rory suddenly, pointing.

'Where?' Belle stooped down to his eye level and followed his pointing finger.

'There! And it's not one. It's two!'

'Where?' shouted Conor. 'Mummy, I can't see. Lift me up. Lift me up?'

Belle lifted him off his feet in front of her, holding his small body against her. She could feel his heart pounding, or was it her own? She pointed. 'Do you see? There!'

He nodded. 'Oh, yes, very interesting!'

'What do you think they are doing? With guns?' Rory asked, looking at her earnestly.

'I don't know . . .' Belle said, too quickly, 'probably out shooting, for rabbits, or ducks maybe, down by the lake.' A simple explanation. But as they watched it seemed to her that the figures moved with care, stealthily, through the thickets of hazels and alders. The men seemed engrossed in each other, oblivious of the three figures in the distance. The light was fading fast, the trees losing their definition, there was a blur of mist over the marsh and the wind seemed to have dropped. Corey had faded from sight, and the men too, so soon. She was unnerved. There was a simple explanation, there must be. People went shooting in the country. In the city a gun meant something else entirely. But she wasn't sure. They could be . . .

'Time to go home,' she said abruptly and turned, hurrying, heading for the copse and beyond it the deepening shadows of the orchard. The boys followed, quiet now. They would be in no mood for fighting any more today, the earlier aggravations had been forgotten.

'We'll go down the other side of the orchard, to the other side of the house, it's quicker, it's getting dark, we should hurry.'

The orchard was not so steep here, and in the gathering dusk less brambles and fewer unsure footholds, the maze of trees stretching ahead.

'Why are there marks on the trees, Ma? Look, white marks.' Rory was pointing at a series of white flashes on the tree trunks. They showed clearly in the half light.

Belle gave them a cursory glance. 'I expect they are just a reminder to the Johnstons, when they are spraying. One tree would look pretty much like another. I expect they marked them out last spring and the paint or whatever they used hasn't washed off yet. It is a sensible idea, saves spraying the same trees twice. Let's get home.'

'I see,' replied Rory thoughtfully, pausing and running a finger over one of the marks. 'It doesn't rub off all that easily.'

'Yes, yes,' said Belle impatiently. But Rory persisted, running to catch up with her.

'It's a bit like the Minotaur, isn't it?'

'What do you mean?'

'Well, the ball of string and all that. If you got lost among all the trees you would be able to follow the marks you had made, especially if it was dark. You could find your way out.'

'What on earth made you think about that?'

'Oh it's something we were doing at school before I left. There was this man Theseus who went away down into a maze of dark passages to find a monster called the Minotaur and kill it. Theseus had this ball of string which he unwound as he went so that when he was trying to get out again he wouldn't get lost, he just followed it.'

'I think I remember something about that,' Belle said slowly, thinking, but pressing onwards, 'yes, when your father and I went to Crete on our honeymoon there was some place there where it was supposed to have happened.' She shook her head. 'I've forgotten.'

'If you look at the marks,' went on Rory, waving his arm, 'you can see that they are in a definite line, down. And look here! Marks on this tree, moving over to the left, and here again, there's a definite turn . . . and here too!'

'Now who would want to be up in the orchard in the dark following marks on the trees?' she laughed.

'Och, I don't know. It was just an idea.' He waved his hand dismissively.

'I know,' Conor piped up in a small voice. 'If you were a soldier and you were planning an attack in the dark . . .'

'Shut up, Conor! That's stupid,' Rory scorned.

'Now you boys. That's enough!' Belle warned.

Down by the house there was a break in the boundary wall by the end of the stable block, a narrow passage of laurels led into the yard. And there was also a passageway, a crack between the boundary wall and the side of the house that led out on to the front lawn. It was now dark and Belle, from experience knowing how fast the laurels grew each year, thought that perhaps coming down this way was a mistake. But surprisingly the thick growth was neatly trimmed. They emerged easily into the yard. She searched in her pocket for the key and stood in the growing dark by the door feeling for the keyhole.

'You should have left the kitchen light on,' Rory said, 'then you would be able to see.'

'It costs money for electricity. In future I want you to check that you don't leave any lights on. Do you hear?'

'Yes, we hear,' Rory said defensively, wondering at her brusque tone.

Belle wanted to get indoors and pull the curtains tight, close the shutters, build up the fire.

'Are you going to get the television going tonight?' Conor tugged at her sleeve as they stood in the kitchen.

'Yes, we'll have a go, but I don't know whether the aerial will work,' she told him as he looked at her anxiously. 'You boys go and organise a bath while I see to the tea and try the telly out,' she said.

She went over to the door and locked it. She was indoors for the night. She slid the bolt across eventually, lifting the door with a wrench, wedging it up with one foot. Then she went from room to room on the ground floor unfolding the heavy wooden shutters stuck with paint and forcing the locks across them. And out in the porch where dead leaves had spun through the cracks around the door, she tugged the handle to make sure it was secure. It was.

Eventually she got the television going in the kitchen but with no picture.

'Two bombs went off in Belfast today. No one was injured in the explosions. One bomb was in a van parked outside the Law Courts. It was estimated at 500 pounds. Considerable damage . . .' She switched over quickly. There was a Western on BBC2. Gary Cooper, when she got the picture, was looking tall, silent and comforting.

Yes, this house is a fortress, she told herself when she eventually went upstairs to bed all in the dark, having switched off the lights, feeling each step with her feet. I must be safe here. Where else can I go, anyway?

Chapter 5

THE HOUSE WAS TOTALLY silent when she awoke next morning. A dull light was coming through the curtains, and she felt frozen, chilled, where she had turned and tossed the bedclothes aside in her fitful sleep.

Belle turned over on to her back and lay supine, feeling the flat of her stomach with her hand. She cupped each breast in turn, thinking disconsolately about herself. Not voluptuous, not ever, just adequate. It had been no help to her over the years. Her girlfriends had grown and ripened as they grew together to the exploratory years of adolescence. She had just grown, envying the others their obvious charms which the boys enjoyed. She had tried to keep apart, her relationships with boys had been on equal terms, she trying to beat them not only in academic subjects, but in sport too. They regarded her thus the less for her sexual charms. And as the years progressed she had grown aloof from them, only on the fringe of the female circle. She would not be interested in new hair-styles, or frocks, or even in a new chocolate cake recipe. Falling for Sam had been a deliberate act on her part, an attempt to be drawn into the circle, to be accepted. She had become his willing slave, more feminine in her behaviour than any of the other girls had hoped to be. They had all lusted after Sam, but she had snared him, for good or evil . . . till death us do part.

Had she heard voices in the night?

She sat up in bed drawing the covers about her, rocking her body. No, that was just silly, she had dreamed it all. Who would come around the house in the middle of the night? In the city, voices were commonplace, along with the buses that spun by regularly and the patrol cars. Some sounds you got used to, even the patrol cars, but sometimes they played games, zooming round the corner at the top of the street, accelerating madly, then braking furiously at the bottom of the street. A way to break the monotony of long wet dull streets, rows of sleeping windows, and the possibility of a sniper's bullet.

Who would come around? Had they found her already? She held her breath to listen. Silence. It was no good, she had to go downstairs, face it, whatever it was. She had convinced herself that the house was virtually impenetrable. But could they come around checking things out? Did they come around last night? Would every morning be like this?

She took a deep breath as if she stood on the high diving-board of a swimming-pool and swung her legs out of bed to stand on the worn rug. All her clothes seemed to be inside out, the way she had thrown them off last night. She groaned. She would wash later.

Later. She would have to go into town and see about a job, and she needed to go to a bank, talk about a loan. She needed a job. In Belfast she had coped by letting one of her rooms to a student. Anne Rooney had become one of the family, contributing to the cost of the food but paying for her room by helping out with the boys. Now she would have to recalculate her finances.

Belle went downstairs carefully to find the kitchen just as she had left it the night before. Voices? She had been mistaken. She was poking up the range when there was a tap at the door. There had been no sound of footsteps outside over the scraping of the coals. She listened, but held the poker firmly in her hand. Then she heard the sound of Mrs D singing to herself on the other side of the door. When she finally got the door open, Mrs D was dancing a little unsteadily on the cobbles as if she was following an Orange band on the Twelfth of July.

'It is old, but it is beautiful,' she lingered on the 'beautiful', her voice quavering, 'its colours they are fine. It was worn at Derry, Aughrim, Enniskillen and the Boyne . . .' She looked up and laughed.

'Och, Mrs D, you're mad, now don't be singing *The Sash* too loudly, you never know who might be listening.'

'Och yourself! Never worry. I'll sing whatever I like to whomever I like and when I like. I know there's no Fenians listening here.'

'You're terrible, you always were,' scolded Belle.

'You were bolted and barred up well and truly, shutters and all, I see,' Mrs D observed, 'and I see you have had visitors.' She pointed.

Hanging on a hook on the wall beside the back door, rimed with frost, the coloured plumage dying, was a brace of mallard ducks.

'Somebody was thinking about you. I won't say who though.' Mrs D shook her head in mock surprise. 'Those will roast up nicely, won't they, but you would need to hang them a few days before you could eat them.'

'Well, hallo there!' said a man's voice cheerfully. Belle jumped. A stocky young man in a blue overall came round the corner of the house with a milk bottle in each hand. 'I thought you'd want milk, now that you're here. How many pints do you think you might be needing?'

'You gave me a fright! Let me think,' Belle said, her eyes wide.

'I'm sorry. You'll have to get used to me every morning, bright and early, around eight o'clock,' he went on, 'there's three of you, and Mrs D who I know fine well will drink so many cups of tea you would need a pint of milk a day for her alone. You'd need four I think, yes four. Growing boys need their pintas . . .'

Even he knows all about me, Belle thought.

'And if there's anything . . .' he smiled knowingly and jokingly, 'that you need, missus, I'll do my best, my very best, to provide it.' He looked her up and down and whistled.

That was enough for Belle, she had met men like him before, charmers all of them. 'Yes, four a day please. Can you leave them at the front gate please . . . it would save you traipsing all the way down the drive every day,' she explained. And I would not have to put up with your charms too, she thought, or your inquisitions, and your nosiness. I don't want strange men walking around the house.

He put his head on one side. 'At the gate?'

'Yes, it would save you, wouldn't it?'

He walked to the corner of the house, looked up the drive to the gate, and then looked at her thoughtfully. 'Well . . .' he said slowly, 'yes, why not?' He looked up the drive again. 'The best thing would be to put it in a biscuit box, with a lid, hidden, so nobody passing would be tempted to steal it . . . you never know who might be passing . . . and if you wanted anything else like . . . cream maybe of a Sunday, or yoghurts for the boys, or even eggs, they would be safe, and in all weathers too.' He nodded, she nodded, it was a good idea.

'We'll start tomorrow then? Have you a box there now?' he asked.

'Yes, I know just the one,' said Mrs D, scurrying inside. Belle waited for her to find it, standing in the cold, aware of the critical eyes of this young man, wondering what to say to fill the conversational silence that dropped between them.

He looked at her and nodded his head again, smiling. 'Fine day that.'

'Yes, but cold,' she replied.

'Soon have you fixed up.'

Mrs D appeared round the doorpost, breathing hard. 'Sorry, it was at the bottom of the cupboard, I had to stoop to get it and you know I'm not such a dazzler,' she smiled knowingly at the man, 'as I used to be.' She held out a tall square biscuit box.

'If you could just take a walk with me down to the gate,' he insisted, looking at Belle, 'you could see where we could put it. You go and put us on a cup of tea, Mrs D, and we'll be back in a moment.'

They walked down the drive side by side. He covered the awkwardness by whistling desultorily. At the gate he paused, looked up at the house, and chose a nook beside the gatepost, brushing aside the rhododendrons to make a space on the top of the wall.

'There now,' he rearranged the tin and stepped back to survey its position critically, 'you can't see it from the road. You would never know it was there. It will be our secret. You can leave me a wee note to say what you want . . . and I'll do my best . . .' He leaned towards her conspiratorially.

She drew back. 'Yes, I see. You're right, very neat.'

'If the weather's bad, it's sheltered, d'ye see?' he ended in triumph.

'Yes.' She turned and walked up the drive.

He followed her into the kitchen. Mrs D had three cups of tea poured, the sugar bowl at the ready and a tin of biscuits.
'All the comforts of home,' he murmured, and looked Belle up and down.
'Get on with you!' Mrs D said, giving him a shove. 'She's a married woman!'
'That's not what I heard,' he replied.
That's enough, Belle said to herself and went upstairs to rouse the boys out of bed. Her cajoling produced only grunts in reply.
'I'm staying, it's cold,' was eventually Rory's response. Followed by 'Can't I?' when he saw the frown on her face.
'Oh all right, but I have to go to town to see the bank manager, and see if I can do something about a job. Will you be quite happy here with Mrs D? I'll be back at lunchtime or soon after it.'
'Don't worry. We'll be fine. We won't get in Mrs D's way, don't worry. Anyway we have to get all our things tidied. There's an awful mess.'
'Yes, that's a very good idea,' she replied, stepping over a pile of clothes and toys to where Conor was still sleeping soundly. She kissed his flushed cheek. He murmured, putting out his arms to encircle her.
'Mama. Mama.'
'Yes, love. I'll be back soon. Stay with Rory.'
She paused at the top of the stairs listening. Mrs D and the milkman were having a long conversation.
Some time later, by the time she had unpacked and put away the clothes, washed and dressed, brushed her hair and put on some make-up, the voices downstairs had ceased. She went down to the kitchen.
'I had to throw your tea out, it was stone cold,' Mrs D complained.
'Oh, I expect you have another cup in the pot,' Belle said.
'It'll be stewed. But you just went off. Is anything the matter? You seem worried this morning.'
Belle wanted to reassure her. 'No, not really. I'm sorry. I just don't feel much like talking to people. It's not you . . . I just . . . look, I need to go into town and fix up about money. Can you keep an eye on the boys for me, I won't be long. They are still in bed, and it won't do them any harm to stay there for a while.'

Mrs D looked pleased. 'Well, I did have a wee job to do but it can wait until tomorrow – I'll stay home and do it then. Never you worry. Just you go on.' She smoothed her apron. 'There now. That's fixed. You didn't get a chance to talk to young Cathal.'

'Cathal? Oh, the milkman.'

'Yes. He's quite a lad with the girls. He's not all that bad, and he'll see you right, you can be sure of that. Poor lad, he comes from one of those . . .' she lowered her voice, 'mixed marriages. He was RC, the mother the other. Nothing would please the father's side but that he be Catholic too. It's a pity, he's a nice lad.' She lowered her voice further. 'The father is in the Maze, they found him with guns it seems. But I think he's all right, the boy I mean, he looks after his mother just grand. They have a herd of Friesians which they keep down at the O'Briens. You know that pair never had any sense about the land or anything and there's all that good land going to waste down there. Anyway . . . that young man is up at all hours to do the milk round, then get the cows in for milking . . . he never has a day off.'

'Where does he milk them?' Belle asked.

'Down at the O'Briens. You know there used to be a farm at the back of the big house there. He's in there. Done it up, worked hard. Would you believe it?'

Belle gathered up her handbag, a cheerful red jacket which made her feel bright and confident, and took the car keys off the hook. 'I had better get going, I don't really want to go, but I have to.'

'Don't you hurry back. The boys and I will be fine.'

Belle got in the car, but sat for a moment before she started. It must be done, she told herself. It must be done.

There was a light coating of frost on the hedgerows, but the road surface was dry and she drove along quite fast. She thought hard about what she needed to tell the bank manager. She needed a small loan to tide her over. Staying in the House wasn't going to cost her much but there was a limit to how long the money would last. All her confidence seemed to be slipping away. Going to town meant the possibility of being recognised. It was no good, she couldn't hide for ever. Yet she felt in a void, waiting for something awful to happen.

Soon the town's familiar landmarks came into view. The town, set in a hollow, had the square tower of the Church of Ireland cathedral surrounded by fine nineteenth-century houses on one hillock and in the distance the twin spires of the Roman Catholic cathedral, standing out silver grey, each proclaiming its own brand of Christianity.

Belle drove into the top of the Mall by the grey stone gaol built two centuries before and shrouded in protective wire, then turned left down the side of this green oval, once a racetrack. A full mile round its perimeter, skirted by two lines of trees, there was room in the centre for football, and cricket in the summer. At the far end was the courthouse in the Greek style with a fine pediment and fat columns supporting the law. It too was wrapped in fencing.

'Just here, Mrs Johnston, the room on the right, if you please.'

Sergeant McEvoy has me firmly by the elbow. Can he feel me shaking, I wonder? My knees feel like the proverbial jelly.

'Just in here, for a moment,' he explains.

It's a small bare office, two desks, two filing cabinets, the windows glazed with that strange bomb-proof glass so that it is hard to see out.

'Take a seat.' He points to a chair. 'I want to explain the procedure. There will be eight women next door. I want you to go and take a good look at them. Take your time. If you think you see the woman, I want you to go up to her and touch her on the elbow. Do you understand?'

'But . . .'

'What?'

'I didn't realise that I would have to go up to her, touch her. I thought that I would just point her out, from another room, that there would be one of those two-way windows, you know . . .' I am trying to keep calm.

'Like in the movies!' He laughs. 'No, not here. In America maybe. But here you have to do it personally.'

'I see.' I must be sensible, cool.

Minutes later, I am walking back down the corridor to the front door. It's done. I have committed myself.

'I'll be in touch,' the sergeant says to me as we reach the

passageway that leads through the security fencing to the open street outside.

There was little traffic. Belle drove past the courthouse until she found a parking space. She sat looking out on to the green expanse. She could almost smell the cut summer grass, hear the click of the cricket ball against the willow. A jogger passed her making his way around the perimeter. He passed three times before she gathered courage to move.

She locked up the car and walked to the security gates, passing by a soldier on guard who looked briefly in her bag. Did he notice a strange face? She did not detect a flicker of interest as she looked at him.

The bank was some distance up the street. She went in through the heavy mahogany doors with their brass fittings to the marble-floored emporium inside, then squared her shoulders and walked up to a side booth, ignoring a small queue for the cashier. She kept her face turned resolutely, refusing to be intimidated and stare back at the three pairs of eyes who watched her progress.

'Is the manager in?' she asked a girl who eventually appeared.

'Yes. What's the name?'

'Johnston.'

'Sorry,' the girl said pointedly, 'I didn't quite hear . . .'

Belle cleared her throat. 'Johnston,' she said, fractionally louder.

'Ah. Johnston,' the girl enunciated loudly. 'I'll see if Mr McKinney can see you.'

'It used to be Mr Bell, I knew him,' Belle said.

The girl smiled deprecatingly. 'No, Mr Bell has been gone this long time . . . years.'

'Well, can I see Mr McKinney then?'

'Just a moment, I'll see if he's free.'

Belle waited. She stood on one foot and then on the other. There were now five sets of eyes in the queue. The girl reappeared and nodded, leading her behind a flap in the counter top to a room in the back.

Mr McKinney was of medium height, about forty, with hair

brushed carefully over the top of his head to disguise a thinning patch. As he rose to shake her by the hand she noticed how limp and moist his hand was.

'Mrs Johnston.' A statement, not a query. He motioned to a chair. 'I was at school with your husband, Sam Johnston, am I right? I was in a higher form of course, older . . .'

'Yes. I have been living in Belfast for some years now . . .'

He held up a hand. 'I know the circumstances. Two boys, that's right? What can I do for you?' He seemed to have sensed her unease, like some doctor recognising symptoms.

'I had a good job, but I only managed to make things meet. With luck Rory, that's the eldest, will get the eleven-plus exam in the spring and then I'll not have to pay for him to go to grammar school . . . he's going to go to the local primary school in the mean time . . .'

'I know all about the cost of a good school,' he said, 'I have three boys at the grammar school but what with uniforms and all that . . . you still have to find money for it.' He was smiling with pride.

'I know there will be more expense. That is really why I came to see you. I came for your help . . . it may be some time before I can get another job. Is it possible for me to have a small overdraft?'

He leaned across the desk and put his hand over hers in a comforting gesture. 'I think that's possible, quite possible. The Johnstons are good for credit, I know, I know. Give me your account number in Belfast and we will take it from there. Don't you worry now, don't you worry at all.' His hand closed over hers again.

'I shall try to find a job at once, perhaps you might hear of one? Secretarial.'

He rose and walked around the desk. She stood up and took a step towards the door. 'Yes, I'm sure we can help out. I'll do a bit of detective work . . . if I get any ideas . . .'

'Yes, yes, thank you.' Belle backed away, hand on the doorknob. He followed and she retreated, then he nodded to her as he lifted the flap and she slid past him.

She stood on the doorstep of the bank breathing in the cool air, thankful for a moment. She didn't hear the doors swish behind her, only felt a hand on her arm. She started.

'Now, Annabelle,' the formality of the voice took her unawares, 'dear Annabelle, you didn't see me waiting in there, you were so concerned with other things. How are you? Silly question. Fine, I can see you are fine, just as beautiful and alluring as ever.'

Marcus. He didn't look a day older. Shortish, plump, immaculately attired in a plain dark pin-striped grey suit with a waistcoat, a pale pink silk shirt with a maroon-striped tie, his hair cut into a slightly schoolboy fringe across his forehead, horn-rimmed glasses, yes, Marcus was the same. In Ulster terms he would be described as 'old-fashioned'.

'Marcus! What a surprise! How are you?'

'As well as ever,' he replied, 'and why have you suddenly appeared in our midst? We thought that you had run away to find fame and fortune in the big city, though your real friends never thought that to be really the case. Your real friends still love you, I hope you realise that.' He took her hand. His grasp was firm, controlled. This man professed to be her friend, and over the years he had been devoted to her, until she had gone to Belfast, away from his immediate territory. She thought of him in those terms because he seemed like some predator, waiting for her when she was at her most vulnerable, seeking to comfort and reassure her, and devour her with his own brand of love should she let her guard slip. 'You know I have always cared for you . . . for your interests,' he added quickly, 'all these years.'

'Yes, I know, Marcus.'

'And if I can help at all, you know, I am here. Are you staying?'

'Yes, I think so.'

He looked at her sadly. 'All those years away, away from me . . . from us.' He held her hand still.

'I know. I know.' She looked up into his face, trying not to let the façade slip. His tone had been enough to set her on a slippery slope of self-pity.

'Well now, I think you need a bit of lunch. A quiet drink. Come with me? Let's talk?'

'No, Marcus, not this time,' she said, 'I just came into town briefly to see the bank manager. That's all. I need to get back. Another time.' He had that look in his eyes which she remembered from years ago. She couldn't cope with his probing into her life, not today, even though she knew he would only want to help her. 'Thank you for the thought.'

'I'll come and see you.'

'If you wish.'

'I do. I do,' he said quietly.

'Thank you, Marcus. I must go now.'

A streak of silvered sunshine was warming the pavements, casting long shadows between the buildings. It shone in her eyes, made her blind for the moment. She felt surrounded by alien things she could not see. It was disconcerting. She almost ran back to the car, opened the door and slid into the driving seat breathing hard. Home. She had to get home.

As she left town she checked the mirror to see if she was being followed. Silly. Of course not. She thought about Marcus, thought about how he had been with her when she had gone to identify John's body in the mortuary. She could have married him, all those years ago, he had asked her often enough. Too staid, too solid, she had thought, but he had stuck with her, in the background, all these years. Had Sam resented him? Maybe he had.

Sam. Why did her thoughts turn to him so often? Was it because she was back in the familiar countryside they had seen together? Was it simply that if she took her eyes off the road ahead and studied the landscape, the neat farms, a newly ploughed field, a tractor in the distance, a stubble field with a flock of white geese . . . it all served to make her think of him, and the Johnstons and the farm at Ballinmore which backed on to her family's land? The Neills and the Johnstons. How well they fitted. The Neills had only the past to look back on, and their dreams. The Johnstons worked hard on their farm, unrelenting, loving the land, looking up at Top Hill for what it could be, not at what it had been allowed to become, a few fields for cattle. When she and Sam had married he had talked to John of what might be made of the land that wasn't orchard. But it was John's land, he was the Neill of Tannaghmore. Only the apples counted for him.

The fields became a blur. She was crying. A flicker of black caught the corner of her eye and she saw two crows flying alongside her just above the hedgerow, keeping at her speed, like some sort of escort, or even an omen. Then there was a flash of light in her eyes and she blinked, forcing her eyes back to the road ahead. A car was coming towards her, shining its headlights even though it was daylight. She understood. There was a roadblock ahead, this was the way to warn of it, one driver to another.

She slowed as she came round a corner, seeing two Landrovers parked, and the familiar camouflaged figures. She wound down her window, steadying the wheel with her elbow, then she felt around for her handbag. In it was her driving licence, her identification. They would also want to know where she was going, and where she had been. It was an unnecessary exercise, she realised, when the UDR soldier stooped at the car window and saluted her.

'Good-day to you!' was all he said.

She could not fail to be charmed by that familiar smile, could she? That boyish smile, that thick dark hair? It was unfair. Keep out of my life, Sam.

'Been to town then?' he asked.

'Yes.'

'How are the boys?'

'Fine.'

'Not with you today?'

'Obviously not,' she said coldly, and regretted her tone at once. 'I left them with Mrs D. I had to see about . . . things . . .'

'Do you need any help?' He paused, at a loss for words for a moment. 'I mean, you know . . .' His voice died.

She looked steadfastly down the road ahead of her. 'I know.'

A car approached, coming in the opposite direction. The soldier turned his face away from her and looked at it as it drew near, adjusting his rifle. It gave her the excuse she needed. She pressed the accelerator with an impatient foot.

'Belle . . .' he started to say.

'I must go,' she said, letting the car move forward from him as he stood in the middle of the road.

'I'll call . . .' she heard him say.

She shook her head, but could not look back over her shoulder at him. She pressed the accelerator and heard the engine respond with a roar. She was crying now, tears flooding down her cheeks as she gripped the wheel in front of her, trying to focus her eye on the road. This was impossible. She must stop this, at once! When she felt more in control of herself, she took a deep breath and looked in the driving mirror. She had turned a corner. That familiar strong square figure had gone.

A car coming towards her flashed its headlights at her. Another check? The lights flashed again, she could see a long arm come out of the driver's window as the car approached, waving her to stop. What? Stop? For a moment she was going to accelerate, drive past the car as fast as she could. It was them, they had come to get her! Then as the car drew level with her she saw that it was Pat Quinn. She stopped the car and rested her forehead on the steering wheel and started to laugh hysterically.

He came across to her as she sat bemused. 'I recognised the car . . . I called in to see you . . . are you all right?' She looked up at him now, face streaked with tears. 'No. You're not, I can see that.' He walked around her car and motioned to her to unlock the passenger seat so that he could get in beside her. She had rested her forehead again on the steering wheel. She could not speak. There was no laughter either. 'What's happened?'

She raised her head. 'You don't have to concern yourself with me and my problems,' she said bitterly, 'they're not important.'

'I think they are,' he said gently, looking at her. 'Whatever they are, you're upset, and I'd like to help.'

'It's not important,' she repeated, 'I'll be fine in a minute.' She brushed her cheeks with her sleeve.

'Tell me?' he said.

'You said that you had called in to see me. Is there a problem about the boys?' she sniffed.

'No,' he replied in the same quiet tone, 'no. I had an idea. About a job for you.' He paused. She waited, not speaking. 'Our secretary has been off for a week now, will be off for the rest of the term it seems, varicose veins, she has to rest up for a few weeks . . . what I called to ask . . .' he looked down at his hands for a moment, hesitating, 'would you like to take the job on until she returns?'

Belle's eyes widened in surprise. A job! With Pat Quinn!

'I'm afraid that it is only part-time, mornings mostly, and the pay is not great . . .' he smiled apologetically, 'but I wondered if you would be interested.'

'Interested? Of course. If you think I can be of use, it

would . . . I would . . . oh . . .' She smiled a watery smile at him. 'Thank you.'

'What a difference a smile makes,' he chided, leaning towards her.

'Thank you,' she repeated.

He held up a hand in protest. 'Now you'll probably not say that in a week's time, once you've started, you'll probably think I'm a terrible man to work for . . .'

'No, I don't think so, I don't think I will.' She shook her head, smiling broadly now.

'That's better!' he said. 'I must get on, I only slipped out of school for an hour and I have someone to meet . . .'

'And I have delayed you. Thank you once again.'

'You're welcome,' he said, getting out of the car and walking over the road to his own. He waved cheerfully. 'I'll see you on Monday with the boys, anyway.'

'Yes,' she nodded, smiling still.

As she drove on down the road, round the last corner and saw the House ahead, for the first time she felt like shouting out loud. A job!

She put the car into the garage and walked briskly indoors. Mrs D took one look at her face and demanded, 'How did you get on?'

'Great. A loan from the bank. And a part-time job . . . down at the school at Corey. Apparently the secretary is off sick.'

'So that's what he called for,' Mrs D said thoughtfully. 'He didn't say. To tell the truth I thought there was trouble over the school.'

'No, it's all very straightforward. With luck the boys will start next week, and me too. I can't believe it.'

'I said he was a nice man, didn't I? You can always rely on the schoolteacher when there's trouble.'

'You did tell me and you're right. Now where are my boys?'

'They are stuck in the sitting-room in front of the television set. I moved it in for them, Rory helped . . .' she hastened to add when Belle raised her eyebrows. 'Sure, you can't live in the kitchen all the time?'

'No. I suppose not.'

'I must get on. My Willy is waiting for his dinner. You get the boys fed. There's eggs there. I'll just get my coat on and be off. Don't you be coming out with me.'

'Yes,' Belle replied, suddenly thinking. She felt deflated. Yes, she had a job, but the old fears were still there.

'Now make sure you lock yourself up safe and sound tonight,' Mrs D warned. 'Don't be answering the door if someone comes late at night . . . did you not hear the news?'

'No. What?'

'About that wee woman in Belfast. Sure it will be on the lunchtime news. Isn't it near enough time for it now? I'll go away on.'

Belle joined the boys in the sitting-room where they were watching television.

'A woman in south Belfast is recovering in hospital today after what was described as a savage assault in her home in the early hours of this morning. Three masked men wielding cudgels burst in when she answered the door and attacked her. Nails hammered through one of the cudgels left her with severe gashes to the legs and head injuries. The condition of the woman, who has not been named, was described as fair today. Police are trying to establish a motive.'

Rory looked up at her. 'Hallo, Ma. Do you see that? It's just as well you do lock the doors, isn't it?'

Chapter 6

ON FRIDAY MORNING it rained. Belle drew back the curtains of her bedroom and looked at the sodden landscape. Ahead the village sat in a shroud of mist and rain. A small stream of water was running down the road on one side till it reached the corner in front of the house where it crossed in a furious flood. A tractor went by throwing up a flurry of spray. Down the drive the pine trees drooped to the ground, heavy with rain, dripping on to the mat of pine needles. Rain streamed down the window-panes in front of her. What a day!

She decided she would have to go into town again today to find a supermarket to indulge in some judicious buying. She felt reassured by the trip in to the bank yesterday, and the job, but she knew that she needed to build up some stocks of groceries so that forays to the shops on a daily basis were not necessary. She needed to fill the cupboards – for a rainy day. She smiled at that, how appropriate it seemed. Not many folk would be about, she could push a trolley up and down some reasonably anonymous shopping aisle, with no questions asked.

Two patrol Landrovers passed by the house, up to the bend and out of sight. They moved slowly, but were gone before the fact registered. Could she see the biscuit box? Surely she could from here? No, not at all. She looked up the road again. It was empty. A storm of rain beat on the window making her retreat to the warmth downstairs.

The boys were impressed by the idea of going shopping and

were soon galvanised. Belle was getting them into the car when the phone rang.

'Ma? Isn't that the phone?' Rory asked, his hand on Conor's collar, pushing him out of the rain.

They stood for a moment. Belle shrugged her shoulders. 'It doesn't matter.' She got in. 'I am not going back now. And anyway by the time I get the door unlocked, they will have rung off. Nobody knows we're here anyway, do they?' She felt then in her pocket for the key, it reassured her of her impenetrable home. 'Let's get off now.'

The supermarket was on the edge of town. It was anonymous and at this time of the morning and on such a wet morning deserted. It was quick shopping, and the bill at the end was not quite what she had expected. She felt quite cheered. And she had bought a tin of cheap emulsion paint. Daffodil yellow. She would treat herself to a bottle of sherry, she decided, a small reward.

The off-licence was just within the shopping segment, a few yards up the street. She would be able to drive in and park since she had the boys with her. To leave the car unattended while she shopped could create a bomb scare, and the likelihood that the army would blow up the car in what they called a 'controlled explosion', just in case it was boobytrapped. The least consequence would be that she would get a ticking-off from the police. She had had enough of them and people who asked interminable questions.

So she drove in, a soldier checking her car and boot as she passed. She settled the boys and set off up the street, back in moments clutching the sherry. Rory asked her if he could look in the window of a nearby shop.

'I can see trains in the window. I just want to have a look. I won't be long, I promise,' he said.

'Go on,' she said, 'don't be long, two minutes, that's all. Conor and I will wait.'

'I want to go too,' Conor cried, jumping up and down in protest.

'OK. Anything for a quiet life. You go too. But on one condition,' she put mock severity into her voice, 'that you let me have one of your sweeties you got in the supermarket. And don't be long.'

'You can have the whole packet,' Conor said in a fit of magnanimity. Belle smiled and settled deeply into the seat. She sat there idly chewing, watching the few people walk to and fro, through the windows which were misting up more as she breathed. The moments passed. She sat hidden, watching, noting how people behaved, pausing to look in windows, stopping to greet each other, admonishing their children, their dogs. Her mind became a kind of blank, lulled by the sweetie chewed slowly and laboriously to see how long she could make it last.

A girl with long blonde hair came down the street. Belle held her breath. It's that girl, she thought, it's her. I know her. But what is she doing here? No, it couldn't be her. There are an awful lot of girls with blonde hair in the world, in Belfast, in this town. I must be sensible! The girl was standing still now, looking in the window of a dress shop, about Belle's height, a little fatter.

I know that I really don't want to go to this party, I haven't been to one in weeks, even months, but Anne says I must stop hiding myself. So that is why I am standing in this shop trying to find something to wear. Maybe I'll find one here if I take a good look along the rails . . . Now this one, in blue, with a full bodice, might make me look as if I have bigger breasts than I have. I'll try it.

A communal changing-room is no way to make me feel confident. There is always someone in there trying not to show their knickers, their white bra that got into the coloured wash by mistake, their bodies . . . at this rate I don't know why I bother . . . I know I shall look awful.

There's a fair girl there already, in the corner. She has a sniff, sounds as if she has a cold. As I struggle out of my clothes I watch her out of the corner of my eye. She is watching me. She stoops and brings another handkerchief out of the big shopping bag she has deposited at her feet. She is not trying on the black and white dress that she has hanging on the hook beside her. Maybe she feels shy about undressing in front of me? Maybe she just feels awful?

This dress won't do. But I fancy the black and white one. Back amongst the rails I am looking for the black and white dress. Then I find it, but not in my size. The one that girl was trying on won't be my size either I think, but it's worth checking. I wonder if she is out of the changing-room yet? They usually hang the garments that have been tried on, on the rail outside the door. I'll see. I reach the doorway. The blonde girl comes out, she has the dress in her hand. She walks through the shop with it, I follow. There's another girl, tall, ginger-haired with slightly protruding front teeth and freckles. They meet.

'I thought that woman would never leave the changing-room!' says the blonde, laughing, she seems happy now. 'Thank God! Let's go!' She puts the dress on a nearby rail.

I look at the label. It is the wrong size. Probably wouldn't have suited me anyway. Maybe there's another dress, I'll take a look . . .

Minutes pass, searching minutes, I'm going to give up on this search.

Suddenly there's a dull explosive thud near the back of the shop. And screaming, wild screaming. An assistant fights her way past me, screaming like a siren. Smoke billows about us thick, black and choking.

'It's a bomb!' another assistant shrieks beside me. 'We have to get out!' She pushes me furiously, pummelling my back with her fists as we crowd out, pushing roughly past the rails of dresses, choking, coughing, gasping in the smoke, out of the door.

Outside in the street there is a fine mizzle of rain coming down. I stand with a handful of people about twenty yards away from the shop and watch. The crowd grows as the smoke continues to billow out. They want to see the show. We can hear the klaxons long before the fire brigade arrives in a rush. Seconds later the bomb squad arrives. There could be another bomb. The brigade will have to wait. The fire is burning nicely. I don't want to wait any longer. I don't want to know any more.

The world is full of girls with long fair hair. Like Belfast is full of men with limps. If you did not know how many hundreds of men had been kneecapped over the past years you would not know to look for them. The same with yellow-haired ladies. Belle swallowed hard. Forget it.

Rory was tapping on the car window.

'Come on now, Rory, you've been ages, it's time we went

home.' There was an edge to her voice and she sighed impatiently.

'OK, Ma, can we come another day perhaps?' It was as if he understood why she wanted to get home. He bundled Conor into the car, hauling him by his coat collar. Conor protested momentarily, but accepted his fate.

The telephone was ringing as they walked across the yard. Conor, Rory and Belle all had their hands full of shopping. By the time Belle had unlocked the door, the phone had inevitably stopped.

Later, when they had got all the packages inside and were sorting them out, the phone rang again.

'Someone seems awfully mad to get talking to us,' observed Conor.

'Yes, I'll answer it,' said Belle, not hurrying to answer it.

Rory looked at her, puzzled. 'Ma? Aren't you going to . . . ?'

She carefully pulled the kettle forward on to the hotplate.

'Ma?'

'Yes, all right,' she decided, moving now. The phone stopped ringing. Rory and Conor both looked at her now, frowning.

'I could do with a cup of tea,' she said, dismissively.

Half an hour later the phone rang again. They were sitting toasting themselves in front of the range, a smell of damp clothes steaming in the warmth.

'Oh, I'll get it,' Belle decided, but Rory pre-empted her.

'Yes,' he put on his best voice, 'yes, she's here. Who's speaking? Oh, Mr Quinn. Just hold on a moment.'

Belle took a deep breath in relief.

Pat Quinn's voice was deep and somehow reassuring. 'I tried to get you this morning earlier, a couple of times. Were you out?' Before Belle could reply he went on, 'I just wanted to make sure . . . after yesterday. Were you out? Or is there something wrong with your phone?'

'We're fine,' she said. She wasn't going to explain that she was reluctant to answer the phone because it might be the IRA.

He paused. 'Ah, I see, I'll see you on Monday morning then?'

'Thank you, Mr Quinn,' suddenly Belle felt that she had to be formal, 'thank you for thinking of me, for the job,' she added hastily.

'You will have to call me "Pat",' he said, 'I'll see you on

Monday and we will get the boys fixed up, then perhaps you can start . . . ?'

'At once. There's no reason why not,' Belle said.

'Good. I'll be relieved if you can help out. I just don't have the time between classes to answer letters . . . the phone . . .'

'I hope that I can be of some help to you . . .'

'Monday then,' he said.

When she put the phone down she smiled to herself. I'm behaving like a teenager.

'Ma?' Rory was looking at her. 'Ma . . . you're blushing.'

'No, I'm not,' she retorted. 'It's only the warmth from that fire.'

She went upstairs to change out of her clothes. It was the same skirt and shirt, she realised, from that day months ago in the shop. But she was being really stupid, she really was imagining things.

The rain had stopped. She could see cracks in the grey above with rags of blue in between. A figure moved at the gate. Who was it?

Cathal. The milkman. So he was delivering late today. He disappeared. Funny man. Yes, it had been a day for strange foolish things.

Belle wanted to start painting the kitchen walls. She went out to search in the various outhouses for a scraper and a paint brush. Luckily she found just what she needed. Cleaning up after scraping the walls took more time than she realised and it was only when Conor came to stand in the kitchen doorway looking somewhat bleakly at her that she looked at her watch. The boys had spent the afternoon lounging on the battered flowered settee in the sitting-room, watching television. During the afternoon she had put her head round the door to find them lying together, their legs interlinked in a quiet peace pact, the empty sweet packet on the floor.

'I just wondered, Ma,' said Conor, 'if we could have tea in there, with the telly?' He waved his arm. 'There's a great film coming on . . .'

'Yes. OK.' She wouldn't have to clear the kitchen up for tea, she could keep on at the task, maybe even start painting.

By nine o'clock she had finished the first coat of yellow on the walls. The boys, once fed, had melted back to the somnolence of the television set, and only the murmur of it disturbed the stillness of the house. The smell of paint, she decided, was slightly lemony, it smelt fresh and clean. Despite the stiffening of her shoulders she felt a sense of ease, and when the boys went off readily to bed the feeling of contentment grew.

It was surprisingly light outside as she stood in the porch looking out. A clear moon had risen high into the sky. She could pick out the occasional glow in a village window where somebody was home again, the fire lit, the tea made. Then she opened the door and stood sniffing the air like some wild animal caught and caged in the dark, sensing freedom.

She stepped out into the gloom, to the vegetable garden which she had not yet inspected. She unlatched the gate and walked between what remained of beds in the weeds, bending now and again to where she thought there might be remains of currant trees, a patch where mint had grown thick and aromatic. Would she plant some cabbages for spring? She turned and went back slowly to the house, smiling to herself. Spring. It wasn't all that far away. This awful darkness would not last.

The fire in the sitting-room was low, but the room was warm, so she retreated there to subside into the comfort of an armchair, idly switching on the television set.

It was a late film, but too late for her to join it. As she reached to switch off she stopped as if paralysed. As the words POLICE MESSAGE were flashed on screen she heard: 'Reports are coming in from Armagh that a number of incendiary devices have been found in shops. Key-holders are requested to return to check their premises . . .'

Yellow-haired ladies . . . the world is full of them, is it? she asked herself desperately.

Belle snapped off the set, walked into the kitchen and checked the bolts on the back door. Then she walked steadily upstairs. When she got into bed she did not feel the cold even though she had not paused to make herself a hot water bottle. She pulled the bedclothes up over her head so that she was entombed in a blackness that obliterated all sound.

It was my imagination. It was not that girl. Not again. That is impossible. And anyway . . . what is the point? Now? What if it was her? I have done enough. I don't want to get involved again. Please let me just be an ordinary housewife, a mother, in my own world of domesticity. That's all I want. I don't want to get involved. Not again! Eventually she slept.

Chapter 7

BELLE HAD NEARLY FINISHED painting the kitchen walls when Rory awoke and made his way downstairs the next morning. He came round the kitchen door, opening his sleepy eyes wide.

'It's tremendous, Ma, you've nearly finished. I heard a few bumps earlier but I thought that maybe it was the bats in the attic.'

'No, they don't make any sound. You needn't worry about them, though they do fly about quite fast. If you find one, just pick it up gently, it will cling on with its sharp claws.'

'Were you ever afraid of them, Ma?'

'No. When I was small I used to go to see them nearly every day and tell them what I had been doing. They were my friends. They just hang around in the dark listening to everything that goes on in the house, you, me, Conor . . . everyone. I liked to clap my hands to make them fly, but not very often.'

'Have you been in to talk to them since you came home?' This was going to be one of Rory's interminable question sessions.

'No. I stopped talking to them when I grew up.' That was when John died. We would visit the bats together, even when we got older. There were times when I only really felt close to him if we were standing in the attic.

'What can I tell him? What can I tell him?'

I am standing in the dark warmth of the tank room. I have

been standing here some time, whispering, asking the same question.

I don't hear John coming up the last flight of stairs. He is right behind me. He puts his hand on my shoulder.

'What are you talking about? What must you tell him?' he murmurs.

'Sam. Sam. He's going to join the Ulster Defence Regiment. I'm afraid. I can't stand guns. I can't stand the uniform. Something will happen.'

'That's stupid. What about all the others who join?'

'They get killed. You know they do. Eventually the IRA get them.'

'If he feels that he must, you should back him, not stand in his way,' John whispers at my ear.

'He'll be killed. I just know it,' I repeat stubbornly.

John puts both arms round me and holds me close. He nuzzles my neck, kissing my ear, my hair. 'Silly, silly, silly woman,' he mutters.

I turn round. It's very dark. I can't see his face, only feel him beside me.

'Oh, hold me John, hold me.'

'Where do they go, Ma, how do they get out?'

'The bats? There must be a gap under the eaves, they go out that way, at night-time, out into the orchard, to catch insects.'

'What are they doing in the attic then, in the dark? Just sleeping?'

'Yes, yes.'

'Why did you go to talk to them in the attic?'

'Because I didn't have many friends, I suppose. It's different in the city, lots of houses there . . .' Her voice died away.

'But we didn't have many friends in the city, did we?'

'No, not all that many.'

'Maybe I might start talking to the bats,' he persisted.

'You could try, I suppose.' There was a finality in her voice. He recognised it.

'Do you want me to make breakfast while you finish that bit of wall?'

'Yes, that would be a great help. The kettle is nearly boiling.'

'If you don't mind my saying it, there is a bit of wall there where you might do another coat, it's a bit blotchy.' He frowned at her.

'Sometimes the paint doesn't seem to stick on too well. It will dry out all right.' Yes, I know I rushed the job, she told herself, but it will do perfectly well. I just had to get it finished.

'Are you going to paint any more rooms? Conor's room and mine are all right really, except for the paper peeling off in places. If you like I could try painting them, to save you the trouble . . . you look awfully tired this morning.'

'I think that I shall take a rest before I do any more painting.' What was the point of painting any more rooms? It was useless, all of it.

Rory started pulling the table and chairs into place across the the floor. There was a scraping sound which somehow seemed to put her on edge. She had done enough.

She stood at the sink letting warm water run over her painted fingers, rubbing them with the pot-scrubber. For a few moments she made her mind a blank, thinking of the water trickling through her fingers and how useless it seemed, one moment she seemed to have progressed, the next she was back, fearful, afraid.

The smell of toast broke her thoughts from their determined path and brought her back to reality. Rory had started making toast, but he had left it to burn. He was standing out in the hallway looking down the drive, a puzzled expression on his face.

'There's a man out there!'

Belle looked out. 'It's only Cathal with the milk,' she snapped, 'he puts it into a tin at the gate to save him coming all the way up to the house. Didn't I tell you? Your toast has burnt.'

'No. I didn't know. I just thought it a bit weird, that's all.' He looked at her, deeply offended.

'It was all fixed up the other morning when you were still in your bed, you lazy boy.' She ruffled his hair but he still looked serious. 'I collected it yesterday because you had your nose stuck to the television set. He seems to come with the milk at odd hours, yesterday it was almost lunchtime. I must ask Mrs D when he is supposed to come with it, or at least try to pin him down to a regular time, otherwise when will we know to collect it?'

'Shall I go down and get it now?' Rory had the door open and was running helter-skelter down the drive before she could reply.

When he returned he informed her, 'It was him. Cathal says that he always delivers the milk early in the mornings, about eight o'clock, not in the afternoons.'

'Then what?' She stopped. 'I thought I saw him yesterday, by the gate, yesterday lunchtime?' If it wasn't Cathal, who had it been? It must have been Cathal.

'Maybe he meant to say that he normally comes in the morning but that yesterday he got delayed because of something. He's a funny man, he's not very friendly, is he? He was quite cross when I asked him.'

'Well, that's probably the explanation. Something did delay him yesterday, his van broke down or something and that made him cross and he didn't fancy being reminded of it.'

'I suppose so . . .' Rory replied very thoughtfully.

'There's no other logical explanation, is there?' she said, changing the subject. 'Let's try to make some more toast . . . and not burn it this time, OK?'

The day, when she had cleared the table, seemed to be stretching inexorably ahead of her hour after hour. She had done her bit of painting and did not intend to do any more. She had tidied their various possessions in the house and bought a stock of food. What more could she do? Dig the garden, plant some cabbages for spring? No, she did not know if she would still be there for springtime. What about television? The thought of spending the day in that way, half slumbering, watching on the offchance that there might be a 1957 film with William Holden in it would not do.

There was a brisk rap on the back door. She looked out of the kitchen window trying not to be seen, but could not see who was standing at the door. The yard appeared empty. If it had been someone who knew her they would drive up to the back door and she would hear that. For an instant she hesitated, then went to the door.

Pat Quinn was standing on the doorstep, bending his head because of his height when she opened the door. 'Good morning,' he said cheerfully.

'Oh hallo . . . I didn't . . .'

'I know, you didn't expect me.' For some reason he emphasised the last word.

Belle didn't know what to say. She opened her mouth, closed it again, and felt her cheeks redden.

'I'm sorry, I'll say that again,' he smiled. 'What I meant was that we have only just met and surely you have had visits from lots of your friends since you got home here.' He had spotted her awkwardness.

'Yes, you're right,' she said expansively, 'I have had a lot of people dropping in, old friends who have heard that I'm home . . .' Her voice died. She wanted to tell him the truth, that she felt hemmed in, in this house, isolated, afraid, and that she was honestly glad to see him, yet she smiled and kept up this bravado.

'There's a football match this afternoon in Armagh and I'm off to it. I wondered if your boys would like to go? I could pick them up . . . say about two, which would give us time to get into town.'

'That's a great idea.' Rory was beside her, grinning all over his face, listening to the conversation. 'I'm Rory, by the way, we spoke on the phone yesterday. How do you do?' he added as a formal afterthought.

'Oh, so you're Rory, right then. Your mother is bringing you over on Monday to talk about school and what you've been learning. I talked to your headmaster . . . no,' he had noted Rory's grimace, 'he said you were pretty sound. You'll probably get a place in the grammar school at Armagh but you need to keep studying in the mean time. Do you think your wee brother would like to go to a football match?'

'Yes, great! He's still in bed, but I'll dig him out, you'll see. He'll be pleased. He's still a bit of a baby, three years younger than me, but he is quite good at football. Not as good as me of course . . .'

He was looking at Pat, totally assured, and laughing in a way that Belle had not seen him do for a long time. Maybe it was just that he was bored with her company and that the chance to get off to a football match was a good way to brighten his day. That was the answer.

Rory went off upstairs calling out the news to Conor excitedly, to get up at once, they were off to see some football.

'Sounds as if he likes the idea,' Pat Quinn laughed at her. He had put one hand on the doorpost and because of his height was leaning towards her as he talked. For a moment she felt his breath warm on her cheek . . . She hesitated and moved backwards into the room.

'I'm awfully sorry, I feel terrible . . .' she said to cover her embarrassment, 'I haven't even asked you in . . .'

Pat laughed and walked in through the door. Belle had hoped that he would excuse himself at this conversational gambit but instead he continued to advance, surveying the room.

'Aha! I thought that I could smell paint. It looks very bright and clean. You have been working hard.'

And I am behaving like a fluttery teenager, she told herself severely, but felt that her breathing had quickened as if she was not entirely in control of her emotions. What had come over her? Had leaving Belfast and coming here entirely upset her normal calm, unruffled, uncommitted manner? For the first time in years, she had to admit sheer physical attraction for this man who was intruding, so very charmingly, and she was not quite sure how to handle it.

He was looking at her and smiling again, a smile which reached into those cold grey eyes of his. There seemed to be a spell between them which she did not want to break by speaking, but caution told her she had to.

'Yes,' she said, matter-of-factly. 'It needed cheering up a bit, especially at this time of the year when everything is so dark and dismal. It seems to get dark so early . . .' She checked, aware of a wistful tone in her voice.

'It must be quite lonely for you here, particularly at night-time.'

'Yes,' Belle said, forgetting what she had said about all her friends dropping by. 'But the boys are really great company for me.'

'Would you like to come to the match too?' he asked.

'No. No,' she said awkwardly. 'It will do the boys good to be off with someone else for a change. They have had enough of my company lately, I think. It will be better when they have started school.'

'You trust me with them, then?'

'You're the teacher around here. And anyway, you're not precisely a stranger to the district,' she countered.

'Oh, yes, I'm the teacher, I'm automatically an upright citizen.'

'I hope my boys will settle into school,' she said quickly, noting a wry tone to his voice.

'I don't think you need to worry about that. They sound like sensible boys to me, don't worry.' He put his hand on her shoulder and she flinched. He took it away instantly and his expression hardened. 'I'll call back around two, OK?' He headed for the door.

She followed, wanting to say something, not knowing what. By the time she got out on the doorstep he was heading for the corner of the house, his back firmly to her, his shoulders hunched into his tweed jacket. He did not turn to wave at the corner, but strode on.

Belle went back into the house, ran to the porch window and looked out. Still he did not turn, simply strode to the end of the drive, got into his car, slammed the door shut and drove off fast up the road.

There was one bright white envelope on the hall floor where it had spun through the letter box.

She picked it up curiously, recognising the handwriting. It was from Anne who was continuing to live in the house in Belfast until she herself could find a new home.

The envelope was bulky. Belle tore it open with suddenly clumsy fingers.

There was short note, and another envelope.

'Dear Belle, this came last night and it doesn't look like a bill. I thought you should have it at once. The police have been here looking for you. I have told them nothing. Don't you think you should talk to them? You can't hide for ever? Love, Anne.'

Belle's name was carefully printed in block capitals on the enclosed envelope. There was no address. It had been hand-delivered. She opened it with recalcitrant fingers.

'We know what you have done. The next thing you will get will be a bullet.'

Quickly she tore the envelopes and the letters into shreds, rushing to the kitchen where she could lift the front plate of the range and stuff the fragments into the hot coals, watching the paper flare and flicker and flame and finally dissolve into red ashes.

Chapter 8

BELLE LET HER MIND drift against the background of the boys' conversation, trying not to think about how she would spend the afternoon. She didn't want to stay in the house. She needed fresh air. 'I know!' She put her cup down.

Rory looked puzzled. She had been so quiet. 'Yes?' he asked, rolling his eyes in mock surprise.

'I think I'll take a wee walk down the road to see the O'Briens – it's only just down the road for two minutes, and then into their demesne. That's the answer, while you boys are gadding away to the football.'

'The O'Briens?' Conor squeaked.

'They live down at the Lodge, on the way to school. You won't remember them, Conor. I'll just slip down to see them on my own.'

'I thought you told me that they were a bit weird?' Rory said accusingly.

'Well, not exactly weird,' she emphasised the word 'weird', 'they really are quite nice people, once you get to know them.'

'Isn't Uncle Marcus a brother or something? I remember Uncle Marcus, he came to see us a few times after we moved to Belfast, didn't he?'

'Yes, he's a younger brother.'

'Are they married?' Rory demanded.

'No, they are brother and sister, do you not remember, Rory?'

'If Uncle Marcus is their brother, does he live with them?' Conor asked curiously.

'No, he lives in Armagh.'

'Ah, yes,' Rory sounded very authoritative, 'he's a solicitor, isn't he? Wasn't he a friend of Dad's?'

'In a sort of way.' Belle was momentarily irritated. She got up from the table, pulling the cloth which she had put on it 'to make it more Protestant-looking', as Mrs D would say, awry, and tipping over a cup of cold tea. 'You boys will need big jerseys, it's going to be a cold afternoon,' she said unnecessarily, mopping up the tea.

Rory took one look at her set face and left her. She heard his steps up the staircase, measured, slow, and a low monotone, as if he was thinking out loud to himself, but she could hear no other sound. Conor had disappeared in that silent way of small children who have discovered that they can make themselves invisible even for moments. She listened for the click as he switched on the television set in the sitting-room.

'Now you have to keep an eye out for Mr Quinn,' she told him, sticking her head round the door.

He was already curled into an armchair, watching the set with a glazed look in his eyes. He did not look up. 'Do I have to go to the silly old football match, Mama?' he asked without turning his head in her direction.

'Yes, Mr Quinn has taken the trouble. He will be calling here soon. Please go upstairs and find your big blue jersey, the one I knitted for you. You know you can watch television any old time.'

'I'll go . . . in a minute,' he muttered, eyes still fixed on the screen.

'Now!' Belle's hand thumped the edge of the door.

He scowled, got out of the chair stiffly as if he had been there for hours and walked towards her, not meeting her eyes with his own.

Why do I have these confrontations with him?

John has his hand on the sitting-room doorpost. He is laughing at something he can see on the television set. The kitchen door is open and I am standing stirring stew for the tea, for all of them. The phone rings.

'John?' He doesn't turn his head. 'John?' He doesn't seem to have heard me.

It's no good, I'll have to stop this and go to the phone. It's right beside him. Can he not see I'm busy? I know that the call will not be for me. If it's not for Sam, it will be for John. Sam has taken Rory over to the Johnston house, they took the tractor. Muck-spreading.

'Yes? Hallo?'

'Belle? It's Jimmy. Is John in?'

'He's right beside me.' I hold out the receiver, saying loudly, 'It's for you.'

I can hear the stew boiling over on the range. I can hear it spitting.

John turns his head very slowly, laughing still.

'What does he want?'

'I don't know. Here, take it!' I thrust the receiver at him. 'My stew's boiling over.'

Why did I do that? It was a mistake. I know somehow that I should have said he was not at home. Where's Sam? He's been gone for hours. Since breakfast. He just went off with Rory. He won't talk to me today. He slept hunched away from me in that big bed all last night. I know that I retaliated by not getting up to make his breakfast this morning. I know that I pretended to be asleep. Then when I came down, he just said, 'I'll take the child.' It is just one of those awful days, I know it. Everything is going wrong.

The stew has boiled over. I have to scrape the stove with a knife. Mrs D will notice and she will scold me. And this child, this child that I am carrying. Why does it have to dig and dig me just under my ribs?

John puts his head round the kitchen door. 'I'm just off down the road to pick up Jimmy. I thought I'd borrow Sam's car, he's not using it, and I won't be more than a couple of hours.'

'What about your own car? What's wrong with it?'

'Och, the battery's flat again,' he smiles. 'What's wrong?'

'It's just the baby. He kicks. I wish that it was all over.' I am trying to smile back. 'I don't want it to be like the last time, with Rory. I couldn't bear that.'

John puts his arms round me and I bury my head in his sweater. I can smell sweat and spray from the orchard, he did the apples yesterday.

'There's no reason at all why it should,' he soothes, 'now is there? Sure I'll be here, you know that, and the doctor says everything is going well, so why worry? Go on now. Who's the brave one around here? You. You are. You're the brave one . . .'

He is gently stroking my back, running his fingers up and down my spine, pressing me to him, talking softly like I've heard Sam talk to his cows . . . but not to me, not to me, not Sam.

'You're right. I am silly.' I draw myself away from his arms. 'Will you be back for supper?' I say because he is just looking at me, questioning.

'Yes. I won't be late. A couple of drinks, that's all.'

'You won't drink too much? And take it easy on the road home. You will be driving and it's Sam's car.'

He strides to pick the keys off their hook on the wall by the stove. Then he turns and puts a hand to my cheek. 'Och, stop worrying. Stop worrying. I'll be all right. You'll be all right. We'll all be all right.'

'I've just put this stew on.'

'I'll be back for it, didn't I say so?'

I hear the car start, reverse and turn in the yard. The house falls silent. Why did I tell him about Jimmy being on the phone? I could have said he was out. But that wasn't true. There was no other way.

'I'll go,' muttered Conor, slipping under her arm as she stood there holding on to the doorpost. 'I'm going . . . now!' He pounded up the stairs.

There was a lot of shouting.

'You will go!' That was Rory, the tones slightly deeper.

'I'm going. I said I would, didn't I? It's bloody useless anyway, football! I'd rather stay and watch television but then you,' he spat out the word, 'you and Mummy have decided that I have to go, have to go. Nobody asked me. Just assumed. There's probably a great programme on about cars and chases and all on the television and I'll miss it.'

There was more sound of stamping feet on bare boards, then coming downstairs, thumping down.

'Ma?' Rory was looking at her from the foot of the stairs as she stood still at the doorway. 'Ma?' Rory was looking very angry. 'We're going to wait down by the gate for Mr Quinn, Conor and I!'

He grabbed Conor who was behind him by the sleeve of his jersey and pushed him out of the front door. Conor looked back at her in reproach.

'Go on then,' Belle nodded, trying not to smile. 'Go on!'

She stood at the sitting-room window with both hands stuffed into the pocket at the front of her apron, clenching her fists, watching and waiting until Pat Quinn's green Ford Cortina drove up. He did not get out. She could see his shadow as he swung the door open and the boys climbed inside.

Minutes later she had the apron off, the red coat on, and was walking, what she thought initially as cheerfully but then as the cold wind bit into her bones, grimacing, down the drive. Those boys will be cold, she thought. Well, they were well wrapped up, bomber jackets, scarves . . . they could stand it.

Maybe she should have phoned the O'Briens, made sure they would be home. But then they always seemed to be. Jean only dashed out once in a while for last-minute shopping, a bottle of whiskey for James when he got morose. On a day like this they would surely stay home.

Her footsteps echoed on the tarmac surface and the pine trees hanging over the demesne wall beside her seemed like a black barrier. Soon she would be off the road and into the demesne. She would feel less conspicuous then. Maybe she should have brought the car? No, she needed the walk. Would it snow? She turned thankfully off the road at the gates as they hung open, one gate off its hinges. She carefully navigated a route through a thicket of nettles to the gate-lodge and peered through the window. The room was full of corn, high as the cornices, submerging the fireplace. There was a rustling noise. She retreated quickly. Rats, probably. She set off down the drive.

The first half-mile was closely forested with pines planted right up to the edge of what was now just a track. Below the trees the ground was littered with pine needles, branches, debris of the years, red-brown like the squirrels that inhabited the place, even the light filtering through the trees seemed reddish too.

Eventually she came out on to wide expanses of what had once been parkland. Relics of 'oul dacency' people called it. On one side a straggling electric fence contained a bunch of Friesian cows. That must be Cathal's herd. In the distance was the dark bulk of the Lodge. As she neared it she saw stumps of trees where once there had been great chestnuts. It had been a great conker-hunting ground for herself and John, sneaking in, hoping they would not be spotted by the O'Briens and have to account for themselves. Pedantic conversations with James and Jean could be avoided. The cows stopped grazing, eyeing her, then moved towards her. That old fear grasped her, despite the electric fence. How foolish it was. If John were here he would protect her. She stopped, stood stockstill. The old ploy. John would be proud of her. The cows resumed grazing, stopped moving towards her. She walked on a yard or two and realised the cows were moving again, and she quickened her step. Such irrational fears in a woman of her years.

The Lodge was in total darkness for the light was beginning to fade as she reached the imposing flight of steps that led to the front door.

Built asymmetrically, as her own home, the Lodge was three storeys high. While the House was about fifty years younger, built with less money, just on the bend of the road, not in this wide park, there were little touches of extravagance in the urns on each side of the front steps, a balustraded balcony before the main window on the first floor. There was a basement too; but the window embrasures were gaping holes without glass and had been for many years. Down there were the remains of wine cellars, cool rooms for haunches of meat to hang, the kitchen complete with worn wooden benches, and a copper boiler to help keep linen table-cloths and napkins and sheets brightest white, linens that would be spread over the front lawns to bleach and dry each week. There were rooms there too where the servants had lived in domestic gloom but it was all open now to the elements.

James and Jean did not seem to notice the cold that seeped up from below. They had covered the floors with layers of newspaper, then lino. James called it great insulation, commenting, 'And we just don't feel the cold.' But Belle could not fail to notice that Jean's fingers were thickened with chilblains, even in September. How could they live on in that house? They had inhabited only the ground floor for thirty years or more. The rooms above were stacked with piles of rotting furniture, crumbling to dust under the attack of woodworm and damp. It might come in useful one day. They lived on year after year simply because they couldn't move elsewhere. A small annuity from their father's days in the British Army was enough to keep them, and Marcus no doubt helped along, now and again. Where could they live otherwise? And why bother?

The O'Briens were not at home. Perhaps it was just as well. Belle was beginning to feel uneasy, as if the isolation of the house and the park about it threatened her. She retraced her steps hurriedly.

It did not seem quite so dark out on the road. Perhaps it was simply the thickness of trees in the parkland and along the length of the demesne wall that made it all seem so glowering. As Belle walked, the first really big flakes of snow started to fall, drifting down aimlessly. Belle tossed off a few that had settled on her hair, but felt the dampness as more fell. The boys would think this was great fun.

A Morris Minor was coming down towards her. She recognised it at once. The O'Briens. The car stopped by her.

James, gaunt-faced as ever, was in the passenger seat, for he hated driving. He wound down the window saying in an almost bored voice, 'Well, I do declare. It's Annabelle.'

Jean was getting out of the driver's seat. The car moved forward slowly. 'Whoops!' she said breathlessly, slipping back into the seat again and pulling on the handbrake. Her hair is now quite white, thought Belle.

'You'll do that once too often, Jean,' said James in a harsh voice, then the tone changed as if he remembered Belle's presence. He laughed. 'She's always doing that. Did it on the village street a couple of weeks ago but fortunately I was able to put the brake on in time. She was at Crawford's. I was just reading the paper waiting, you know how long it takes in there to buy even a packet of sugar. One moment I was in the middle of the golf, and the next the car was taking off down the hill. You know I haven't driven in years, but I do know how to put the handbrake on, even if Jean doesn't.' He added the last bit crossly, but glanced at Jean as he did so with a sly smile.

They are like some old married couple, Belle thought, married and stuck in some kind of time warp, never middle-aged, more like retirement. Their lives are intertwined like two old trees which have been planted too close together.

'Don't pay any attention to him,' Jean said vexedly. 'He's an old silly. It wasn't really as bad as all that. The car did not run away. You stopped it before it could hit anything.'

'But if I hadn't . . .' James interrupted.

'Oh go on, stop romancing about it,' Jean scolded. 'It looks as if it might snow.' She was changing the subject swiftly as if he were a child.

'Yes, it does look very like it,' Belle agreed.

'Nonsense,' James said, 'far too early in the year for snow. It'll never lie, it'll never last, you'll see.'

'You see,' sighed Jean, shaking her head, 'still the expert. I can't do a thing with him.'

Belle realised that James had taken hold of her hand and was squeezing it, looking anxiously at her.

'You're home . . .' he began, 'you're safe . . . we wondered how you were doing in Belfast. Marcus dropped the odd word at the beginning, but not such a lot lately. He's too busy . . . making a lot of money.' He spoke like a conspirator. 'You went away without a word . . . and your Sam . . .' His voice trailed away and he shook his head.

'That's enough, James.' Jean spoke severely. 'She's home.'

'Are you staying?' James quavered, his watery eyes fixed on Belle.

'I expect so,' Belle said.

'But all that time in Belfast, and hardly a word . . . we wondered . . . and we worried, didn't we, dear?' James went on.

'I managed fine well in Belfast.' Belle spoke in her best reassuring voice. 'You ought to see the boys. They have grown up quite a bit. Rory is very like Sam, stubborn, a bit serious, set in his ways. And Conor – he was only a baby when I went, but you will see that he is quite like John.'

As soon as she said that she was regretting it. Why bring up John, now?

Two Landrovers appeared out of the snow which was now flurrying down.

'Watch out, Jean. Look! You'll have to move the car,' Belle warned.

Jean had parked the Morris Minor in the middle of the road. She got into the driver's seat and tried to start the car but stalled it. The Landrovers waited in the roadway behind her, their side-lights on, standing like two large cows, heads down, staring and waiting. Eventually Jean got the engine running and drove to the edge of the road, Belle retreating to the pavement.

The Landrovers moved past slowly and as they went by there was a sound of soft cheering that was almost jeering.

'That lot!' Jean said breathlessly as she hopped out of the car again and came over to Belle. This time she had remembered to put on the handbrake. 'They are a lot of . . . well, you get used to them I suppose, there's a mixture. Sometimes it is the local lads, they are not too bad, the UDR you know. The regular army officers are all gentlemen, but the ranks . . . well, some of the things they say wouldn't bear repeating.'

'What do you expect?' James demanded. 'They're soldiers, not here for a charm school!'

'Oh James, don't be silly, you know what I mean,' Jean said.

'Bloody army!' James said succinctly.

Belle waited for him to say more, but he seemed to have made his statement.

Jean waved a feeble hand in the air and said, 'He's biased. He's got nothing good to say about the army.'

'Have you noticed the way they look at her?' James fired at Belle.

'What do you mean?' Belle couldn't understand what he was talking about.

'The army. The soldiers. Her major. For a start,' he continued his verbal attack.

'Whose major?' Belle asked.

'Jean's. Jean's,' James insisted.

'Don't be silly, James.' Jean put on her best schoolmistress voice.

'Oh yes,' James went on, rolling out the words with relish. 'Jean has an admirer. Yes. An admirer. A major. Went through Sandhurst. The real thing. Isn't that right, Jean? And he comes to call. And Jean makes him tea.' He waited for Belle to respond, but watched Jean slyly.

Jean reproved him coldly. 'Don't be silly, James, it's not like that at all. He is just a very lonely man. Yes, I know he is a widower, but his family are all in England – and he misses them so much.'

'So you give him tea and sympathy,' James continued in the same mocking tone.

'I am only providing him with a little of the home comfort he is missing, that's all,' Jean said. There were bright spots of colour in her cheeks. Was it anger or discomfort? Belle could not decide. She felt that she was party to a conversation which was between only two people.

'That's not the way I see it,' James went on.

'Well, that's the way your silly mind thinks, isn't it?' Jean said shortly. Belle realised that Jean was angry, something she had rarely displayed in the past.

James attacked again. 'Hm . . . he's a very handsome fellow.'

'Oh be quiet. That's all nonsense and you know it,' Jean snapped back.

'I was on my way back from calling with you,' Belle interjected before the conversation could go further in its accusing way. 'I know that it would have been sensible to phone you before I set out . . .'

'Well, why don't you come to lunch tomorrow?' Jean said, smiling like some automaton, putting on her instant hostess look. 'I only have a wee chicken, but I have a piece of boiling bacon would go on the side and I can easily cook up some more potatoes. Yes, and I could bake an apple tart. James just loves a tart.' She smiled winningly at him, as if to cajole him out of his sulks, for he had subsided into total silence. 'It's hardly worth making a tart for one, but if you're coming . . .'

James brightened, having seemed, once he had lost dominance of the conversation, to have lost interest in what was being said. 'Yes, I shall look forward to a tart. Haven't had one of those in ages.' He chuckled suddenly. Belle looked at him severely and he looked back at her sheepishly. 'Oh, you know what I mean,' he excused.

'Well, we won't keep you, dear.' Jean was smiling her best sweet, tremulous smile that Belle had forgotten. How pretty she must have been once. Belle could not remember when. 'We'll see you around twelve thirty tomorrow, all right? James doesn't like to be too late having his luncheon.'

'Yes, that'll be grand,' Belle smiled back. 'We'll be delighted to come. It looks as if the snow is easing off now,' she added, looking up at the sky.

'Told you it wouldn't last,' James said.

'Oh, you always know, don't you,' Jean shouted suddenly,

getting into the car and slamming the door shut. The car started with a jerk and sped off into the distance, Jean accelerating madly in first gear.

Belle made her way quickly to the house, let herself into the warm kitchen and gloried in the heat with a mug of tea. It was very quiet, a heavy lethargy outside as if the sudden fall of snow, however slight, had coated the earth with a blanket, stifling all movement. She heard the clock ticking across the stone-flagged hallway, a sudden gust of wind in the chimney. For a moment she felt calm, her life in order.

A car door slammed, there were high-pitched, excited shouts. Opening the door from the kitchen to the hall, she peered out of the porch window into the gathering dark. The boys were running, dancing up the drive, scooping up handfuls of thin snow and throwing them at each other.

Pat Quinn was standing by the gate, illuminated by the side-lights of his car. He was, she realised, talking to someone, a shortish stocky figure. It looked like Cathal. What was he doing here at this time? He couldn't possibly be delivering milk now. They must have just met at the gate. Cathal must have been passing by when Pat dropped the boys off. At any rate, they agreed on something and parted quickly, Pat ducking into his car and speeding off down the road to Corey. There was the sound of another car but she could not see anything in the darkness.

Rory slammed the kitchen door shut with a sigh and shouted, 'Ma? Where are you?'

'I'm here, I heard you,' Belle said, coming out of the gloom of the hall.

'Hey, that was tremendous, simply great!' Rory said. 'Even Conor thinks so. And Pat Quinn ('Pat?' Belle thought with amazement) is the greatest. Ma, he really is the greatest.'

'I'm not so sure about that,' Conor interrupted briefly.

'You're only saying that because you are a baby and you don't understand what he's talking about half the time.' Rory pushed his brother aside importantly.

'Oh do stop you two,' said Belle, 'I gather it was a good match even though it snowed?'

'Yes. Great, great,' Rory repeated. 'Great.' He headed for the television set.

'Yeah, great,' Conor said in a scathing tone, for once not

following him. 'My fingers are frozen off, you see? Look, Mama!' He thrust out his hands; the tips of his fingers were white and stiff.

Belle gathered Conor on to her knee and rubbed his fingers in front of the heat. He moaned as they ached, the circulation gradually returning, but she wanted to mother him, smother him with comfort. You're my baby still, she reminded herself silently, my baby, wrapping her arms round him.

There was a firm rap at the door, the sound of the latch being lifted and a gust of chill air broke into her reveries as she sat there with Conor in her arms. She hadn't locked the door. She caught her breath, lifted her head, turned it and looked across the room.

Pat Quinn stood by the door which he had shut behind him and as she opened her mouth to speak, he lifted his hand apologetically.

'You didn't lock the door. Were you expecting someone?' He stopped, as if he felt an intruder on her warm languor. Her cheeks were flushed by the fire, her small son's body was moulded close to her own as he sat on her lap, his cheeks flushed too and his eyes half closed in a sleepy stare. 'I'm sorry, I didn't mean to intrude . . .' Pat's voice died, he gestured to the door. 'I didn't want to let too much of the cold in . . .'

'Come in, Mr Quinn, I'm sorry I didn't hear your car. Did you leave it at the gate? I heard you drop the boys off. I thought you were away off home.'

'I'll not disturb you,' he said uncertainly now.

'It's a cold night. Has there been any more snow? Come on over here to the stove.'

'No, there's been no more snow.'

'Come and sit down. I think the heat has made us a bit sleepy,' she smile downwards at her son's head.

'Is he asleep?' Pat asked, lowering his voice. He had come to stand beside her.

Conor opened his eyes disdainfully. 'I am not indeed, I was thinking, that's all.'

'Can you pull a chair close, Mr Quinn,' she said, pointing to the carver. 'As you can see, this big baby has me pinned down . . .'

Conor straightened up and looked at her wide-eyed. 'I'm not . . .' he started to say reproachfully.

'No,' she said, brushing his hair off his forehead tenderly. 'No, you're a big boy now. And didn't you enjoy the football match this afternoon?'

It was a conversational signal he recognised. 'Oh yes,' he said, 'I never thanked you, Mr Quinn. It was kind of you to take us. It was a good match. Very enjoyable.' He slid off Belle's lap and stood stiffly beside her.

'Yes,' Belle said. 'It was very kind of you, Mr Quinn.'

He held up a hand in protest. 'Didn't you say you would call me Pat?'

'Oh, yes. I forgot, I'm sorry . . . Pat.' She said his name firmly.

Conor tugged at her arm, turning and looking up at her bright eyes. 'Mama?'

'I must say that you look very . . . what is the word? I can't think,' Pat acknowledged at last. He wanted to say that she looked like some ikon of a mother and child, the encircling arms, the serenity, but he couldn't for that instant put it into words. He sat down in the carver chair beside her and spread his fingers out to the flames. A silence fell between them.

'Mama?' Conor said again. 'Mama!'

'What is it, love?' she asked, not turning her head to him. She found herself still looking at Pat and he at her.

'Och, nothing,' Conor muttered, twisting his fingers in the loops of her sweater.

'Do you want me to start making the tea?' she asked, and looked at her watch. 'The time! I didn't realise. You boys must be raving with hunger. Maybe Mr Quinn would like to stay too?' She looked at Pat.

Conor looked smug. 'Och, sure we had chips on the way home.'

'What's this?' she asked, her eyes widening.

'Mr Quinn. He bought them,' Conor explained.

Belle looked at Pat in consternation. 'Oh, you are too good to them, you really are. How can I . . . ?'

'There's nothing like a bag of chips and a pasty after hanging around in the cold and sleet for an afternoon,' Pat said grinning.

'But . . .' Belle didn't know what to say.

'But if you have any hot water in that kettle I wouldn't say no to a big mug of tea,' he said quickly, sensing her disquiet.

'You really are too good,' she said again, shaking her head.

'It was nothing. I enjoyed their company. They're great boys. To tell the truth, I miss the kids at the weekends.'

'You and your wife . . .' Belle blundered, 'you don't have children?'

'I'm not married,' he said.

The kitchen door opened. Rory stood there waving his arms urgently. 'Conor! Do you want to see that programme with the cars or not?'

'I thought I missed it,' Conor cried excitedly.

'Well, you just didn't check the time, did you,' Rory said in a superior tone. 'I knew we would be home in time to see it. I knew.'

'Has it started yet?' Conor asked.

'Just now.' Rory stood back as the small boy pushed past him in the doorway. Rory nodded his head at his mother knowingly. 'He's stupid. I knew all along. Oh hallo, Mr Quinn . . . you're back?' he said as an afterthought, seeing Pat by the fire. 'That was a great match, great.'

'Well, maybe you'll come with me another afternoon,' Pat said.

'Yes, it was great. And the chips. Thanks,' Rory lingered, 'thanks.'

'I'll see you on Monday then,' Pat said.

'Yes, on Monday.'

'Oh go on with you, Rory, go back to the television. There's a terrible draught coming in through that door. Is there a good fire yet?' Belle scolded.

'Oh yes, I got it going in no time,' Rory replied confidently. 'OK. Cheerio, Mr Quinn.' He shut the door with a bang.

Belle sighed, then she looked a trifle uncomfortably at Pat.

He was sitting with his elbows on the arms of the chair, resting his chin on his hands looking into the fire. She heard the sitting-room door shut and the sound of the television softened and died to a low murmur. She felt awkward, that she had to say something, and in the end it was her practical streak that showed. She stood up abruptly.

'Yes, I think I could drink another cup of tea myself,' she said, brushing her jeans straight with her hands. 'And if you let me take your jacket . . .' She held out her hands to Pat. 'You will feel the cold, you know, when you leave, if you sit here in the warm with your jacket on.'

Pat stood up. Once again she was conscious of how tall he was. He slid out of his jacket, unwound his striped scarf from his neck and handed them to her. Their fingers touched. She looked directly at him, feeling the fire on her cheeks. She stepped away then across the tiled floor to the back door where she hung his jacket on the hook on top of Mrs D's apron, then the scarf, smoothing it flat with her fingers.

When she turned she saw that Pat had pulled the kettle forward on the hob and was standing looking at her quizzically.

'Mugs,' she said, 'I'll get them. Give me the teapot and I'll empty out the teabags.'

'You sit down,' he said, 'I'll make the tea.' Taking the pot from her he walked into the scullery.

'Well, you seem to know where everything is in this house,' she joked when he reappeared. 'The mugs –'

'Are in the dresser,' he said, 'and the teabags are in the caddy on the shelf.'

'You don't by any chance live here yourself, do you?' she laughed.

'No, but one house is like another.'

Belle sat down and watched him make the tea, pour the milk, ladling two generous spoonfuls of sugar into his own mug. He sat down then and stretched his long legs out in front of him, cradling the mug of tea to his chest, sipping slowly now and again, staring into the fire.

Belle tried to stare into the fire too, but her eyes slid sideways to look at him critically, his iron-grey hair curling at the nape of the neck, his Aran sweater fraying at the wrists, his legs in their worn grey corduroy trousers.

Sam is dead dog tired tonight. I know it. He is sitting in that chair as if it were glued to him. He has been out all day ploughing. He kept at it. The weather's right, he says, it might rain at any time, there's a depression coming in from the Atlantic, and if there's too much he won't be able to get that field at his father's finished. He has ploughed more than half of it and looking at him, I hope it rains and rains. If he goes out again tomorrow he will be dead on his feet.

Given some mild weather we could have some silage. The

Johnstons have a big herd of store cattle, for fattening up. They need feed. Sam says that if John would let him plough up the front field on Top Hill, it would give them all the feed they would need next year. But it's been fallow too long, John says, it's not worth it, all reed. Sam says it can be ploughed. They argued all last night over supper. Sam gave up in the end. It's John's land. He decides. He's only interested in the orchard.

Maybe Sam is thinking about that now. He looks so defeated. He hasn't changed out of the clothes he was working in and I can see mud caked on the knees of his corduroy trousers as if he has been praying out there amongst the furrows, praying for the right weather, a good crop.

He is looking at me now. With such a look. I reach out and touch his knee and he puts his hand over mine.

'Do you want some more tea?' I ask, taking the empty mug from his other hand where he has it propped on his chest.

'No. That was good. I needed it.'

I stand up and put the mug on to the mantelpiece.

He takes my hand again. 'Here, woman, how are you?' he says quietly, pulling me towards him. I stoop and kneel down beside him, laying my head on his knees. 'How are you?' he asks again, touching my hair. I can feel the strength of his arms and his thighs, a hard urgency rising against me quickly as he leans and gathers me up to him, his hands pressing my hips to him so that I can feel my body surge and urge with his. 'How are you, my woman?' he whispers into my ear.

'I'm fine . . . I missed you, oh! how I missed you. I worried that you were working too long. You were off at the farm for such a long time and Rory has been in bed these ages . . . you were very late coming home to me tonight.' I am trying to keep the reproach out of my voice.

'You know I had to get as much done as possible, before the rain comes,' he explains, kissing me gently on the lips, my neck, his tongue seeking my ear. 'Don't worry,' he breathes, 'I'll get it done.' He slides one hand up under my sweater, cupping my breast, pulling at the nipple till it goes erect. His other hand follows, cupping the other breast, teasing till I can hardly stand it. Something inside me begins to move and gather momentum.

'You're tired, you're tired,' I remind him.

'Not too tired,' he says, his lips close to mine, his teeth teasing my lips, 'not too tired at all.' I can feel his stubble on my face as he kisses me hard, peremptorily, his tongue sliding between my teeth so that I catch my breath at its sweetness. 'Come on, woman, I fancy you, here, by the fire . . .'

We are kneeling together now, the tiles feel hard on my knees but it doesn't matter, for I can feel him close, hard, compelling against me, my hand quests and feels and caresses.

The door latch clicks, the wind rushes across the floor as the door opens and shuts with a clang. It's John. My brother John. He looks white, furious . . . is it only the cold?

'God!' he says, clutching his coat collar around him. 'It's bloody cold out there. And wet. Did you not know it's raining? A downpour. Bloody hell! Coming down! Oh, don't let me disturb you two lovebirds,' he continues angrily, 'move yourselves! Let me get a look at the fire!'

Oh John! Get out of my life! Leave me alone! Why do you always get in the way? Why do I feel this way? I love you really. Why should I wish you out of the way?

Maybe that bomb was my fault. I wanted it. Maybe I made it happen.

'Mrs Johnston . . . Mrs Johnston!'

Belle blinked and looked at the speaker.

Pat was leaning towards her. She saw the slight stubble on his chin, how cold his grey eyes were, how they crinkled at the corners and a strange searching look in them as he stared at her.

'What is it?' he asked. She looked so desolate in that moment, but as he stared at her she changed, became aware of his presence.

Belle sighed. 'I thought that I was going to call you Pat if you were going to call me Belle,' she said quickly, filling the void.

'Well, I had to get through to you somehow, you were miles away.' He took her hand in both of his and looked at her very intently. 'Tell me, do you mind being in this house on your own, with the boys, you aren't afraid?'

'Do you mean, do I check under the beds and behind the doors before I go to bed at night?' she asked, trying to appear nonchalant.

'It's very isolated here. This house has been empty for so long. You should lock yourself in at night . . . sure tonight I just walked in . . .'

'Och, just up the hill there's not only the police but the army as well,' she said, conscious of the pressure of his hands on hers.

The door from the hall opened quickly. Rory stood there. 'Ma! Ma!'

'What is it?' Belle turned and took her hand away from Pat's.

'There's a newsflash! It's the Red Crown, the pub just down the road from where our house is . . . a bomb!' His voice rose.

'Was anyone hurt?' she asked.

'No. Someone carried it out of the pub and threw it over a wall or something, it said . . . it was just down the road from home . . .'

'You forget,' she said, 'we don't live there any more, do we?'

'But, Ma?' he protested.

'It was just another bomb, Rory, another one.'

'I just thought,' he muttered, shutting the door with a bang.

Belle looked at Pat and took a deep breath. 'Sorry, it goes on and on. What's the point any more?'

'Yes,' he said without any emotion.

'Would you like more tea?' she asked, reaching for the pot.

He stood up now. 'No. That was fine. I only dropped by to . . . I came back,' he laughed, 'but I forgot why I came back.' He strode across the kitchen to his jacket, lifting it and the scarf off the peg, feeling in one pocket and coming out with a brown paper bag. He held it out to her.

'For me?' she asked in amazement.

'Yes, I thought this morning that you looked as if, well, that you needed a little . . .' his voice slowed, 'a little token of my esteem,' he finished with a flourish.

'This morning?' she asked.

'Yes. You looked half dead. Forgive me, you looked . . . as if you had been painting these yellow walls all night.'

'I was tired, you're right. But I went for a walk. Thank you for that. They really needed to get away from me. They have been with me too long . . . What is this?' She felt the package with her fingers. She peered in, then drew out a box of chocolates.

'You really . . .' she started.

'Yes?' he said, putting his fingers under her chin and drawing her to him. 'I figured that a box of candy would do the trick, would bring some colour back.' He noticed the sudden flush in her cheeks. 'How long since somebody bought you a box?'

Belle caught her breath. At that moment she wanted him to hold her, bury his face in her hair, to feel him caress her neck with his lips, feel his long lean body against hers. She swallowed hard. 'A long time,' she whispered, wondering what more she could say, and lifted her eyes shyly to his.

'A long time? Yes, I thought so,' he said, as if talking to himself, reassuring himself.

His stare was disconcerting. 'Do you know the O'Briens?' she asked, hearing starchiness in her voice and regretting it at once.

He looked away, let her go. 'Oh yes. Not well. Funny pair.'

The moment had passed, she realised. She had broken the thread between them.

'Yes,' she said sadly, 'they are a bit old-fashioned.'

Pat was winding his scarf round his neck in a deliberate gesture and she found herself taking his jacket in her hands and holding it for him as he eased his long arms into the sleeves. He turned and put his hand on her shoulder. She didn't flinch this time.

'Are you sure you're happy being on your own?' he repeated.

'Yes, I am.'

'All the same,' he paused, 'it's different to living in the city.'

'You can be very lonely in a city,' she said, thinking out loud. 'It's quiet here. When I lie in bed I can hear the sounds of the apple trees, the wind, the foxes in the orchard.'

'So you lie in bed listening for foxes?'

'No. Generally I sleep very soundly, it would take a very loud noise to wake me up,' she said ingenuously.

'And you lock yourself in at night?' Belle looked at him, wondering why his voice was now harsh and questioning.

'Why should you be bothered?

'Because . . .' He sighed and put his hand on the latch. 'I'd better go.'

'Thank you for the chocolates,' she said, wishing that she could say more to keep him with her a little longer.

'You're welcome, you're welcome,' he said, leaning towards

her, then straightening. She realised that she had not responded to his gesture.

As he opened the door and stepped out, telling her to stay inside, it was far too cold and that he would see her on Monday, she felt her body go limp in defeat, a defeat she understood.

'Thank you,' she said, in a low voice.

'You're welcome,' he repeated. 'Now, lock the door, and keep it locked, no matter how many foxes you hear tonight!'

'Don't tease me?' she implored.

'I'm not,' he said, disappearing into the night. She listened for his footsteps on the cobbles but all she heard was the wind in the orchard, gusting down the long rows of trees.

Chapter 9

THE SUNDAY MORNING silence was broken only by a single bell tolling slowly, the sound flooding down from the top of the village street.

Early Communion. The smell in the church of damp and dust, polished pews, hassocks once embroidered by the good ladies of the parish in a fit of zeal, now balding and scenting the air faintly with mothballs as if that were to stop the siege of time. The sound of feet on the stone flags, hushed tones, the slapping sound of prayer books placed down on pews as each and every one gathered there in Christ's name.

Belle used to go with her mother. John steadfastly refused, but Belle for the sake of peace would go. In the years before her Confirmation she would sit in their pew while her mother and the others gathered there in the morning chill would take their places, each in turn to kneel at the altar rail and receive the Sacrament, the rector repeating the words to each recipient in a monotone half sung, but not quite, for singing, chanting, was frowned upon. Too much like the Catholics.

The palpitating, rough sound of a helicopter broke Belle's reveries as she lay there, warm this morning for the covers had magically stayed in place. For an instant she thought she must be back in Belfast, lying in that front first-floor room, buses going by the door, a helicopter above. But the bell was wrong. Somehow in Belfast she had not heard the bells, though she lived in an area of the city which was full of churches. Maybe she simply had not noticed them before. Maybe the background of city traffic blurred the sound for her.

'On the Sunday morning sidewalk, wishing I could be home . . .' Kristofferson haunted her this morning.

The Belfast sidewalks had been far from the romantic dream that she had dreamed far back in her bed in the country. The big city, the slick city. She had tried not to miss the countryside, but on warm nights she longed for the smell of the cut hay, the swallows and martins dipping over the land after evening midges, the sound of doves in the distance echoing each other's slow low call over the darkening fields, the trees heavy with leaf, the dew thick and wet underfoot.

She missed the nights, those special nights, when she had walked up under the orchard boughs growing heavy with fruit with Sam, arms linked firmly though they had occasionally to duck their heads under the low-hanging branches. Sometimes they had made slow sweet love there together in the tangled dew-laden grass, feeling a freedom they could not feel within the four walls of the big bedroom back in the House where it seemed as if something or someone held their breath, listening for the sound of their loving.

Sam. Why should she think of him now, other than with a cold compassion born out of so many nights without him, first in the empty bed in Belfast, now in the bed which they had shared so many years ago? She had made the decision, made the break. It had seemed right at the time. Had he loved her? Did he ever love her? Yes. She thought so, but still the doubts came back. He had let her go, her departure had been greeted with stone-cold impassivity. He was a proud man. Sons or not, he had let her go, and hadn't followed her. Why? Why? Why was she thinking like this now? It's the bells, the bells.

'The bells! The bells!' Conor came creeping round the bedroom door, the thick Connemara rug about his shoulders and a definitive hump on his back – it was a pillow stuffed up his pyjama top. 'The bells!'

'You fool!' she laughed and buried her face in her pillow, choking. 'All right, Quasimodo . . .' she choked again, 'when you've finished we might get ourselves organised for lunch, we're going out to lunch today.'

'Aargh!' Conor clutched at his throat and fell on to the bed.

'It's not as bad as all that, we're going down the road to the O'Briens.'

'Aargh!' he said again, rolling his eyes in terror, sliding off the bed and roaming round the room, taking giant steps from one window to the other, pushing back the curtains with a dramatic gesture. 'The bells, the bells,' he intoned.

The bell sounded louder now that the curtains were back. Belle could see a greyish landscape. The sound of the helicopter had faded.

'What happened to the snow?' she asked him as he swept past a window.

'There's no snow, it's no joke!' he intoned again, then fell on the bed giggling.

'If that's the best joke you can come up with at this hour of the morning, then go back to bed,' she said in mock severity.

'Och, Mama,' he was putting on a little-boy voice, 'och, Mama, do we have to go? To the O'Briens?'

' 'Fraid so,' she replied in her best American accent. 'It's on the cards, baby!'

He winced and stopped his gyrating, serious now.

'Well,' she decided to soften the blow, 'your Auntie Jean . . .'

'She's not my Auntie Jean!'

Belle went on, 'She's got a chicken, and a ham,' she added hastily, 'and she's going to make an apple tart.' She waited.

He looked at her knowingly. 'If we go, we won't stay long, will we?'

'Well, we can't rush away afterwards, but since it gets dark early, we won't be staying much after four, I'd like to be back, just in case the weather does get bad.'

'Four!' he shouted in despair. 'But there's a programme on TV . . .'

'You are the limit!' she shouted back at him.

'Well.' He sulked a moment. 'Did you say chicken?'

'Yes. You like chicken.'

'I suppose it's all right then. But we won't stay long, you promise me. Rory says they are creepy people. I don't like creepy people.'

'What about the snow?'

'No more snow,' he replied, shaking his head sadly. 'It was only a thin layer.'

Later, after breakfast, Belle opened the back door, looked out on the yard and sniffed the air.

It was crisp, cold, with a piecrust of snow coating the gables on the roofs of the stables across the yard, and the cobbles shone with a glazing of ice. She retreated to the kitchen. Above her the house was silent, for the boys had snatched breakfast and disappeared back to bed again. She would have to dig them out before long, polish their faces, get them snugly dressed and off down to the O'Briens. And she would take the car.

It look longer than she anticipated to rouse the boys. Conor lingered, grumbling about what clothes he was going to wear, and which shoes and where he had left them last. She was glad when she got the boys into the car for even Rory had seemed reluctant to set out on this particular expedition. Eventually, by twelve thirty almost to the minute, she was drawing up to the front door of the Lodge. There was a white Mercedes parked there, she noticed. Another visitor to lunch? It might be quite a party.

She was concentrating on getting the boys out of the car when the door opened and Marcus appeared on the doorstep. Of course, Sunday lunch, it was his duty. He came down the steps quickly and before she realised what he was doing, he had gathered her into his arms, kissing her firmly on the lips. He had never in all the years kissed her in this fashion. He looked woebegone, and she wondered why he should be. Materially he looked prosperous enough, the clothes, the car. She also, to her surprise, felt the bulk of a revolver against her as his arms tightened. He was carrying a revolver, under his armpit. It was ridiculous. What on earth kind of work was he doing now that he felt he had to have this kind of protection? She wanted to ask but Jean had appeared behind him on the steps. Marcus released her quickly, casually, his expression became guarded as if he was afraid Belle would say something, remark upon his sudden loving act, or did he sense she might ask him about the gun?

'Well, Annabelle, it's good to see you,' Jean said warmly, taking her arm. 'You see it did not snow after all. James was right, yet again.' She led Belle indoors, exclaiming about the boys, how big they were, how right Belle had been about them, Rory was so like Sam, and to be sure Conor so like John. Uncanny it was, she fluttered, but so true.

'What's this about snow?' James, tall, thin, wearing a grey loose cardigan which was darned at the elbows, a shirt open at the neck with a bright green cravat, a baggy pair of flannel trousers and brown tartan felt slippers, appeared in the hallway from the room he liked to call the library. More honestly it was stacked from floor to ceiling with not only a mouldering collection of books, but suitcases full of odd possessions mostly belonging to himself for he could not bear to throw anything away in case it came in useful. It was a storehouse of memories, of experiences once suffered or experiences he wished fatefully upon himself but would never encounter or dare to encounter.

So there were exercise books from his senior terms at the school, full of essays about countries he would like to visit but had only read about in books, a worn set of cricket pads, a pair of leather gauntlets for the motor cycle he had for four months, along with goggles. The remains of the motor cycle were in a stable at the back of the house, taken apart one reckless day when James decided it didn't fire too well and he was the mechanic to fix it. He had misplaced a part here, a part there, lost heart and left it in bits. There was a box of electric light fittings and plugs from another time when he planned to rewire the house. And at one time he had gone through a kind of literary twilight, collecting posters and photographs of leading writers of the day. These had been pasted on to one wall over the old paper, making a collage of faces staring down at him, peeling and yellowing like the paper on the walls of the rest of the room, for all in time through days of gathering dust and desolation had fallen into decay. It was in this room that he would sit, the door closed from Jean and her domesticity, dreaming perhaps of another day ahead or days behind, sipping his favourite Bushmills whiskey, his own elixir of life.

Jean rarely entered this room except to take him his tea on a tray. Certainly she would never dare try to clean it. She had her domain at the back of the house, where the sunshine sneaked into the tiny kitchen, once a pantry, over the worn red tiles, the battered electric cooker which she had persuaded James to let her have but which she had never had the heart to clean properly, the long kitchen table covered in oil-cloth, the edges tacked underneath, a wooden airer slung from the ceiling that could not be pulled right up out of the way so that you had to duck under assorted tea-towels, underpants, and tired shirts which she might iron for James if the fit came upon her. Only the row of geraniums on the window-sill provided the brightness of colour, the solace, and the company she wished. Most of the day she spent here, warmed by a small electric fire in winter, sitting in a battered leatherette armchair by the window, knitting sometimes, with swollen reddened fingers, producing cardigans with drooping pockets into which she stuffed balls of string, hankies for her dripping nose (it had always dripped) and odd keys which might open something some time. Occasionally she made forays into the rest of the house, to the dining-room where she guided them now in almost hushed tones like some guide in a country house.

'This is the dining-room,' she twittered unnecessarily, 'do take a seat while I dish up. James will see to a small sherry, I'm sure you'll take one? So good to see you, so good. Marcus? Come with me and help me dish up, you can push the trolley in. I do find a trolley most useful for it is so far from the kitchen . . . yes, so far . . .' She smoothed her Crimplene dress nervously. It was a dowager's purple, surprisingly smart, and it brought out the colour in her cheeks, made her hair a white halo.

Marcus looked at Belle and shook his head in disbelief at Jean's performance as the perfect hostess and followed her out of the room.

James was occupied, talking to the boys about a collection of guns in a cabinet, explaining the technicalities to an enraptured audience.

Belle let her mind go blank, listening to the sound of James's voice describing each piece in turn. She had heard it all before many times.

'Are you going to unlock the case and let me touch them?' Conor's voice broke into her reverie.

She looked up, almost said the words with James as he replied, 'Oh, I don't think that's possible. We've lost the key of the case, d'ye see? We have looked everywhere, but never managed to find it. Sad, isn't it?'

'So how do you keep them so well polished?' Conor went on.

'Oh, it's an airtight case, d'ye see. The dust just doesn't get in, or the air . . . much.' James shrugged his shoulders helplessly.

Conor still looked puzzled. He knew, John had known, that

James had a key, of course he had a key, but those guns were his private possessions, only his to touch, take out, polish, adore. 'Would they still work, d'you think?'

Rory was beginning to get impatient. 'Yes,' he broke in, 'would they still work?'

'After all these years?' James raised a sceptical eyebrow. 'No, I wouldn't think so.'

It is the first day of the school summer holidays, ten weeks. I stayed in bed until nearly lunchtime, I felt lethargic but then Mother came roaring in. She was very cross. I tried to help her get lunch, but she kept telling me to get away from under her feet. She said she was glad it was sunny. John and I could go off for a cycle ride somewhere.

So that is why John and I are standing outside Quinn's, down at Corey, eating ice-creams.

'Which way will we go from here?' John asks.

'Not far. Not today,' I say lazily, looking down the straight street.

'Och, come on now,' John growls. 'We could go to the Johnstons'.'

'But there are those three big hills – it's a long way. Not today, John, I just don't feel like it.'

'It's not that far, don't exaggerate!' He goes very quiet.

I turn my head and look at Top Hill. It looks cool and serene under the trees. But you can't take a bicycle up there.

'Well,' he says at last, 'what about going along the lane at the back of the demesne to the old cottage by the mill stream, you know,' he describes the route I know only too well, flailing his arms in the air, 'the lane that curls round and ends up at the top of the village.'

'Och, it's too far, it's too hot today,' I complain. It's nice that way, I know. The cottage still has its roof and it's very old, all wooden beams and a fire with one of those hooks you hang cooking pots on. There's the remains of an orchard with plums. Some days in summer we go swimming in the stream, the water is not very deep, but it's sheltered and warm and nobody would know you were there.

'Let's go to the O'Briens' then?'

I had better agree. He is beginning to look ferocious.

Down in the park it's cool and shady when we ride in through the gate, and as usual the Lodge looks deserted. We throw our bicycles down on the grass by the front door. Then we can hear someone snipping a hedge. Jean is at the side, by the garden hedge, wearing an old straw hat and a shapeless flowered dress. She is trying to trim a bush into what she calls her peacock. John says it still does not look like one, even though she seems to have been trimming it for at least five years.

'Well, you two? Isn't it hot?' She is quite pink in the face. She looks rather pretty today. I think that she is quite pleased to see us. 'Where have you been?' she asks cheerfully, putting down the shears.

'We thought we would go for a cycle ride –' I start to say, but John interrupts.

'It's too hot to go far and Belle is feeling lazy today. We had ice-creams down at Quinn's but then we thought about going over to the ruined cottage, the secret one, you know, round the back of the demesne. We thought we might go for a swim some time. But not today, in the end we decided to come and see you.'

'Oh, you call it the secret cottage do you? Yes I know where you mean. You're right, nobody ever goes there. Now when James and I were young . . . we went there . . . quite a lot. There was one particularly good summer just before our parents died. We must have been teenagers . . . well, nearly twenty I suppose. We went there several times, it was hot I remember, very hot . . . and so handy because you could change in the cottage . . . not that anyone uses that road, it's really only a track, but you could shelter there too if it rained . . . ever . . . it was very cool in the river, I remember . . . James and I used to . . .' She pauses, then clears her throat. Is the remembrance of her parents' death still hard to bear, I wonder? She is looking disconcerted, flushed.

'What did you do?' I ask.

'Do?' Her voice rises in alarm. 'Do? Nothing . . .'

'I don't mean . . .' My voice dies in embarrassment. Why do grown-ups have to misunderstand me?

She now looks at me distantly, and clears her throat again.

'I was just hoping someone would come along and interrupt me,' she then says, changing the subject. 'And I was thinking about a nice glass of home-made lemonade, from Aunt Grace's recipe, you know.' She is looking at me. She gave me the recipe last summer but I haven't tried it out yet.

'That would be nice,' says John, sounding polite.

'If you're looking for James,' she says, 'he disappeared after lunch. I don't know where he has gone. My! It's hot. Now just you sit down here, yes, by the steps, and I'll go for that lemonade.'

John sits down on the top step. I sit the next one down, leaning my back against his left thigh.

Jean is back in a moment. 'Here we are now, isn't this a good idea?' she says gaily. I think she is really pleased to see us. She pours the lemonade. It is not precisely ice cold. She doesn't have a refrigerator, just a cold room downstairs where all the old kitchens are, but it tastes nice, and I'm thirsty.

We sit for a while. The sun is hot on my face.

'Belle? Belle?' Jean breaks into my daze.

'Yes?'

'You have a birthday coming up soon, haven't you? Next week.'

'Yes. I'll be twelve,' I said proudly.

'And John is?' She wrinkles up her nose. When she does that she looks years younger.

'I was seventeen in January,' says John.

She looks him up and down critically. 'You are getting old, quite old, John. Have you got a girlfriend yet?' Jean asks.

'No,' he says.

'Well, you have Belle,' she smiles.

He looks at me fondly. 'Yes. I have her.'

Jean sighs suddenly. 'I just don't know where James has got to, I suppose he had some letters to write, or some such thing, he keeps busy you know.'

I don't understand why he hasn't got a job. Mother says they live on the interest on the interest on the interest.

The sun is beginning to sink towards the forest. I begin to think about tea and whether we ought to get home to help Mother get it.

There's the sound of a shot, close by.

Aunt Jean goes, 'Tut, tut, tut,' under her breath. We look at her, startled. 'Drat him!' she says in explanation. We look at her enquiringly. 'James must be after the rats again. They come out at this time of the evening. He's probably upstairs round the back. He gets a gun out sometimes. There are a lot of rats this year. It's since that old terrier of his died, last winter. A lot of rats. Why don't you go and say "hallo"?' she says brightly.

We go in and up the threadbare carpet on the wide sweeping stairs that go up to the first floor. More shots. We follow the sound.

James is at a broken window, sitting with one of his precious guns, the ones from the case that is always locked. 'Not bad! Not bad!' he is saying when we come in the door of the cluttered room. He is crouching down, sitting on a faded red velvet chair. 'That's four so far. Blighters! Bloody blighters!' he says.

John squeezes beside him at the window, looking down. 'Where?'

I stand back. I don't like guns.

'Come here? Come here, wee Belle?' James invites me, waving his arm.

I creep to the window and look out. The yard below is full of rusting bits of metal that once were ploughs, cars, oil drums, bits of gate, something that looks like a motor bike, falling apart, leaning on each other. They are corroded, crumpled, clumps of weeds springing up through the twisted tortured metal. I can only see decay. No rats.

Then there is a movement.

'There! D'ye see? There! They come out of that bit of drain there. D'ye see?' James points the gun and fires quickly. I step back, banging my leg on a bit of table sticking out. 'Got him! Another! This is excellent! Excellent!' says James, his eyes gleaming. 'Just watch! There'll be another one. See!' He fires again. 'Aha!' he shouts.

Something grey bundles, jumps and trembles bloodily amongst the weeds.

'What kind of gun . . . ?' John starts to ask.

'It's one of my specials. My father's specials. He was in the Second World War, came through it without a scratch you know, in the regular army, commissioned of course, none of your volunteers. Now there was a real fighting man.' He opens his hand and spreads his fingers to show off the gun. 'One of my father's wee beauties. Takes a bit of skill to get a rat, boy, a bit of skill with a gun like this. Did you know I was an expert? Thought I might join the army one time. But then . . . never mind . . . this is my target practice. The rats come out and I'm the man to get them. Did you know I was good with a gun, boy?'

'I thought . . .' John starts to say. He wants to say something about the locked case, I know. But he doesn't.

James is smiling inanely. 'That's six so far, and the light is still good,' he says.

James was seated at the head of the gleaming mahogany table while Jean bustled round fussing over the assorted dishes.

This room has been exhumed for the occasion, thought Belle, the table out from under the thick green baize, the chairs dusted off, all for this Sunday lunch.

James started to carve the chicken slowly and laboriously, Jean standing by his shoulder with each plate in turn, telling him to hurry up, it was all getting cold. It was quite chilly in the room. A small log fire in the grate looked as if it had only just been kindled, a flame or two was flickering in a half-hearted way.

Marcus had seated himself beside Belle. She felt her hand being taken in his under the table. 'I've missed you,' he whispered.

Belle looked at him, trying to gauge this new demonstrative mood. 'I'm grand, Marcus, grand. And you?'

'Grand. It is good to see you.' He brightened.

Jean put a plate down in front of Belle. As she did so, Marcus let go of Belle's hand under the table and straightened in his seat. Silence fell. James said Grace as they all bowed their heads.

The boys were tucking into the food disgracefully – as if they have not eaten for days, Belle thought. Certainly the chicken did taste good, and the potatoes were roasted to a light golden crispness.

'This is all very splendid,' she commented, 'it's so good to see you again. You both look so well.'

'I thought we were going to have wine with this meal?' James said peevishly.

'Oh, I'm sorry, James. I forgot,' Jean said, jumping up. 'It's in the kitchen. I was hoping Marcus would open the bottle for me. I'll get it.'

'No, I'll get it,' Marcus said, rising to his feet. 'You sit down, Jean.' He went out of the room sighing.

'I am stupid,' Jean said in an undertone.

'Yes, you are,' James said loudly.

Marcus returned and filled their glasses one by one. James drank deeply in his and looked at Marcus hoping he would fill up the glass again before he sat down. He didn't.

'Now,' Marcus said heavily, 'is everyone happy?'

'Yes,' the boys chorused. 'Great.'

'What are your plans, then?' James demanded, pointing his knife at Belle. 'What are your plans?'

She paused, her mouth full at that moment. 'The boys should be starting school next week, down at Corey.'

'Corey!' James sniffed. 'Funny fellow in charge down there. Fancy accent. Born here, reared in the States they say. Catholic you know. How he got the job I do not know. All comes of being educated elsewhere. Sounds better. Did you know he was a Catholic? Funny family. The whole family went out eventually, one by one. Bit like Noah's Ark.' He laughed mirthlessly.

They all had stopped eating and were staring at him, waiting for him to say more. And he surged on.

'Funny family, like I say. The father was a villain . . .' He stopped, took a quick forkful of food, chewed it briefly and continued with his mouth full, gulping on the words. 'More wine, here, Jean,' he pointed to his glass, 'more wine.'

Jean poured him another glass. He took a deep draught, then continued. 'Funny fellow that teacher. They knew what was best. They stayed out. Apart from a sister who married some doctor and lives over the Border. She'll stay there, and the rest of them'll stay in the States if they're wise. We don't want their kind here. Catholics! Terrorists! That man's probably one of them.' He stopped, looked at the faces around the table, and loaded his fork with food.

It was as if he had thrown down the gauntlet, and now he waited for someone to pick it up. Everybody was eating, eyes on their plates.

Jean did, apologetic, placating.

'Now, James. That's not quite fair. The man has a university degree. He was educated in a Christian Brothers' school over the Border first I hear, then a big grammar school in England.'

James pounced. 'The man's a Catholic. That's enough for me.'

'Don't be foolish, James,' Jean adjured. 'The family is a mixed one. The father was Catholic . . .'

'The offspring are always Catholic, the Church of Rome makes sure of that. He's a Catholic.'

'He wouldn't be in that job if he was one,' Jean pursued doggedly, 'you're being unfair, James. He's maybe an agnostic now.'

'You know nothing about it. You don't even know what the word agnostic means. Once a Catholic, always a Catholic, you couldn't trust any of them,' James growled contemptuously, taking another forkful of food.

Jean was not prepared to accept defeat. 'I heard that he has very good qualifications, he's been a teacher for a lot of years. Maybe he didn't want to teach in a Catholic school,' she said.

'They bent the rules for him. He shouldn't be there. He should be with his own kind. He's teaching Protestant children. That's not right. It never could be right,' James continued, tapping his fork on his plate to emphasise his point. 'You can't trust Catholics, you know that. They want us all in a United Ireland and then where would we be?'

Jean was silent. James looked at her under lowered eyebrows and frowned, waiting for her to respond again. She stayed silent.

'So your boys are going down there to school?' He pointed his knife again at Belle.

'Yes, for the mean time,' she replied.

'The sooner you get them into a decent school the better. My father always said that a good school stood you for the rest of your life. And my father was never wrong.'

'Yes.' Marcus, who had been silent all this time, but, Belle realised, keeping himself very much under check, intervened. 'But he's been dead these thirty years or more. Times change. People change. Society changes. The situation isn't the same as in his day . . .'

James pounced. 'My father? If he were alive today he would be appalled, sick at this . . . this . . . appeasement.' He stopped, then rushed on again before the amazed company could fill the conversational breach or even divert its course. 'My father knew a thing or two about the army. He knew about strategy. He knew how to let the enemy know who's boss. None of your lily-livered appeasement for him! That's what's wrong today. Too weak, right from the start. If in 1969 we had gone in like we did in the 1950s when the IRA tried a few tricks, there'd be none of the nonsense we have today. But today's soldiers, see them? They're a waste of time, a waste of time. They haven't got the guts that won the war, both wars, I tell you.'

'Now, James,' Marcus interrupted smoothly. 'Our army is the finest in the world. They are working under extreme provocation . . .'

'If it had been Father . . . your father too may I remind you . . . the whole thing would have cleared up years ago. And the cost . . .' he decapitated a roast potato, 'it's ridiculous. Nobody's ever done any sums about how much all this has cost. But every time there's a bomb, every time a hotel gets blown up and then has to be rebuilt . . . who pays? The bloody Government! And in the end, it's the taxpayers . . . even us, with our income, we pay. Bloody Government.'

'James, James,' Jean said anxiously. 'Not that kind of language. Not in front of the boys, please.'

'The bloody Government! The bloody army!'

'Och, James,' she implored. 'Now stop! Don't let us talk politics.'

'You're only standing up for them because of your bloody major,' James roared.

'That's enough,' Marcus said quietly and with authority.

James looked at him balefully and put down his knife and fork deliberately. 'I've finished,' he announced.

'That chicken was really delicious, Jean,' Belle said. 'Wasn't it, boys?'

'Yeah, terrific, terrific,' Rory said. Belle looked at him sharply, recognising his pained tone of old, but he looked back at her unconcerned and did not say any more.

Jean asked tremulously, 'Would you not like a little more?'

'We're all finished,' James said, 'let's get this mess off the table.'

The boys were shaking their heads, not daring to speak, staring at James, wondering what he might say next. He looks so mild mannered, Belle thought, and suddenly out comes . . . all this hate, as if he has been rehearsing for days. He and Jean used to get on so well, now he talks to her as if they were once lovers and now it's only bitterness at the remembrance.

The plates were cleared, Jean brought in the apple tart, a big bowl of whipped cream, and proceeded to serve them all. There was desultory conversation about how big a slice 'wee' Conor could eat, and whether Rory should be allowed to have a second spoonful of cream. James sat looking sullen. Belle sensed that he had not had the last word.

'Did you notice the flashy car Marcus has these days?' he muttered eventually having scraped his plate clean, as if he had licked it.

'Yes,' Belle said. 'A Mercedes, Marcus. You must be doing well.'

'Not too bad,' Marcus acknowledged in an undertone.

James was undeterred. 'Makes a lot of money. Don't you, little brother?' Marcus gave him a warning look. 'Do you know how he makes his money? No? Well, I'll tell you . . .'

'He's just a solicitor,' Belle said calmly, 'you're not going to suggest that he's a crook, are you?'

'He makes all his money from crooks, con men, thieves, villains, terrorists, thugs . . . the scum of the earth!' James spat out.

'Well, I suppose that is one part of the job,' Belle agreed easily. So that was why he carried a gun. He must be dealing with some terrorist cases. That would explain his sporadic visits to Belfast. He had never mentioned work.

'But he's making money out of the Troubles, he's overworked, overpaid and getting fat on it! And he knows all the right people,' James tapped the side of his nose, 'know what I mean? When all this is over, when we have the Catholics under control, young Marcus here is going to be one of the top men. He's in with the hard men.'

Marcus in league with the Protestant paramilitaries? Belle was amazed. But it was impossible. As a solicitor he couldn't take sides. 'He's just doing a job,' she said, looking at Marcus for corroboration. Marcus looked pained. He has heard all this before, she realised.

'Ask him,' James pointed to Marcus with a shaking bony finger, 'ask him who his friends are. Hard men, I tell you. Thugs. That's the kind of friends he has . . . but he keeps his hands clean! See him, devil a bit he does only talk and scheme and plan for the day . . . THE DAY . . . like the bloody Second Coming! Bloody politicians!'

Marcus still looked pained, but said nothing.

'If I had my way,' James went on, 'I'd root the Catholics out, the lot of them . . . shoot the lot of them . . .'

'But your guns don't work,' Conor piped up suddenly.

Belle looked down at his anxious face. 'He's only talking politics. He doesn't mean it. Och, James, could we not talk about something else?'

James was not to be silenced. 'Money, money, money,' he said, on a different tack. 'That's the root of it all. Everybody wants money and all the wrong people have it! Look at us. In my father's day we were well-to-do. Father didn't even need the army money, the family had investments. And now look at us!'

'We're doing all right,' Jean said defensively.

'You're a fine one to talk,' he rounded on her once again, 'and you're the one wants to put up new curtains in the sitting-room. That tomb next door which nobody in their right mind would want to sit in. Three hundred pounds it's likely to cost. And all for your bloody major.'

Jean leaned over to Belle, and mouthed the words carefully. 'I know it sounds a lot, but the place is threadbare, and we never spend any money on this place. I just felt that we owed it to ourselves, to not let the family down . . .'

'I hear you. Shut up, woman. Shut up talking about the family. That doesn't mean a thing. You just want to show off, for your major,' James jeered. 'Your sweet, loving, understanding major . . . has he made love to you yet?'

'Stop it, James. That's enough, quite enough!' Jean's voice was icy calm.

James looked at her and smiled wickedly. 'You see, I can still upset her,' he said triumphantly. 'I can still get through to her.'

Jean sniffed and looked at Belle who looked at Marcus for support. Marcus had his pained expression on his face once more.

'Aha!' James laughed. 'Got you all going, didn't I?'

'You're not very amusing,' Jean said coldly.

'And you've said all this before,' Marcus chimed in. 'It's just getting very boring.'

'You've been very rude to our guests,' Jean continued. 'Really, Belle, I don't know what you think of us. Please don't take James seriously, he doesn't mean any of it,' she averred, shaking her head.

'You needn't talk about me as if I'm a child,' James said in annoyance.

Jean withered him. 'You don't set a very good example for the boys, now do you? First you say what a bad school they're going to . . .'

'The teacher, the teacher, that's the trouble,' James grumbled.

'Then you attack the very nice man who has been so kind as to take an interest in us . . .'

'You're not talking about your beloved major, are you?' was the scathing reply.

'Don't let's get on to that subject again,' Marcus interposed. 'That's enough, quite enough. You don't like him, James, now we know.'

'Is there any more wine in that bottle, woman?' James asked, looking at Jean.

She lifted the bottle. 'Only the dregs. And we don't have another bottle.'

'Stupid woman,' said James.

'Yes, James,' she replied, clearing the dishes.

'Stupid woman,' he said more loudly, 'I don't know why I live with you.'

'Because there's nobody else,' she cried.

'Come on, Jean.' Belle stood beside her. 'Let me give you a hand?'

'I hope you don't take any notice of James,' Jean commented as the two women reached the kitchen, Jean carrying the tray full of dishes and Belle following behind with the last handful.

'No, I don't really,' Belle replied. 'But he seems crosser somehow than I remember him.'

'Oh, you wouldn't know what mood he would be in from one moment to the next. I have learned to deal with him, but he's a difficult man to live with,' Jean said, whipping up a lather in the sink and sliding in the first glass.

'You should have married,' Belle said in her direct way.

'Yes, I suppose I should. But I never found anyone . . .'

Belle leaned towards her conspiratorially. 'What about this major?'

'Oh, him.' Jean washed a glass with great care. 'He's a nice man. But it's too late.'

'It's never too late,' Belle said, laughing. 'I know it's corny to say so, but it's true. Lots of people get married at your time of life. Look at this place, it's awful, you know it! Maybe you could get away, find another life with your major. Tell me about him?'

Jean pressed her lips together.

'James is the problem, isn't he?' Belle said.

'Oh, the whole thing is ridiculous. James is impossible. I'm old, oh I'm so old. Just look at me! What's the point? It's useless. Don't let's talk about it.'

Belle bent and kissed her cheek. Jean's face was very red.

'Jean?' Belle said softly.

Jean kept her head bent, washing deliberately. 'It's no good. It's no good,' she said in a muffled voice. 'I don't want to talk about it.'

Belle sighed and slipped a tea-towel off the airer above her head, starting to dry the dishes that were now piling up on the drainer. The major was not discussed any further.

As she washed, Jean launched into a torrent of other topics. She seemed loath to stop talking, stop telling Belle about all that had happened in her absence, and reminiscing about the things past. She seemed lonely, or was it simply that she wanted Belle to explain about how her life had been in Belfast, why she had come home?

This is one area of my life which I will not talk about today, Belle decided. Jean doesn't want to discuss her major, and I am tired of talking of Belfast. So Belle had parried the questions, stalled others, turned the conversation around, but it still took longer than she had anticipated before the two women had finished washing up and returned to the dining-room.

There was no sign of James, he had obviously retreated, but Marcus was sitting at ease with the boys, talking quietly.

'You have a grand pair here, Belle,' he said, getting to his feet. 'They have been telling me all about themselves and how they liked the life in Belfast. Rory here, was telling me –'

'What?' Belle interposed sharply.

Marcus spread his hands apologetically. 'What?'

Belle looked at Rory who raised his eyebrows. 'Nothing, Ma!' he said. There was no disguising the mock innocence.

Belle walked to the window and looked out. 'We had better make tracks,' she said with finality. 'It's a pity the dark closes in so early these days.'

'Oh, you're not going,' Jean protested.

'I'd better. These boys will have to be up on time tomorrow to go down to the school. I have things to do for the morning,' Belle excused.

They stood in the hall, muffled up. Still there was no sign of James.

'Thank you for the lovely lunch,' Belle said, squeezing Jean's arm. Behind her, the boys concurred enthusiastically. Belle sensed that Conor was thinking about his television programme, and Rory had had enough of these old friends from the past.

'What's this? Going?' came James's voice behind her. She had not heard his approach because of his carpet slippers.

'Yes, we're off, James.' She held her hand out to him but he put his arms round her instead of taking it. She could feel how thin he was, how bony his body, and smell the reek of whiskey.

'Don't be too long before you come and visit us again,' he said as he released her, 'we don't have too many visitors these days, not the kind I welcome anyway.' He gave Jean a bitter look.

Belle was glad to get the car safely parked in the garage and go into the house. The range had burnt low. Rory put a match to the sitting-room fire but it was loath to light and she found him and Conor crouched over it, still in their coats and scarves by the time she got the range glowing again.

'It's freezing!' they said. The television set was already on.

'It's warmer in the kitchen.' Conor waved his hand at the television set, looking miserable. Belle tried again. 'Do you want tea or anything?'

'After all that lunch?' Rory groaned.

'Scrambled egg. What about it? Maybe some bacon on the top?'

'OK, OK,' Rory said, 'but there's this programme we want to watch.'

She went out into the kitchen. She was standing with an egg in one hand when she heard the sound of a Landrover engine, the feet outside the door stamping in the cold, the rap at the door. She guessed who was there. She unlocked the door, then opened it slowly.

'Good evening.' The soldier at the door had his face blacked up but she knew him. He put up his hands in protest. 'Don't, don't say anything. I'm not staying long. I just have a few questions to ask you.' She backed away. 'No, no. Look, I'm sorry about the other night. It shouldn't have happened, I know. I just thought . . . well, I apologise.' Belle stared at his face. 'Can I come in . . . even?' he asked earnestly. 'There's a problem, an enquiry. Do you understand?'

'An enquiry?' she said at last, standing now in the middle of the kitchen floor, her arms folded across her chest.

He closed the door behind him, saying, 'I'll just keep the cold out.'

'An enquiry,' Belle repeated evenly.

He looked at her seriously for a moment, then smiled. 'From Belfast.'

'From Belfast,' she said.

'Well, it's only in the manner of a check.'

'A check?' Belle's eyes widened.

'To see if you are all right.'

'I'm fine. There's nothing wrong with me. Why should there be?'

'Look!' He looked angry. 'You know and I know what about. You left suddenly. They wanted to know . . . we need to keep an eye out for you. Do you understand?'

'I'm fine. The boys are fine. We're all fine. Why are you so concerned, now?'

'I've always been concerned!' he retorted, then sighed abruptly. 'Look, Sergeant McEvoy . . . he was worried . . . he asked us to check you out.'

'How did he know I was here?'

'Logical . . . possible . . . he asked us. We knew of course, straightaway you got here. You can't hide in the country. Your sergeant –'

'Excuse me . . . my sergeant?'

'McEvoy . . . he thought you might have come here because somebody threatened you. Did someone . . .'

'Now, why should someone threaten me?' Belle said expansively.

'Don't pretend. Not about this. We know all about it. I'm on your side, remember?' he fumed.

'No. I don't remember. I don't want to remember. Not you, not any of it!' she blurted out.

He backed towards the door, and opened it without turning from her. 'That's the way you feel?' he asked.

'Yes. That's the way. I'm fine. Forget about it. Forget about me!' she insisted.

'I see. That's the way of it.' He shrugged his shoulders. 'Well, I'd like you to know . . .' he said formally, 'that . . . we're here . . . we're watching . . .'

'I don't want to know. I'm fine. Leave me alone . . .' She bit her lip, realising she was not far from tears.

He seemed to sense this and went out the door. A gust of wind made her shiver. 'It's cold,' he said quietly, glancing at her. 'You're all right then, really?'

She nodded. 'Yes, yes.'

'We'll keep an eye open anyway.'

'Yes. If you must. But leave me alone. Leave us alone!'

'Yes, I see.' He looked downcast. He shut the door, she locked it quickly after him.

Time for scrambled eggs, she told herself, the boys will wonder what on earth I have been up to. No, they won't, they're too busy watching telly, too busy to hear even.

She heard the Landrover start up and leave, but she kept cracking the eggs into the bowl, eight in all, two for Rory, two for Conor, two for herself . . . and two more . . .

Chapter 10

IT FROZE VERY HARD in the night. Belle made her way down the drive for the milk and hurried back to the house clutching the bottles to her chest, her fingers going numb. She would be lucky if the milk wasn't frozen on the top, she thought, reminded of her school days and compulsory milk in small bottles which if they were delivered very early in the morning, would have an icy cork by assembly time.

The boys were sitting like fledgelings in a nest, waiting for her, with bowls of dry cornflakes before them. Conor looked sheepish, as if Rory had been bullying him again. Belle looked at her watch. Ten to nine. Pat had said to come at nine thirty. She poured the milk on to Conor's cornflakes noting it wasn't frozen. So Cathal had delivered the milk not long before her trip to the gate. She had not heard or seen his van stopping or starting. But she had heard something. Voices. Last night. No. In the early hours, maybe four o'clock. Maybe not. Maybe she had dreamt it. There had been voices . . . and sounds. What kind of sounds? She couldn't remember. Perhaps someone had found her, last night. No. No. No. This was foolish. She must have heard Cathal with the milk and it had seemed like four o'clock. Since it stayed dark for so long at this time of the year it was hard to gauge what time it could have been, but she definitely, now she thought more about it, had heard quiet voices. Maybe Cathal had someone to help him with the milk round.

'Ma?' Rory stood up. 'I'm ready. I don't know about that squirt there,' he looked at Conor with disdain, 'but I'm ready. I suppose he'll want another bowl, just to be awkward.'

'No. No. Why should I?' Conor asked defensively, his voice rising.

He's a bit worried about the new school, Belle thought, smoothing his hair with her hand. 'It's all right, Conor, there's plenty of time, Mr Quinn said about nine thirty.'

He did not have a second bowl, but slipped off his chair and went out of the room without another word.

'Go easy on him, Rory, for goodness' sake. He is only little, you know. And he is worried about school. It's all right for you . . .'

'What do you mean?' he asked. 'All right for me . . . I don't fancy it either. What's the point in going to this silly school . . . James said . . .'

'Never mind what Uncle James said. It's sensible and you know it. You'll have the results of the exam in the spring. It's silly to let things get rusty. You would be only under my feet here, and when I get a job you couldn't possibly stay here on your own.'

Rory was still in an argumentative mood. 'I could stay with Mrs D.'

'You could. But she's not as young as she used to be and you would get bored. But I have a temporary job at Corey so I'll be down there. We can all be there together.'

He sighed. 'You have decided it all, haven't you?'

'It's the best thing we can do at the moment.'

Rory put his arm round her shoulders. How tall he was getting. 'I don't want to worry you, but I thought I heard voices last night.'

Belle's heart missed a beat. But she replied calmly, 'You probably heard Cathal delivering the milk.'

'Oh,' he sounded offhand, 'I thought maybe it was very early.'

'You heard Cathal,' she heard herself say firmly, as if she was convincing herself as well. 'Away and get your coat,' she said.

Minutes later the boys clambered into the car, joking with each other. How could they be fighting one moment, friends the next, Belle thought. She locked the door and put the key in her pocket. Mrs D would not be coming today. She checked again that she had the key in her pocket. The car seemed reluctant to start. She pulled the choke out a bit more, tried the starter again, then realised by the smell of fuel that she had flooded the engine. That was what happened when you were not thinking.

'You've flooded it,' Rory commented sadly.

'Yes I have.'

'You'll have to wait a while before you try it again,' he added.

'Yes,' she sighed in exasperation.

She tried again. This time the engine started but fluttered hesitantly into life. There was a very strong smell of petrol and a lot of white smoke belched out from the exhaust. The car struggled out on to the road, lurching and firing badly, but once down the hill towards the gate-lodge, it seemed to go better. She felt relieved. Ahead she spotted Jean's car. It was stationary, and beside it was an army Landrover. A camouflage figure was leaning, talking to Jean, head bent to the window. At the sound of Belle's car, the figure straightened. Only when she drew close did she see that he was quite an old soldier, with a bushy greying moustache. This must be Jean's major, she decided. As she reached the vehicle she slowed, not daring to stop for fear her car would not start again. She explained, winding down the window, shouting above the noise of the engine.

'I can't stop . . . on my way to Corey with the boys, and the car's playing up this morning, wouldn't start for ages . . . lovely lunch yesterday . . .'

'Ah . . . yes,' Jean said, beaming, obviously wanting Belle to stop so that she could go through the pleasantries with her army friend. He waved Belle past with a practised hand, bowing in a courteous gesture.

'Will you come by again?' Jean called after her.

'Yes, later in the week if it's suitable,' Belle called back.

'Come for lunch . . . Thursday?' Jean's voice was barely audible.

'Yes, yes,' Belle shouted, winding up her window.

'Come on, Ma, it's late,' Conor scolded from the back seat.

Pat was holding open the front door when she got to it, trying to straighten her coat collar and smooth her curly hair. The cold had brought colour into her cheeks, Pat thought, and a freshness about her. Last time she had looked as if painting the walls of her kitchen yellow had painted her face yellow too. She looked apprehensive, and he was quick to try to put her at ease.

'Great to see you, boys. And your mother. Come in out of the cold and we'll get the door shut. My office is right there.' He pointed to a door across the corridor from the classroom he had been in.

Belle ushered the boys in, conscious of Pat Quinn behind her.

He shut the door and pointed to a chair for Belle. 'You boys won't mind being without a seat for a moment, will you?' They shook their heads shyly in unison. He turned to Belle. 'I had a great talk with the boys on Saturday and I think I have a fair idea of how far they have gone in their studies. They could start today, if you like. It's a bit unorthodox but no problem. I will start Rory in the top class, and Conor along with the nine-year-olds because I think he's a wee bit ahead of his own age group.' Conor looked pleased.

'Today?' she asked. 'So soon?'

'I don't see why not,' Pat said, 'I'll just go and get them settled, introduce them, and then I'll be back.' He smiled reassuringly.

'Yes,' Belle said, not knowing what more she could say. She felt out of her depth, unsure of herself, matters had been taken out of her hands, settled, just like that. As the door closed after them she sat back in the chair and sighed. Fixed up. That was that. Then she thought about working for Pat and just what might be involved. She had been pretty efficient as a secretary, so surely it would not be too difficult to learn what was required in this job and it was only a temporary one. But she felt that she would have to be efficient. 'Could try harder.' That was what her school reports had said. She was capable, but she was beginning to doubt herself when the door opened, Pat came in smiling and sat down on the edge of the desk.

'There now, that's them settled. I don't think you need worry too much about them. They are very bright kids. You should be proud of them.'

Had he sensed her feeling of inadequacy, of disquiet? Belle pushed her hands into her jacket pockets and shifted in her chair uneasily.

'Now, about you . . . can you still start here tomorrow?' he asked.

'Yes,' she nodded, 'OK. I can.'

'Well, look pleased about it,' he chided, leaning towards her.

She coloured. 'I'm sorry. I don't wish to sound as if I don't want the job, I do. It's just . . .'

'I understand,' Pat nodded, 'don't worry. I have faith in you to sort all this lot out.' Belle looked around the office for the first time and noted the disorder of books and papers. 'Mrs Jamison, the secretary, has only been off a week and already the place is getting out of control. I need help. I am useless at office work. Teaching is totally different, I enjoy that . . .' He was deliberately putting her at her ease now, being charming and she was being charmed.

'I'll do my best.'

'Now it's agreed, you're going to call me Pat. I'm not going to have any formality . . . and I'm going to call you Belle . . . is that OK?' he continued in the same assured manner.

'Yes,' she laughed, 'please call me Belle.'

'Well now,' he stood up, 'I'm sure you have other things you want to do this morning now you have got the boys out of the way. And I really must get back to class. School finishes at twenty past three. But I wouldn't expect you to work the full day. You'll probably work four half days a week, or something like that.' He held the door open for her and, as she passed him, he leaned confidentially towards her. 'I'm sure you're going to be very good for me.'

They went out into the schoolyard, standing side by side on the step. Pat looked down at her with an expression on his face which she could not read. She felt she had to say something.

'You know Cathal then?'

He turned his head sharply and looked down the road. 'Cathal,' he said in a flat disinterested voice.

'Yes.' She wanted to sound conversational but somehow it sounded inquisitorial. 'The milkman. Didn't I see you on Saturday, at my gate, talking to him?'

'Oh, yes, that Cathal.' He turned and looked at her. 'That Cathal.'

He's thinking he ought to get back to classes and I'm holding him up, Belle thought. 'I'll be off now, then, I won't keep you,' she said hurriedly, stepping out towards her car.

'Yes, sorry, I was miles away,' he said, shaking his head. 'I must get back to class. See you tomorrow. About the same time.' He saluted her with his hand and turned back into the building.

She might have known that the car would not start. Faces in the nearby classroom were turning to stare out, curious at her predicament. There was a tap at the car window and when she looked up, Pat was there.

She wound it down, shaking her head. 'She's been playing up this morning. I had trouble starting her in the first place. I don't know what's wrong. She just doesn't seem to be firing.'

'Have you had new plugs lately?' he asked.

'Yes. Sure she was only serviced four weeks ago and it cost a packet.'

'I think the battery might need a charge. How old is it?'

'I've had her four years. The battery was new when I bought her.'

'I reckon it's the battery. Of course in this cold weather it is kinda more difficult to get her going.' He was relaxing into American vowels, she noticed. 'Can I have a shot at starting her?'

'Yes. You might be more lucky.' Belle slid out of the car as he held the door open, and watched as he curled himself into the driving seat. The engine would not respond. He got out and opened up the bonnet.

'I have a jump lead in my car,' he told her. 'It's just over there. Don't worry, we'll soon have your car started.'

She waited while he reversed his car in her direction, aware, with a touch of annoyance, of the audience at the classroom windows.

He was right. Deftly he connected the lead from his own battery into her car and the engine sprang to life instantly. It was almost as if there had been nothing wrong in the first place.

'There, you see, no problem,' he said, beaming at her.

'Thank you.'

'You're welcome. Look, I have to go into town after school so I'll drop the boys off for you. You had better not risk bringing the car out again if it's giving trouble.' He held up his hand before she could demur. 'That's settled. Now I really must get back to class.'

'I'm sorry,' Belle said, blushing again.

'Don't worry. I'll see you later.' He strode back to the building.

Belle drove out of the schoolyard feeling furious with herself, the car, the whole thing. She was useless. Useless. She thought she was so calm, so well organised, efficient. But it was all a façade. The slightest thing would crack it. She was useless and as for this wretched car, she hated it. Absolutely hated it. Had done, for months . . . years.

I can hear voices, snatches of laughter, a car door slamming, then revving up quickly and driving off down the street. It's Friday night and warm for early June. The students in the flats around have finished their examinations and are waiting for the results, which means now is the time to throw a party. There are bursts of sound from open windows, stereos blasting out on the soft night. It would be nice to go to a party. No. That's not true. Not for me. I would rather stay at home with the boys. Anyway Anne, who could have stayed to keep the boys company if I had wanted to go out, has gone off with her boyfriend, a medical student. They are getting serious about each other. She said she might stay over with him tonight. It makes me feel old. I'm Cinderella in a way, waiting for my prince to come. It's no good, Belle, as far as men are concerned, you have just packed yourself away like some old suitcase. No style, no charisma . . . I wish I could sleep . . .

'Ma!' It's Rory. He's pounding up the stairs two at a time. 'Ma!'

'What is it?' I raise myself on my elbows as he rushes into the room. I look at my watch. It's eight forty five!

'It's late!' he squeaks. 'But . . . but . . . I just went to bring in the milk and there's no car!'

'No car! No car? There must be. Did you really look?'

'It's not there! Honest, Ma!'

I look out of the window. The car has gone. Then I am phoning '999'. It's commonplace, car stealing, joyriding, dozens of cars a week they say. They'll phone me when they get word, if they get word, later.

I feel bereft. My little car. Conor appears and looks as if he might start crying. Neither he nor Rory will eat any breakfast. It's very late. I call a taxi and send them off to school.

Now what do I do? Wait. I phone work. They tell me to stay home, wait. I walk round the house, watering the pot plants, shining the brass knocker on the front door. I wait. The kitchen is spotless. Anne comes in, a bit bleary-eyed. I tell her about the car. We drink tea.

It's four o'clock and the boys come in from school, grumbling about having to travel by bus and then walking the last bit by themselves. Maybe I've spoilt them.

'Where's the car?' Rory demands.

I don't know, not any more. 'It's not been found. Do you want some tea?' I ask him. I'll make yet another pot of tea.

'Yes.' He is distracted, Conor is distracted, and I am . . .

The phone rings. It's my boss. 'Have you heard anything?' he asks.

'No.'

'Well, keep in touch,' he says. 'They'll find it.'

The phone rings again. This time it's the police. The car has been found. Up in West Belfast. 'Tiger Country' people call it. I have to report to the nearest army base, on the edge of this Sinn Fein area. I phone for a taxi and he takes me up.

The base is surrounded by high corrugated walls, wire fencing to repel lobbed bombs, security cameras, two checkpoints before I can get inside. The taxi driver has disappeared at speed. Yes, they know where my car is, they will take me up in a 'pig'. That's one of those armoured vehicles with slit windows. It's gloomy inside the pig, and the soldiers already there do not say much. There are strips of light through the windows, guns on the knees of the soldiers.

'You'll be glad to get it back,' says one, his voice raised above the sound of the engine.

'Yes.'

'Might not be right, though. It could be burned out, the battery stolen, the tyres . . .' They talk of other cars on other days. I am trying to work out their accents, where they are from. The pig stops.

We are in a small street, redbrick, dusty, narrow, slogans on the walls, 'Brits Out', 'Up the Provos' and more. I am trying to see my car, see if it's all right. The soldiers pile out and three go to crouch in doorways up the street, rifles at the ready. Apart from one stringy dog, the street is totally empty. And there's my car. The sergeant in charge of the squad is walking round it, checking, and I follow him round.

'Is it OK?' Four wheels, no visible damage. Just the driver's door is half unlocked.

'Unlocked,' says the sergeant, bending and squinting to see

inside the car. 'Looks OK.' He bends again and looks carefully under the car.

'Yes. Looks OK.' He kicks the boot lid casually with his foot. It falls open. The boot is empty. 'No problem there,' he says, slowly moving round the car again and peering closely at the bonnet. This is taking ages. It could be a trap. The sergeant shrugs his shoulders. 'Probably a joyrider,' he says, 'or somebody who didn't fancy the walk home, been to a party. Dead easy to steal these cars. Dead easy.'

'You mean it's all right?' I ask, sighing with relief. 'I can take it home?'

'Well, not quite so sure about that. Could have boobytrapped the ignition. Don't fancy trying to get the bonnet up to check the engine, but there's no sign of anything underneath . . . now that's the quick way to do it, just a line, a fishing line, underneath, with the bomb attached. It can do terrible damage. Takes the legs off for a start. Can kill you.' He peers underneath again. 'No, no. Probably all right. Have you got the ignition key there?'

'Yes.' I fumble in my pocket and hold it out in my hand.

'Now hold on, hold on,' he says, backing away.

'What's the matter?'

'The ignition. Could be boobytrapped, they think of everything.'

'But you said it looked all right. And it was probably some joyrider?'

'Probably,' he says laconically.

I'm getting angry. Maybe I'm getting afraid. Maybe I'm remembering John.

'It's up to you,' he says. 'It's your car. Do you have a man, a husband or anything, would come and see to it for you?'

'What do you mean, "see to it"?' I ask.

'Well, like I said, it looks OK and I reckon it is. But it's up to you . . . or your friend. Maybe we'll just trying blowing the bonnet to make sure, a controlled explosion, you know . . .'

'My car! Blow it up?' I'm furious, horrified. Before I know it, I'm in the driver's seat, putting the key in the ignition, turning it. The engine coughs a little and starts reluctantly.

The sergeant is some distance away where he has jumped when I got into the car. Now he strolls back. 'You're a cool one,' is all he says.

My little car. When I get home I wash it, inside and out, vacuum the carpets. It looks spotless, only it's not.

Belle sighed as she rounded the corner and saw the familiar gateposts. Home. Safety. She turned into the drive at speed, sending gravel flying.

There were two Landrovers in the drive and two soldiers from them crouching by the gate. A familiar figure detached itself from the shelter of the rhododendrons. Smiling yet again. She felt sick.

'I told you we would keep an eye open for you, didn't I?' he said cheerfully. 'Now what are you looking so worried for? Sure, we know the number of your car.'

Chapter 11

IT WAS AT TIMES LIKE these, with her arms up to the elbows in foamy washing-up water, that the best philosophical thoughts should be enjoyed, thought Belle.

Yes, there was quite a lot to be pleased about. The boys had started school, she had a temporary job, but why had she not cornered Marcus to see if he could find her a more permanent job? She could have asked him about a job, but she had hesitated. Why? Because he had not seemed quite like his usual stolid self. Something had happened insidiously to him over the years, something she had not noted on the rare times he had dropped in to see them in Belfast. He didn't look any different. But then neither did James. He seemed so irascible, contrary, very contrary. Jean seemed the same, one moment girlish, the next uncertain. Belle wondered if she herself had changed.

She would have to do something about the car. Without it she was isolated, relying on others for help. What else was wrong besides the car? Nothing and everything. What had she done in Belfast? Could she escape it? She felt the vestiges of fear creep up on her once again, feelings she had been suppressing for days. They were only feelings. They might go away, slide away like morning mist up over the orchard. What she needed now was some simple domestic task which would not require much mental activity but which would occupy her physically for a while. The washing. That was a good idea. There was an old but serviceable twin-tub washing machine in the scullery. She hauled it out from under a shelf, pulled out the hoses and pushed them on to the taps at the sink with some difficulty because the rubber links were hard and unyielding with age. Soon she was sorting the washing into whites and coloured in a practised way, two neat piles on the stone-flagged scullery floor. She pushed the bundle of whites into one side of the machine and turned the water tap, hearing the water seep quietly into the machine. She sprinkled in the detergent, pressed the switch, and watched as the clothes agitated slowly. She looked out of the window and thought about the voices she had heard, shook her head, and stuffed the thought away crossly. What was Pat Quinn really like? Mrs D had said he was a 'good man'. Was Belle too guarded now to be able to judge who was and who wasn't? She had armoured herself for too long. But he was a teacher, and her mother had been one . . .

Belle's feet were soaking. She looked down. There was water all over the scullery floor. Quietly, greedily, it had been leaking out through the dozed hose, or some wretched rusted part of the machine.

'It's only water, simply water, turn off the taps, mop it up, it's only water.'

She gathered the half-washed clothes out of the machine and stuffed them into the spinner part on the side. The water was still running out of the machine.

'It's only water, it can be mopped up,' she told herself aloud again. 'This is silly. Don't let it worry you.'

But as she stood there gripping the edge of the sink with both hands, feet wet, she started to sob, deep shuddering sobs which she knew had been gathering within her for hours, maybe days.

'This is silly, silly, silly,' she cried between sobs, her face wet with tears. 'It's nothing. It's nothing.' She stopped sobbing, switched on the spinner of the washing machine, and watched as the sudsy water trickled out of the end of the hose that hung over the edge of the sink. The clothes would have to be rinsed, somehow. Not now.

'First mop up the water,' she spoke sternly, 'dry your eyes, girl, dry your eyes. This is futile, and you know it.'

She found a mop, slopped it over the puddles on the flagged floor, drying up the water after a fashion. It would do. She left the clothes in the machine. She would see to them later. Later, not now.

Belle went upstairs and peered at her face in the bathroom mirror. She was a mess. Red-eyed, pale, blotchy. Where was the confident lady who had looked out of the same mirror an hour or so ago?

I hate this old house! I hate this kitchen! I hate it!

John is coming down the stairs. He is off to his beloved orchard. Again. Sam has just gone out, over to the Johnston farm. Again. And I'm left here with Rory, all day long. In this house. 'I hate it!'

'What do you hate?' asks John, laughing, taking my arm. I snatch it away.

'This house!'

'What's wrong with it?'

'What's wrong? Look at it! It's awful. It's so old-fashioned, everything! It needs painting, every room. It's too much for me to do on my own. Will you help? Sam is always busy, over at his parents' place.

'I have the orchard. Sam is busy because it's the family farm, his farm, it will be his when his father dies, it won't belong to his sisters even if they are older than him. Sam is the son, the Johnston son. It will all be his.'

'This house is ours.'

'Strictly speaking, it's mine,' he says. His expression is cold.

'And I look after it for you.'

'You decided to come to live here, you could have lived with the Johnstons.'

'I came back . . . I came back to look after you, when Mother died.'

'Yes,' he agrees reluctantly.

'Well, don't you agree, it's impossible, it smells of old age and decay and . . . look at this kitchen, it's a mess, it needs a new stove, an Aga like up at the Johnstons'. And cupboards . . .'

'Like up at the Johnstons',' he finishes for me.

'Let's do something about it.' Why do I have to beg?

'You decided to come and live here. Why not go back to the Johnstons'? You belong there, you . . . and Sam!'

He has retreated from me, mentally and physically. He is standing very still at the kitchen window, looking out, up at the orchard, very still, his lips tightly together, white with determination. I'm a nuisance, I know it.

'Do you want me to go back?' I cry behind him, putting my arms round his waist, pressing my face to his unrelenting back.

He turns slowly and cups my chin in his hands. 'No,' he breathes very quietly, 'no,' kissing my lips.

Belle felt drained and chilly, spent, as if she had just come off stage after a great performance, the mask had been removed, this was her old self looking at her. She felt untidy, frayed, just like the house.

It was a different person who went down to the sitting-room to put a match to the fire an hour later. Smooth, calm, face glowing from a long leisurely bath, a touch of lipstick, eye-shadow, her eyebrows had been freshly plucked, her nails had a coat of transparent nail-varnish, she had slipped into a treasured silk blouse, navy blue with a matching skirt, a slit up the side seam. Underneath there were deep navy stockings, and she had found her black stiletto patent shoes from amongst her baggage. A city slicker. She looked it. The touch of musk behind her ears and at her wrists was the final embellishment.

As if on cue a white car came up the drive. She saw it out of the corner of her eye as she straightened up after attending to the now crackling fire. Marcus. He came to the front door, knocking even though he had probably seen her through the window as he passed.

Belle held the door wide and smiled with pleasure. 'Marcus. It is good to see you, really good.'

He was as neatly and impeccably dressed as ever. He held out his hand to her, looking at her with a kind of amazement which turned into a solemn stare.

'I was coming this way with some stuff for Jean, from town, the new curtains she ordered for the drawing-room,' he explained. 'She has gone ahead with them, despite what James thinks. There'll be ructions about that. I had to sneak them into the house, on tiptoe, for fear he'd see them. He was shut up in his room, she said, wasn't to be disturbed. I don't know how Jean copes with his rages, but she smiles sweetly at him, and he seems to love it. He doesn't like her army friend, hates her major. I don't think he approves of Jean having any menfriends. I don't think she ever had any in the past. Maybe James chased them off. He always was very possessive about her . . . about everything when you come to think of it . . . look how he can never throw anything away.' Marcus shook his head, then brightened. 'Anyway, I was coming up the road and I thought that I would call on you to see how you are settling in, and if there was anything I could do for you.' It was a long speech for Marcus who rather tended to talk in short sharp sentences. He seemed ill at ease with her today. 'You look different today.'

'Different?' She raised an eyebrow.

'Yes. Different. Well, I mean to say, yesterday you looked very . . .' He sought the right word.

'Motherly?'

He nodded, staring at her. 'Yes, motherly . . . yesterday. But you look different today, yet again. You've changed you know.'

'I'm sorry, Marcus, but I am seven years older,' Belle replied drily.

'But you have a glow today . . .' he insisted.

'I've just had a hot bath,' she laughed. 'Oh, do come in.'

He followed her into the sitting-room where she motioned him into an armchair by the fire and then settled herself into one on the other side of the fireplace, crossing her sheer legs, conscious that she might seem a trifle overdressed for the country life. Marcus stared at her legs.

This is ridiculous, she told herself, what's wrong with him? I have never seen him behave this way before.

'You look good, Belle, you really look good,' he said slowly, still staring at her.

'I'm grand, thank you. And what about you? I never got a chance yesterday to ask. James seemed so . . . difficult.'

'Him? Yes, he's difficult these days.'

'He had a lot to say . . . about . . . about you. Marcus . . .'

'Yes.'

'I couldn't help noticing . . . you carry a gun. I didn't think . . .'

'Now don't you worry your pretty head about that. Commonplace. For my own protection,' he soothed.

'But . . .'

'And I haven't it on today. It's in the glove compartment of my car.'

'I just don't like guns,' she said quietly.

'I told you. Don't worry. Don't take any notice of what James says. We're not going to talk about him today. I came to see you,' he leaned towards her, 'I came to talk to you.'

'Look, would you like a cup of tea, or coffee . . .? No, I know you. You would rather have a whiskey but I don't have any in the house, only a sherry. Would you like a glass?'

'Stop there!' Marcus stood up quickly. He held up his hand as she started to speak. 'I'll be back.' He went out of the room, out through the front door to his car, and opened the driver's door, emerging with a brown oblong paper bag twisted at the top. He came round the drawing-room door, triumphant, sliding off the paper packaging to reveal a bottle of Bushmills whiskey. 'I had this for James, but with all that nonsense about the curtains, I forgot all about giving it to him. Get some glasses. We'll celebrate.'

'Celebrate what?' Belle asked curiously.

'Your return.'

'I've been back since Wednesday, nearly a week,' she reminded him.

'So you have. So you have. But what matter, we're going to celebrate.'

'I don't really . . .' Belle's voice died. She wanted to say that she did not really like drinking whiskey unless she had a cold coming on. To refuse would be rude. Marcus was too dear a friend to be upset today.

'Get some glasses, get some glasses,' he demanded.

'I think I have a couple of tumblers in the kitchen,' she offered, going to the door. She found two heavy-bottomed ones and put them on a tray.

Marcus was standing with his back to the fire when she returned, he was rocking backwards and forwards on his heels warming himself. 'This is cosy,' he reflected, as she slid the tray on to a small table by his chair. He lifted the bottle from the mantelpiece, unscrewed the top and poured out two generous measures.

'You don't take water in it, do you,' she asked, 'or have you changed your tastes?'

'You're right. You remembered,' he said, looking at her seriously. She held up her glass and surveyed him through the pattern glinting in the flickering fire. 'You don't have water either?'

'Well, I don't really drink whiskey . . . a hot one with water sometimes . . . or soda water and ice . . . but we don't have either of those. The refrigerator is not working properly, it doesn't seem to freeze up the way it did . . .' She was conscious of a wistful note in her voice. 'I don't have soda because I didn't think I would need any . . .'

'Well, if I'm going to pop in to see you, you will have to, won't you?' Marcus said, raising his glass. 'Cheers.'

'Yes, cheers, to you,' she said, raising her glass in salute to him.

He nodded and took a sip. She hoped that he would sit down, but he stayed standing there in the heat and she stood beside him, sipping very slowly.

He had finished his glass and he poured another one quickly, a hefty dose, looking at her over the rim as he took the first sip. Then he walked to the settee and sat down heavily.

He is more thickset these days, Belle thought. But then he must be nearing forty. What has he achieved in life except for a successful practice, a place in society, such as it was, and probably a lot of money? The Mercedes is an indication of that. He fits in at long last. His job has made him acceptable to people around here.

'Sit down here beside me,' he said, patting the settee.

'Oh yes, sorry, Marcus, I was thinking . . .'

'It doesn't do any good to do that,' he joked, 'sit down, woman. Tell me about yourself and why you are looking . . . I have now got the right word,' he said rather solemnly, 'alluring.'

'You called me that the other day. You have always called me that whether I was or not.'

'Did I? Have I? Well, today it really fits. You do look very alluring, very . . .' He leaned towards her. She caught the smell of wine on his breath. He had been lunching with some crony, she decided, that was the explanation, that was why he was behaving in this strange unreserved way. 'I am not drunk,' he asserted, noting the look in her eyes.

'I didn't think . . .' she said hurriedly, 'oh Marcus, don't be silly.'

'Yes, I did have a good lunch, but I have a rule now, only one glass of wine, and I stick to it.'

She moved uneasily on the settee.

'Belle, you look so good . . . and I begin to feel so old . . .'

'Don't be silly,' she chided. She put out her hand unconsciously and he caught it up in both his own, pulling her towards him, gathering her tightly into his embrace.

'Belle, oh Belle, my lovely Belle!' he muttered, kissing her around her neck, behind her ears, murmuring into her hair. He became more demanding, his hands running over her shoulders, down her back. She could feel a sudden heat through her thin blouse, a heat which seemed to intensify as he brought one hand round under her arm and on to her breast, feeling it, fondling it between his fingers, muttering her name over and over again. She felt her nipple harden, a stirring somewhere within her, smelt a sweet aroma of lemon cologne as he kissed her now, softly at first, then hard, hard on her lips. 'Belle, oh Belle,' was all he kept saying. His hand moved to the buttons of her blouse and he undid them rapidly, but clumsily, sliding his hand in and underneath her bra to feel the rounded swell of her breast. She felt herself responding to him, bit by bit, her body curving at his touch, her lips finding his in an urgency that surprised her. It was the whiskey, it must be the whiskey, she told herself.

But Marcus? He had bared her breast and was kissing it, running his tongue over it, licking and sucking. She was cradling his head in her hands and saying his name, 'Marcus, Marcus, Marcus,' over and over again. He raised his head to her, his lips to hers, and they kissed long and hard. His tongue sought its way between her teeth. She put a hand on each side of his face and drew away. His glasses were askew. She straightened them. In response he took them off and stuffed them in his top pocket. She stared at him as he bent his head, his lips seeking hers again, his hands becoming anxious.

'Marcus?' she asked, looking at him with wonderment. He looked back at her, calculating, then cold and hurt, she realised. He drew away. She put a finger to his lips tenderly. 'Stop. It's not like that, it's not that, you know it. I care for you, I always have, you know that, but not this way, not this way.' He turned his face away. It was set. 'Marcus, please, Marcus?' she urged him to reply, to respond in some other way than this hurt reproach.

He turned his head eventually, and nodded. 'I see, Belle,' he took a deep breath, 'I see. I've always loved you, always. Even when you chose Sam, I've wanted you. Why did you choose him? It never did any good, you know that. Why did you not choose me?'

'Because I chose him,' she answered, shaking her head.

'I thought you might have changed, might feel differently. You look so different, especially today.'

'I am older, Marcus, that's all.'

'But you feel the same way . . . about Sam . . . about me?'

'I don't know. I just don't know. Not any more. Don't you understand? Coming back here . . . it's just impossible, all of it.'

'Where does that leave me?' he pleaded.

'I don't know, Marcus. I'm sorry. I have taken your love for granted all these years, never doubted it. It wasn't fair of me, I can see that now. But I just did not think . . . until now.'

'Have you ever loved me . . . at all?' he asked, a catch in his voice.

'Yes, but I don't understand why or how.'

'Can you not forget Sam?' he asked. 'Can you not start again, with me? It's not too late, my lovely Belle, start again with me?' A tear had run down his left cheek leaving a wet trail.

Belle wanted to wipe it away and kiss him, she realised, but that was not the answer. 'I don't know, Marcus, I don't know how I feel, or if I feel anything any more.'

'That's the past still with you, the past. You know that. Start again with me, Belle, please?'

She wiped his cheek with a gentle finger. 'Marcus, dear Marcus. Don't talk like this, not now. Maybe another time but not today, please?' she begged quietly.

He gulped. 'You're right, of course you're right. I just wanted you to know that I love you . . . deeply . . .' His voice choked. 'I want to make you happy. I could. I have a lot of money. We could go anywhere you like. Leave here. You would never have to worry about anything ever again. You know I love the boys like they were . . . always have done . . .'

'Yes, you have been their favourite uncle.'

'Uncle!' He spat out the word. 'That's all I have ever been! I love you, Belle, I want to sleep with you, make love to you, I want you to have my children. I can take Sam's, love them as if they were my own, but I want some too, I want you, Belle, I need you . . .'

She did not reply, but buttoned up her blouse and stood up, tucking it into the waistband of her skirt. She had unconsciously slipped her feet out of her shoes. Putting them on again made her suddenly two or three inches taller. Marcus stood up beside her. Their lips were inches away from each other. He looked very determined.

'Marcus,' she began, 'Marcus?'

'Damn!' he said, looking over her shoulder out of the window, wrenching his glasses out of his pocket and putting them on, staring.

Belle realised that she had heard a car door slam, and then another one. She looked at her watch. It was nearly four o'clock. There was a green car at the gate. The boys were home from school, and by the look of it, Pat Quinn was coming up the drive with them carrying something heavy. It was a car battery. Marcus was straightening his tie beside her, tugging at his impeccable waistcoat, drawing himself up into his role as solicitor, solid citizen, emotions in check, guarded again.

'Marcus?' She took his arm, sensing his withdrawal, the finality.

He drew away. 'It's the boys. And you have a visitor. Who's that?'

'It's Pat.'

'Pat?'

'Pat Quinn. From the school. Down at Corey. I took my boys down to start this morning but I had trouble with my car. He said he would leave them off home on his way into town after school.'

'Pat,' he said again, flatly, cold.

'I'm going to work there, temporarily, only for a few days, his secretary is off sick. Oh Marcus!' She read his expression. 'Stop it! Don't be silly!' She shook his arm and laughed at him and suddenly he smiled back. 'Now there is something you can do for me,' she continued, 'like you did before, Marcus! Are you listening? You got me a job in Belfast.' Marcus was looking at her with a strange wistful expression in his eyes, now clouded by the glasses. She shook his arm once more.

'And you want me to find you another one – in Armagh – is that what you mean?' he said in measured tones.

'Yes, please.'

He put his hand under her chin and turned her face up to him. 'Very well. I'll see what I can do,' he said, his lips once again very close to hers. 'I shall expect some reward of course . . .' He smiled benignly.

They were standing very close. Pat Quinn could not fail to see them as he came towards the house. He recognised Marcus.

Belle was standing at the front door. Marcus was standing behind her looking proprietorial. Belle put a hand up to straighten her hair in a gesture which Pat recognised instantly. So that was the way of things. Pat was suddenly aware of his worn cord trousers, the tweed jacket with the button missing, and behind him his rusty car. Marcus nodded as if from a great height although Pat was a head taller.

Belle intervened formally. 'Marcus, this is Pat Quinn. He's in charge of the school at Corey.'

'Yes,' Marcus nodded, 'I think I have seen you around the town a couple of times. You haven't been here long, have you?'

Oh stop it! Belle thought. The man was born and reared here, just down the road, he's not a stranger, he only lived down the road from us when we were children, why do you not accept him now, there's no need to make him out to be stranger, that's not fair.

'A year or so,' Pat was answering easily, nodding, looking down at Marcus.

'Well, Belle my dear . . .' Marcus turned to her and kissed her cheek fondly. 'I must be off.' He looked into her eyes. 'I will call again soon. Better still, come and have lunch with me, maybe Thursday, I'll pick you up, I'll take you off somewhere really special. You deserve the best. Yes, why not Thursday?'

'I can't. I'm going to see Jean . . .' Belle began, then she looked at Pat. 'I'm sorry. I never really checked with you about lunch hour or whether you needed help at the school with the kids then . . .'

'It's all right,' Pat said. He looked directly at Marcus. 'You just take what lunch hour you like.'

Is he talking to me or to Marcus? Belle wondered. She didn't understand. Pat sounded fierce although he did not look it. Just under control, tight control she realised, as she watched him watch Marcus get into the driving seat of his great white car. There was a quiet hum as Marcus opened the electric window, started the car, then reversed on the driveway so that he was pointing towards the road; then he paused.

'Goodbye, Belle, my dear,' he called softly, smiling. 'I'll ring you.'

Belle stood beside Pat as Marcus drove off down the drive. Pat was looking down at her. He still held the battery in his hands, lightly, as if it was no weight at all. He did not speak for a moment but just stared at her fixedly. Eventually he said, 'Where's your car?'

'In the garage,' she replied. 'You've brought a battery?'

'It's a spare. With luck it will do your car in the mean time. There's only a bit of life left in it, but you're welcome to it if that will solve the problem for the moment.'

'That's very kind of you . . .' she began stiffly.

He shrugged his shoulders. 'I just thought it might help.' He turned away from her. 'Rory, will you come with me?'

'I'm coming too,' Conor squeaked, pushing between Pat and Rory as they headed for the corner of the house.

Belle went back into the house and tidied the bottle and glasses into the scullery. Then she lifted the car keys, went out of the kitchen door and across the yard to the garage. Pat had the bonnet of the car up and was sliding the battery carefully into place, checking the leads.

He looked up. 'Simple, easy. No problem,' he said. 'Now we'll see how she sounds. Do you have the keys there?'

'Here.' She handed them over.

The engine responded instantly, purred into life. Pat switched off, took out the key, got out and stood up, slamming the door shut. 'That seems to be it.'

'Wow!' said Conor beside him. 'Wow!' He was looking at Pat with an adoring expression. Rory struggled to lift the old battery, which was sitting on the ground beside the car.

'It's a bit heavy, boy, I'll take it,' Pat said, lifting it. 'We can get this recharged and then we'll try it again, maybe there is a bit of life left in it yet. There's no point spending money on a new one if the old one can be made to last a bit longer. In the mean time my battery should do you.' He put the battery on the kitchen window-sill. 'I'll take it with me, into town, get it recharged.'

'It's very kind of you . . .' Belle began hesitantly.

'It's nothing. You're welcome,' Pat replied.

'Would you like a cup of tea? I've just put the kettle on.'

He nodded. 'That would be fine.'

As they went into the kitchen he said, 'I need to wash my hands.'

Belle looked at his oily hands proffered towards her in explanation. 'Oh yes, the battery. Do you want to go upstairs . . . it's the first –'

He walked into the scullery. 'This will do fine,' he said over his shoulder.

She followed him in, noticing how untidy it was, the pile of dirty washing, the damp floor, the tray by the sink and her dressed up like some floozy! She must stink of whiskey. Yes, floozy was the best word to describe her, she thought, frenzied. Pat turned to look at her as he rinsed his hands. She handed him a towel and he dried his hands vigorously. 'You look as if you had a flood here,' was all he said.

'The washing machine. It packed up. There must be a leak in it somewhere. Just when I thought I was getting somewhere . . .' She stopped, she had said enough. Pat waited for her to continue. 'The water came out all over the place. It's ages old. Maybe I didn't fit it together properly, or maybe I connected up the wrong hose . . .'

'I'll take a look.'

'No, really, there's bound to be a simple explanation. It's probably something very silly and simple that's wrong and I have been stupid.'

'I'll take a look,' he repeated, 'it's no trouble.' He had his hand on the top of the machine, and bent his head to look more closely.

Belle put her hand firmly on his and said, 'No. I won't let you. You have done enough to help. You will be late getting into town. I insist. Thank you, but I cannot . . .' She wanted to say that she couldn't accept all this help, not all at once from someone she had only just met, even though they had been children together.

Pat straightened up, drew his hand away slowly and stood looking at her for a silent moment. 'You're sure?'

'Yes. Mrs D knows its foibles, there'll be an easy explanation.

If not I'll have to abandon it and buy another one, reconditioned or something.' She wanted to say: Look, I'm sorry, I cannot impose on you, take more from you, I cannot. From his expression she knew she had said the wrong thing, though he was pretending it didn't matter. He went into the kitchen and stood with his hands thrust into the pockets of his trousers, looking at the boys who were warming themselves by the stove. There was the clatter of mugs as Rory made the tea.

Awkwardly she said, 'Great, Rory, I'm dying for a cup of tea. Now, Mr Quinn –' It came out before she could stop it.

Pat looked at her sharply. 'Pat!' he said, taking a deep breath.

'Yes, Pat,' she said, feeling like one of his pupils, 'yes, Pat. You still have time for a cup?'

'Yes. I could do with one.'

She pointed to a chair. 'Please sit yourself down.'

Pat took off his jacket and hung it over the back of the chair. He did it so casually, it was as if he was at home. He sat down and stretched out his legs.

Belle poured the tea and found the tin of biscuits. The boys were talking about school, telling her what they had been doing. Pat interjected now and again with a wry comment or joking remark. She began to feel at ease. Then Pat caught her eye above the boys' heads and was silent, staring at her critically. The boys kept talking, now to each other.

Belle was disconcerted by the direct look. 'Do you like wild ducks?' she asked abruptly. Pat blinked. 'Mallards,' she said. 'They were left for me the other night. Someone must have been out shooting. There's a hook by the back door, outside. Friends, in the old days, used to leave ducks, maybe rabbits, for my mother. She was a widow, you see, for many years, and I suppose it was one way in which people thought they could help, quietly, without a fuss, without her feeling indebted to them. Well, anyway . . .' she was breathless, 'someone left me two fat ducks and it is time they were eaten.' She stopped, then plunged on. 'What I mean is, if I cooked them up for dinner tomorrow, would you come and help us eat them?'

'I'll be delighted,' he said, nodding, 'yes, delighted.' Then he asked thoughtfully, 'Where were they shooting the ducks?'

'Oh, I don't think they do it often, but there's a bit of lake at the other side of Top Hill, near the railway line, the viaduct. It's over the hill from here, where the Neill land meets the Johnstons'.'

'And they left them on this hook at the back door . . . did you hear them come around?' he probed.

'I thought I did . . . the next morning . . . when I saw them. The sounds here are so different from the city. Imagination can play tricks.'

'Somebody obviously knew you were here,' he said.

'Well, you knew, and you're only the schoolteacher.' She spoke without thinking how it might sound.

'Schoolteachers get to hear all the news,' he replied, standing up. 'I guess I ought to be getting on my way.' He reached for his jacket. 'I'll see you tomorrow, day one of the new job.'

Belle noticed the missing button. She suddenly had an urge to take the jacket from him and sew on the button. It was the familiar role of a wife, and that was a role she could not play with him.

'Do you have far to come? I mean, will you drive over or do you live nearby?'

'I'll drive over, I expect. I live down at Corey. If it's icy I can walk, it will only take twelve minutes, or so, if I walk briskly.' He was buttoning his jacket. When he reached the missing button his fingers stopped. He looked at her and for a moment she was tempted to offer to sew it on.

'Yes, well, I'll see you tomorrow then,' was all she said, 'if you're sure?'

He laughed. 'Sure about what? The job or the dinner?'

'Oh both!' she said, shaking her head in dismay.

He said goodbye to the boys and went out through the kitchen door bending his head. Sam was tall, but not quite so tall. Sam. Why must she remember him now? She went out after Pat into the gathering gloom. He took the battery off the window-sill. She found herself walking beside him down the drive. She did not feel the cold, or notice the first shades of darkness beginning under the canopy of pines.

Pat put the battery into the boot of his car, and walked to the driver's door, then he stopped and looked at her beside him. 'Aren't you cold?' he asked. 'It's freezing. Go in!'

'I hadn't realised,' she replied.

'I'll see you tomorrow. Go in,' he dismissed her.

'Yes,' she said obediently, turning on her heel, grinning to herself.

He watched her walk all the way back to the house. As she reached the corner she turned to wave at him, and he waved back. But he still did not move when she disappeared from sight. He stayed a moment longer at the gate before getting into his car and driving off.

Chapter 12

'MA! THE CAR STARTED,' Rory said in awe next morning when she turned the key in the ignition.

'Yes, thank goodness, thanks to Mr Quinn.'

'Is Mr Quinn our friend?' Conor asked in a small voice from the back seat.

'Yes, why not?' Belle asked.

'I hope so,' Conor said, 'I like him a lot.'

'Do you like him, Rory?' Belle turned to her elder son who as usual was sitting in the front seat, itching to drive the car. 'Rory?'

'Oh Ma, I wish you'd look where you're going. Yes. I think he's pretty good. He's not really like a teacher.'

'In what way?' she asked, curious at this observation. How like a child to notice things about adults which they themselves did not.

'Och . . . just, well he's very friendly, to us and all that. Teachers in Belfast didn't seem to want to know so much,' he explained.

They were at the school gate. There was no time for further discussion, the boys were too interested in scrambling out of the car and heading for the door, calling out to their new friends.

Pat was in his office, behind his desk, seated, clad in a grey suit and wearing steel-rimmed glasses over which he peered, not getting up as she entered. 'Morning,' was all he said. Then he looked down at a piece of paper in front of him, a letter of some kind she surmised.

Problem with a parent, she wanted to say to break the ice, but she stayed silent, slipping out of her red jacket and hanging it up on a peg on the back of the door. She sat down at the other desk, her back to the window. For an instant she just sat, waiting for him to say something. He didn't. She smoothed her hair from her forehead with a nervous hand and placed her hands side by side in front of her, palms flat on the desk. Still he said nothing. Then he folded the letter, and half rising pushed it into his trouser pocket. He glanced at her, then he nodded.

'Now then. You want to get started, I suppose,' was all he said. His voice was expressionless, without any warmth. She looked at him, but said nothing. 'Sorry. I'm sorry.' He shook his head. 'I'll have to go up to Belfast tomorrow, somebody to see. It's a nuisance, but I need to get some information about something . . .' He stopped, as if he had been thinking aloud to himself and now recognised her presence. 'It's not all that important, it could wait I suppose, but I should find out, pretty soon.' He looked at her again, the same impersonal look. He looked at his watch. 'I had better go and get classes started, take the roll, I'm a bit late today.' He rose. 'Make yourself at home, I'll be right back,' he said, going out of the door. The background noise of children in the corridor outside and in the classroom banging lids, shuffling feet and schoolbooks, voices, died to a soft murmur. Belle stood up and walked round her desk to Pat's, standing looking at the pile of papers. It really was a mess, but where should she start? She was still standing there when Pat returned.

'Don't worry about the mess on my desk, I'll clear it now,' he said quickly, 'some letters need answering, some just need throwing in the basket, circulars, you know.' He gave her a fleeting smile.

That's the first time this morning, Belle thought. 'I wasn't reading your mail,' she said defensively. 'I was just waiting for you to come back and tell me where I could start.'

'Well, let's get on with it then,' he said in a brusque tone.

Back to your place, Belle, she told herself. He's the boss, you're only the secretary. She went over to her desk and sat down, staring at the smooth wooden surface.

'I'm sorry,' Pat said. She looked up at him. 'I'm sorry,' he said again, and sighed. 'It's one of those days. Just when you think that everything is going smoothly, something happens to wreck your organisation, stir it all up.'

'Stir it up?' Belle asked. 'Thanks to you my car started at once. Thank you for that. What's gone wrong for you?'

He looked at her curiously and for a moment she thought he was going to explain. But instead he put on his cold matter-of-fact voice and proceeded to outline where everything was generally kept in the office, as far as he could remember, except that Mrs Jamison had her own mysterious methods, details of the timetable so that she would know when he could be interrupted, and finally he thrust a pile of letters at her, ones that he said he had answered but that needed filing. Then somewhat irritably he departed to teach. She was aware in the final minutes of her briefing that there was a growing sound of discord in the nearby classroom, possibly the one he ought to be in, and she was keeping him back while he had to explain everything.

He's busy, she consoled herself, after he had left and the sounds became muted again. And having to go to Belfast tomorrow may mean complications about classes, I suppose. Maybe he won't want to come over for dinner tonight. She felt a pang of disappointment at the last thought.

At tea break Pat brought in a shy young man who looked around twenty-two years of age – the other teacher, Alan, who sat nervously drinking tea and eating Nice biscuits like a hamster. Pat explained that Alan had just come from college and that he was getting on fine. Alan just nodded and kept nibbling. She would have to pick up the mantle of Mrs Jamison neatly and unobtrusively, she thought, not Belle Johnston, just the secretary. When they went back to class she felt isolated and very unsure of herself, trying to motivate herself in her various tasks.

When lunchtime came it was almost as if Pat had realised he had been withdrawn, cold and unresponsive, for he came into the office with a broad friendly grin on his face, whipped her coat off the back of the door and insisted that she put it on.

'Time's up,' was all he said in explanation as she looked amazed.

'What do you mean?'

'Enough is enough. Especially on day one.'

'But . . .'

'I do hear that there's going to be a very special dinner served at a very special restaurant in the town tonight, in which case it's time the chef went home.'

'I don't need all that much time to pluck, clean and dress a couple of small ducks.'

'Dedication. That's what's needed. And no distractions. When those boys come in from school, and they can walk home today, good for them, it's not far, you'll have your hands full getting them to do their homework, and laying the table, and polishing the family silver, and the Waterford glass and . . .'

'How do you know I'm going to do all that?' she queried in mock awe, infected by his sudden joviality.

'Well, aren't you? Wild ducks need special treatment, don't they? A touch of class, you might say.'

'Yes,' she replied, still bemused by this change of mood.

'And what time does Madam expect the guest?'

'I suppose about seven. But do you really want to come? I thought you said you had to go to Belfast tomorrow? What time are you going?'

'Oh that,' he was offhand, 'that. Not to worry. Not important. I'll not go up till after school anyway. It's no problem . . .'

'When will you be back? I mean, will you be back for school next day?'

'Of course.' He looked surprised. The guarded expression in his eyes had returned but it changed again to a mischievous twinkle. 'Of course,' he held open the door, 'I'll be back. Now off you go.'

'I'll see you around seven then?'

'Yes, ma'am,' was all he said.

The first thing that she spotted when she got home was the long line of washing drooping in the cold air of the garden. Mrs D had been at work but she was obviously far from well.

'I have the flu coming on,' Mrs D excused herself. 'I just couldn't get on me this morning, and Willy's not well neither. The both of us have it. It's the cold does it, the cold and the damp, them houses is full of it.' She looked sadly at Belle.

'Please go home, Mrs D. I don't like to see you like this. Thank you for doing the washing. What was wrong with the machine?'

'Everything. It's done, broken.'

'But there's all that lot on the line. You had to do it by hand,' Belle exclaimed fretfully.

'Och, it didn't take all that long. But I haven't done much else in the house,' Mrs D replied, hunching her shoulders.

Belle gave her a hug. 'You're marvellous, but you should not have done all that washing, especially when you were not feeling right. We'll have to find another machine, a second-hand one for I haven't much money . . .'

'We'll do rightly doing it by hand, my mother never bothered about it, and she raised seven of a family . . .' Mrs D sniffed loudly.

'Will you please go home?' Belle said. Mrs D smiled wanly while Belle helped her on with her coat. Then Belle remembered the whiskey. She thrust the bottle into Mrs D's hands. 'Mr O'Brien brought this yesterday. It would do Willy a power of good, now wouldn't it, whiskey is great for the flu. And maybe you might take a wee drop yourself?'

'Would you put that bottle into a bag for me? It wouldn't do for those ones, up the village, to know I was taking strong drink into the house.'

Belle walked up the yard with her, then along to the gate. She stood for a moment while Mrs D made her way up the road, a small dumpy figure. How old was she? She would not give in, not to old age. I am still a child to her, Belle thought, her child in a way.

Belle walked about the house from room to room, forgetting about lunch, looking around her with critical eyes. Each room seemed worse than the other, worn and decrepit. She got as far as the attics and found a desultory clump of toys scattered about the floor of the apple attic, left by the boys. Even they had lost interest.

She went into the tank room and listened. There was no sound. But she knew in the dark that the bats were there, listening to her.

Belle bent down to look out of the landing window, to the road, the lawn, and the trees outside, then went downstairs into the garden where she cut some green pine branches with cones on. They would help to lift the gloom of the house. The boys arrived home just as she finished cutting the branches. Faces flushed from the walk in the cold air, they wanted something to eat, they were starving, they said.

'We're going to eat the ducks tonight,' she reminded them, as they tucked into the biscuit tin.

'Oh, is it tonight?' Rory asked carefully.

'Yes, don't you remember?'

'Oh yes. Would you not rather just eat with Pat . . .' he paused to see if she would react at the use of the name, 'and we could just chew the bones . . . we wouldn't be in the way, and then you would be able to talk to Pat . . .'

'In the way? Don't be silly, Rory. What's all this about?' She frowned.

'Yes, yes,' Conor chimed in quickly, 'we wouldn't be a nuisance . . . it's just . . . well, there's this television programme . . .'

'I don't believe it! You two are awful. I suppose it all was Conor's idea and you are doing the talking for him, Rory. It will seem very rude if you sit and watch television and we eat in another room . . .'

'Oh, it's OK,' Rory replied, 'I have already asked Pat, if he minded. He said he didn't, if you didn't.'

'Well, really!'

'Och, Ma! You know it would be better. And you'd like it better that way, wouldn't you?' Rory cajoled. 'We talked about it, discussed it all.'

Belle was getting angry. 'Do you mind telling me who all you have been talking to . . . about it all?' she demanded fiercely.

'Just Pat, just Pat. I haven't been talking . . . I haven't been talking to anyone . . . only him, and the stupid O'Briens!' He turned away from her.

'Ma! Ma!'

Rory is coming in through the kitchen door from the yard.

'I'm here,' I call to him, 'I'm here. What is it?'

He is standing now at the door, red-faced, breathless, his schoolbag hitched on one shoulder. He shakes it off. It falls to the floor. Clump.

'Nothing.'

'Oh. I thought . . . well, you sounded as if you had some news . . . about school?' I ask carefully.

'Nothing at school.' He scowls now and turns away from me, standing at the stove, fiddling with the gas taps, on and off, on and off. 'Nothing.'

'Oh.' I try to meet his eyes. He'll tell me, sooner or later, I know. 'How was school today? Do you have much homework?'

'Nothing . . . much.' He walks over to the window and peers out into the garden, taking a long look up the rows of houses on one side.

'What is it?' I ask.

'Oh nothing. Nothing,' he says. He sighs deeply and turns back to me.

'You keep saying that!' I go to the window . . . I look out. I cannot see anything, or anybody, in the long lane that runs down between the gardens. I look at my son then, my big son. He has a bloody graze down one cheek. Somehow he has hidden it from me in all these moments.

'What happened to your face?' I ask.

'It's nothing. Just two big boys, in the entry.'

'What did they do?'

'They asked me if my name was Johnston and if I lived at number ten.'

'Then what happened?'

'They said we were scum. They said we were informers. That we were better dead.'

Now it's out! 'What else did they say?' I ask gently, afraid.

'Oh, they just pushed me down. Kicked me. There was a man coming down the entry. They saw him coming. They ran away.'

'Did you ever see those boys before?'

'No. Never,' he assures me, trying to keep his voice steady.

'You must not talk to strangers ever again . . . about anything!'

Belle put a hand on her elder son's shoulder as he headed for the door. 'I'm sorry, Rory, I didn't mean to shout at you. OK. If you want to watch television, and Pat says he doesn't mind, why should I?' She gave him a gentle dig in the ribs, trying to make him laugh.

He did not even smile. 'Yeah, great,' was all he said.

Chapter 13

BELLE MOVED AROUND THE kitchen as if under some enchantment. The boys seemed to melt away with their attendant untidiness, melting to the sitting-room where, she discovered later, they had surrounded themselves with all kinds of favourite things. Even a special bear of Conor's was propped up in an armchair in the viewing position. They were ready for a siege. It all happened so quietly, so surreptitiously, as if they wished to melt away out of her life for this one evening which was to be hers.

Only Conor had lingered for a while when she spread newspapers on the table so that she could pluck the ducks. The papers were old and yellowed, a bundle she had found at the bottom of the scullery cupboard. When she started pulling off the green and black and blue plumage and he had placed the more beautiful feathers in neat rows, his eye wandered and he started reading the newspaper in slow halting words.

'Suspect bomb. A car found parked illegally in Scotch Street, Armagh, yesterday was found not to contain a bomb. Troops examined the vehicle which was discovered at 3 p.m. using the robot device. A package in the boot was found to be a hoax. Traffic was diverted for four hours until the vehicle was made safe. A man was found on waste ground behind the ABC cinema in Belfast with severe leg injuries last night. He is believed to be the victim of a punishment shooting. A spokesman for the Royal Victoria Hospital reported that he had undergone an operation for the removal of bullets from one leg. His –'

For a moment the spell was broken.

'Oh stop it, Conor!'

'Och, Mama, it's only old news. Look, the paper says –'

'I don't want to know. Have a look to see what was on television.'

Conor pushed and pulled at the papers trying to find the right page.

'Watch! There'll be feathers all over the kitchen at this rate.'

'Well, you did ask me to look.'

'Do you want to see their insides now?'

Instantly diverted, Conor watched bright-eyed as she slit the body with a sharp knife and drew out the entrails.

'Phew! It stinks, doesn't it?'

'Well, that's to be expected.' She pointed out the heart, the intestines and the stomach, picking them out with the knife point.

'I didn't know there were so many things inside.' Wonderingly Conor put out a finger and poked. 'There's not much blood, is there?'

'Only where the shots went in, the lead shot, do you see?'

He picked up the small lead pellets and rolled them between his finger and thumb. 'And that's enough to kill them?'

'If there's enough and they hit the right place.'

'What about a human being? How much lead shot would they need? Could you kill a person with these wee bits of lead?'

'I don't know. I suppose it would depend on where they hit.'

'Well, Uncle James's bullets . . . how many of those would you need?' he went on interminably as Belle disembowelled the second bird.

'Just one of those, if it is in the right place. A bullet is much bigger.'

'You could kill a person with any kind of a gun then?' he asked, his face screwed up in determination to get the facts absolutely clear.

'That's enough, Conor.' Belle pulled the papers up from under his hands and rolled up feathers and intestines into a tight amorphous bundle.

He exclaimed in dismay. 'Och! And I wanted to keep those feathers.'

'You should have put them to one side. I'm not unwrapping it all now,' she said firmly, going out to the scullery and dumping the bundle into the waste bin under the sink.

She had put the newly plucked birds side by side on a roasting dish. Now they were food. The unpleasant part, the reminders of dying, were gone. She realised that she had acted out a scene which she had played with her mother, curious, as Conor had been, to see what lay inside the birds, the rabbits, what made them live and what had made them die.

Conor walked round the table and poked one of the birds.

'Leave it alone. It's going into the oven soon and your fingers are far from clean,' she scolded.

'Could I . . . ?' he started.

Rory appeared at the doorway.

'We've been doing the ducks,' Conor said importantly. 'Cutting out their guts and all. Mama told me all about what kills them, what kind of shot . . . I know all about it . . .'

'Sure I've always known,' Rory scoffed, coming over to the table and looking at the birds, 'I know all about guns, I talked to Uncle James.'

'Well, so did I!' Conor echoed.

'Hey, Ma, did you know Pat Quinn knows all about guns? I was talking to him . . .' He stopped when he saw Belle's expression, then hastily continued, 'We were only talking . . . not the whole class Ma, only him and me, after school . . . I was waiting for Conor . . . we were only talking about Sunday. I told him how we had gone to the O'Briens for lunch and how Uncle James had those guns. He knew all about what kind of guns they were, I mean all . . . Do you know he was in Vietnam?'

'Vietnam?' Belle asked, amazed.

'Yeah. A coupla tours,' Rory said nonchalantly in an American accent. 'At the end of the war, he said.'

Pat in Vietnam? It seemed so unreal put into the Ulster context. The idea of Pat fighting just did not seem to match the man she believed him to be.

'Mama?' Conor tugged at her sleeve. 'Does that mean Pat Quinn killed people? Does that mean he . . . ?'

Belle looked at Rory. 'Now look what you have started,' she groaned.

'Hey, Conor, you're missing it,' Rory said grinning.

'What? What?' Conor shouted.

'*Top Cat*. I came to tell you –'

'*Top Cat!*' Conor pushed past Rory and rushed out of the door. Rory followed, giving his mother a sly look as he left the room.

Now she had the kitchen fully to herself, Belle got busy peeling potatoes and parsnips for baking. A tin of salmon became a quick pâté, a tin of peaches became a pie. Yes, Americans liked pies, she recalled, from some movie. Her pastry had always been light and airy. This time she surpassed herself.

She smiled to herself when laying the table, digging into the china cabinet to find the fine bone china plates that had been her mother's, the crystal glasses which would have to hold water since she had not had the time to get in a bottle of wine, silver knives, forks and spoons which were wrapped in blue tissue paper, and a pair of silver candlesticks. She had some emergency white candles in the kitchen, ready for a power cut. They would do.

How strange it was that it all remained the same, how the whole house had, all these years, been waiting for her to bring it back to life, the doors firmly closed, the cupboards, the drawers. Only the still pervading smell of damp betrayed the closed windows, the stale air where spiders spun their webs undisturbed, beetles trundled across floors and moths fluttered, enmeshed, and died.

A candle-lit dinner. That was something from the past, something from those early days with Sam.

I can smell something cooking. But there's no one in the house, unless Sam is home. If he is, he will be sitting, waiting for his tea.

I am standing in the upstairs room of the Johnston house, the room on the right at the head of the stairs. This is our home, just this room. I positively hate the wallpaper. Granny Johnston says that if I like I can change it. If I like . . . I wish I could, but being precisely eight and a half months pregnant tends to restrict what you can do. This child will be born eventually. The Johnstons all want it to be a boy. Both Sam's sisters have wee girls so far. Now it's up to me.

They have already picked out a name for him, James. I can only think of poor sad James up at the Lodge, drinking his life away. I will not call my son, if he is a son, James. No way. I told

Granny Johnston that I thought Rory was a good name. She nearly had a fit. That's not a good Protestant name, she said. Well, what about Patrick, I asked her. That was as bad. But lots of people whether they are Protestant or Catholic call their children Patrick. So long as it's not abbreviated to Paddy they are all right if they are Protestants. I'm sure there's a Rory way back in my family somewhere. As for girls' names, it's just as bad. I suggested Siobhan to Sam, just to see how he would react. He must have known I was teasing him when I suggested it, but he just went silent, humpy. He doesn't say much here, in this house, when he's with his mother and father. His father doesn't say much either. He has continual heart trouble but he can't stop working. It's as if he is driven by some awful spirit. He'll drop dead one day, just drop, out in some field somewhere. And Sam will be the same. This is his inheritance. There will come a time when we sleep in the bigger room at the other side of the landing. I hope the bed is better than this one.

I have been snoozing. Granny Johnston sent me up to rest before they went off to the agricultural show at Balmoral, in Belfast. She and Sam's dad are going to stay over, in an hotel if you please. She has a new suit and hat, bought specially. They need the break, Sam's dad particularly. I can't call him Grandad, not yet. They are nice people really, it's just we never get away from them, until now, half a day, a night . . . Granny Johnston said she would leave a pie for our tea. That's what I can smell. Sam must be heating it up.

Sam is in the kitchen by the stove, and he's cooking! He has a cookbook propped up, the one I got as a wedding present, I can see when I lean over, he's cooking Chicken Kiev.

'Why don't you cook more often?' he asks.

'Because your mother won't let me. This is her kitchen.'

'That's no excuse. If I can do it, so can you. Cooking is easy.'

'That's not fair. She's not here to argue with. You know I can cook . . . but your mother thinks that my cooking is a bit fancy. She wouldn't like Chicken Kiev . . . is that what you're doing?'

'Have you ever tried to cook something here, anything at all?' His voice is suddenly scornful. He must be very tired and I have been lazing, he thinks.

'Yes, yes, I have. She won't let me. It's not like my own house. This is not my home, you know it!' I cry at him. I feel lumpy, ugly, fat, pregnant and touchy. I'm going to start weeping all over his wretched Chicken Kiev if he's not careful.

'This is your home,' he says slowly and deliberately. 'You know it. It's all yours. Why can't we be happy?'

Tonight this feels right. This is my home, Belle thought. Since the boys have arranged it, I am going to play out this ritual.

She wondered what to wear and decided on a dark green wool dress, cut straight with long tight sleeves and a simple belt worn loosely at the waist. It emphasised her narrow shoulders, narrow hips, made her face glow peach-coloured under her mop of auburn hair.

As she opened the door to Pat Quinn, sensing rather than hearing his steps in the yard, the light streamed out behind her into the dark, bright warm light, rich cooking smells. She knew it was him even though it was ten minutes to seven. He had on a bulky black tweed coat, the collar turned up against the frosty air, and he carried a package which she realised was a bottle of wine. From the other hand, held behind his back, he produced a bunch of chrysanthemums, bright yellow, aromatic. He bowed. She invited him in with an expansive hand. Neither spoke at that moment.

She took the flowers into her arms and buried her face in them, sniffing. 'They are lovely. How did you manage . . . ?' The wine, the flowers, he would have to take a trip into town to get them.

As if he could read her mind he said, 'Oh, I collected your battery. The guys at the garage reckon it will do you for another few months.'

'You have gone to a lot of trouble . . . I don't know what to say . . .'

'You're welcome,' he replied solemnly. He was looking at her in a way that distracted her. This man was stirring feelings she had buried.

'Did you walk, or did you come in your car?'

'I brought the car, in the end.'

'I thought perhaps you might walk it, you said it only took twelve minutes. Can I take your coat?'

'Yes, sorry, I was thinking,' he replied uneasily.

Belle was glad that she could take his coat into the hall to hang it up. She felt that she was blushing, again. She stuck her head round the sitting-room door.

'Mr Quinn is here, boys, do you not want to say hallo?'

They trooped in side by side to the kitchen. Belle stood between them, a hand on each head, not knowing how she looked with them, and how much her love for them showed.

'Hallo there,' Pat said cheerfully. 'I gather you have decided to take up my suggestion about dinner tonight.'

'Your suggestion . . . ?' Belle began.

Pat smiled sweetly. 'Well, it seemed like a good idea at the time.'

'I thought –' she said.

'Pat thought,' Rory interrupted, grinning from ear to ear. 'Pat thought that we would be bored with your conversation and he said that you deserved a bit of special attention, since you had had such a lot of troubles lately . . .'

'And what else did he say?' Belle asked, staring at Pat.

'Nothing else,' Pat answered for him. 'My, that smells good!'

'My mother is an excellent cook,' Rory explained.

'Yes, I know, you told me,' Pat said. Then they all laughed.

'You are awful, the lot of you,' Belle said, 'this is a set-up.'

'You're dead right,' Pat agreed.

Conor turned on his heel. 'I don't want to miss the end of this programme.'

Rory lingered. 'Will you give us a shout when you dish up the ducks, Ma? We can just eat them with our fingers in there,' he pointed to the sitting-room, 'can't we?'

'Well, that's what you planned to do, isn't it?' she said with a smile.

'Yeah, great,' he said, hurrying out of the door.

'Do you usually organise people's lives like this?' she asked.

'Only some people's,' he replied, then in an undertone he said, 'only those I care for.'

Belle turned quickly to the stove, wanting to hide her face from him. 'Dinner won't be long,' she muttered.

'It certainly smells good,' he said, leaning over her shoulder.

She turned her head and said brightly, 'Would you like a drink?'

He stepped back. 'Yes, that seems a good idea.'

'I only have sherry I'm afraid . . .' She stopped. That seemed like a lie for yesterday there had been an almost full bottle of whiskey in the scullery. She felt she had to explain. 'I gave the whiskey to Mrs D. She seemed so full of the flu this morning and her husband is sick too. Marcus brought it anyway.'

'Ah yes, Marcus.' It was a statement.

'He's a very old friend. I've known him for years. He was sent to school in England. He always seemed a bit shy. We only saw him in the school holidays but he lived with James and Jean and they always seemed so old-fashioned . . .' Belle was talking on, wondering how to keep the conversation going. Pat was nodding wisely as if he knew it all already. Her voice died. She concentrated on pouring two glasses of sherry, and they stood together sipping, Pat remarking on what a fine job of painting the walls she had done, then as she dished up the ducks browned and succulent and stirred the sauce, he stood beside her, not talking, just watching her as she worked.

'You're ten times better than a wife.' John's tone is teasing, he is standing behind me as I cook.

He puts his arms round me. He is very warm, soft, plump these days.

I am trying to cook tea for the two of them. Sam and John. Sam is sitting in the carver chair reading the farming section of the morning paper. Only now is he getting time to do so. John is now prowling round, hungry, lifting the lids of saucepans and sniffing hopefully. He has already eaten the heel of a loaf of bread on the table liberally spread with butter. He has been up and down the orchard about a dozen times today. Restless. Waiting for the apples. Some of the eaters are coming on well, but the cookers, the Bramleys, are going to be late this year, and not good, he says gloomily, because they got apple scab this year. I told him about spraying but he put it off and when he finally did spray it was too late. Why does he not go and help Sam? Today he could have done, instead of wandering around, restless.

Sam is lifting new potatoes over at the Johnston farm. It is going to be a glut crop, he says. He has got some help at long last, a new man, from near the Border. He's called Willy John McDowell. He is not a young fellow by any means. He had his own farm, but Granny Johnston says he was intimidated out, he's a Protestant, too near the Border, the IRA said they were going to kill him and his wife and three kids. So he left it. They are all living with the wife's mother somewhere the far side of Armagh. We have no accommodation for them. Sam is awkward tonight. I can't please him. Maybe he'll be in a better humour when he has had his tea.

I'm late tonight. Rory is in bed at last. He's a terrible handful for a three-year-old. It takes me all my time to keep up with him, keep this house and then start in and cook tea at the end of the day. I wish Sam would understand. He wants another child, he says, another son. That's all the Johnstons are keen on, more Johnstons to keep the farm. Continuity. That's what they want. They have had it for generations, and they want it for more. The land. They are obsessed by it. I suppose that if you have worked a piece of land for a long number of years you get to know it well, how much it will yield, how the weather changes it from season to season. It's part of the family. There now, the potatoes are cooked at last. I'm going to roll them in lots of butter, John likes them that way.

'Aha!' John says, sneaking up behind me. 'We're almost there!' he says triumphantly, putting his arm round me and poking the potatoes.

'Get off! Let me do it! Who's cooking this tea, you or I?' I laugh.

'Is the tea not ready yet?' Sam asks, raging, getting up suddenly from his chair and throwing the paper down on the floor.

'Yes, yes, it's ready,' I tell him.

'I'll just go and see if Rory is asleep,' he says, going out of the room, shutting the door with a bang.

There was the quiet sound of a cork coming out of a bottle. Belle turned. Pat had found a corkscrew and had opened the bottle of wine which he now set at the side of the range.

'It won't have time to warm up, even there,' she told him. 'I'm nearly ready to dish up.'

Pat ran his hand down the side of the bottle. 'It's not too bad, I had it inside my coat all the way here.'

She went out into the hallway and opened the dining-room

door with a flourish, glad that she had made all the effort earlier, the glasses gleaming, the silver and the candlesticks.

Pat had followed her. 'Aha!' he said. 'Matches are needed. I have some in my coat, I think. I don't smoke, but I acquired some the other day thinking they might be useful.' He walked to his coat hanging in the hall and fished in a pocket. 'Yes, here we are.' It was a flat presentation pack from a smart restaurant in Belfast.

As he leaned over the table to light the candles she had a momentary misgiving, as if her small effort would seem shabby for a man used to more elaborate places. He noticed the look of worry on her face and put out his finger, touching the tip of her nose. 'Hey! Why so serious? This is splendid. I'm starving, and it really smells good.'

'I'll go and dish up, you sit yourself down, please,' Belle said.

When she came back with the two plates of salmon pâté, with brown toast quickly made, he was standing looking at some faded photographs on one wall.

'Those are my parents,' she explained, 'and Great-Uncle Samuel. He is the one who built the mill.'

'The ruin at the end of Mill Row?'

'Yes. A lost dream. Totally impractical. My father was just like him.'

'Your father just kept the orchard, he didn't farm the rest of the land?'

'Just the orchard. It's a very big one, tons of apples in a good year. He rented the other land to the Johnstons. They always wanted it.'

'You married Sam Johnston. That was . . .' He stopped.

'In the scheme of things. Now, which end do you want to sit?' She motioned with her hand.

'The end I can see you best by,' he joked, pulling out one chair with mock aplomb. 'Will madam sit here?'

As she sat down he slid the chair expertly to the table. 'Yes,' he nodded, 'one of the many jobs I did in my youth was a waiter.' He sat down opposite her, and put his head on one side, eyeing her quizzically.

'What other jobs have you done?' she asked as an opening gambit, the two of them sitting, each waiting for the other to start eating.

'I was a pump attendant too. It helped pay the way to college. We didn't have too much money in those days although my father is comfortably off now.'

'What does he do?'

'He's retired now, he says, but he can't give it up entirely, my mother's still with him, you know. He started as a car salesman and it went from one thing to another, he was always good at charming the customers, he has a good business, buying and selling machinery.'

'You never thought of following in his footsteps?'

'Following . . .' Pat seemed puzzled, as if he had misunderstood the question. He spread some pâté on his toast very deliberately.

'Yes, taking over the business when he retired.'

'Ah, I'm with you now . . . I have helped, but now I'm a teacher.'

'What about the rest of your family?'

'They're all out there, except for my sister Maureen. She married a doctor and she's living over the Border now. They moved.'

'Moved? From where?'

'From Belfast. They had problems with their kids, three sons. They were living up the Antrim Road but the boys travelled to school. There were a few punch-ups, you've heard about it happening I dare say.'

'Yes, it happens,' she said, thinking about Rory. But she did not expand. 'Your father never thinks of coming back?' she asked instead.

'Sometimes. But he's old and he couldn't live with the changes.'

'I think it's very much the same here. People are better off . . . there's just the Troubles, they get in the way.'

'Yes,' he laughed shortly, 'as you say, they get in the way. Nobody has ever put it quite like that to me before.' He bit quickly into a piece of toast.

'Why did you come back?' she went on.

'This is good,' he answered, munching. 'Are you not eating yourself?'

'Sorry. I have been asking a lot of questions,' she said, crestfallen, biting into her toast.

There was a minute or two's silence while they concentrated on eating. Then as she looked up, her question unrepeated, he finally responded.

'I came back because . . . I wanted to see how it all was. I taught in London for a while, then I came over to see Maureen and the kids. There was a job going in a primary school in north Belfast. I stayed there four years. This job at Corey came up. I thought I'd do it . . . for a while anyway.'

'Rory tells me you were in Vietnam?'

'Oh did he? Yes, at the end.'

'What was it like?' She stopped, shook her head and looked at her plate. 'Maybe you're tired of answering that question.'

'I was only there a few months. It was just another war. Like here.'

'But it's not like Vietnam here,' she protested.

'It's another war. Hey, that was good.' He arranged his knife neatly on his now empty plate.

'Rory said you know all about guns . . . we were up at the O'Briens the other day. I gather he told you about it. James has a fine old collection of his father's pistols although I think only one of them really works . . .'

Pat looked distant. 'Yes, I do recall Rory saying something about guns.'

'Do you have a gun?' Belle had asked the question in her usual direct manner without realising the implication.

He looked at her hard. 'Why should I, of all people, have a gun?'

She shrugged her shoulders. 'I thought that all Vietnam veterans had them as souvenirs . . . or something . . . it was a stupid question.'

Pat stood up, gathering the plates together. 'Not all Vietnam veterans carry guns.'

She stood up beside him, feeling that her attempts at conversation had led her into a no-man's-land. 'I'm afraid of them,' she said, smiling nervously at him, hoping that his expression would change. 'I'm afraid they are going to go off and kill someone. I was never happy with Sam . . .' She stopped. Pat looked at her. 'I was never happy with Sam having one in the house. It was when he joined the UDR. One moment he was a farmer, the next he was different, in that uniform, totally different.' Pat was regarding her with compassion now, she felt. 'I'm sorry. Sam Johnston . . . my husband.'

'Yes, I know about him.'

She turned abruptly, taking the plates from him. 'I'll dish up the ducks,' she muttered, glad to get away from his direct look. But he followed her to the kitchen. 'I won't be a moment; you pour the wine.'

'OK, I'll do that, ma'am,' he said, lifting the bottle from the warm.

Belle stood for an instant and took a deep breath. Sam was in the past. She must be able to talk about him without feeling anything. Mechanically she cut each duck in half and took one on a large plate into the sitting-room where the boys greeted it with glee. Back in the kitchen she garnished the remaining portions with oranges and carried them into the dining-room on a tray along with the vegetables.

Pat was sitting, turning his glass round and round on the polished table with his hand, his head bent, looking very serious. But when she came in he looked up and smiled.

'Here we go then? The *pièce de résistance*? My . . . what a sight!'

'Yes.' She felt quite proud of herself in that brief moment, but she told herself she must stop asking questions, stop prying into his life.

He poured the wine. As she helped herself to vegetables he asked, 'And you say someone just left the ducks for you?'

'Yes, on the hook by the back door. I haven't found out who left them. It was probably the people we saw down by the lake the other night.'

'The other night? When was that?'

'Och, one night . . . well it was late afternoon really, just before it got dark . . . we were up Top Hill . . . last Thursday I think it was.'

'Thursday,' he mused. 'What did you see?'

'Just two men. It's a strange part of the country, by the lake. Very few people go that way, it's a kind of wilderness. Only people passing by in the train would see it normally.'

'What were the men doing?' he pressed.

'Shooting I suppose, although we didn't hear shots. It was getting dark and when we came down through the orchard . . .

it's funny . . .' She stopped, then continued. 'Have you ever been to Crete?'

'No, that is one place I have not yet gone to.'

'And you came all the way back here.'

'Yes. You're right about these ducks being special, this is really good.'

'It's strange . . . coming back, isn't it?' she asked. 'I felt the same way last week, coming down the road, seeing this house . . . it all brought back the past . . .'

'I remember you and your brother.'

'Yes. John. He and I were very close. He wasn't a farmer, he just had the orchard. It was his life, his passion . . . The Johnstons look after it now. But it's not the same as living beside it, day by day, like here, watching for every bud and leaf almost. John spent hours up there, among them, just looking and pruning and looking . . .' She cleared her throat. 'They are mostly cookers, Bramleys. We could have done with some apple sauce tonight. Come back this time next year, and I'll give you apple sauce with your wild duck.'

'I'd like that. I'd like that a lot.'

'It seems so strange to be in the house without John. When my father died, oh we were quite young when it happened, John took over as head of the house. I did leave when I got married, Sam and I lived over at the Johnston place and Rory was born there. We came back here after my mother died, cancer, it was over in a few weeks. John needed someone . . . so I came home.' It seemed logical at the time, but maybe it would take too much explaining why. 'Sam was never happy here.'

'Did he not get on with John?'

'Yes, oh, yes. Most of the time. Why not?'

'Well, he was the outsider.'

'He was my husband. It was his home too,' Belle protested.

'Your brother . . .'

'He's dead,' she said flatly.

'I know.'

'He got blown up. It was Sam's car. He should have been killed. Someone thought it was Sam in the pub, they booby-trapped it while he was in the pub. John had only borrowed it . . . for a couple of hours . . . that's all. It wasn't fair!'

'But it could have been Sam,' Pat said carefully.

'Sam! John! Are you asking me which I should choose?' Belle demanded, bewildered.

'No,' he shook his head, 'I didn't mean it that way, please . . . I didn't mean . . .' He shook his head again. 'Why did you leave Sam?' he went on very quietly.

'Because of John. Sam didn't have to get involved, he didn't have to join the UDR, be a soldier. He could have stayed being a farmer. If he hadn't got involved John would still be alive . . .'

'But Sam didn't put the bomb under the car . . . a terrorist did . . .'

'Sam got involved, he got involved . . . don't you see?'

'People do get involved. For various reasons. Very reasonable, ordinary people. Sam had his reasons. The IRA have theirs,' Pat said determinedly.

'He didn't have to,' Belle said, putting her hands over her ears like a child does when its mother scolds. 'He didn't have to.'

'And you were happy with him?'

'Yes, yes . . . most of the time. But we were never alone together . . . I look back on our life together and see that we were never alone, never free, just to be with each other. At first it was his parents, then back here it was John. And then later on Sam joined the UDR . . . he was always off somewhere with them . . . or else he was over at the Johnston farm . . .'

'He could have left the UDR, afterwards, after John died.'

'He didn't. And anyway, what would be the point? The IRA never forget. Once in the UDR, always. They get them years afterwards . . . they never forget . . . we would never be safe again . . . I would always be wondering if they would get Sam next. We would never be safe . . . me . . . or the boys . . . I had to think of the boys!' She shook her head and looked down at her plate, feeling tears gathering, upset that what had promised to be a happy meal was becoming sad. She had not meant the conversation to go this way, she had wanted to talk of other things, of Pat and his life, but she had blundered in that direction and they had ended up talking of her, and it hurt.

He sensed her distress. 'What was life like for you in Belfast?'

She took a deep breath and looked Pat squarely in the face. 'I had always lived in the country. I had never gone to the theatre, to the art galleries, met people who cared about something other than the land and the weather.'

'But what about the politics? They talk about them there, more than in the country.'

'I'm not interested in politics. I just want to get on with my life, teach my boys about the world and people so that they can grow up and stand on their own anywhere in the world.' She was conscious of how many times she had made this statement, this protest of her own, and now it must sound rehearsed.

If Pat recognised it, he did not respond, but went on, 'What about the bombs, the shooting, you can't forget them.'

'I try not to watch the news bulletins on the television, or listen to the radio. It's always about killing, or politics, and if someone is shot the television always has to show the place where the blood has soaked in . . . or the soldiers and police going round after an explosion with those plastic bags, picking up the bits . . of people. I shut it out of my life if I can.'

'Have you ever been near an explosion?' he probed.

'Yes. I was in a shop once that went on fire, another time in a coffee shop where a bomb injured two people. I don't want to talk about that. I could have been hurt. I wasn't. I was just lucky.'

'Were you on your own, I mean . . . the boys . . . ?'

'Yes, yes.' She shut her eyes tightly. 'Yes, on my own. It was the only time I was in danger there, the only time, in all those years.'

'You can't shut your eyes and pretend it's not happening. Do you not know what this is all about?'

'I only know that a united Ireland is a romantic thing. It's for sentimentalists. If people were to be there when a bomb explodes, if they were to see what was left of John . . . I think they might change their minds. Some people get involved for the wrong reasons.'

'The wrong reasons?'

'They don't realise . . .'

'Are you saying that people have no right to fight for something?'

'I don't know . . . not any more,' she said wearily, 'you have seen killing, you must have done in Vietnam. Did you ever kill anyone?'

'Yes.'

'I cannot imagine you hurting anyone, not anyone,' she said vehemently. 'You're a teacher, teachers see all sides, they don't take sides.'

'What do killers look like?'

'I don't know. They probably look . . . just ordinary. I saw one once, a girl who planted the bomb . . . in the coffee shop. I recognised her, later . . .' Belle stopped, regretting her words. Why was she telling him?

'You saw her? You recognised her?'

'Yes. You see she had been in a dress shop, one I was in that went on fire. It was sheer coincidence, I suppose. I know she was in the shop with a blonde girl, the one who planted the incendiary bomb. I was right beside her, she must have planted it in the changing-room, they do that. Then months later I saw her in the coffee shop that was bombed, she wasn't with her blonde friend that time, but I recognised her, she was so striking, red hair, freckles, teeth . . .'

'How could you be sure that she put the bomb in the coffee shop, how could you be sure?'

'I just am sure. The two events fit precisely.'

'Did you tell anyone . . . the police?' he asked abruptly.

'No.' The lie was easy. 'I had not the courage. And anyway I did not want to be involved. I don't want to be reminded of all that, it's over.'

Inside she was crying: I've put it away, it's behind me, it was madness to get involved, to go to the police, madness. I put my boys in danger, something I said I'd never do. Why am I discussing all this with him? Why did I ever tell him anything about it? Madness. And yet he seems to understand, in some strange way. Maybe I should tell him the truth, tell him what I really did, see what he thinks about it all, what he thinks I should do now. I've hated the IRA for all these years for what they did to John. That's why I went to the police. At last. I felt I had to. And look what happened. No, I daren't tell him.

'Surely you should have gone to the police, helped catch her. She could plant another bomb, hurt more people, maybe kill them?' Pat pursued further.

'I didn't want to be involved,' Belle reiterated.

'You just let it lie then? You did nothing?'

She did not answer, she was thinking aloud. 'The strange thing is that I saw that red-haired girl recently, on a bus, the day my car went in for servicing. She must live in my area . . .'

'Do you know her?'

'No, I just recognised her, that's all.'

'And still you did nothing? You have every reason to hate the IRA.'

'It takes a lot of courage,' she said, unable to lie directly a second time.

'I find it hard to believe you didn't go to the police,' he debated.

'Do you? I'm a coward, didn't you realise that? I only want the easy way out.'

'No, I don't see you in that light at all.'

'Do you think I should have gone to the police?'

'Would you go? Tomorrow?'

'It's over, that part of my life is over, whatever I have done, or not done, does it matter now? I have to start again, don't you see that?'

'Are you going to stay here?'

'I don't know. I loved Sam when I married him. Now I don't know how I feel. I've locked my emotions away for so long. I only know that I must think of the boys, see them safe . . .' She drew herself up very straight in her chair and took a long sip of her wine. Pat remained silent, waiting for her to continue. 'I once thought that if I loved a man I would want to be with him . . .'

'No matter what he did? But you left Sam?'

'Can't you see how difficult it was! I loved him, but he chose to go where I couldn't follow. If there hadn't been the boys . . .'

'You would have stayed . . . no matter what he did?'

'He caused John's death.'

'No he didn't. He probably thought that by joining the UDR he was protecting you and the boys.'

'He took sides.'

'What's wrong with that? What's wrong with taking sides, following a cause if you think it's right? He was man enough to. You have to admire him for that. If John hadn't been killed, and there hadn't been the boys, would you have stayed?'

'Yes,' she whispered. 'Yes. But that's all hypothetical, isn't it?'

'He could be a killer. Maybe he has killed already. If you join the UDR you have to be ready to kill. Would that make a difference?'

'You tell me you have killed. Even now I find it hard to believe.'

'I killed . . .'

'I don't want to know how many men you killed, you're a schoolteacher now,' she said vehemently, rising from her chair, gathering the now empty plates. She had eaten the duck and all the trimmings yet she could not remember how it tasted. She had blundered into this conversation. She wanted it to stop. Deliberately injecting a note of frivolity she said brightly, 'I have a surprise for you, made it specially because Americans are supposed to love pies.'

'Even killers?' he asked behind her.

She sighed and turned to him, her hands full of plates. He took them from her. 'Yes, even killers, don't be foolish, you're not . . .' she said, smiling sadly, unable to say more.

'I understand you. Very well,' he breathed, leaning towards her. 'Yes, I understand, you're quite a lady.'

Belle headed for the door, she had to hide her face from him.

Out in the kitchen she brought the pie out of the oven, juicy and golden brown.

He was right beside her again. 'Yes, I do love pie, just like my Momma used to bake.'

'It's a peach pie, canned I'm afraid . . .'

'Looks just dandy. Mind you I prefer apple pie . . . maybe if I come . . .'

She grinned. 'Back next autumn . . .' He nodded and grinned back.

They went back to the table, the candles burning low by now, and she served the pie. There seemed to be an understanding between them, as if old sores had been unwrapped, bathed and soothed and bandaged again, and were healing slowly.

After they had finished they sat back in their chairs regarding each other without realising it for some seconds, or was it minutes? Then they smiled at each other, replete, comfortable in each other's presence.

There is a spell, a spell hanging between us, Belle thought, please don't let it be broken, not yet, not yet.

Pat leaned his elbows on the table and bent his face towards her. 'I haven't told you this yet . . . but, you look very beautiful tonight,' he whispered.

She laughed. 'Don't be . . .'

'Silly? I mean it . . .'

She leaned towards him to catch his softly spoken words. Their lips met, just touched. There was a sudden chorus of cheers and clapping from the sitting-room, from the watchers across the hall.

Belle laughed shyly and drew away. 'Those boys . . .' She shook her head. 'Where would I be without television?' She shook her head again. 'Do you want coffee?'

'No, not now.' He was looking at his watch.

'Do you have to go? Now?'

'Well . . . I don't want to be too late. There's someone I have to see before I get home tonight. A problem has come up . . . if I can get it answered, I won't have to go to Belfast.'

'Do you want to go now?'

'Not right now. It seems rude. I don't mean it that way.'

'I understand. I'll walk down to the gate with you.'

'There's no rush,' he said, as if suddenly deciding. 'Look, we'll wash the dishes first.' He was gathering the dishes together.

Belle protested. 'No, honestly, I can do the dishes, this is ridiculous.'

'I am a very rude guest, I apologise,' he said. 'We'll wash the dishes. It's the least I can do.' He had decided. He lifted the tray and went through to the kitchen, Belle following.

'Very well, if you're sure you won't be too late, if you have to see someone . . .' she said doubtfully.

'It won't take long to sort out,' he said easily, leading the way to the scullery. 'Please forgive me for seeming churlish. It's been a beautiful dinner. You wash and I'll dry.'

As she filled the sink full of hot water, squirted in the detergent and washed the dishes, he wiped carefully and expeditiously.

'You're really quite good at it,' she joked.

'Naturally, I've had a lot of practice.'

'Don't you . . . haven't you . . .?' Belle felt awkward. It seemed that every time she steered the conversation round to him he would turn it back to her again. She knew nothing of the man, but she wanted to know.

'No. I don't have anyone,' he replied frankly, 'I haven't had room in my life. I've been pursuing my own solitary course.'

'I'm sorry. I didn't mean to ask you, it's rude of me,' she said, wondering why she had to be so direct at times. 'I have no right . . .'

'You do have . . . I want you to have the right . . . I want . . .' He sighed. The last dish had been dried.

'I'll get your coat.' Belle had dried her hands and now she went to the hall. She stuck her head round the sitting-room door. 'I'm just going down to the gate with Pat. I won't be long,' she told the boys.

They rose to say goodbye. Pat bowed to them in mock politeness. 'A grand dinner, good-night, gentlemen.' He held her red jacket ready and she slipped it on. Then he shrugged himself into his black coat and they went out through the kitchen door together.

Outside the sky was clear, the stars bright pinpoints above. Belle and Pat stood stockstill on the step, gazing up, their breath hazed around them in the cold. They started up the yard, walking slowly because the cobbles were slippery with ice. Pat took her arm. It seemed so natural, to steady her, and by the time they got to the corner of the house he had put both his arms round her and they were kissing passionately.

'I –' she started to say.

'Don't speak, don't say anything . . .' he said, his lips on her eyelids, the lobes of her ears, teasing her lips, softly then hard and harder. Somehow she knew this was right, this man was right, he was the now, for ever, that all evening she had waited and hoped that he would do this, that they would come together like this, body to body, laughing, breathing, tasting each other's lips, breath to breath, tongue to tongue, it was right.

There was the sound of a car on the road, headlights swung in their direction as a car came round the corner picking up their entwined figures. They spun round in each other's arms, oblivious.

'This is . . .' she gasped. 'You'll be late.'

'Does it matter?' he asked, kissing her again, more urgently.

'No . . . but you did say . . .'

'Do you want me to stop?'

'No. Not now.'

'To the woods! To the woods!' he said dramatically. 'Only it's too cold tonight and if I take off your clothes because I want to make love to you, you will freeze to death in minutes!'

'Is that important?' She tossed her head. 'What a way to die!'

'You really mean that, don't you?' he said, serious for a moment.

She shook her head. 'You're here, now.'

'I want you, you know that, not just for a moment's passion . . . I want you, but I can wait . . .'

'You just want to be comfortable, it's too cold, and you have someone else to see,' she teased, nestling against his chest.

'You think that matters to me tonight?'

'It mattered a while ago. You said you had to go, you said so.'

'That was really only a plot to get you out here so that I could get hold of you.'

'I see. Another plot. Another set-up.' She spoke in mock severity.

'Belle . . .' He kissed her once again.

'You said you had to see someone, you'd better go, it's getting late.'

'And leave you? How can I leave you? I want to stay with you. What does it all matter? Nothing matters any more.'

'No, nothing matters.'

'Stop it!' he groaned and kissed her again.

Then he took her by the hand and bowed. 'Will you have this dance?'

Beyond the corner of the house the drive and the front lawn were pale in the moonlight. Pat put his arms around her and they waltzed slowly down the drive, deep in the shadows one moment where he would stop to kiss her yet again, and then out into a patch of moonlight where she could see him smiling, eyes shining, strangely elated.

But I feel it too, she told herself, I feel it too.

A crackle underfoot by the gate stopped them both dead. A dark figure detached itself from the shadows, two others beside it.

'Sam!' Belle whispered. 'Oh Sam!'

Two Landrovers were parked just around the corner of the gate, hidden by the pillars and the clump of rhododendrons, their lights off.

'Good evening!' was all he said. The moonlight on his face was quite clear, on his dark curly hair. She could see the hurt, the bleak hurt, she had seen it before, but this time it was closed, pale in the light.

Pat put his arm in hers and led her to his car parked on the other side of the gate. She looked over her shoulder at Sam, Sam in that awful uniform that made him inconspicuous in this light, but made him stand out by day, and he stood still staring at her, not moving. Then he turned his back on her. A quick movement. Dismissive.

'Well, now,' Pat was saying, 'I put the battery on the kitchen window-sill. I'll put it in for you . . .' He stopped. 'I'll put it in for you,' he said deliberately, 'when I next come over. It won't take long and you won't worry about the car not starting. Thank you for the dinner. The duck was really delicious.' He put his arms round her and kissed her very firmly on the lips.

'I can't,' she breathed at him.

'You can and you will, I'll see to that,' he whispered, his lips on hers. 'I'll see you tomorrow,' he said loudly, casually releasing her, then he gathered her to him again and kissed her once more. It was hard not to respond, but the spell had broken, the music had died.

I died, Sam, she said to herself, John died, I died, you died, this is my resurrection, it has to be.

Pat got into this car. 'Don't be late in the morning,' he said cheerfully, 'you know I can't do without you.'

She put her hand flat on the window by him as if she wished to touch, to caress his head, his lips once more, as though this was goodbye. As Pat switched on the headlights the two Landrover headlights were switched on too. Pat moved off slowly, up towards the village. The Landrovers followed. She watched as Pat's car reached the corner. But it did not proceed further upwards. Instead she saw the car turn, neatly, in the width of the road. Then he was coming towards her, past the house, past her as she stood there. He went on down the road, fast, followed by the two Landrovers who had turned in their tracks also, they were hard on his heels, down the long hill to Corey. Pat had changed his mind. He would not be meeting whomever it was, tonight, after all.

Chapter 14

THERE WAS THE SOUND of a helicopter, overhead, whirring, grinding.

But there were no echoes from the dull frozen surrounding countryside, the hummocky hills, the patches of flat marshland in between, the wirebrush hedgerows stiff with ice, the orchard and its tangled thickets. Another day. Oh to be able to pull the bedclothes over her head and start again, to be reborn with no guilt, no people with guilt in her life, no problems in theirs. Sam had intruded despite her efforts to shut him out. And Pat? She recognised how much she was attracted to him. It had been a physical thing from the start. She had not felt that way for a long time. She had shut herself away from such sensations.

We are coming out of the Crown Bar. It's just after eleven o'clock and Belfast is simmering under a kind of sullen heat. There is no air between the tall grim buildings and the pavements seem dusty. But then isn't every city like this in late summer?

We came into town to see a new film, about Vietnam, *The Deerhunter*. There was a bomb scare about ten minutes from the end. What does the end matter anyway?

We, I should explain – I am with a lecturer from Queen's who looks like a student. I think that he gets all his clothes from War on Want. He lives down the road, some friend of Anne's. He's a Scot although his granny came from Northern Ireland. Everybody says that.

He has been sitting for the past forty minutes talking about Nietzsche and feeling my right knee under the bar table. At last I have escaped.

And now as we stand here there's a helicopter. It's just up above our heads, and it has its searchlight on, picking up the streets nearby. The sound goes on and on. I am standing looking upwards.

Suddenly he pounces and, grabbing me by the shoulders, he kisses me hard. His beard is soft not bristly.

'I've been wanting to do that all night!' he says, kissing me again.

'Everybody is looking!' I protest.

He looks around. 'Everybody?' he asks, spreading his arms out wide. 'Everybody? Where?'

The helicopter is still grinding and whirring up there. What can they see? What is important?

'Belle! Have you no heart?' Tom asks dramatically.

'Yes, of course,' I tell him.

'Well, don't you feel anything about me?'

'It's too soon,' I tell him. I wish the helicopter would go away.

'Belle!' He pounces and kisses me again. This is ridiculous.

I tell him so. He looks sad.

'What about . . . ?' he starts to ask.

'I think I will just go home. The boys will be waiting up for me, I expect.'

'OK,' he sighs. 'You have no heart at all.'

Meryl Streep gets de Niro I decide as we go towards the bus stop.

Rory was already up and in the kitchen making toast for Conor. They were in a world of their own, just the two of them, joking quietly to each other. This morning she felt an intruder on their communion.

'Ma?' Rory asked. 'Ma? You look a bit pale . . .'

She now had to admit it. She did feel pale, shivery, eyes laden as if she had wept under the bedclothes all night. I don't do that any more, she reminded herself.

'Yes, I don't feel the best. I suppose I might be getting flu . . .

Mrs D has it. Pour me a cup of tea, will you, Rory? I'll take a couple of Disprin. My head feels a bit thick . . .'

'Ha! You've got a hangover,' said Conor cheerfully. Rory hit him sharply on the ear. 'Ow!' he protested.

'You little squirt!' Rory looked fierce. 'That's not funny!'

'I'm sorry, Mama.' Conor looked pleading. 'I didn't mean it, I was only trying to be funny.'

'Well, it's not funny!' Rory said sternly. 'Go and get your coat on, and your books, and shut up!'

'I'll be fine soon. Yes, you go and get yourselves ready for school, it won't take me long to get dressed,' Belle protested, sipping her tea quickly and swallowing the pills in a gulp. They seemed to stick a few inches down. She swallowed another mouthful but they still stuck.

The boys stood looking at her anxiously. 'I'll be great in a little while, you know me, I'm old and tough, I'm . . .'

Rory nodded his head wisely. 'Yes, we know you are.'

She drove them down to school feeling fractionally better, but conscious that her hair was not right, that her make-up had been hurried, and that she looked . . . wasted . . . that was the best word. After last night! She had wanted to look her best this morning, for Pat, yes, she acknowledged.

He was waiting at the door, smiling smugly. 'How are you this morning?'

'Great,' she said breathlessly, forgetting her flu.

'Come on, you boys, time to get indoors, the bell will go for assembly any moment,' he said, putting guiding hands on the boys' heads and herding them towards the classroom.

Belle followed behind, remembering the night before and how she had felt. Once inside Pat's small office she felt a moment of restraint. But as soon as he got the door shut, Pat put his arms around her and kissed her very firmly.

'Aha!' she said between kisses. 'So this is how you get on with the hired help?'

'Stop talking, woman, this is serious!' he said.

'We have to work, Pat,' she scolded.

'Och, forget it!'

'Aren't you going to Belfast today, you said . . . this afternoon, you said?' she reminded.

'Not at all! Couldn't be bothered. I would rather stay here, with you,' he said, kissing her again, her eyelids, her hair, her lips.

'Pat! I thought you said it was important?'

'Och, no hurry. I have other things on my mind . . .'

'Did you get to see your man last night?'

'No. Couldn't be bothered. You see what an effect you have had on me. You have me mesmerised, my woman. I could get to like your kisses.'

Bemused, Belle responded, sighing. 'You're a terrible man . . . but I like you. And we can't do this all day, we have work to do.'

'Ah! Yes!' He let her go. Then he sat down at his desk and flicked the post over in his hands. He kicked the waste paper basket out from under the desk and dropped the unopened letters in it.

'You're mad!' she laughed, bending to retrieve them. 'There might be something important there.' She stood up quickly and danced out of his long reach. 'No, there's work to be done and what would your pupils think, and what would the parents say if they went home to tell them that the headteacher was grappling with me? And what about my reputation around here?'

'Aha! Yes, we have to think about your reputation, don't we?'

'Och, be serious!'

'You're right, I shall be dying to get my hands on you all day, but you're safe. It will be difficult to resist you, but within these four walls I promise I will try not to kiss you . . . I'll only try . . .'

'You'd better get along now, your pupils await,' she teased.

'You're a terrible boss woman, did I ever tell you?' he retaliated, going out through the door.

Belle could not settle. She opened Pat's mail and laid it out for his inspection, rearranging the pile of sheets a second time.

His tweed jacket was hanging on the back of the door. She rehung it and rearranged it as it hung there, straightening the sleeves, running her fingers down the knobbly wool.

The phone rang. She lifted it and replied brightly, 'Yes, can I help?'

The voice at the other end brought her down to earth with a bump. It was Sam's mother, speaking carefully as one who is unfamiliar with a telephone is apt to do.

'Is that you, Annabelle?'

Belle took a deep breath. 'Yes, hallo, Granny Johnston. How are you . . . ?' she tried to anticipate the conversation.

'Oh, it is you then. Are you well? I heard about you . . .' Her voice died uncertainly.

'Yes, I'm back home. No doubt Sam told you . . .' Belle paused, regretting her icicle voice.

'Sam? Oh he never said a word . . . I heard it, I was in Crawford's. Sam wouldn't talk about you.'

'How are you,' Belle reiterated, 'and Grandad?'

'Oh we're fine . . . we just wondered . . .' Her voice died again. Belle had the feeling that Grandad Johnston was in the room with her, gesturing, talking quietly, propping up the conversation as a strong man will support someone who has only one leg.

'We're fine too. We have been settling in. You know how long it takes. The boys are grand. They have started here, at the school . . .'

'Oh, we did hear . . .' Granny Johnston's voice faded once again.

'Yes, at the school here in Corey. Only temporarily of course, but Mr Quinn, the teacher here, he has found room for them, till I get them settled into the grammar school if I can.'

'So you plan to stay?' The question was abrupt, to the point, raw.

'Yes. I plan to stay.'

'What about Sam?'

'What about him?'

'Well . . . he's known about these parts . . . you coming back, and the boys . . . there'll be talk . . .'

'So?'

'It's not fair on him.'

'What do you mean?'

'Well, what do you expect him to do?'

'Nothing!' Belle said flatly, feeling that this conversation was going in quite the wrong direction.

'Well, you can't just come back here and pretend that nothing has happened, that nothing has been going on.' Granny Johnston spoke fiercely all of a sudden.

'What do you mean, "going on"?' Belle asked.

'Well, you left him. Now you're back. What is he supposed to do?'

'I don't expect him to do anything,' Belle enunciated carefully, beginning to feel stirring anger.

'You're just going to move back into the House and live there, with the boys . . . my wee grandsons . . .' Her voice broke now.

Belle waited a moment or two, but Granny Johnston was silent.

She went on, hurriedly. 'We're here. And you know you are welcome any time to come and see us. But this place was my home, once . . . and I decided to come back to it. What happened between Sam and me is past.'

There was still silence. There was not even a soft background murmur that might have been Grandad Johnston prompting again.

Belle went on. 'You'll notice a big change in the boys. They are really growing fast . . . Conor is very like his father . . . please come and see us some evening, or maybe at the weekend, why not?'

Granny Johnston's voice was uncertain. 'You're sure?'

'Yes, come any time. You know you will be welcome.'

'No. You're sure this was the right thing to do?'

'It had to be done. Anyway . . . the boys should be back here. This is where my roots are, where the family comes from, mine and Sam's. We're back home. Maybe we should have come home long ago. It does no good to hide.' Belle spoke determinedly now.

'Well, then . . . we'll maybe take a wee run up to see you . . .'

'Great. The boys will be pleased. I've told them a lot about you, about the farm, about my mother and father, about it all. They are just learning, finding out. It's good for them.'

'Any time then?'

'Any time.'

'And what about Sam?'

'What about him?'

'Well, will he not want to see the boys . . . call and see . . . the boys?'

'He's been. Did he not tell you? He hasn't seen the boys yet, but I suppose he will sooner or later . . .'

'You don't mind about him . . . ?'

'He's their father, isn't he? Maybe I have kept them without a father for too long.'

'Yes . . . but you?'

'Leave it, Granny Johnston, please leave it. We'll work something out.'

'I suppose you will.' Suddenly Granny Johnston's voice sounded weary, as if she had spent all her emotions now.

'Yes, come and see us . . . soon?' Belle pressed.

'Yes, yes, we will.'

There was a click. Belle sat for a few minutes staring out of the window and seeing nothing. She did not realise just how long she sat immobile, her mind dithering to and fro, until she heard the bell for breaktime and the thud of feet in the corridor outside. The door opened and Pat's head came round the edge.

'You look very thoughtful . . .' he said.

Belle looked at him a little wanly and forced a smile. 'Yes . . .' I was just thinking . . .'

'We're brewing up, in the other room. Do you want a cup? We'll have to get you trained to produce the tea at the precise moment that the bell rings for break. I'm dying for one right now, two sugars, come on, woman, hot and sweet, that's how I like it!'

'OK, yes, I'll come,' Belle nodded, getting up stiffly and following him out of the room.

'You have the great experience of the school dinner ahead of you,' Pat joked. 'Or did you pack sandwiches for yourself?'

'I never thought, to tell you the truth, I suppose it will have to be school dinner if there is some for me?'

'Oh, we'll get you fixed up. After break I thought of just the task for you. The school reports will be going out in a few days. You could do all the envelopes, and generally sort it all out for me. I shall have to spend an evening filling them all in, it's quite fun trying to think what to say . . .'

'But I thought it was all heartfelt.'

'Of course, of course, but we run out of remarks, we're bound to. Could do better, promising start, disappointing start, there is a formula.'

Belle laughed. 'Don't try to fool me. To think that when I was small the remarks the teachers put on my report had me in tears often.'

'Well, now you know. We're all con men . . .'

'Where's that tea?' Belle asked.

As silence descended once more on the schoolrooms after break, Belle seemed to be more relaxed but worked as an automaton. When the bell finally went just after three and there was the rush and growl of noise as the children departed, Pat's reappearance round the door served to further her desire to wrap the past and the future of her existence around her. She suddenly wanted to know how she stood with Pat, how he felt about her, but she realised such thoughts were fanciful and premature in the extreme. She was regressing, behaving like a teenager. Yet when he held her elbow as they stood on the step of the school together, that seemed an answer of a kind to still her impatient thoughts.

'Conor tells me that you are brewing flu,' Pat said in her ear.

'Oh, did he?'

'Yes, I must say you have been a little abstracted, a little pale today . . . after last night . . . are you feeling as if you are getting flu?'

'Yes. I think I must be. Mrs D is full of it. But I'm tough. I never get it badly. I can shake it off, never fear.' She spoke firmly but recognised now the physical symptoms which she had been trying to keep at bay all day.

Conor appeared by her side and tugged her sleeve, looking up at her anxiously. 'Mama?'

'Yes, love, what is it?'

He did not reply, but stood grasping her hand tightly. Across the yard Belle could see Rory deep in conversation with a friend who ran off when Pat and she approached, Conor still clinging to her.

'Ma?' Rory asked. 'Could we go down the road to the shop?'

'The shop?' Belle queried.

'Yes, McGuigan's. Tony says you can get snares there. I thought I might put some up in the orchard . . . for rabbits . . . for eating . . .'

'Catch them?' Conor asked in a curious voice, his eyes wide.

'Yes. Everybody does it in the country. Why not?' Rory's voice was assured, authoritative.

'Do you know how to set snares?' Pat asked in some amazement.

'Oh, it's quite simple. Tony there,' he pointed to the disappearing friend, 'has told me all about it. There are bound to be rabbits, aren't there?' There was a note of cunning in his voice.

'And where precisely do you intend to set all these snares then?' Pat went on.

'Oh, on Top Hill . . . I'll only set three or four, half a dozen at the most,' Rory said confidently.

'When are you going to set them?' Pat asked. He looked thoughtful. 'It's not really the right time of the year. The spring's the time.'

'Well, I thought about Saturday . . . I thought we could go up then . . . would that be all right, Ma?'

Belle was going to mention the Johnstons but she changed her mind. Better that they turned up out of the blue without any preamble.

'Well, now,' Pat said, 'snares the boy wants. Let's take a dander down to the shop and see if they have any. It's a long time since I set a few snares.'

'Did you ever catch anything?' Conor asked him. He let go Belle's hand and danced around to Pat's other side, looking up at him in wonder. 'Did you ever catch anything big . . . really big . . .'

'Like what?' Pat laughed. 'They are not man-traps, though if you did get your foot in one you could trip up, break an arm if you weren't careful.'

'Oh.' Conor sounded disappointed.

'They're only bits of wire, you silly,' Rory told Conor bossily.

'Oh,' Conor said again, open-mouthed.

They were walking down the road from the school to the shop. They went into the grocery and hardware side, the doorbell clanging just like up at Crawford's shop in the village. There the similarity to Crawford's ended. Inside it was all bright shelving bulging neatly with goods. And on one side of the shop the hardware section showed the only remains of Quinn's shop, the old store, for there were rows of shelves stretching up to the ceiling with strange and unfamiliar objects vying with the bright and shiny. Spades and forks, boxes of screws, hinges, electrical fitments in plastic packs, while as Belle raised her eyes, she saw lamp mantles, yellowing boxes with obscure cooker fitments, scythe blades and more yellowing boxes without an indication as to their contents.

Jimmy McGuigan was behind the till, stout, in his fifties with a dome-shaped shiny head, for his hair grew like a tonsure. He had a brown overall on, two pencils well sharpened in the breast pocket and one behind his ear.

'Right, Pat,' he said as they stood by the hardware counter. 'Right, Pat. I see you have company today.'

'Aye,' Pat said briefly, nodding his head. 'Aye. You won't know of the Neills up at the Big House . . . Neill the man has been dead these long years, and the wife, she was a teacher . . . this is the daughter . . .' He looked down at Belle standing beside him.

'Neill . . . that wouldn't be the young fella that got blew up, would it?'

'Yes,' Belle said shortly, 'my brother,' and swallowed.

'I never knew him myself but I wasn't living here then. My brother had this place. You probably knew him . . . Michael . . . gone to the south . . . it's Mrs Johnston, wouldn't that be right?' The man was looking at her curiously, his hands in his pockets.

Belle swallowed again.

'We were looking for snares . . . for rabbits?' Pat said.

The man still stood looking at Belle. He didn't move.

'Got blew up, yes, I remember. UDR he was.'

Belle eyed him coldly. 'No. He had nothing to do with the security forces. Nothing at all. It was a mistake.'

'Oh, I thought . . .' the man continued.

'He wasn't. I should know, shouldn't I?'

The man took his hands out of his pockets and rubbed them down his expansive chest nervously. 'Well, that's what I heard . . . but then I was away over –'

'Do you have some snares, Jimmy?' Pat broke in.

Jimmy McGuigan stared at him for a moment and then coughed. 'Snares? Right enough. Yes, I have some somewhere. Are you thinking of taking up snaring rabbits, sir?' He turned and stood with his head back, surveying the topmost shelves.

Pat pointed to one end where an elderly box sat, the label half torn off. 'Would that be some?' he asked.

'You're the one with the sharp eyes,' Jimmy said. 'He can see in the dark, you know,' he whispered, leaning towards Belle. 'Where are you going to set them?'

'I'm not,' Pat said, 'this young fellow here is. Young Rory here, the big boy.'

'Oho!' Jimmy eyed him critically. He had found a step-ladder and placed it against the stack of shelves. As he climbed it slowly he looked down on them and again put a question. 'And these must be the Johnston boys? You need to be careful where you set them snares. You might catch more than you bargained for. You'd better not be prowling around. Not after dark. Not in these parts. Does your mother know that?' He talked as if Belle was not there any more.

Rory nodded, looking upwards as Jimmy fastened his large hand on the box and started down the ladder again clutching it. 'I have a friend . . . he knows all about it . . .' he started to say.

'Sure, you should ask Patrick here. He's a man knows everything. About everything. Isn't he the schoolteacher?'

'Could you show me, Pat?' Rory looked at the tall man eagerly.

'Yes, some time. But it will have to wait this week, I have a few things to see to the next couple of days,' Pat replied.

'Oh, that's right,' Jimmy said knowingly. Pat gave him a hard look.

'Would you know where to set the snares . . . up on Top Hill even?' Rory demanded.

Pat broke in quickly. 'It's just a question of seeing the lie of the land, and where they run . . . how many snares did you say you wanted?'

Jimmy was levering off the lid of the box. Conor was standing on tiptoe trying to see inside it. Belle lifted him up.

Rory surveyed the contents. 'Would there be four there, do you think?'

'Four rabbits?' Conor's voice piped up. He had been following the conversation with growing excitement. 'You'd catch four rabbits?'

'No, silly. Maybe one, but not four, not at once.' Rory gave his brother a disdainful glance. 'You have to spread them around . . . be selective . . . isn't that right, Pat?'

'Yes . . . it might take a few days to catch one at all, especially at this time of the year. Maybe it would be better to leave it for a few weeks.'

'Ma?' Rory looked at Belle.

'How much are they?' Belle asked.

'They won't break the bank . . .' Jimmy turned the box round and peered at the label. 'Seven and sixpence it says. Shows you how long they've been up there. When did they change the money?'

'Nineteen seventy-one,' Belle said.

'There now,' Jimmy pursued, 'all that length of time ago. You think about it. We were already fighting then.'

'Fighting? What do you mean?' Belle asked, bemused.

'The Troubles, missus. Nineteen sixty-nine. That's when they started. Two years even before they changed the money . . .'

'How much are you going to charge, Jimmy?' Pat Quinn intervened.

'God alone knows . . .' Jimmy was saying wonderingly. 'All those years ago. You forget.'

'How much?'

'Och, say a pound,' Jimmy said, pulling a bundle of wire out of the box and trying to unravel the snares one by one.

'How many are there?' Pat asked.

'Looks like four, or five, or maybe six . . .' Jimmy said. Suddenly he put the lid back on the box and thrust it into Rory's hands. 'Here, I couldn't be bothered. Call it a pound.'

'Thanks,' Rory said, red-faced with expectation.

Belle put Conor down on his feet and then felt in her bag for her purse and extracted a pound coin. 'Maybe you should wait a while before you set them, Rory, maybe it isn't quite the right time of the year, like Pat says.'

Rory looked downcast. Belle sensed his disappointment. He was trying so hard not to be a city boy. The country boys would be up the hedgerows soon looking for birds' nests. Maybe she ought to get him a dog, a border collie, to follow his footsteps up Top Hill and lick his heels as he went through the long grass.

Pat seemed to sense it too. He put a hand on the boy's shoulder and said cheerfully, 'We could wait until this cold spell is over, and then set them. You never know. Could be over in a few days, by the weekend even . . .'

Conor interrupted. He had slunk into a corner of the shop and found a pile of comics. He pressed against Belle's legs. 'Can I have a comic, Mama?' he asked softly.

'This is turning out to be an expensive trip,' Belle said. 'First Rory wants a whole pound for the snares, and now you.'

'Och, Mama!' he said, pleading.

She laughed, and bent down to him, straightening his coat collar in an automatic reflex. 'How much do you want? Would fifty pence be enough?' She felt in her purse and then counted five ten-pence pieces into his sticky palm. He clenched his fingers quickly as if the coins might escape of their own accord.

'I'll go and take a look,' Rory announced. 'He knows nothing about comics, he's only a baby!'

'I'm not! I'm not!' Conor cried.

Rory was striding across the shop, Conor following, putting his feet down determinedly.

'I think that a glass of lemonade is the answer,' Pat said.

Belle looked at him in surprise. 'Lemonade?' she asked.

'Next door.' Pat looked in the direction of the pub. 'Since you are brewing flu and obviously need some medication, I'll buy you a hot whiskey to ward it off, and these two thirsty fellows can come over later when they have chosen a comic for a lemonade. Is that OK, you guys?'

'Yes, yes,' Rory said from the other end of the shop. 'Great!'

Pat took Belle's arm and guided her out of the shop. As they went in through the adjacent pub door, Belle was astounded to see Jimmy McGuigan behind the bar of the dim brown-painted room. He nodded at her.

It was a long thin room, the bar at the far end, and warm with a small turf fire burning in a fireplace halfway down one long wall. A large Jameson's Whiskey mirror hung above the fireplace. There was a long wooden bench on the opposite wall, with above it, high on the wall, two stuffed foxes' heads, and one hare's. She stood and read the words on the plaque on which the hare's head was mounted: 'This hare was caught and killed on 1 April 1905 after being followed for four hours and thirty-three minutes.'

'How could anyone chase a live thing for so long?' she asked.

'Some people will never give up the chase . . . never give up an idea . . .' Pat said drily, pointing to two tall stools that stood by the bar. He gave her his hand while she perched herself on one, tucking her feet on the rung below.

'Right, Jimmy,' Pat said to the fat man who stood impassively, his hands flat, his fat fingers spread on the bar top.

'Hot whiskey?' Jimmy asked.

'You're on your own today, I see,' Pat observed, just as Belle was about to make some remark about Jimmy looking after both ends of the store.

'The wife's off. Over the Border. To see a cousin. Took bad he was. Yesterday.' Jimmy's explanation was brief. He plugged in an electric kettle, stooping low, then stood up breathlessly. 'What are you on today?' he asked, looking at Pat.

'It's a cold day. Make it two,' Pat said, 'I'll keep the lady company.'

Jimmy turned and slowly filled two glasses with whiskey, scattering in some cloves and spooning in sugar.

Pat sat on the other stool and rested his elbows on the bar top, turning his head and looking at Belle. 'How is the flu?'

'Oh, it's there. But I told you, I'm tough and your remedy is bound to help,' she assured him.

Pat touched her forehead with gentle fingers and said softly, 'You do feel as if you have a temperature. We'd better get you straight home after this.' He cupped her cheek in his hand then. She saw concern in his eyes.

The kettle boiled and Jimmy filled the glasses, stirring vigorously so that the sugar was dissolved, then he set the drinks before them.

'*Slainte,*' he said.

Pat raised his glass. '*Slainte,*' he repeated. 'Would you not take one yourself?'

'Och, well thanks. I'll take a half" un later.'

'Cheers,' Belle said. She sipped her whiskey slowly, feeling its warmth slide down. 'With a name like McGuigan, you wouldn't be any relation . . .' she started.

'Barry,' Jimmy anticipated. 'No, he's from Clones way, we're from Monaghan mostly. Great boxer though.'

'I suppose everybody asks you that,' she said.

'Och aye, a few does. Strangers. Like yourself,' he replied.

Belle wanted to protest, but she said nothing. She was a stranger. She was beginning to see that now.

There was silence between them. Then Jimmy cleared his throat and said, 'Right, sir,' looking at Pat. 'I'll just go. See if those boys have got that comic chosen yet.' He went out through the door behind him that led to the other part of the store.

'Is that doing any good at all?' Pat asked, leaning towards her.

'Yes, definitely.'

'It's just as well I didn't take you to the woods last night,' Pat laughed, 'you'd have pneumonia by now.'

'You're awful!'

'Well, that got a smile out of you. You have been looking too serious today. Is everything all right?'

Belle felt she had to tell him. 'Granny Johnston phoned. It's all so complicated. I thought coming home would be easy, straightforward. I never thought about Sam really . . . not at all.'

'Not at all?' Pat asked her, puzzled.

'I just decided. That's all. I had other things to worry about . . .' She stopped then, feeling that she was saying too much.

'Other things?' Pat prompted.

'Not important, not really . . .' Belle shrugged her shoulders, trying to appear nonchalant.

'There is something, isn't there?' Pat insisted, staring at her. 'What are you afraid of?'

Belle was saved from having to reply by her two boys coming through the door in a rush. They slammed it behind them and Conor hurried to her side holding up a comic for her inspection.

Rory set his box of snares down on the bar counter with a sigh. 'Did you say something about lemonade, Ma?' he asked.

'I did,' Pat said. He was still watching Belle's face.

Jimmy McGuigan appeared behind the bar again. Two glasses of brown lemonade were set up for the boys with straws. Rory refused to use his. He was in a bar. Big boys didn't use straws in bars. For a time the only sound was of Conor sucking noisily through his straw. Jimmy stood looking impassive, saying nothing, arms folded.

Belle felt awkward. 'You live . . . here . . . isn't that what you said?' She was looking at Pat.

'Me?' he asked after an instant's hesitation.

'Him?' Jimmy answered for him. 'Sure he's over there.' He jerked his head over his shoulder. 'Did he not tell you?' Belle looked at Pat, waiting for him to explain. But Jimmy went on. 'He's in the back room. Over the store. At the side. He used to have it. Years ago. When he was a boy. You know. There's an outside staircase. Runs up the side of the shop. He had nowhere, when he came. And like, he and I are connected . . .'

'He means we're distant cousins,' Pat put in quickly, 'but then isn't everyone connected around here?'

'Like I was saying,' Jimmy continued, 'I put him up with me and the wife. Our kids are grown. Left. We only came here because of my brother. He was . . .' for once his staccato conversation slowed, 'retired. We live upstairs. Then Pat cleared out the old room. Seemed a good idea. He has it now. Just like the old days, he says.'

'That's right,' Pat agreed. 'It's two rooms actually, bedroom and a living-room, a small stove to cook on, with a bit of bathroom next door. It's all I need. I don't need much room.'

'Had it when he was a boy,' Jimmy intervened.

'Well, there were quite a few of us, brothers and sisters, it was quiet so I could study, I liked reading a lot in those days. I wasn't here much, really.'

Belle looked at him and tried hard to remember more about the tall gangling black-haired boy who had stared at her.

'I went away to school,' Pat continued. 'I think that my mother feared I might be following in my father's footsteps.'

'So she sent you away?' Belle asked quietly, sensing something hidden and bitter.

'Yes,' Pat replied. He did not meet her eyes with his own.

There was the sudden sound of a Landrover outside which became the louder sound of two engines. A door slammed. There were snatches of conversation.

'Jeez!' Jimmy McGuigan said under his breath. 'Jeez!' he repeated.

The door opened and four UDR soldiers came in, their large green bulks filling the doorway. Sam was the first to enter the bar. He stopped in his tracks when he saw her.

'Sam,' she said. She slid off the stool.

He gazed at her impassively. Then he looked at Jimmy McGuigan, ignoring Pat Quinn who stood looking laconically at him and his companions. Belle caught sight of a yellow Labrador dog.

'Mr McGuigan,' Sam began, 'we're on a check. All premises. Upstairs too.'

Jimmy looked at Pat. Pat said nothing. 'Upstairs?' Jimmy said eventually, and he cleared his throat again. 'And the wife's away!'

'Take the man up,' Pat drawled, 'take him with his dog. What have you got to worry about, Jimmy? He's got nothing on you!' He stared at Sam and it seemed to Belle that they were like cowboys in a saloon in some Western, facing each other out, waiting for the draw.

Jimmy lifted the bar flap and stood aside as Sam Johnston, followed by a soldier with the dog on a lead, stepped past him and through the door at the back of the bar. Jimmy followed the soldiers, casting one last glance over his shoulder at Pat. Belle watched as the soldiers passed her, silent, only watching, seeing that green uniform, the flak jackets, the guns. In time they heard footsteps overhead.

Then it was Rory who spoke. 'Hey, Ma? Ma?' he whispered loudly. 'That was Dad!'

Conor squeaked, 'Dad? Which one? Which one?'

Belle's eyes suddenly filled with tears. Was it rage or self-pity, she asked herself crossly. Two soldiers stood in the bar looking at her, staring at her and the boys, hearing Conor's voice repeat shrilly, 'Which one, Mama?'

'He's busy,' she said. 'He's gone to check the premises for explosives, that's what the dog is for.'

'Which one?' Conor's voice cried out.

'The big strong one, the one in charge,' Rory said. 'Silly, imagine not knowing . . .' Belle heard the contempt in his voice and realised that it was purely defensive.

Poor Conor. He had been only a baby when they had left. He only remembered his father from a photograph. It was all her fault – or else it was Sam's for being so proud, for not coming to see them in Belfast. Numbed, she said, 'We'd better get outside, you've finished your drinks, haven't you? We're in the way. We had better get outside now, it's time to get on home, anyway.'

'But Dad!' Conor's voice was a wail.

'We'll wait for him outside. But he has to search here now, and we'll be in the way.' Belle moved to the door. Pat was beside her, unspeaking. He held open the door while she and the boys went out, his face a mask.

They stood uncertainly on the pavement outside. There were two Landrovers parked, drivers keeping the engines running and two soldiers were positioned on guard, crouching, one by the edge of the building, the other by the door of a terrace house across the wide street, his eye to the sights. A handful of small children stood about staring. Belle saw a curtain twitch in the window of a house opposite. Two women stood some twenty yards away, coatless despite the cold, and motionless. Apart from the sound of the engines, and the fitful crackle of the radio strapped to one soldier's back, there was no sound. Then the door of the pub opened quickly and Sam Johnston with the dog and its handler, followed by Jimmy McGuigan, and the other two soldiers, came out. Sam walked to the corner of the shop and surveyed the side of the building where the staircase ran upwards to the old storeroom, now Pat Quinn's small home. He turned and looked at Jimmy. Jimmy looked nervously at Pat as if seeking some response from him.

Pat Quinn stepped forward. 'That's my . . . flat . . . I suppose you'd call it. It's not much, but I call it home . . .' He smiled deprecatingly at the old phrase.

'Right,' Sam said firmly, and gestured to the handler to go up the stairs. 'Is it locked?' he asked. His voice was harsh.

Pat looked at him coolly, fishing in his pocket for the key which he held out. 'Yes, here's the key.'

Belle could not help comparing them as they stood glaring at each other. Pat stiff as a ramrod, a little taller but more slightly built than Sam who stood, legs apart, aggressively strong, and in command.

'Are you going to search the whole village?' Pat's question was direct.

'Only this. We have instructions to search these premises,' Sam said, taking the key from Pat's hand and going to the foot of the staircase. The dog handler followed him.

Something on Pat's face made Belle act at once. She stepped quickly to Sam's side. 'Sam!' she stormed. 'Sam!' He stopped and looked down at her impassively, but did not reply. 'This is ridiculous! You know it is, Sam.' She lowered her voice, trying not to let the other soldiers hear.

'What is?' Sam asked.

'All this! Don't be ridiculous. Do you really think that Pat Quinn is likely to have explosives in his flat? It's only two rooms!'

'It's OK, Belle,' Pat said, spreading his arms in an expansive gesture. 'He has his job to do, like anybody else. I'll not stop him.'

The dog was standing halfway up the stairs, sniffing with interest. The handler had his head turned, trying to catch the conversation which was almost too low for him to distinguish, but he sensed an argument.

‘Sam!’ Belle said again. ‘There’s no need to take it out on Pat . . . please, there’s no call for this . . .’

‘Oh, you’ll vouch for him then, you know all about his flat, do you?’ Sam asked, giving her a look.

‘Sam!’ she reproached him. ‘There’s no call for this,’ she repeated. ‘Please don’t be daft.’

‘Dad?’ Conor spoke. A whisper.

Sam Johnston stared down at his small son and looked at him with an expression Belle could not read at first. Then she understood. It was not surprise, or affection, or even distaste. It was, she realised, recognition, for beneath the dirty fair hair that was so like her father’s, Conor’s face was just like Sam’s, not John’s, after all, the frank expression in his eyes, the stubborn chin, the full bottom lip. She bit her lip, and felt Pat beside her.

‘I’ll be up . . . later . . .’ Sam said gruffly. He ruffled the boy’s curls, then he caught Belle’s eye, seeking her approval.

She nodded. ‘Dad’s busy. He’ll drop by later. Sam, you will?’

Conor nodded, breathing, ‘Later, later,’ still staring at Sam.

Belle’s eyes searched Sam’s face. Abruptly he turned.

‘Right, that’ll do, we’ll leave this one for another day,’ he told the handler. She saw him nod coolly at Pat as he handed him back the key.

Belle took Conor’s cold hand in hers and led him up the road towards the schoolyard where she had parked the car. He dragged his feet, his head turned, staring at his father. Each step she took away from McGuigan’s seemed a din in her ears. Why oh why? Was there never going to be an end to it? Last night she had been happy. But it could not last, she might have known that. Happiness for her was only to be snatched, as if she was a pickpocket, and if she was caught there would be retribution.

She heard a quiet exchange of words and looked back, seeing Rory at Sam’s side speaking to him. She wondered what he was saying. Pat was standing with one hand paternally on Rory’s shoulder. Pat and Sam still stood as if weighing each other up. Then Sam turned on his heel and climbed into one of the Landrovers.

Seconds later the two vehicles passed her, accelerating, going up the road towards her home and the village beyond. The street was empty. The two women had gone indoors, the children too, the excitement was over for another day. Only the solitary fat figure of Jimmy McGuigan standing at the pub doorway watching and looking. And she saw Pat and Rory following in her footsteps towards the schoolyard.

Belle reached her Mini and unlocked the door with impatient fingers. She bundled Conor inside and waited until Pat and Rory eventually reached her. They seemed to be walking very slowly. Rory was carrying the box of snares carefully and she heard them talking about Top Hill and where to set them. Had they talked about Sam? she wondered. Why had it all gone wrong? she asked herself again. She got into the driver's seat and waited while Rory seated himself beside her. She shut the door.

Pat leaned down at the window. 'You're off then?' he asked.

'Yes. Thank you for the whiskey. I'll go home. I've had enough of soldiers.'

'Yes.' Pat nodded, his eyes narrowed. 'That was plain stupid back there.'

'Sam was being unreasonable.'

'He has his job to do.'

'He had no right . . . oh, what's the use . . . I'll see you tomorrow.' She tried to smile at him.

'Thanks,' he said.

'Thanks?' she said, puzzled.

'Dad's gone, hasn't he?' Conor said in a low sad voice.

She cajoled him. 'Only for now. He said he would drop by later, when he's not on duty.'

'Belle?' Pat started, then paused as if at a loss for words.

She looked at him and waited.

'Thanks,' he said again. She wanted to ask him what for. He had paused once more, and was looking up the road where the Landrovers had gone. Then he straightened up and said decisively, 'Take care, Belle.'

She started up the engine. As she turned out of the schoolyard she saw Pat standing immobile looking after her. I don't begin to understand you, Pat, she said to herself.

Chapter 15

DAWN CAME TO THE village, to the House sitting blindly at its foot, the curtains drawn, no lights showing at the windows. Behind it the orchard stretched grey and crisp and breath-biting all the way up Top Hill, the long lines of trees shrouded in the early morning stupor of ice, the sinuous branches of blackberry and late robin-run-the-hedge intertwining with dun-coloured dying grasses. Spiders had spun their webs glimmering among the tall fronds. A lone fox stalked from tiptoe to toe through the ice-laden grasses, bright-eyed and watching.

'Ma! Ma!'

Rory found Belle on the stairs, stiff, asleep with her head on her folded arms. She was on the third step from the bottom. It was morning, it was Thursday.

She had put herself there when she had finally got the boys to bed because from this vantage point she could see the driveway to the house. She had been waiting for Sam. And then when he didn't come, she had gone to bed. But she couldn't sleep. So she had got up, wrapped her dressing-gown round her with an old rug for extra warmth, and had put herself on the step again, on guard. She had felt vulnerable, in danger, but she could not rationalise why. Her life was beginning to fall into a pattern here. Belfast was miles away. Was it the tension she had sensed when the soldiers had searched Jimmy McGuigan's? Was it merely the hated uniform that had stirred her? Or had even that uniform reminded her of her reason for running away, reminded her of

Sergeant McEvoy and his small cramped office at the station on Donegall Pass? It was there, still, lurking, possible and impossible.

'Mama?' Rory said, standing beside her. He was already dressed for school. She raised her head and blinked, forcing herself awake.

'I'm fine,' she assured him. 'Put the kettle on. I'm just cold. Is Conor awake yet?' Her voice seemed loud in the empty silence about her.

'No. He's sound asleep . . . Dad didn't come at all?'

'No,' Belle said flatly. 'No, he didn't come.' She looked sceptically at her elder son.

'Ah well,' he said, sounding like a grown-up, 'he had his reasons . . .' He started down the stairs. 'I'll put the kettle on. You go and get some clothes on, you must be foundered.'

Belle went upstairs and into the grey gloom of Conor's room. All she could see was a tuft of his hair sticking up beyond the blankets. She knelt beside him and turned back the edge of the covering and looked at him as he slept. His hair was plastered to his forehead. As she stared his eyelids quivered, and he was aware of her presence.

'Mama?' he said slowly.

'Yes, I'm here. It's time you were up. Rory is already dressed and downstairs. You don't want to be late for school, now, do you?'

He turned over and faced the wall. 'I don't want . . .' he started.

'Conor,' she said gently, caressing his head, 'come on now?'

'He didn't come.'

'No, he didn't . . . I expect something happened, he had to work late . . . and then he probably thought you boys would be in bed asleep. He'll come another day, today maybe, you'll see . . .'

'He didn't come,' Conor said again.

'Now, don't start all that again,' she warned. 'He didn't come, I know, but there was a good reason why not, I'm sure. I explained all this last night.' And I'm tired of explaining, she said to herself.

There was the sound of a Landrover. And it was coming from the village. It paused. She heard it coming up the drive.

Conor heard it too. 'It's Dad!' he squealed, tumbling out

beside her and running to the window. He pushed the curtains aside impatiently. 'It's Dad! It is Dad!' he said with certainty.

Belle stood up and went to the window. 'So it is,' she said, seeing the driver of the vehicle which was approaching the house slowly. 'So it is. Now you,' she grabbed Conor by the arm as he headed for the door, 'you are going to get dressed, now! Do you hear me?'

He looked up at her and gulped, 'Yes! I'll get dressed,' wrenching away his arm and going to the pile of clothes on the floor by his bed. He pulled off his pyjamas and fought his way into his vest. She stooped to help him get his arms through the armholes. Then she dressed him while he stood on one foot and then the other, hearing first the knock on the door, the bolts being pulled back, the sound of Rory's greeting, the voices, one pitched high with excitement, the other low, slightly hesitant. 'It is Dad!' he whispered to himself. 'It is!'

Belle watched him run to the door when he was dressed and she followed him out on to the landing, listening then to his feet thudding down the stairs to the kitchen. She stood at the top of the stairs watching him go. A figure was standing in the hall, looking up at her.

'Belle?' he said.

'Dad! Dad!' Conor shouted.

Sam was still looking upwards although his small son was now clutching at his trouser leg. 'Belle?' he called again.

'I'll get dressed,' she said and went into her room. She dressed with care, and splashed cold water on her face in the bathroom. The face that looked back at her from the mirror was blank. She applied some make-up, her fingers moving automatically. She raised an eyebrow at her reflection, but there was no response, no understanding in the face that looked back at her.

Sam was standing with his back to the range warming himself. He was in uniform. Rory was beside him with the toasting fork. She looked out of the window to the Landrover. It was empty. Sam seemed to be on his own.

'You're not on duty?' she asked, going to the table where Conor was spooning cornflakes into himself, eyes on his father, not on the bowl.

Sam's glance followed hers. 'I am, officially, but I'm alone, it's against the rules I know. I just dropped by for a moment.' Then he nodded in Conor's direction. 'A big man like him needs a good breakfast before going to school. Rory here is making toast for us, and the tea's made.'

'Good,' she said, choosing a chair and sitting down at the table beside Conor.

Sam poured her a mug of tea and set it before her. 'You look as if you could do with this. Rory says you weren't well yesterday, getting flu he says . . .' She heard concern in his voice and steeled herself to reply.

'Yes, that's right. But the hot whiskey helped . . . Pat . . .' She had said the wrong thing, she knew instinctively.

'Oh yes, him,' Sam said.

Belle turned her attention to Rory. 'Have you even started your breakfast?' she asked crossly. 'You can't make toast all morning!'

His eyes reproached her. 'Yes, Ma, I've finished toasting this piece,' was all he said, going to the table with a plate piled with toast. He selected a slice and started to spread it with butter, crunching into it with relish.

'We'll never have time to eat all that toast,' she went on.

'I hope there's enough for me,' Sam said, drawing up a chair and sitting down at the table too. He spread a piece of the toast with butter. He had seated himself opposite her, and Belle was conscious of his scrutiny.

'Apart from looking tired,' Sam answered her expression, 'you look well, not a –'

'Not a day older, you're going to say?' she interrupted.

'No, not a day older. And your hair . . . it's different . . . curlier . . . like in the old days, when you were at school . . .'

'That's in the past, Sam,' she said firmly. But she ran her fingers through her hair.

'Are you going to take us down to school . . . in the Landrover?' Conor had finished his cornflakes.

'Do you have time to take them, Sam?' Belle asked. There was no disguising the sarcasm of the question. Last night's wait, the long agonised wait when her small son had watched for Sam to come, followed by his hysterical crying, finally silenced by exhausted sleep, was uppermost in her mind now.

'It's awkward, I have to . . .' Sam started.

Rory seemed to sense his father's disquiet. 'You're going on patrol then?'

'Yes,' Sam explained. 'We have information . . . an alert. You boys mustn't say anything about this at school, mind you . . . if they were to know we know, then we mightn't catch them at it. So not a word! Not a cheep!' he warned severely.

'I'll take you boys,' Belle said, and sighed audibly.

'Look, Belle . . . about yesterday . . . last night . . . I was out on patrol . . .' Sam said.

'Are you boys going to get yourselves ready for school, get your coats on?' she asked. 'What time is it anyway?'

'Time enough, Ma,' Rory said. He had been eyeing the toast and thinking about another slice.

'Look at the time, Rory,' she said, pointing to her watch.

Rory sighed. 'Come on, Conor.' He poked his brother who was sitting staring at Sam.

'Stop it!' Conor protested, moving his body out of reach. 'Stop it! Leave me alone!'

'Have you finished?' Belle asked him gently. Conor nodded. 'Well, away and find your things then, that's a good boy.'

'Is Dad . . . ?'

'Dad will be here for a wee while. He won't go without saying goodbye.'

'OK then.' Conor slid off his chair and went out of the kitchen with Rory close behind, one finger pressed into his small brother's back. 'Och, stop it!' he said again.

'Get on, Rory, don't bully him!' Belle said.

'They're grand boys,' Sam said. He stared directly at Belle now. She saw that he had grey hair at his temples and that the lines at the corners of his eyes when he frowned were deeper. 'About yesterday . . .' Belle stood up. 'Look, Belle, I'm trying to talk to you!'

'What about?'

'Yesterday.'

'What about yesterday?'

'Pat Quinn.'

'Pat? What about him?'

'What do you know about him?'

'What do you mean?'

'I asked you what do you know about him,' Sam reiterated. 'Sit down, woman. We need to talk about this.'

Belle sat down again. 'Well?'

'Have some more tea,' he said.

'I don't want any more tea. I don't have time for any more tea.'

'Pat Quinn is –'

'He's the schoolteacher. He's been there a year or so. His family had the shop, you remember, years ago . . .'

'His father –'

'His father was interned, a Republican . . . does that matter?'

'His father was a womaniser and a Republican.'

'So?'

'I'm concerned about what you could be getting involved in . . .'

'What I'm getting involved in?' Belle cried angrily.

Sam looked at her furious face and said sternly, 'Yes.'

'It's no business of yours,' she protested.

'If it involves my boys, it is!'

'You are the limit! You are suspicious of everything, aren't you? Everyone?'

'I suppose . . . yes, I suppose I am.'

'Can you just not accept that there are some people who don't want to get involved in politics . . . and everything?'

'Not any more. It doesn't pay.' His face was stony.

'You're very hard,' she spoke bitterly, 'very hard.'

'No, I'm a realist, that's all. Pat Quinn comes from a funny family . . .' He held up his hand as she was about to speak. 'No . . . a funny family . . . neither one thing nor the other. Neither Protestant nor Catholic. But both, if you like, all mixed up. He's not like one of us . . .'

'You're as bad as James, down at the Lodge, as bigoted!' she cried indignantly.

'Ha! James. That fool!' There was scorn in his voice.

'You are as bad,' she insisted.

'Thank you for the compliment.' Sam stood up. She had struck home.

'Look, I don't believe Pat is interested in politics, or fighting . . .'

'How do you know?'

'We've talked . . . the other night . . .'

'Ah, yes, the other night.'

Belle pressed on. 'Maybe it's because he was in Vietnam . . . he's seen enough of it . . .'

'Ah yes, Vietnam.'

'You know about that?'

'We know a lot about everyone . . . I shall have to go. I can see that it is of no use whatsoever talking to you. You are as awkward as ever!'

'You said I hadn't changed,' she threw at him.

'I thought that you might understand what I've been trying to tell you . . .'

'Oh, I understand,' she nodded, 'I understand . . .'

'Look, Belle . . .'

'No, you look. I'm home. But I have changed. It's all changed. Don't you see that? We can't step back and pretend that nothing ever happened between us . . .'

'It wasn't between us, you know that. John was between us.'

'Oh, why must you bring him up? Why must you remind me?'

The kitchen door opened with a rush. The two boys flung themselves with their schoolbags into the room. Belle stood up quickly and looked once again at her watch. 'I'll get my coat,' she excused, conscious of Sam standing beside her.

'Dad?' Conor said, standing on tiptoe. 'Will you be coming again?'

'Of course, don't be stupid,' Rory chided, before Belle could speak.

Five minutes later they stood together in the yard.

'It's icy, I should warn you . . .' Sam said, but stopped, seeing the guarded look on Belle's face.

'When are you coming again?' Conor demanded.

'Some time. Tomorrow maybe. It depends . . .'

'He's busy. Understand, boys, busy,' Belle said pointedly.

'I'll come again,' Sam said resolutely, lifting Conor high in the air so that he squeaked and depositing him in the back seat of the car. Rory slid into the front seat while Sam now gravely handed Belle into the driver's seat. His grasp was very tight. She had forgotten that.

'I will come again,' Sam called as Belle started up the car and headed for the road.

Halfway down the hill to Corey a small white car shot out of the Lodge gates in front of her at such speed that she had to put her brakes on suddenly. Her car slewed on the ice.

Conor and Rory drew in their breath. 'Wow!' said Conor. 'Christ!' said Rory in an unexpected oath.

Both cars were now stationary; the white car had spun around also in its efforts to avoid Belle's Mini. It was Jean.

She looked a bit flustered. She got out of her car and came over to Belle who now stood beside hers, trying to stop her knees from shaking.

'I'm sorry, Belle! I'm sorry! Are you all right? Oh, I am so stupid!'

Belle put her hand on Jean's arm. 'We're all right. Don't worry.'

'I was just going down to town to get something for our lunch. You haven't forgotten?'

'Would it be more simple if I didn't come to lunch today? Please don't go to any trouble because of me. Look, the roads are awful, don't go into town, please.'

'Oh, you must come to lunch! You must! I need you there . . . you're the only one can talk to James!'

'What's up with him, anyway?' asked Belle.

'Oh, it's all so difficult. First he gave off about the new curtains. We needed them so badly, they cost so little really. I never spend money on the house, he never lets me . . . and my major, as James must call him, came over for dinner last night. He was absolutely furious about that.'

'I had a dinner party the other night,' Belle said brightly. 'We had wild ducks. Do you know who might have left them for us? They were on the hook by the door, the usual place.'

'Your Sam I should think,' Jean said shortly. 'He has left me some on several occasions, sometimes a rabbit too. Ducks are a bit of a treat. He doesn't get out shooting very much.'

Sam. Belle hadn't thought that he might have left them. And that night, the night of her return, how he had looked at her. 'Look, Jean, maybe I shouldn't come to lunch today, I have been feeling low. Flu I think. I could come another day. What about next week?'

'No. No. I insist. You have to come. You see . . . it's about . . .' She suddenly reddened.

'What is the matter?' Belle demanded. 'What has happened?'

Jean gave a nervous, almost joyous laugh. 'It's my major, you see,' she said succinctly.

'What about him? Jean? You not going to tell me . . . ?'

'He has! He has!' Jean nodded, eyes wide with suppressed excitement. 'He has! Last night! After dinner. We were washing the dishes. It doesn't sound romantic, but . . .'

'And you've told James. That's another reason for him being cross. What did James say?' Belle asked in her direct manner.

Jean whispered conspiratorially, 'He doesn't know . . . not yet . . . I haven't told him.'

'You'll have to tell him soon enough. You are going to marry your major, aren't you? Don't worry about James . . . Marcus can sort him out in the long run . . . it's time you had a life of your own.'

'I don't know whether I can leave James. It's so difficult. Last night, when he asked me, I was so sure, so positive . . . And now I don't know what to do.'

'And you're going to tell James over lunch, is that it, when I'm there?'

'Yes. I thought your presence would help . . . you are such an old friend, Belle. He would listen to you,' Jean implored.

'You said he was in a foul mood this morning. Do you think this is the time to tell him?'

'Yes. Yes. I must know, have it settled. I can't wait.' She seemed childlike now in her determination, hugging her secret in glee. 'Don't worry about James, he has these days. By the time I get back from the shops he could well be his old self again . . .'

'You're sure he has no idea . . . about your major proposing and all that . . . you didn't give him a hint?' Jean's demeanour was so frantic and pent up, surely perspicacious James could not fail to notice.

'No, I don't think he has guessed. He's cross every time my major comes, my James . . . oh, I didn't tell you . . . he's called James! Isn't that strange . . . James. I'm in love with a man called James.' She smiled that silly smile again.

Belle laughed now with her. 'Yes, how strange and how . . . no wonder James is bemused. I'm so glad. Oh Jean, I'm so glad about him.'

'Now promise me you will be there. I need you. Do you understand why? James – brother James – oh, this is all so confusing . . . he is just being silly and demanding and possessive. I have my own life to lead.'

'Well, if you're sure . . .' Belle was doubtful.

'Of course I'm sure. You have to come. Promise me! Now, that's all settled, I'll see you later.' She was climbing back into her car.

'What on earth was all that about?' grumbled Rory.

Belle decided not to elaborate on the conversation. 'Oh, it's only Jean getting into a fluster. She has got herself into a panic and James is in a foul mood.'

'I don't like James. He's creepy,' Conor said in a small voice from the back seat.

'So you've said,' Belle said drily.

'Yes, creepy, very creepy,' he said again. 'I like Mr Quinn, though.'

'Do you? I do too,' Belle said, smiling to herself, wondering how Pat would be today, and how he might greet her.

'I like Dad too,' Conor added confidentially in her ear.

'And how is the patient today?' Pat asked when she got in. He helped her off with her coat, then cupped her chin in his hand and studied her closely. 'Mmm . . . a little tired perhaps . . . but otherwise . . . let's feel the forehead . . . mmm . . . a little feverish. Is there no cure I can provide at all?'

'Och, Pat!' She shook her head in mock dismay.

'How are you really?' he breathed in her ear.

'You said we had to behave . . .'

'You said,' he explained. He put both his arms round her and held her tightly to him. 'You said . . .'

She felt her body respond. She had negated these feelings for so long that now she was surprised and elated by them. She lifted her face to his and murmured, 'Well, you agreed . . .'

The bell went for assembly. Pat took his arms away at once. 'Ah, time's up,' he reproved her.

When he reappeared at breaktime she reminded him that she was going over to thc O'Briens for lunch.

'I'll probably be gone by the time you get back, you could finish off those reports for me, if you feel like it,' he replied.

'Gone?' Belle was puzzled.

'I shall have to go to Belfast after all. I don't have a class after lunch today, only games, and Alan says he'll take it for me. They can play handball in the gym, it's too cold and slippery outside for them. Somebody might fall and break something. I might as well get off as early as possible if I am to get back tonight.'

'I thought you thought it wasn't important.'

'No, it can't wait apparently. I'll have to go. They rang this morning, early. It has to be settled.'

'Is this the same thing you had a letter about?' she asked, trying not to sound too curious.

'I'm going to have to give them my opinion. Look,' he sounded suddenly brusque, 'it's not something that can be handled over the phone. I'd better get on, I'll see you tomorrow, bright and early. Tomorrow is going to be a special day.' He caught her by the shoulders and spun her around.

'Pat! In what way special?' He was looking strangely exhilarated.

'Just special. Take care.' He kissed her lightly on the lips.

There was no sign of Pat when she left to go to the Lodge for lunch, but she could hear his voice in the classroom talking to Alan, so she supposed that he was sorting out some last-minute arrangements and should not be disturbed. She got into the car wishing for the moment that she could get a last look, another look at Pat before she left, to imprint him on her memory once again.

Belle drove up through the demesne and as she neared the Lodge she saw that the front door was open. There was no sign of anyone outside. She went up the steps and stood inside the hall, feeling it cold, as if the door had been open for some time and what little heat had been in the house had quickly dissipated.

'Jean?' she called. 'Jean?'

There was no reply. The door to James's room lay open, open wide this time to anyone's gaze. Belle looked inside. It was empty except for the paraphernalia of the years, the wallful of faces staring and vacant. Back in the hall she called again, 'Jean! Jean! Are you there?' a bit louder. Still the silence in this strange listening house. She stepped up to the dining-room door which lay half ajar. She peeped in. The table was laid for lunch for three. Everything looked as usual. But where was Jean? Out in the kitchen, busy with pots and pans, making too much bustle to hear her at the door, she just hadn't heard her.

Belle went down the dim narrow corridor which led to the kitchen, red-tiled, uneven, dank. She had some difficulty getting the kitchen door open. The door from the kitchen into the backyard with all its collection of relics was wide open, a draught whipping in.

Behind the door from the passageway, the door she had pushed open, she found Jean sitting with her back against the wall, looking. Belle could not see her eyes, for there was a great meaty hole in her face, and a lot of blood spattered on the clothes drooping from the airer overhead, shirts to be ironed, tea-towels, a flowered dress.

I feel nothing, nothing, nothing, she said, then realised that she was screaming it.

When the police arrived, roaring up the long drive, racing up to the house, Belle was sitting on the top step outside the front door. She had not remembered dialling '999', she was sitting sipping cool lemonade with Jean, and John, poor John, and waiting for the sound of shots which she knew she had heard already.

Two UDR Landrovers arrived shortly afterwards. One soldier picked her up in his arms, put her beside him in the passenger seat of her car and drove her the short distance up the road to her home. He carried her upstairs and undressed her until she was naked and shivering before him, then he wrapped her in her dressing-gown, tucking her up with two hot water bottles.

She did not speak. He stayed with her, stroking her hair, calling her name which she did not seem to hear, until Mrs Donnelly came and took over, holding her tightly, rocking her to and fro, clasping her to her bosom with work-worn hands, calling her name over and over again. 'Come on, my baby, my baby, my baby.'

It was then that Belle cried.

Chapter 16

IT WAS PITCH BLACK dark when Belle awoke.

The house was silent, silent as the grave. Two hot water bottles lay like cold stones on her chest. She was like some Niobe, full of tears.

She slipped out of bed and felt her way to the end of it, to the round black knob of the bedpost, grasping it with dead fingers, feeling like a blind person in the dark. For a moment she thought that she could no longer see, that some great catastrophe had struck her down, stone blind and deaf, for she was in this total void. Spreading her hands in front of her she walked flat-footed to the door and felt around on the wall beside it for the light switch. The click of it, the flood of light overhead, denied her fears.

She opened the bedroom door and went out on to the landing, walking barefooted, on tiptoe, to the boys' rooms. She moved like some pale spectre, gliding through the half light of the landing, hardly pausing. The boys' rooms were empty.

Oh God! God! Why has it got to be?

I am standing at the doorway of John's room. The room is empty, of course it's empty. There is the bed, his bed, the trousers he wore yesterday hanging over the end of the bed, two crumpled socks on the floor, a paperback he has been reading lies open, upside-down on the floor beside them. There is that picture, the print of Monet's garden in Giverny with the trees, the one I gave him for Christmas, on the wall. I can see the apple trees, they look like apple trees. That is why I bought the picture for you, that is why. Because of the orchard.

I can feel a strange shudder in my body. I have felt it before, several times. It is as if some giant hand is taking me, squeezing me, tearing me, oppressing me. But I know what it is. I have felt this kind of sensation before. 'John! Oh, John! And where's Rory? He's not here, not in bed!'

'There, there now,' Mrs D is beside me. She has her arms about me and is leading me away from the doorway, from this room, from John. But John is not here. In bits. In bloody bits. I could not even look at his body when they took me to see him, in that mortuary at the hospital. I could not look. I told them, I said, I must look, he is my brother. But I could not. Marcus looked. He just said, 'Yes. It's John Neill.' He did not say any more. I looked at Marcus's face and he looked at me. And nodded his head. Now I know it. I have seen it in Marcus's face. He is dead. That's it.

'Come away now. Come into bed. Rory has gone over to Granny Johnston's, your Sam took him over.' It's Mrs D leading me into that big room, to that bed, and urging me to get into it, lifting my feet on to the mattress, tucking me in, smoothing the coverlet. 'There now, you need to get warm, get comfortable, there, there,' she is saying. She sits patting my hand. 'There. There.'

'I feel . . .'

'It's the baby, isn't it?' she asks, but she knows. This baby I have been carrying, this second son for Sam, it is going to be born, and soon. 'We've phoned for the doctor. We phoned him as soon as Marcus brought you back from Armagh. I told them. So we phoned. He'll be there soon.'

'Where's Sam? He's not here?'

'You know what he did. He had to take Rory over to his mother's, get him out of the way of all this. You know.'

'But he didn't come with me.'

'He didn't because you wouldn't wait for him. Now he has gone, he's gone out on patrol . . . after what happened to John, do you blame him?'

'He was away so long . . . I had to go.'

'It was lucky Marcus was only down at the Lodge. He took you.'

'Hold me, hold me,' I am crying. I know that the doctor will not be here in time. He will not be here to see my son born. Conor. Why must I exchange one for the other?

'John!' Belle cried out. She heard her voice echo somewhere else in the house. She heard footsteps on the stone floor of the hallway and went to the banister rail, gripping it, looking down. A solitary figure, a soldier, was standing in the light of the open kitchen doorway, looking up, running one hand through his rumpled hair as if he had just been awakened from sleep, fitful sleep.

'Belle!'

'Yes, it's me,' she finally whispered and went down towards him one step at a time, like a child who has only just mastered stairs, stiff and unsure, holding on tightly to the banister rail. At the bottom she stopped and swayed and the soldier put his arms round her, drawing her into the kitchen and the bright heat.

'Sam?' she asked unnecessarily. 'Sam?'

'Yes. Sit down. Sit down where it's warm. I'll get you a cup of tea.'

'The boys are gone. Gone!' she said, her voice rising.

'They are at my mother's. I took them over. To give you peace.'

'To your mother's?'

'Yes. They are safe and sound. But it was better for you.' Sam poured her a cup of tea and held it between his large hands for a moment while it cooled. Belle did not speak. She sat there looking at the fire.

'Here,' he said eventually, 'take a sip of this.' The tea was hot, but she sipped first tentatively then steadily as Sam held the cup to her lips. She was awake now, awake fully to everything and everyone, for ever and ever. Amen.

'That's better.' Sam said it for her. She took a deep breath, and he went on. 'You remember now, do you?'

'Yes.' She was remembering the body and the blood, the deathly hush of the Lodge as she had stepped inside.

'How do you feel?'

'I'm fine. Fine. As long as I don't think about it, see it.' Then she shook her head. 'Where's Mrs D? She was here, wasn't she?'

'She's gone home. She's worried out of her mind about you. She wanted to stay but she's dying on her feet with flu. I sent her home to Willy. I thought she would never go, but she did in the end. It was for the best, and you were sleeping at last.'

'And you were here,' she said, looking at him sadly.

'Yes, for once I was here.'

'Poor Jean.' Belle saw her again, that awful picture flashing into her mind's eye. She shook her head as if to dislodge the image.

'Belle.' Sam put out a hand over her clenched fingers, clasping firmly. 'Don't, don't think about it, not now.'

'But I must, how can I not? It was awful. I can still see it when I shut my eyes.'

'It's done. You must try to forget.'

'No, I have to know what it is all about. You have to tell me, explain what happened,' Belle demanded fiercely.

'I don't think that . . .'

'Sam. I'm not a child to be humoured. Tell me! Tell me about Jean! Poor Jean.' She shook her head again and moaned, 'What happened, what on earth happened? Who would shoot her? Why, oh why? It's something to do with the IRA, isn't it? It's to do with Marcus?'

'What?' Sam was astounded, incredulous. 'Marcus?'

'Yes. He's tied up with the paramilitaries and he carries a gun. You know there have been occasions when people have been shot by mistake or as a punishment. I thought maybe . . .. they had come for Marcus, to kill him, and got Jean instead.'

'Hah!' Sam's voice was scathing. 'Marcus is comparatively harmless. Yes, I know he carries a gun. He hasn't a licence for it, but then he's like a lot of other people who feel they need the protection . . . if that's the word. No, he knows a few villains, and he's probably on somebody's list for demolition some time, but no, it wasn't Marcus. It was James.'

She stared at him. 'James? He wouldn't . . . no, I know he's weird, but it's only the drink. He wouldn't go that far. How could he?'

'Well, it looks as if he did.'

'When I went in the door, when I found her . . . I thought maybe it was some punishment or something to do with Marcus.'

'No, it was James apparently,' Sam asserted.

'Where is James now? He wasn't at the house . . . I didn't see him. Have the police found him? He must have gone mad, or been very drunk.'

'Oh, they've found him. They found the car, easy enough to spot, that white car. Then they started searching.'

'Where did they find the car?'

'Do you remember the cottage at the back of the demesne? By the stream. Derelict. You and John used to go swimming there in the summer. You told me about it. And you used to pick plums there too, you said.'

Belle looked at him strangely. 'Yes, I remember the cottage. Did I tell you about it? I don't remember telling you . . .'

'They found his car there, in the lane by the cottage. Then they went to the stream. They could see his body in a pool. He must have drowned himself.' Sam spoke unemotionally, it was better for Belle that way.

'The pool,' she said, 'but there wasn't much water, it wasn't all that deep.'

'He must have been very determined.'

'Determined . . . yes, he must have been desperate.'

'You and John used to go over there for a swim the odd time, didn't you? It was a secret place, you said, we Johnstons never knew about it.'

'Yes, it was a special place for John and me.' Belle could feel her face burning. But it was only the heat from the range, surely. 'I remember Jean telling me how she and James used to go there too. It was so . . . quiet, I suppose, shut away from the world, from other people, you could pretend . . .' she said.

'He must have been out of his mind with drink. Why shoot Jean? She looked after him all these years.'

'He always had a thing about guns, even as a child I remember that. He used to shoot rats. It was a kind of game to him.'

'This was deadly serious. We'll probably never know what happened to set him off. He was obviously unhinged.'

'I met Jean, on my way to school,' Belle started to remember. 'Yes. She was going to town to shop, something for lunch . . . you know she was always doing that, at the last minute. Yes, she said James was in a terrible temper, about the new curtains and – of course!' She stopped in amazement. 'Of course!'

'What?'

'Her major. She said she hadn't told James. But he must have found out. James must have guessed. That's it. That's the reason.' She nodded her head in understanding.

'Belle. Would you please explain?'

'Her major. She was in a fine old state. Her major was over for dinner the night before and he proposed. When they were washing up, she said.'

'What?' Sam was amazed. 'He proposed?'

'Yes. And she was going to marry him. She said so. Quite definitely. She wanted to be sure I was coming over to lunch so that she could tell James then, she said he would listen to me. I suppose she thought my being there would help . . .'

'And you think James guessed already.'

'Yes. She was so excited. He must have guessed. It was the final straw, I suppose. He must have been furious. Poor Jean. She had so much to look forward to after all these years.'

'They always were a strange pair,' Sam said as if thinking aloud. 'Together all those years. Unnatural in a way. When I heard abut Jean's major I wondered if she might have found herself a husband at last.'

'They were too long together, they were the last of another generation, the genteel kind, who lived in the past, not in reality.'

'You're a fine one to talk,' he chided, putting his arm across her shoulders and ruffling her hair with his fingers. 'You and John were the same, really, dreamers . . .'

'That's not fair. You don't understand,' she said abruptly, staring angrily at him. 'You never did understand John and I.'

'Didn't I? I think you're wrong there. Very wrong,' he said sourly.

'You don't understand. How can I make you understand what I felt when he died? He was my brother. I loved him.'

'Yes, I know how much you loved him, I know, but what about me?' Sam said. He stared into the fire, a lost, hopeless look.

'Sam. Don't look like that. How can I tell you? It was as if part of me died too, which sounds silly, doesn't it? He and I . . .'

'No. I do understand. I think I understand better now. You have told me all I need to know . . .' He stopped and looked at her, his voice dying.

Chapter 17

SAM AND ANNABELLE SAT ON together in the kitchen until a pitiless light started to seep in around the curtains. Maybe they slept, but they did not speak if they stayed awake. The life in the range died lower and lower, until it was finally Sam who stood up and put a shovelful of coal on it, poking up the embers. He went to the window and drew the curtains. There was a bleak day outside. Still it had not snowed. James had said that it would not. He had been right even to the end.

Belle stood up and pulled the kettle to the front of the hob, an unconscious gesture born of habit. Sam looked at her. 'I'm fine,' she answered his look.

'You'd better take it easy today.' He stood beside her, looking down with an expression she could not read.

'Why? I'm not going to stay cooped up in this house . . . not all day!'

'Don't you think . . . I won't leave you for long . . . Belle . . .' He put one arm round her shoulders.

'I've heard that before. I can't stay here. I couldn't stay here. I'll go to work. That will occupy me.'

'Down to Corey,' Sam said morosely.

'Yes.'

He drew away. 'To him.'

'If you want to put it that way. Does it matter?'

'Belle.'

'No, tell me, does it matter to you, now?'

'Yes.' He stared at her as if seeing her with new critical eyes.

'I don't understand. You didn't come near us in Belfast . . . a parcel at Christmas, on the boys' birthday . . . that was all.'

'I know.'

'Why? Didn't you understand the reason I took the boys away, the reason I couldn't stay with you?'

'I thought I did. But I didn't think you would stay away. I thought you'd come back . . . you have . . . but it took longer than I expected . . . Belle . . . I've missed you.'

'Has anything really changed? You're still the same! In that uniform!'

He turned his head away from her accusing eyes and was silent.

'I'm going to work,' she said, heading for the door. 'I'm going to get dressed.'

'Belle . . . we have to talk.'

'Perhaps it's too late for talking. I have to go to work.' She started up the stairs.

'Belle . . . stay a moment?'

'No,' he heard her reply.

He stood in the kitchen, disconcerted. 'I see,' he said eventually to the empty room. 'I can't argue with you, I know you only too well.' He went to the door and called up the stairs, 'I'll make the tea, don't be long.'

Belle found some warm clothes to wear, but still felt cold. She drew the bedroom curtains and watched Sam walk down to the gate, his shoulders hunched, tired, not the proud straight-backed man she had once known. Where was he going? She could see the top of his head as he got near the gate, then he paused and stopped. Did he know about the box for the milk? Apparently he did. Or did he? She watched him walk back up the drive in the growing light. He had a piece of paper in his hand.

She went downstairs and was opening the kitchen door when he came round the corner of the house. 'It's freezing,' she said. 'What have you got there? Is there no milk? How did you know to collect it from the tin? Cathal thought it would be safer in a tin.' She looked at her watch. 'It won't be here for another half hour at the least.'

'Oh, we found the tin the other night when we were waiting at the gate for you. Seems like a good idea, so long as . . .' He stood on the doorstep and thrust the piece of paper into her hand. 'Do you know what that means?' He watched her curiously as she read it aloud.

'Friday's Milk: 4 yoghurts, ¾ pt double cream, 50 lb potatoes. The bill must be paid. It's just a note for Cathal.' She waved a hand dismissively.

'Did you put this note out? I have to know.'

'No. I have never seen it before. What's it for? Let me see it again. Who would want fifty pounds of potatoes anyway? Fifty pounds? Why not two or three stones? That's daft.'

Sam was standing there with the note in his hand, reading it over again and then looking at her, his dark eyes intent.

'What does this mean?'

Sam is standing in the yard shouting at me.

'What does this mean? You thought that I wouldn't come home early today, didn't you? You thought that I wouldn't get this until you had gone, didn't you? Even when I came in from work you just looked at me and told me you were going shopping with the boys in Armagh, getting a lift from Marcus you said. And you just walked out the door, leaving this note upstairs, on our bed. You're going, aren't you?' He is standing over me, bending over me, shouting and waving the note. 'Dear Sam,' it says, 'I'm going away with the boys. I can't stay here. Not now. Love. Belle.' He reads out the words in cold fury.

'Ssh! The boys are in the car, with Marcus, he's waiting for me. Do you want everyone in the village to hear you? The boys don't understand, not yet. I'll explain to them. Later.'

'The boys. Is that what it's about? The boys?' He lowers his voice a little.

'No. Not just the boys. But I can't stay here. I've tried.'

'You're just going!' he shouts again.

'Yes.' I wish he would stop shouting.

'That's final?'

'Yes.' It must be, I tell myself.

'Where are you going may I ask?'

'To Belfast initially. Marcus thinks he has found me a job.'

'Marcus? How long has he known about your intentions? You'll tell him, I notice, not me!'

'Only a few days. He's taking us to Belfast. I've packed the main stuff, all I think we will need.'

'You could talk to him, but not to me.'

'He said he would help me. He's an old friend,' I plead.

'I see.'

'No, you don't. You never have.' I am beginning to weep, I try to stop, gulping on the words.

'Haven't I?' he asks, sadly and quietly now.

'No. You haven't been able to talk to me for years.'

'For years you say?'

'Well, since John died. It's no good, Sam.'

'Is that my fault? I've tried to make it up to you, I've tried.' He is looking at me with such hopelessness.

'It's no good!' I am crying now, once more, I can't stop.

'It's still my fault?' he goes on.

'Yes. Yes. Your fault.'

'And there's nothing I can say?'

'No. You'll never change, you're too stubborn and too proud.'

'Then that's it.' He stuffs the note into his pocket, turns on his heel and walks quietly to the back door, going in and shutting it.

'This is the second note,' Sam muttered thoughtfully. Standing in the yard and unbuttoning his top pocket, he stuffed the note in. 'I made the tea. I'll not stop. You'll have to take yourself down to work, if you're going.'

'What's the matter? Are you in a hurry?'

'I'll have to go up the hill, see someone.' He strode to his car.

'Now? Have some tea.' Why can't he wait? she wondered.

'I'll not. I'd better get off at once,' he said.

'What's all this about?' she asked, incredulous. 'I don't understand.'

'On second thoughts, I don't think you should go down to Corey today,' he said, 'I think you would be safer here.'

'Why on earth not, Sam? This is ridiculous. I have to go, you know that. I can't stay in this house.'

'I'll try not to be long, I told you, wait for me here, please?' he pleaded. 'I'll be back. We can stay together.'

'I have to go.' Belle stamped her foot like a small child thwarted.

'To see Pat?'

'Why do you have to put it that way? I need to get out of this house.'

'I understand,' he said, speaking slowly. He took her face in both his hands and bent to kiss her lips tenderly. She had forgotten how sweetly his kisses tasted. 'I understand,' he repeated.

Belle spoke as firmly as she could although there was a lump in her throat. 'Do you really understand?'

Sam took her chin between thumbs and forefingers, hard, it hurt. 'Don't tell anyone about the note . . . or anything.'

'About the note? No. Why should I?'

'Just don't. Promise me!' he reiterated.

'Yes, I promise.'

He climbed into his car, slammed the door and drove off at speed.

Belle drank her tea very slowly, then eventually she got into her car and drove down the road to Corey. Sam had not returned. She drove unseeing past the gate-lodge down the road to the school.

Chapter 18

PAT HAD GOT TO SCHOOL before her. He looked tired, grey, drawn. She went into the office, ducking her head, but he had removed his arm as if he wished to distance himself from her. He turned back into the office behind her and shut the door, leaning against it, folding his arms across his chest.

'You look tired this morning,' he said without emotion or warmth.

'I was just thinking the same about you,' Belle replied, looking up at his set face and wondering what words to use, or even what more she could say.

'Oh, I'm fine. Dandy.' He clipped the words.

'So am I . . . really . . . I still think that the flu is going to get me, but it's not too bad . . .' Her voice tailed off. 'How was Belfast? Did it take long for you to sort out the problem? I suppose you were pretty late getting in last night?'

He looked at her for an instant, uncrossed his arms and turned from her. 'How can you be so calm?' he asked over his shoulder, hiding his face, standing at the desk and turning over some papers absently.

'Calm?'

He walked to the door, turned the handle, opened it an inch or two, then shut it again, and turned to face her once more. 'Yes . . . calm.' Belle looked at him but did not speak. 'I understand you found Jean O'Brien's body yesterday.'

'Yes, I did.' She nodded slowly.

'Why are you here today?'

'I couldn't stay at home, not there. I wanted to be down here . . .' With you, Pat, with you. But perhaps that was best left unsaid, looking at his stern face, his stiffened shoulders. 'How was Belfast?' she repeated, determined to turn the conversation.

'Necessary.'

'Did you manage to sort it out . . . whatever the problem was?'

'It wasn't a problem. It was a clarification. They wanted some information. I supplied it. And I had a question. They answered it.'

Belle waited for him to say some more, but he merely buttoned up the two buttons on his formal grey suit, drew his steel-rimmed glasses out of his pocket and put them on, each movement measured, calculated, as if he was avoiding speaking. 'Look,' he said, 'I'd better get off to class now.' He opened the door once more. Halfway out of the doorway he stopped and looked at her. 'I meant to ask you . . .' he began.

'What?'

'What about your phone?'

'What about it?' She was bemused.

'I rang you a couple of nights ago and it didn't seem to be working . . . is there something wrong with it?'

'No . . . nothing, I just didn't feel like answering it,' she said airily.

'I see. I see.' He frowned.

'Do you?'

'Well, if there was an emergency, one of the boys was ill, or something . . .'

'It's perfectly OK. I didn't answer because I thought it might have been . . .' She stopped, wondering what this questioning was all about.

'Were you worried . . . that it might have been Sam?' he said, eyeing her.

'Yes. You've guessed. Of course.' If he needed an easy explanation she could give it. She had wanted to tell him the whole truth today, when he had time to listen, but he was so cold and unresponsive.

'I see,' he said. 'I'll go off now.' He shut the door after him quickly.

Belle stood in the middle of the office and looked at one desk, and then the other. What was all that about? she asked herself.

She felt disinclined to work. She looked out of the window. The yard was empty, the road was empty, the village, like her own, had died. Jean had died. Two army Landrovers sped down the road; she craned her head to watch them. They sped through Corey and on down towards the Border and were soon out of sight. They were travelling fast, not the usual cruising speed. Was there trouble on the Border? Sam had said something about an alert, that they were expecting an attack of some kind. She wondered if he was in one of the Landrovers.

She took off her jacket and hung it up on the peg on the door, each movement slow, deliberate, as if she felt she must tranquillise herself and not let other images intrude on her consciousness. She wondered about the boys, whether Sam's father had brought them to school, playing grandfather after all the years of separation, and whether the boys would be shy with him. She felt regret now for the years that she had denied Sam's parents the chance to play that role, hiding away in Belfast. She had not asked Pat about the boys, she had been diverted by his cold manner. Where was the man of the night when they had waltzed in the starlight? Was it merely that the food and the wine had brought a madness into their relationship? Was he merely flirting with her, following in his father's footsteps, and regretting it? Would work and school and the daily routine now be the norm? She had armoured herself against all feeling for too long.

At breaktime Rory's head appeared round the office door. Conor slipped in a few moments after Rory and they stood side by side at her desk, not saying much, Conor fiddling with a ballpoint pen and staring at her.

'I'm fine,' she told them, 'these things happen.'

'I said I didn't like Uncle James,' Conor said quietly. 'He's creepy . . . I mean, he was creepy.'

'Shut up, Conor!' Rory said. 'Shut up!' He grabbed his brother by the arm and squeezed it tightly so that Conor's face screwed up in pain.

'Stop it!' Belle said. 'It happened. These things do. It's just another killing, another death, that's all. James went a little mad . . .'

'I thought they were married, I mean, him and Jean,' Conor said, determined not to be put off by his brother's physical admonition.

'No,' Belle explained, 'sometimes brothers and sisters get like that if they live together for too long.' She tried to divert their morbid thoughts. 'Now what are you boys going to do after school today?'

'Grandad Johnston is going to collect us and take us home after school . . . to the farm,' Rory said. 'I wanted to come home,' he added, 'but Granny Johnston says you'd be better off on your own for a while.'

Grandad. Granny. How strange the words seemed to her. So she was to go home to the House. To do what? she asked herself. At least with the boys in the house she would have something to do, to occupy her thoughts. She was too tired to argue. Maybe it was a good idea. She should go to bed early and try to shake off this lassitude, this malaise. Perhaps there would be an old movie on TV, a Western, a shoot-out, blood on the sand. How ironic it seemed. The school bell brought her back to the present.

Rory was already halfway out of the door. 'It's Pat's class next, history,' he said, 'it's very interesting . . . the way he tells it.'

Conor lingered, looking up at her with wondering eyes, big and round like Sam's. 'Will you really be all right, Mama?'

'Yes,' she said gently, 'you go on ahead. I'll see you tomorrow.' She felt tears of self-pity gathering.

'He's nice . . . Dad . . .' Conor said.

'Yes.'

'He's not as I imagined. I was only little, wasn't I, when we left. I didn't remember him at all. He's quite big and strong, isn't he?'

'Yes,' she said, swallowing hard.

'He hasn't always been a soldier, has he? I mean he used to be a farmer, like Grandad Johnston. I want to be a farmer when I grow up.'

'I thought you told me you wanted to be a soldier? And it was only yesterday!'

'I just want . . . I want to be like Dad.'

'Yes. You'd probably make a good farmer,' she said, 'now isn't it time you went into class?'

'OK,' he nodded. 'But he is nice, isn't he?'

'Go to class,' she barged.

He went out. She heard the sound of children's voices die to a familiar murmur. She closed her eyes. It was no good. Her mind kept coming back again and again to Jean's face, what was left of it, to the hole in her head. She thought that she had put it all behind her, but now it was only too easy to let all the vivid technicolour pictures come into her mind again.

'Belle,' Pat's head was round the edge of the door. She looked at him but hesitated, finding it hard to speak.

'Yes,' she said eventually.

'You just don't look well. Would you please just take yourself off home?' His voice was hard, impersonal.

Belle stood up reluctantly and reached for her jacket hanging behind the door. 'Very well,' she said, realising that her voice was husky, not because of the flu, but because she could not find words easily to talk to him.

He stood beside her, helping her on with her jacket, easing each arm patiently into a sleeve as if she was one of his smaller pupils. She looked up at him. His gaze was impassive.

He doesn't know how to talk to me, she thought suddenly, that is the explanation. He doesn't know how I feel about Jean . . . or anything. I don't think that he wants to know. He just doesn't understand me. He doesn't want to. I thought that he was a compassionate man. I thought that he liked me, even a little. And today, he promised, was going to be a special day. I need him now. Doesn't he realise that? She was disappointed.

Pat looked down on her very coldly. She raised her eyes to fix her gaze with his but he had shut her out in some strange way that she could not understand. She waited for him to respond to her gaze, taking in the details of his face she thought she had retained from memory, and finding out that they were not quite the same. There was the set of his jaw when he was determined on saying something, the curve of his lips when he smiled, though he was not smiling now. All she saw was that his eyes were dead, distant, almost disparaging.

As if he sensed her reaction to him, moment by moment, he put out a hand and touched her forehead. 'You do still seem a bit feverish,' he observed, 'take yourself off home to bed, stay indoors. I understand from the boys that their grandfather is going to take them off to the farm after school. They are better out of the way.'

'I would rather have them with me.'

'No, they're better off there,' Pat said in a decided tone. 'Why don't you go too?'

'I would rather be in my own home, thank you,' she said, resenting his organising manner.

'Yes, why not go over to the Johnstons'? Just for the night?' he pursued.

'No, I'm going to my own home. Don't you understand?'

He seemed to have mentally distanced himself even further from her, standing looking down as from a great height. He said nothing.

'Pat?'

'You go off home. Go up to the House if you must. Go off home.' He spoke in a monotone, not meeting her eyes with his own.

'Pat?' she said again.

He did not reply, but looked in the direction of the front door.

She walked down the corridor. He did not accompany her but stood by his office door, watching as she went, a small but vulnerable curly-haired woman, past the first beauty of youth, demoralised, he saw, by his coldness which he now regretted. She wished that he was beside her, would take her arm, sensing that his touch would be enough to succour her at this moment. But he stood there, watching. He was standing very straight, almost to attention, very much under control, she realised. I am a nuisance, she thought. He is thinking about the O'Briens, thinking how foolish and futile it all is, thinking I will burst into tears, want to tell him all the gory details, fall upon his shoulder and weep. He doesn't want to get involved, and I know it, I sense it. Go home, Belle, go home.

'Go off home,' he called to her. 'Get yourself to bed, keep warm, stay indoors, lock yourself in securely and forget about the world outside, about us . . .'

'Will I see . . . ?' she started to say, realising that he might not hear her voice above the rising sound of the classroom nearby.

'And don't listen for foxes,' he said, and then he brushed a hand to his lips gesturing farewell with it to her. 'Take care,' he said, then strode into the classroom, shutting the door resolutely behind him.

Belle reached her car and then cast a long look over to the school. There was little sign of movement. She was a lone figure, an insignificant part of the landscape. She got into the driver's seat, started the engine and drove home.

Chapter 19

BELLE DROVE UP THE ROAD from school slowly, wondering at Pat's demeanour. She had wanted to stay with him, but for some reason he would not allow it. Reaching the corner by the gate-lodge, she realised that there was something she should do. It was like setting out to climb an apple tree after she had just fallen out of it, like picking up a windfall just after having been stung by a wasp lurking inside the rotten sweetness of another. She would have to go back to the Lodge some time, but not today. No.

When she got to her own home and turned into her drive, a short figure in a flannel coat and headscarf was coming towards her. It was Mrs D. Belle stopped the car and got out. Her legs seemed heavy, full of lead. She put out a hand to the old woman.

Mrs D took it in both of hers and squeezed it tightly. 'That was a bad business, a bad business,' was all she said at first in a broken voice. 'And Miss Jean was such a nice person,' she added eventually.

'Yes.' Belle was seeing Jean's face once again.

'Awful sad, awful sad,' repeated Mrs D, shaking her head, trembling.

'Please . . . don't . . .' Belle put her arms round her and drew her close.

Mrs D sniffed at last and drew away. 'There now, I'm a silly old woman,' she said, almost talking to herself. She dragged a handkerchief out of her pocket and blew her nose loudly, then dried her eyes with determined gestures. 'A silly.' She eyed Belle. 'You're looking . . .'

'I'm brewing a dose of flu, I think, so I'm going into the warm. The boys are staying at the Johnstons'.'

'That's probably the best idea . . . stay in the warm, I just made up the stove for you. I'd better get off, I have the dinner to make for Willy,' Mrs D excused herself. She set off towards the gates.

Belle went indoors. She looked to see if Sam had left a note. He hadn't. She wandered around the house tidying desultorily room by room.

Time passed. The day began to darken. Still there was no word from Sam. The house started to close in tightly about her. Her isolation deepened her feeling of uselessness. Each room seemed emptier, the sound of her movements seemed muffled, her whole body ached. Retreating to the kitchen, she made some tea and waited for it to draw. As she straightened her shoulders she felt a stickiness between her shoulder-blades and across her forehead. The flu which she had fought had caught up with her.

She looked at the clock. It was a quarter to five. The boys would be with Granny Johnston, eating her home-made scones, her blackcurrant jam . . .

Belle heard a dull sound, caught her breath. Yes, the window-panes had responded. An explosion. A bomb. But where?

She went into the porch, and looked up the road in the growing dark to where the village lay, street lights twinkling in two long necklaces down the hill. The army post at the top? For a moment a dozen fingers of fear gripped her. There was no sign of a glow of fire, or a grey cloud of smoke against the heavy sky up the hill where the army post was, or even the police station close by. Two Landrovers appeared over the hill and came down towards her, headlights glaring. They raced past the house, accelerating furiously as they went down the hill towards Corey. The sound of their engines died away. Belle stayed by the porch window, her nose pressed up hard against the cold glass. Nothing seemed to happen for a very long time. While she waited, she thought about the radio. It was too soon for a newsflash.

A solitary figure appeared in the gloom coming down the road. Mrs D. Belle went down the drive to meet her, teeth chattering in the cold wind that was now surging in the pine-tops.

'It's the railway!' Mrs D called out as soon as she reckoned Belle was within earshot. 'It's the railway they think. You can't see it, the hill's in the way, but the UDR boys are away on down. Did you see them?'

'It was a bomb then?' Belle said.

'Och yes. Fifty pounds or maybe by the sound of it.' Fifty pounds. 'I'm puffed,' Mrs D said, 'and I could do with a drop of tea.' She caught Belle by the arm and leaned heavily on it, wheezing. 'Yes, what I need, and you by the looks of it, is a good cup of tea. Come on now, inside.'

The answer to everything, Belle thought. 'I was going to make some.'

'Have you any milk for it?' Mrs D asked curiously.

'No, I'll go up to the gate for it . . .' Belle began but Mrs D intervened.

'There won't be any. Have you not heard about Cathal?'

'No. What about Cathal?'

'Och, I'm silly. Sure I could have told you when I was over earlier but then . . .' she shook her head at the recollection, 'then I had other things on my mind. Yes. The police lifted him this morning, just starting on his milk round he was. I heard it up at Crawford's.'

'What did they lift him for?'

'Och. I don't know. He's a good boy. Sure I know his mother . . . and a nicer wee woman . . . well . . .' Mrs D went out into the hall, into the porch, and looked out.

'Do you want this tea, even without the milk?' Belle asked.

'Och aye, throw a few spoonfuls of sugar in it to take away the taste.'

Belle put the cup of tea into her hand. She took it but held it tilted so that the tea slopped on to the stone floor. They stared up the street. The tea slopped a bit more. It was the only sound for some time.

Eventually Belle stirred. 'I'll put on the radio, for the headlines.'

'Yes, that's an idea.'

They had to wait for a minute or two while the disc jockey signed himself off.

'Here are the five-thirty news headlines. Reports are coming in that the Dublin-bound express train has been derailed at Kilraughter Bridge just south of Armagh. It is understood that there was a bomb on the line. There are no reports of casualties so far. We will bring you more information when it is available . . .' Belle switched off.

An ambulance sped down the road, blue light flashing, siren blaring.

'Look at that!' Mrs D said. 'And did you see the crowd of soldiers this morning?'

'I was down at the school. I only saw one patrol,' Belle said.

'They must have got word about something, they must have done.'

Belle stood beside her thinking, not wanting to speak, watching the village and its lights up ahead of them. 'How are they getting over to the bridge, where the explosion was?' she asked.

Mrs D thought for a moment. 'Well, you would have to go down past Corey and away off down that road. It's maybe five miles or more.' She stopped and looked thoughtful. 'Funny, when you think about it, if you went from here, it would be less than a quarter of the distance . . .'

'What do you mean?' Belle cried.

'Well, there's no road of course, so the Landrovers and all couldn't get through . . .' she considered, 'but if you were to go out through your front door,' she pointed, 'and went up the side, to the opening in the wall, and then into the orchard, and on up to Top Hill, and down the other side . . . it would take no time at all. It's no distance really, when you come to think about it.'

Belle caught her breath. She had suddenly a pain in her chest. The Minotaur. How do you find your way through an orchard in the dark?

'Are you all right, child?' asked Mrs D. 'You're shaking. Come on now. There's no point us standing here, there's going to be traffic going up and down the road all night. You're going to your bed.'

She made up two hot water bottles and bullied Belle into the big black bed, telling her that the only way to beat flu was to get into bed and stay there. 'I did it, and look at me,' she maintained stoutly. 'I'm grand.' She tucked Belle up securely – 'So as you can't escape.' Then she sat on the edge of the bed clasping the radio, waiting for the next news bulletin, waiting to turn it on again. It seemed as if they held their breath together, minute after minute. There was silence on the road outside as if the first flurry of excitement was over and the village had subsided into unconsciousness again.

'It's no good!' Belle cried, sitting up straight in bed. 'I can't stand it, lying here . . . what's going on?'

'Now then,' Mrs D said, putting her hands on Belle's shoulders and pressing her downwards on the pillows. 'What could you do? What could I do? Me with my chest. You'd best stay in bed, stay in the warm.' She straightened the covers deliberately, trapping Belle under them.

Belle struggled up. 'I want to know. I want to know what's going on!'

'Well, we only know there's a bomb, at the train. We'll have to wait.'

'I can't!' Belle said, pushing aside the covers and putting her bare feet to the floor. 'I'll phone . . . I'll phone . . .'

'Who will you phone?'

'Och, Mrs Crawford, she's bound to know.'

'Well, maybe you might be right,' Mrs D admitted. 'We could try her, I suppose.' She was feeling that they were isolated here, cut off from the news, moment to moment. The two women went down the stairs in a rush.

'Mrs Crawford?' Belle had dialled with surprisingly firm fingers.

The phone was picked up instantly as if Mrs Crawford was manning an information line to the whole world. 'Yes?' Her voice was precise.

'It's Annabelle Johnston here,' Belle said cautiously.

'Yes?' came the brusque reply.

'Have you any news? What's happening?' Belle burst out.

'Oh . . .' There was a considered pause. 'Well . . . you know that there has been a bomb . . .'

'Yes, yes,' Belle said.

'Well, it's on the railway line, the viaduct you know . . .'

'Yes, I know that. It was on the radio.' Belle wished that Mrs Crawford would stir herself out of this long-drawn-out agony.

'Well, then, what do you want to know?' Mrs Crawford asked deliberately.

'Is there any more news?'

'It wasn't a very big bomb, not like the one in Belfast last week. They are all away down, ambulances, police, the army . . . and they're bringing in the helicopter, can you not hear it?' Her voice was suddenly backed by the roar of a helicopter engine. Mrs Crawford shouted, 'They are getting the people off the train now, we hear there's no casualties, at least no one is dead . . .'

'No one dead,' Belle reported to Mrs D beside her. 'Is that all?' she shouted down the phone to Mrs Crawford.

'That's all we know at the moment,' Mrs Crawford shouted back.

Belle put the phone down. In the distance the two women could hear the helicopter hovering, up at the top of the village street.

Mrs D seemed to have sensed the futility of the conversation. 'Never worry,' she said, patting Belle's arm. 'Come on now, back to bed, my wee love. There's no good in standing in the cold here.' She was thinking that a couple of tablets and a good night's rest were all Belle needed. If she were to get back up to the village now, she would get the latest word. She was impatient all at once, wanting to get back home, feeling left out of something that was happening, she wanted to learn what was being surmised, proposed, done. 'You go back to your bed, Belle. You have the radio. There'll be another bulletin in a wee while, at six o'clock? Your boys are safe at their Granny's. Away to your bed. Take a couple of tablets.'

Belle went towards the kitchen door wishing that she was alone to work things out for herself. 'You're right, Mrs D. I will go back to bed . . .'

Mrs D took up her flannel coat and thrust it on. She retreated out through the kitchen door.

Belle shut it after her, slid the bolt across and went to the bottom of the stairs. Then she stopped. 'No, I can't wait, that's not enough, I have to know,' she said aloud. Seconds later she was putting on a pair of jeans, a thick sweater, grabbing her red jacket, ignoring the stickiness of her forehead. She had to know.

Outside the cold caught her, took her by surprise as she stood at the kitchen door. There was no sound of the helicopter, or of traffic on the road. Only the wind in the tree-tops. She held her breath for a moment and waited until it was almost bursting inside her. She listened for some sound which would give her a clue as to what was happening on the other side of Top Hill. She let out her breath slowly and stood for a moment longer. Still nothing. She stepped out into the dark, which seemed to enfold her like a big deep blanket. She had no thought of her own safety, the fears that had made her lock herself in at night, the fears of retribution. She knew she was involved in something secret. The note had told her, but she hadn't recognised the fact until this moment. The handwriting had been familiar. Yes. How blind, how unsuspecting she had been.

She went to the side of the house and passed through the black tight passageway of laurels that led to the orchard. Then she was among the trees. She could hardly hear her footfalls in the grasses. She was aware of the dark, deeper and deeper. A gusting wind blew on her face, the trees loomed above and around her. Occasionally she had to duck for a low-hanging branch, but she did it out of instinct, not because she could see the boughs. It seemed to her that the apple trees were surrounding her in a tryst of friendship.

Belle felt in her pocket for the only thing she had thought of sensibly, logically, before she had left the house – a box of matches. She struck one and it went out instantly. She struck another, shielding it with her hand. The flame flickered and went out. She struck another and this time the flame stayed alight unsteadily. She examined the tree trunk beside her, looking for a mark. There wasn't one. The match guttered and went out. She stepped forward three or four steps to the next tree and struck another match. Yes, there it was! A white dash of paint, a mere splash, and glowing strangely in this half light. She lifted the match, which was burning close to her fingers, and looked forward to the next tree in line. Yes, there was another mark. She stepped to the second tree, dropping the match at her feet with an exclamation of pain as the flame caught her fingers. It fell into the damp grasses, instantly extinguished. But she had had time to see another mark.

She could judge the direction now. That and the slight slope of the hill here gave her a clue to the route ahead up through the trees, all the way to the summit of Top Hill. It was surprisingly easy for her. There were only three occasions when she had to stop to strike a match, check the direction. But then, she knew the orchard well, like the back of her hand. All those summers with John, mapping it out in her mind without realising it, familiar yet unfamiliar.

She knew she was nearly at the top by the whiplash of wind

that came eddying through the trees, and then she was out under the clump of beeches and crab trees and the countryside was open before her, the hill dropping away steeply from where she stood, the lake a pale blur at its foot, and beyond it the railway line bathed in a succession of lights, a wreath of smoke lifting hazily into the air above it. In time she heard sounds too and smelt the acrid smoke.

It was as if she was some bird, now gliding, then hovering. She could pick out the outlines of five carriages, yes, she could count five. They were illuminated here and there by lights, some of which moved, some of which flickered. There were people moving, standing still, shadows sometimes. Someone was hammering, an uneven laboured sound of metal against dull metal. There was sporadic movement, but little sound to convey what was happening. She tried to put the sounds together in her head as a person watching a silent movie puts words unconsciously on to lips. Below her lay the train, just beyond the viaduct; two carriages were lying on their sides, one smoking. About the wrecked ruins figures struggled, or stood motionless, and in the background were vehicles, Landrovers, whose headlights, blazing, pinpointed the fields, the marshy swamp and ridges and furrows of the land round about. It had all happened. The destruction lay waiting for the cranes in daylight to move in with a giant hand and tidy everything up. She had no clue to human anguish, who might be hurt, only that she was apart from it all, a watcher amongst the frosted grasses.

Then there was a quick volley of shots. From a sub-machine-gun. Below her the figures still moved, the lights still flickered. But there were shouts suddenly, she heard them on the wind. The staccato sound of returning fire did not come as a surprise, she only waited to hear more.

There was a gunman to her right, at the foot of the hill, in the shelter of the hedgerow. As she watched two figures advanced from the wreckage of the train, running, dodging in the gloom, holding guns. They were advancing towards the hidden assailant. He fired again. A dozen rattling shots. The two figures stopped, and dropped to the ground. Silence fell, engulfed the scene. Then someone in the distance started up a Landrover; its wheels were sticking in the heavy ground, its engine screamed. The two figures rose again and advanced, followed by others.

Belle heard the man's breathing before she saw him. She heard the breaths caught, laboured, someone struggling up the steep gradient of the hill, someone she realised she knew. As his tall figure stumbled into view, a silhouette against the sprinkling of lights below, she knew him. Then the fact that he staggered, then limped, dragging one foot behind the other, impinged on her. She moved.

He stood transfixed, breathing hard, shocked. Then he recognised her. 'Belle!' was all he said; a kind of sob, she thought. Was it relief, or pain in one sound? She stretched out her arms, their hands touched, then they were in each other's arms, clasping, loving, desperate in one moment. She became aware of the hard bulk of his gun hanging on a strap, and flinched. He tucked it behind him, in a casual practised move.

'Belle,' he said at last, 'what are you doing here?'

'I had to come . . . I heard the bomb and I realised . . .' she said haltingly. 'I followed the marks on the trees . . . yes, the marks, up through the orchard.'

'Ah. You spotted them.'

'No, not me. One of the boys. I didn't think anything of it at the time. It was only tonight that it all fitted.'

'You realised . . .'

'Yes, Pat, I saw you with Cathal at the gate. Sam found the note. I began to wonder . . . it was your writing.'

'Your brave Sam,' he said contemptuously. 'So you climbed to the top of the hill . . .' he continued, his breath coming more evenly now.

'To see if I was right,' she finished simply. She tightened her arms round him, burying her head in his shoulder, smelling his black sweater and a sour-sweet body smell. Was it fear? 'Yes, I wanted to find out . . . Why,' she started, then stopped, waited, then went on, 'why did it have to be you?'

'It just happened. It could have been someone else.'

They stood arms entwined, not saying anything. Then there was the sound of a helicopter coming from a distance at speed, great speed. They stood immobilised as the sound of its engine grew louder. Its searchlight roamed over the thickets of hawthorn, the clumps of grass stiff with frost, nearing them as they stood, unable to move.

'Down!' he shouted, and they threw themselves to the ground

together, limbs on limbs, arms still intertwined, awkward. The ground was hard. Belle held her breath as the helicopter came overhead, as the searing bright light played on the ground inches from their bodies. She lay limp like some rabbit paralysed with fear having caught its leg in a snare. The machine roared overhead and she felt the draught of the rotor blades as it whirred over the edge of the hill and back down behind it to her house, down over the sleeping orchard, the cat's-cradle boughs.

'What's the matter?' she asked, in the sudden silence that seemed to fall about them. 'You were limping. What have you done?'

'Not a lot!' he said irritably. 'I've wrecked my ankle. I thought I was the quick-footed one, but I must have put my foot down a foxhole. I had to stay, to detonate the bomb, make sure it would work this time . . . and it didn't.' His voice died. She could hear the disappointment. He went on, 'They sent me here because they failed last time. And of course I was useful for other things . . . what do you think I am?' He laughed. A brittle sound.

'You were brought in?'

'I was handy. They found me only too soon after I came to England. I had . . . credentials you could say, through my father who prefers to orchestrate it all from the States . . . he helps bring in the arms . . . and I had the experience, from Vietnam . . . I am an expert at killing, bombing, didn't you know? An expert! Ha! After tonight's performance I can't claim that any more!'

'I thought . . . you are a schoolteacher . . .'

'So? Does that make me immune from all feeling?' He sat up, then turned gingerly and stood up. 'What was all that worth?' he asked, as if talking to himself. 'A small derailment . . . I should have stayed . . .'

Belle put out her hand to the man she knew was close to her and at this moment enclosed in a quiet misery of his own. 'It's not your fault . . .' she said, not understanding at first the implication of what she was saying. 'It just happened this way.'

He rounded on her as she stood up beside him. 'It was my fault!' he said, each word shouted at her. 'My fault! We had planned a signal, Cathal and I. He was to be down the line. I had to go ahead without him. I exploded the bomb too late.'

'But you could have killed people,' she cried.

'Yes, that was a possibility,' he said in a calculating voice.

'Did that not matter to you?'

'What do you think? This is a war, woman,' he replied. He put a hand on his gun as if to remind himself of its presence. Then he stood away from her, testing one leg carefully, groaning to himself. 'Bloody hell!' he said, easing his weight on to the other leg.

'What have you done?' Belle asked, clasping his hand in hers.

'Bloody hell!' he repeated between clenched teeth. 'Bloody ankle!'

'What have you done?'

'I don't know, do I? Bloody broken it by the feel of it. Bloody stupid!' he said wearily, taking a deep breath. 'Aah!' He ran his hand down one side of his chest. 'Aaah!' he said again, and lifted his hand to his face in the half light. 'Christ!'

'What is it? What is it?'

'Did they get me?' he said in wonderment. 'The bastards must have!'

'What do you mean?' Instantly Belle remembered the men who had been advancing on the hidden gunman, firing on him, this man beside her. 'The soldiers,' she said, 'where are they now? I can't see anything.'

Pat was looking down the hill too. 'Stupid!' he said. 'What am I doing here with this woman? Standing discussing the weather!' he raged.

Her question seemed totally inadequate. 'What does it feel like?' she asked.

'Bloody awful!' he threw at her. 'Who do you think I am?'

'I don't know, not any more. I only want to help you!'

'Then give me your arm, woman,' he sighed philosophically, 'give me your arm till I get away out of this limelight!'

Belle grabbed the arm which he offered to her, felt the weight which he put on to her as he tested his injured leg on the ground, and felt the shudder that went through his body.

'That helicopter will be back. For God's sake, woman, let's get going!'

She felt his leaden weight as she supported him the first few yards of flat ground at the top of the hill before they reached the edge of the orchard where the unnevenness of ground, the brambles catching and the black dark met them, making where they put their feet even more uncertain. His breath was coming in laboured gasps.

'Can you make it?' she asked. 'Where is it, how bad is it?'

He stopped, straightened, moaned, passed his hand over his chest again, seeking with his fingertips for the centre of the pain.

She pressed her hand over his. She could feel a warm wetness. 'You're bleeding,' she said, realising the full implications of his injuries.

'Yes, woman, did you not realise that! They must have got me.'

'But if you're bleeding . . .' she began.

'Och, I've been shot before. It's nothing. Christ . . . I'm bloody useless!'

'Shouldn't we put something on it, stop the bleeding at least?' she asked, touching his chest again. It seemed wetter than before.

'It's nothing! Nothing! Let's get away from here. Christ! It's cold, strikes right through . . .' he muttered, starting down the hill again.

They made their way slowly, haltingly, down through the trees. There was no need to strike matches on the way. Anyway Belle did not have a free hand to do so. She sensed the way unerringly from tree to tree in the darkness.

After some minutes Pat stopped, took a deep sobbing breath and put out an unsteady hand to a tree trunk, leaning against it.

'It's not far, not far now . . .' Belle started to reassure him.

'I know. I know this way down, don't I?' he said between breaths.

'How long have you been planning this?'

'A few months.'

'You used my house, you met in my house, didn't you?' she accused. 'That's how you know all about it, where everything is?'

'Yes. It was suitable. And comparatively isolated,' he said grimly.

'And then I came home. I was in the way. Is that why you kept coming over to see me? Is that why?'

'In the beginning, yes. I have to admit it. I had to find out your movements, what you were up to, who might be calling on you . . . like Sam with the ducks. That was a near one. We wondered whether he might get in the way if he went out shooting down by the lake.' He groaned then. 'We'd better get on. I can manage now I think.'

'So you had to keep an eye on me, that was it, that was all it was.'

'No. No. It started that way, and then it got complicated . . . come on.'

'No. I want to know. Tell me!'

'We have to keep going. They may be following us,' he hissed, starting off again, this time unaided.

She went after him. 'Why did you have to get involved?' She couldn't see his face. If only she could. There had to be truth between them.

'How can you talk to me?' he said. 'You! You got involved, in Belfast. I understand why you did it. But, boy, have you given me problems. Oh yes, why do you think I had to go to Belfast yesterday? They wanted to know if you were here. If you were likely to give trouble. They thought I might be useful. To shut you up!'

'To shut me up?'

'Yes. You were to be my next assignment.'

Belle caught her breath in a sob. 'They sent for you?'

'Well, are you surprised? You didn't think that by running away you would get out of it? The police lifted that girl on your word, your evidence, you identified her. She's in custody now.'

'You know her?'

'Yes.'

'What is going to happen to her?'

'Her case will come up soon. Your evidence is crucial. Without it . . .'

'I see,' Belle said slowly, 'without me she might get off?'

'She might. But her cover is blown anyway. She'll not be much use north of the Border, not in the way she has been in the past.'

Suddenly, ferociously, there was the sound of a helicopter. It was coming back. They saw the searchlight spread out below them as it came up over the house, the rimed stable roof, the frozen boughs, up over the orchard towards them.

'Christ!' he shouted over the roaring engine. 'Christ! My cover's blown now. Stay still! Absolutely still!' he commanded her.

They stood stockstill side by side. Belle was only too aware of her red jacket and wished that it would not stand out in the greyness. But just as the helicopter approached them it veered away and the beam of light passed a few trees' distance away. The machine sped up and over the hills behind them, the engines deafening, the light piercing the branches cruelly. Then it was gone. Only a faint throbbing in the distance indicated how far and how fast it had disappeared.

'Pat?' Belle said cautiously in a low voice.

'I'm here. I'm here. Come here, woman.' He clasped her to him.

'We'd better get going.'

'Yes. You're right. We don't have time to talk . . . but Belle, I have to tell you . . .' He started forward again.

'What?'

'Oh, you know what I want to say . . . about you and me . . . we'll have to sort it all out . . . I want you . . I'm not going to let you get away . . .'

'Pat!'

'No. Not that. I couldn't hurt you . . . ever . . . Oh hell! I'll have to tell you another time,' he decided.

'Do you think anyone will be coming after us on foot?' she asked him.

'Possibly. I didn't get those fellows who were shooting at me. The helicopter covers more ground, and it has the searchlight.'

'If we could get down to the house, you'd be safe there for a while . . . I could take a look at your chest . . . they wouldn't search the house, would they?' she urged.

He laughed. 'No. They wouldn't. Not with your connections.' He choked on the words. 'Let's get on!'

They moved slowly now, stopping every once in a while to listen for sounds of pursuit, or the helicopter. Pat's breath was coming in groans and the only other sound was of their feet dragging through the grasses. Soon they could see the light in the kitchen window below them. They would be in the house soon, in comparative safety.

'Hell!' Pat gasped.

A Landrover was coming down towards the house from the village, its headlights blazing. It stopped at the gate, hidden in the dark blur of the clump of rhododendrons. The engine was revved. They heard the crackle of voices over the radio. Two figures detached themselves from the shadows and merged again into the darkness of the drive.

'They're coming to the house!' Belle breathed, her lips close to Pat's ear. 'What can I do?'

'I'll stay here. You go down, see if you can intercept them.'

'But . . .' she started.

'I'll wait here. I'll be OK . . . really.'

She pressed her lips to his cheek, feeling a shock at its coldness. 'I'll be back . . .' she whispered.

Belle ran down the last few yards to the entrance by the laurels at the side of the house. She realised that her face was wet, but with snow. It had started snowing, big flakes coming down thickly about her in a white cloak. She sped to the back door, listening for the sound of footsteps which would mean that the soldiers had come into the yard. She had the kitchen door open and was standing on the step, trying to breathe evenly, the snow falling thickly about her, when they came up out of the gloom.

'Mrs Johnston?' an unfamiliar voice asked. It was not Sam, this time.

'Yes,' she replied faintly, wondering what the next question would be.

Two burly figures showed up through the snow, coming to stand beside her. She was aware of their guns, the menace of them.

'We just came to check on you,' one man said.

'I'm fine. I just heard you coming . . . and I put my coat on and came out. It's so cold, and all this snow too. I wondered what was happening . . . the bomb and all that . . . is it over? I mean . . .' Her voice died.

'Sam radioed, asked us to drop by. He's over at the train. There was a bit of shooting, did you hear it?' the other man explained.

'I saw the helicopter . . .' Belle started.

'Oh, it's just taking a close look, all around here,' he went on.

'What's happening?' she asked.

The first man shrugged his shoulders against the snow. 'We're looking for the fellows who planted the bomb. They were there when it went off and then they started shooting. You would need to stay indoors, keep the place locked up. Sam said to make sure and tell you. The fellows could be coming this way . . .'

'Here?' she asked. 'Surely not here?'

'Well, maybe not this way. It's some time ago now. We think they must have got away by now, there's no sign of them,' the other man joined in.

'Them? More than one?'

'Well,' he said, 'like, only one was shooting, but you can't be sure. Sam said to warn you. Away inside, missus, and make some tea. I could do with a cup myself but we can't stop. We have to go away on down the road. And with this weather . . .' He brushed aside the falling flakes in a useless gesture, 'sure they'll freeze to death if we don't find them.'

'Thanks,' Belle said, 'thanks for calling. You're right. I'll lock up, safe and sound.' She turned in the doorway.

Inside with the door shut she found that her legs were trembling violently. She had to stand for quite some time before she felt any strength return to them. She sneaked out of the kitchen to the hallway, closing the door behind her so that the light no longer streamed through to the front of the house. Outside the lawn lay clothed in a white smooth blanket. The Landrover had gone from the gate. Ahead lay the village, its lights blinking in a flurry of snowflakes.

Belle walked calmly back to the kitchen and slid the kettle forward on the hob. He would be cold, very cold. She had no spirits apart from sherry in the house. A cup of tea would warm him, she knew. She poked the range and paused, spreading her hands in front of her to the heat.

The fingernails of both hands were stiff and red with blood, blackening at the edges. She turned her hands over and stared in horror. The lines of her palms were engrained with blood. She looked down at her coat, her red coat damp with snow, ran one hand down it, then stared at the dripping redness on her fingers.

'Oh God! Pat!' she cried.

She rushed out into the yard, closing the door behind her in frantic haste to keep in the heat. She strode out into the snowstorm, knowing the way, sure of her route and her footholds and what she must do.

The snow was beginning to gather in thick ridges, blown over the bramble thickets that clustered under the trees. She walked steadily ahead, counting in her mind back to the spot where she had left him. The snow came down heavily, flicking into her eyes, beating against her cheeks, wetting her bare head. It was only when she had gone some distance that she knew in this white wilderness that Pat was not where she had left him. She spun round, surveying the whitening landscape, the dark trunks fading under the furiously falling flakes.

'Where are you?' she called quietly. 'Where are you?' she called louder. There was no sound, except that behind her the wind had risen and was thundering through the pine-tops. 'Where are you?' she called even louder, each word slow, deliberate. 'Pat?' she called, her voice rising. 'Pat?' There was only the sound of the wind, the snow falling, licking around the branches and her face, drifting thickly at her feet.

'Pat? Pat?' she called again. Her feet were cold, she was cold, and wet, her jeans tight on her thighs. She sank to her knees in the snow, calling once more, 'Pat, oh Pat, where are you?'

It was no use. She struggled to her feet and went from tree to tree in a frenzy, calling out softly then loudly. Did it matter now if anyone heard her? But there was no response. Her voice grew fainter. Eventually she retreated from the orchard, where every tree seemed to threaten her, to stand against the kitchen door, weeping and calling out again, 'Where are you?' to the trees, the cobbled yard, the black bulk of the stables.

Inside the kitchen door she stood shaking and weeping, the snow dripping off her clothes on to the red-tiled floor. Was it possible that he had simply gone, not waited for her but slipped away while she had been diverting the soldiers at the House? Or was he under the snow? She had searched and searched in the orchard. It was no use, she was no use.

The kettle steamed. She moved it hopelessly off the heat.

Out in the hallway she took off the red jacket and hung it on the peg. Then she climbed the stairs to her room where she undressed very slowly, making a methodical pile of her clothes on the chair by the bed. She drew on her dressing-gown and slid under the covers of the big bed, sensing the cold stiffness of the sheets, the unyielding bundle of blankets. She lay flat. The soldier's voice drummed in her mind. 'Sure they'll freeze to death if we don't find them.'

'Pat?' she said to the empty room. 'Oh Pat, I couldn't find you. I couldn't. I tried. Where did you go?'

As she lay there she heard the helicopter's insistent engines. It was returning. She heard it come up and over Top Hill and descend towards the house. Then the window was illuminated by the searchlight, four chestnut leaves wide, twelve chestnut leaves deep.

It came over again, blotting out her thoughts, her mind, she closed her eyes tightly. It would go away, like those in Belfast that patrolled night after night. It would go away and leave her. In time it did.

Chapter 20

IS THAT A FOX in the orchard?

I am in the orchard, it's evening, it's summer, the smell of rotting apples, windfalls underfoot, the wasps buzzing happily over the browned and softening fruit hidden in the long grass.

I have been running, running downhill, down the darkening orchard towards the House. A bat flies towards me, darting, fleeting, I duck my head.

John grasps my hand. 'Come back and see the blossom?' he says, his face close to mine, his breath warm on my cheek.

'No. No. I said I'd go with Sam.'

'It's my blossom, mine . . . and yours . . . not his. Why must there always be Sam?' he laments, his voice rushing like the wind past my ears.

'But it's not spring, John, spring is over,' I tell him, wrenching away my fingers. My hands are damp and sticky. I can feel the sweat on my forehead, my breasts. Down in the house there will be a glass of cool lemonade from Jean, Jean with her vague lost look, her faint girlish smile.

Mother will scold me for worrying about the fox. Where is he? He sounds nearby. Mother will tell me not to be afraid, not now, it's only a fox out under the summer moon, baying to his mate.

Hold me tightly, Mother, keep me warm in this big bed.

But I am out in the orchard, the brambles are catching at my gown, my feet are soaking.

I can hear the fox clearly, I'm nearly there. He is calling my name as if he is caught in a snare and cannot get free. I stoop under a tree, my hair catches on a branch, where is he? I can hear him breathing, panting, but it's too dark to see. A cloud has passed over the summer moon and suddenly it's cold, very cold.

I touch him, touch his chest. He is breathing in hoarse ragged breaths, lying in the grass under a tree, but the grass is so cold.

'Belle!'

'You're cold,' I cry, touching his chest with my fingers, feeling for warmth yet there is none, only blood. 'You're bleeding to death, you're dying!'

'No. No. It's nothing. Only a flesh wound. Don't be daft, woman.'

'We must get you up, get you into the house,' I cry, tugging at his shoulder.

'No. Leave me for a moment. I'll be better in a moment . . . better . . . I'm just cold . . . cold . . .' His voice dies.

'You're dying, my fox,' I say, 'get up . . . get up . . . here's my hand . . .' I fumble to find his. It's flaccid, nerveless, stone cold. There's no response. His chest is damp as I run my fingers over it. I know. I know.

The fox is quiet now and heavy, too heavy for me to carry from among the snowy grasses. It's cold. Could it be snowing? Of course it is.

'Early in the year for snow,' James says besides me, shaking his head, 'no, it won't snow, not much.'

'But it is snowing. You're wrong, James, you're wrong.'

I will cover my fox, first with my gown to keep out the cold, then with the snow. He is under the tree. Just here. They say that under the snow it's warm, but my fingers are numb now.

He is under this tree. I will remember which one it is, each summer that comes.

Chapter 21

'BELLE! Belle!'

A hand was shaking her awake. She was tired, let her sleep. A fox had been in the orchard all last night, keening to the moon, or he had been caught in a snare, she could remember the sound of his voice.

'Belle! Please, Belle!'

A cold sponge passed over her hot flushed face, brushed her lank hair on the pillow. She opened her eyes. Sam was leaning over her.

'What . . .?' she murmured. Her body felt limp, spent and, as she moved between the sheets, clammy. 'Sam?'

'Yes, I'm here.'

'What . . . where . . . ?' She blinked. The room seemed very bright, the light pouring in through the opened curtains cruelly picked on the worn wallpaper, the yellowing paintwork, the faded rug on the floor by the bed, the uneven coating of polish down through the years on the bare boards. As she turned her head to look out of the window that overlooked the orchard she could see the snow on the topmost boughs. Overnight the fall of snow had transformed the winter's gloom in the house to an unrelenting reality. She dragged her gaze back again. 'What happened?'

'I called early this morning and found you. The bed was soaking wet. You seemed almost unconscious. But Dr Wilson says you will be all right, now that the fever seems to have broken. Mrs D says you didn't seem too bad last night when she left you. She's downstairs, worried sick.'

'What happened?'

'Dr Wilson says flu. You must have had a very high fever last night . . . he's given you some antibiotics. The back door was lying open. The whole place was freezing. I sent a couple of the boys to call last night and they told me you were locked up safe and sound.'

'No,' she interrupted. 'What happened? There was a bomb on the line.'

'Oh that,' he waved his hand, 'that. Nothing to worry about. They tried to blow the bridge. They tried a couple of years ago. They tried again. There's not much damage. The trains will be running tomorrow.'

'Was anybody hurt?'

'Cuts and bruises, shock. Two carriages were derailed and toppled over. There was a small fire. That's all. It could have been terrible, people could have been killed . . . but it wasn't. It was just another bomb. We've had so many. It's nothing to worry about. Look, you've got to take it easy . . .'

'What time is it?' Belle asked curiously, clearly awake now.

'Just after two. You've been sleeping like a baby.' He sat down on the edge of the bed and folded the sheet over the blanket carefully, straightening it like some nurse would, choosing not to say more. He had been coming off duty when he had called to see her. Now that it was past midday he was tired to a point of exhaustion. After the initial flurry of activity when they had got all the passengers safely off the train, and the outbreak of shooting, he had been forced to stand around for hours at the scene. The engineers had been working on the line all night. Belle had closed her eyes. 'You're tired still, why not sleep some more?' he said.

'No. I feel better.'

'That's good, you seemed so . . .' he said, then was silent again.

'There was a helicopter, wasn't there?' Belle was beginning to recall the events of the night before. 'There was shooting, wasn't there?'

'Yes, at the train. They detonated the bomb when the train came along, a connecting wire. They must have waited to see what the damage was. We saw one of them, then he opened fire on us. He must have had an Armalite. We fired back but we don't think we hit him. We searched, the helicopter searched. He got away . . .'

'You were there?' she said hesitantly. 'You were there?'

'Yes. I was there. It was very dark. We were lucky not to get hit. We were an easy target against all the lights on the line.'

'I didn't think . . .' No. She had been too preoccupied with Pat.

'That's not important, there's no call for you to think about me,' Sam said gruffly. 'Anyway, the helicopter came over this way to look for them, or him, we're not quite sure how many there were.'

'Yes, I heard it.'

He sounded impatient. 'It was difficult to see because of all the trees, and then it snowed. How could anyone find their way on foot down through the orchard? Sure it was pitch dark, one tree is like another, and that snow would have frozen anyone half to death.'

'Yes, it was cold.' Belle rolled over in bed, burying her face.

'Then there was Cathal . . .' Sam went on.

Belle had asked for explanations, but now she didn't want any more. She tried to think clearly. Pat was dead, up in the orchard under the snow, they would find him soon enough. His bones would never have time to bleach.

Sam continued. 'He must have been picking up notes, leaving them, using your tin at the gate. We believe that you spoilt their plans by coming home. They must have been meeting here, planning it. When you came along they had to just leave notes. We found two notes, not just the one yesterday, but we found one on Tuesday night . . . yes, on Tuesday night . . .' Belle turned her face round to stare at him. 'Yes. Tuesday night,' Sam went on, 'the night of your . . . party.'

'What did the other note say?'

'What was it? Oh, yes. Please settle your account on Friday. We cannot allow further credit. Or something like that.' He stood up. 'Cathal was involved. There are others. They went ahead without him. We lifted him, but they went ahead.'

'Cathal seemed such an ordinary person, not a terrorist,' she began.

Sam laughed. 'He had form. We have been keeping an eye on him, but since he's a milkman, visiting houses all over, we couldn't be sure who his contacts were. There's been a terrorist group working in this area for some months now. They must have been responsible for the incendiary bombs in Armagh a few days ago and there was a culvert bomb under an army patrol three months ago – two soldiers were injured. Did you not hear about it?'

'No. I don't watch the news, not any more.'

'You can't run away from it here!' Sam's retort was scathing. 'We knew there was something planned for yesterday. But not what it was. We had the note, but we didn't know where and how it would happen. That bit about the potatoes was quite clear – fifty pounds of explosives. Clever. It's a pity it snowed last night, a lot of clues will be lost, buried.'

'Yes, I remember now, it snowed a lot, an awful lot,' Belle whispered.

'Yes. It won't lie long. Not at this time of the year.'

'James said that it was too early in the year for snow,' she said sadly, hesitating over the words.

'Belle.' He bent down and put out a tentative finger and traced the curve of her cheek. 'Don't think about that please . . . not now.'

'Is there much snow in the orchard?' She spoke as calmly as she could.

Sam straightened up and walked over to the window that overlooked the orchard. He stood for a moment considering before he answered her. He was a broad figure of a farmer in his civilian clothes of open-necked shirt, tweed jacket and worn flannel trousers. It was the first time she had seen him out of uniform in years. She saw again how handsome if stubborn his face was, illuminated by the snow outside.

'Yes, surprisingly,' he said, 'there are some really deep patches under the trees where the wind blew it into drifts.'

'I wonder how long it will lie?' she thought aloud.

'Not long. It's beginning to rain now.'

Belle closed her eyes. Outside the light began to fade. The room was deathly quiet. Sam stood unmoving, looking out on the snow and the orchard. Then she heard him walk back to the bed. He put his hand on the rail at the end and she heard a faint rattle from a loose knob. 'Stay still!' she heard her mother say sternly from another time and she smiled to herself. She kept her eyes closed, but clenched her fists over the folded sheet. She wanted in this instant to be with her boys, to touch them, treasure them, feel their angular bodies tight to hers.

Sam sighed. 'Oh, by the way,' he said, 'I got word to that schoolteacher about you.' Belle opened her eyes, startled. 'Yes,' he nodded, 'I sent word to your friend . . . told him you were ill, you might not be back . . .'

'Pat?' she asked incredulously.

'Yes. I told him.'

'He's all right?' she asked, regretting the question at once, but then she never could hold back sometimes. So Pat wasn't dead.

'Oh, he's terrific! It is only his ankle. Were you with him when it happened? He says he slipped on the ice in the schoolyard yesterday and didn't realise it was bad till later. It's broken apparently, Dr Wilson was telling me, he was down setting it for him this morning. Pat Quinn wouldn't have been much help to us last night. I wondered where he was, to tell the truth. Everybody was down at the train helping, running around, even Mrs D's Willy.'

'Pat broke his ankle.' It was a statement, she said it unemotionally.

'Yes. Didn't you know how bad it was? I suppose you were with him when it happened. It's a bad break. He wouldn't have let on to you how much it was hurting . . . he wanted to be the big strong man . . . to impress you . . .'

'Sam!' she broke in, thinking fast. So Pat had got away safely back to his flat. And he had established an alibi for himself to prevent people getting suspicious. A slip in the schoolyard, a twisted ankle which had not seemed bad enough to require medical attention at the time, but which had turned out to be broken, yes that would be pretty convincing to most people. He would not have been able to drive himself over the Border last night because of the roadblocks. And he would have been weak with his wound. She had felt the blood, her hands had been dripping.

'Ha!' Sam's laugh was contemptuous. 'His dancing days are over for a while! He'll be in that plaster for a few weeks.'

Belle shook her head. 'Stop it, Sam!'

'I'll leave you,' he said, and walked to the door. 'The boys, if you're interested, are still at my mother's. Mrs D is downstairs if you need her. She'll stay and keep you company.'

'Where are you going?' she demanded.

'To the farm, to the boys, my mother, I've had enough here.'

'Wait a moment, please, Sam?' she called, sitting up in bed now, drawing the covers up around her bare breasts as she felt the chill of the room and his explicit gaze as he turned to look at her. The room swam, blurred before her, she felt hot and breathless and enclosed.

'Behold, you are beautiful, my love; truly lovely. Our couch is green; the beams of our house are cedar, our rafters are pine . . .' he declaims, leaning towards me, smiling foolishly.

'You fool! Where does that piece of doggerel come from?' I ask.

We are in the cottage, he and I. Outside is blazing heat, breathless. In here there is a cool carpet of chickweed, ferns and docken.

We have just been swimming, or trying to. The water was quite warm today. It hasn't rained for at least two weeks, so the river is low, just murmuring over the stones. But as I dipped my body I felt refreshed. It's been hot too long.

'Behold, you are beautiful, my love . . .' he starts again.

'Oh shut up. I'm trying to get dressed. Give me that towel,' I tell him.

'Your lips are like a scarlet thread and your mouth is lovely . . .' he continues, standing close to me. 'Your eyes are like doves, your hair is like a flock of goats . . .' He stretches out his hand and touches my hair, fingers entwined in my curls. 'Belle . . .'

'What is it?' I whisper, infected by his strange happiness.

His fingers now caress my bare shoulder, stepping one by one, like I do when practising my scales on the piano, step by step.

'Your two breasts are like two fawns . . .' He pushes the towel away and cups one breast with his hand and stares into my eyes. 'Belle . . .'

His body is beautiful. Naked and beautiful. Ecstatic, stiff, risen to meet me, my bare body.

'What is that coming up from the wilderness, like a column of smoke . . .' he murmurs, his fingers stepping out still, determined to explore me.

'What are you saying? What is this foolishness?'

He kisses me, brushing my lips, then teasing with his tongue. 'You like this, don't you?'

'Yes, yes, I do. But . . .'

'Then I'll give you more. It's the most famous love poem in the world . . .' he murmurs. 'Have you not read it? You're the one who's always going to church with Mother. It's the Song of Solomon. You should know it. You should read it.'

'You and your books . . .' I laugh, mesmerised by his touch.

'I know this one by heart . . . the scent of your breath is like apples . . .' He clasps my hand and draws me to him.

'You and your orchard . . .'

'It's for you, all for you, my beloved . . .' he breathes, his tongue questing urgently now. 'You have ravished my heart, my sister, my bride . . .'

'Why can't you leave me alone? It's over,' Belle cried out. 'Why won't you give me peace?'

Sam stared at her, standing rooted. 'I'm going!' he shouted. Then his voice softened when he saw her awful expression. 'What is it? What's wrong? You'll freeze, woman, you're half naked. Cover yourself up.' He strode back to her side and wrenched the covers around her shoulders. She shook her head, breathing deeply as if she was drowning. 'You need to stay in bed. You're still feverish, just look at you. You're ill.' He stooped and put his arm round her shoulders, grasping her.

'Oh Sam, hold me, just hold me . . . send him away.'

'Who? Who? I don't understand you.' He rocked her in his arms. 'All this business . . . Jean . . .' he said, pressing his lips to her forehead. 'You need to take things easy . . . you need someone to take care of you . . . not this . . .'

Belle shook her head hopelessly, trying to focus on the room, on the brightness, feeling the strength of his hold on her.

'Belle, this is foolish and you know it. You need to take things easy, from now on . . . and I'm not having you going down to work at that school.'

'Stop it!'

Sam took his hands away quickly, stood up, stepped away from the bed. 'Well, your lover boy won't be there for a while. I hear he's going to stay with his sister over the Border, the sister that married the doctor. They'll be well heeled. He'll have every comfort there!'

That was it. Pat was going to get away across the Border. Getting his ankle fixed would have given him time to organise his escape, to get someone to take him over the Border. If his brother-in-law was a doctor, his bullet wound would be tended to, without any questions being asked.

'When is he going?' she demanded.

'Some time today.' Sam waved his hand in irritation. 'I don't know. Does it matter?'

'I must go . . . I have to see him . . . I have to talk to him . . .'

'Don't be ridiculous! You're ill. You're raving. Anyway he's maybe away by now.' He waved his hand again, dismissing her, walking back to the doorway.

'I must go. Please understand? Please . . . there's something I have to settle.'

Sam was standing with one hand on the doorknob, a guarded look in his eyes.

'What do you want to talk him about?'

'I just have to see him before he goes. It's important!'

'This is madness and you know it. You're in no fit state . . . What is so important . . .?' Belle did not reply. He took one look at her expression and sighed in hurt resignation. 'Very well.' He shook his head. 'I know what you're like when you get an idea in your head. I don't know why, but I'll take you. I'm going that way anyway, to the farm, to the boys.'

'Thanks, Sam. You can just drop me off at McGuigan's. It won't take me long to get ready . . .'

Ten minutes later Belle stepped weakly across the snow-covered yard, her boots sliding in the white carpet which was beginning to turn to slush under a shower of dismal rain. Mrs D was at her side, scolding.

'I'm OK really. You go off home, please,' Belle begged.

'Och well, you're with your man.' Mrs D jerked her head. 'You're in good hands now. I'll away off home, like you say.'

'She cares about you, you're like a child to her,' Sam said

baldly as the dumpy figure disappeared round the corner of the house.

Belle stared after her, then got into Sam's battered blue Fiesta. She had put on the forest green dress which made her eyes turn to emeralds. Had Pat told her that? Or had she imagined he did? She had left her red jacket hanging on the peg in the hall. It was still damp, she had told a questioning Mrs D. She had found a tweed coat instead and sat in the passenger seat of the car with the collar turned up, smelling the raw tincture of the wool. She had brushed her hair, but it had refused to curl the way it normally did, and she knew her face was pale and drawn, the carefully applied lipstick was a red gash.

'This is not a good idea,' Sam said, settling into the seat beside her. 'I don't know why I am doing this.'

Belle hunched herself into the coat and looked at him in reproach. How could she make him understand? He drove without speaking down the road.

Corey was typically empty, but as they slowed by McGuigan's shop and drew to a stop around the corner, Belle thought she caught a sight of Jimmy's face peering out between the pyramids of tins and packets that neatly filled the window. There was a large silver Volvo estate car parked by the outer staircase that led to Pat's small flat. Sam stopped behind the other car. He turned off the engine and pulled on the handbrake. Belle looked at him in surprise.

'I'll wait for you,' he said obstinately. 'We can go to the boys . . .'

'But I don't know . . .'

'Like I said. I'll wait. It looks as if he's about to leave, that estate car has a Southern registration.'

So they had arrived already to collect him, he would not be alone, and she might not get the chance to ask the questions she must ask, or tell him what she must tell him. Belle bowed her head in defeat.

'Look at you!' Sam said beside her. 'You should have stayed in bed.'

She lifted her head defiantly, opened the car door and got out, shutting it firmly behind her, and climbed the steps to the flat. When she reached the top, the door opened and Pat stood before her, looking quizzical, looking ashen, standing on one leg, the other she saw was thickly plastered about the ankle. He smiled. Her heart thudded.

'Belle,' he said. 'Come on in. I recognised the car but I didn't expect to see you . . .'

'And I didn't expect to see you . . .' she said. She wanted to add the word 'again', but she sensed, then saw the other occupant of the room and this stopped her mid-sentence.

Pat nodded his head. 'This is my sister Maureen. Do you remember her?'

Belle looked at the well-dressed middle-aged woman who had appeared from an alcove where she had apparently been washing dishes for she had a tea-towel in her hand. Belle shook her head and said apologetically, 'No, I'm sorry, I don't. It was a long time ago.'

The other woman smiled, but she seemed ill at ease.

Pat explained, 'She's come to collect me. I'm going over to Dundalk.'

'Oh I remember you, Belle, cycling by the odd time,' Maureen said. 'I'm just redding up. It wouldn't do to leave the place looking as if he had had to leave in a hurry.'

Belle looked around the living-room. She noted the pale brown, patterned walls, the heavy sedate furniture, the leafy design on the carpet which was far from new. There was a desk by the single window, a large pile of paperbacks on it. Pat could depart with what little was his and leave hardly a sign of his occupation.

'I'm nearly done, like I said,' Maureen said. 'Pat! Would you sit down and take the weight off that ankle for a moment?'

'What it is to be bullied by a woman!' he laughed. 'Sit yourself down, Belle.' He lowered himself carefully into an armchair, levering his injured leg out in front of him with both hands. Then he sat back and grimaced, putting one involuntary hand on his chest.

'How do you feel?' she asked in an undertone.

He nodded in his sister's direction. 'She's patched me up very well, considering she's only a doctor's wife.'

'I heard that,' Maureen said, coming to stand beside them drying a plate. 'We'll get him right. He's a cheeky fool. And he's dead lucky to be alive. The sooner I get him over the Border the better. He has a right wound there in his chest. He's lost a lot of blood. We'll be away in a couple of minutes. This man here has the cheek of the devil!'

Pat looked up at her. 'Get on, woman, stop barging me. You'll make me nervous.'

'Nervous!' Maureen said. 'The sooner we get away . . .' She shook her head and hurried back to the alcove.

'I thought that you . . .' Belle started. 'I thought you were dead!'

He raised an eyebrow. 'Och, it's only a flesh wound. Bled a fair bit. I lost consciousness for a while . . . I suppose that was when you found me. You kept calling me your fox and you wrapped me up nicely. When I next came to, I felt quite strong and the wound had stopped bleeding. I trotted down here, you might say. Do you know, I didn't meet a single car down the road. All the checks must have been at the Border.' His expression hardened. 'But I failed, didn't I?'

'How can you talk like that about something that could have been horrific?' Belle cried.

'That's what it's all about, isn't it, whichever side you're on? Killing, maiming, a bit of bloodletting. It's necessary. Your Sam's as bad, in his way, there's not a lot of difference between us,' he said, shrugging his shoulders. He winced.

'Is he?'

'You've been brilliant,' he said, shaking his head in admiration. 'I have to hand it to you.'

'What do you mean? Are you talking about last night?'

'I owe my life to you probably, lady, not just last night, but the other day too. I have to thank you once again for helping me out.'

'Once again?' she asked. 'When was the other time?'

'Huh! Did you not realise that day your big man came searching . . .' He stopped and shook his head wryly.

'What do you mean?'

'Where do you think I had the explosives for last night's fiasco?'

'They were here?' Belle asked in amazement.

'Oh yes. Right here.'

'Is Jimmy involved in this too?'

'What do you think!' Pat smiled disarmingly. 'We put on a pretty good performance that day, don't you think? Your big man didn't catch on.'

How had she been so stupid? 'What would you have done if they had decided to search the place?' she demanded.

'Oh, I would have thought of something. I'm a good poker player. And if that hadn't worked, well, I would have stopped him.'

'How would you have stopped him?' She looked aghast as he smiled again.

'I had ways and means . . . as it was, you distracted him.'

'How can you just sit there, with a hole in your chest . . .?' Belle cried. 'Sam's outside right now!'

'Yes, I know.'

'Dear God, Pat! Is he there? And you told me he's in the UDR!' Maureen said fiercely, going to the window and peering out. Her hands were shaking. 'Dear God! We'll never get away!'

'Stay cool, Maureen, stay cool. I don't think that Belle is likely to tell him about me,' Pat said, giving Belle a direct look.

'No,' Belle admitted. Her position was only too clear at this moment. To tell Sam would be to implicate herself in the night's work. As well as that she had stopped him from finding the explosives, and she had corroborated Pat's story about breaking his ankle in the schoolyard. She had had no idea what she was really assenting to. She was in a quagmire, bogged in deep. How had it happened? Would Sam ever believe her if he found out? She needed Sam now, wanted him, suddenly.

'Come on, Pat,' Maureen urged, lifting a large blue zip bag that was sitting by the door. 'There's only that wee bag, don't forget it.'

Belle helped Pat into his coat as if in a trance. He was going. It was better that way. Somehow she had to break free of all this madness. Sam had said she was mad, and he was right. She had to put all this behind her, everything, John, Jean and James . . . everything. Pat was a killer. Men like him had killed John, and would keep on killing.

Maureen opened the door and went down the steps, looking back at Pat in the doorway. 'Come on! Can you manage? Do you want my help too?'

'I'll be down in a minute,' Pat called to her, going back inside to where Belle stood and shutting the door. He leaned against it. 'Well, my foxy lady?' he asked, smiling at her. 'Come here, woman.' He reached out and grasped her shoulders, bringing his lips close to hers.

'Pat,' she whispered, 'I cannot . . .'

'I have to tell you, I need to tell you . . . I tried to tell you last night . . .' Pat began, then he kissed her hard.

Belle tried not to respond, and he did not seem to notice her hesitancy. When eventually he drew his lips away, she asked before he could speak, 'What did you want to tell me?'

'I have to explain. This all started out . . .'

'As a joke?'

'No! No! You think all this is a joke?' he raged, turning away.

'Go on,' she prompted. She tilted her head sideways so that she caught his eyes with her own. 'Tell me. I'm listening.'

'I want you with me.'

'Sam says you're a womaniser just like your father was.'

'Sam says . . . what does he know? I want you, Belle, you and I . . .'

'It's too late now. You're going,' she said.

'Only for a few days. I'll be back.' He stared at her. 'You don't . . . ?'

She stared back at him, stunned. 'I thought . . . I thought you wouldn't be back. It would be safer.'

'Look, woman, I have a job here, and I have other things to do as well. Do you think I'm a coward? I know the risks but I'm not getting out. I'm not giving up.'

'You're going to come back and pretend . . . What about Jimmy?'

'What about him?' Pat seemed astounded at her question.

'Well, is he going to stay too?'

'Oh, yes. Why not? He's one of our best operatives, been active for years, well in, you might say.'

'Does he know about me?'

'Aah. That's it. I understand what's bothering you. Yes, he's been fully informed. But you don't have to worry about Belfast, that little problem. Just forget about the case. Get out of it. Tell the police you were mistaken, you won't be the first person who has done so. Jimmy is going to fix it with our boys up there, don't worry. And after what you've done for me . . . well, you're all right, you've reciprocated, shall we say. And besides, you and I . . .'

'I've reciprocated, Pat! Where does that leave me?'

He kissed her briefly. 'Here, with me, I suppose, you are the first woman that has meant anything to me. We'll work it out, you and I . . .'

'You're telling me what I feel. You don't know what I feel.'

'I know what your body feels . . .' he said, his hands caressing her. A car horn sounded. 'That's Maureen, she wants to get on, she's terrified of your man there,' he said, taking away his hands. 'I'll have to go, my darling girl.' He sighed and picked up the small blue holdall.

Belle said nothing. She couldn't speak. She opened the door, then started down the steps, turning to see Pat make his way, halting every now and then, pressing a hand against the wall beside him for support. The steps were icy, he unbalanced suddenly.

'Give me that bag,' she said, taking it from him, 'and give me your hand.' She clasped his hand and guided him downwards.

At the bottom he lurched dangerously and staggered to the silver car. Maureen was already in the driver's seat, the engine running, but as she saw Pat falter she flung open the door and rushed to his side. 'You think you're Superman!' she said between clenched teeth, opening the door for him quickly.

Sam had got out of his car. He strolled over, seeing this tall competitor weak and vulnerable. Maureen was casting anxious looks at Sam as he approached. She slammed the door shut and walked briskly to her own side, slipping in behind the wheel, shutting the door and revving up the engine. Pat wound his window down and started to say something, but Maureen pressed her foot hard on the accelerator, the car's wheels spun in the slush, and the car roared forward, out on to the main road and towards the Border. Pat called out – was it to Maureen, or to Belle? – it was hard to tell. He waved his hand. It didn't look like a farewell.

Belle felt Sam's fingers gripping her elbow. 'He's away then, I see. Looks a bit weak and pale on it too,' he observed, 'and just look at that mad driving! Stupid woman! In these conditions. They'll end up in hospital.' He looked up the road. 'Ah, there's the boys.'

Two patrol Landrovers were cruising down past them. Someone cheered and shouted at Sam. He stood stolidly, legs apart and waved back, grinning. The two vehicles went on down the road towards the Border after the fast-disappearing silver car.

Belle saw then that she still held Pat's small holdall. She stood looking at it in her hand, and then down the road. That's what Pat had been waving about. He had left it behind. He was not likely to come back for it now with the UDR on his tail.

'What have you there?' Sam asked, looking at the holdall.

'Och, it's Pat's. In all that fuss, I was left holding it. I'll leave it in with Jimmy McGuigan, he can keep it for him.'

'Oh, he's away. I just saw him come out of the shop. A fellow came by in a white van and picked him up. God knows where he's gone. Maybe he's off to Belfast for the Sunday. The wife's away . . . and when the wife's away . . . funny . . .'

Belle's voice was sharp. 'What's funny?'

'Och . . . he's very friendly . . . knows everybody's business. I have had a feeling about him for some time now.' He scratched his chin.

'Mrs Crawford knows everybody's business.'

'Oh yes, but she's a Protestant. No, there is something about Jimmy which I think I might investigate. He'll be back after the weekend no doubt. I'll drop the bag in, it would give me a chance to talk to him.'

'I wonder when Pat will be back?'

'I wouldn't think he'd be back till after Christmas,' Sam said, walking to his car. 'The school term ends soon. There's the other teacher. He can take charge.'

She followed him. 'Well, that will do. I'll give him the bag then,' she said quietly. She would have to face up to him, tell him . . . settle it.

Sam opened the passenger door for her. 'I don't want you working down there any more, with him.'

'So you've said,' she replied wearily, getting inside.

He got in beside her, slamming the door. 'What do you think I am?' he demanded. She recognised his hurt thinly disguised as scorn. 'Do you expect me to just let him walk in and seduce my wife?'

'No. I didn't mean that. Please understand,' she pleaded.

'And what about the mess in Belfast?' he argued.

'You know about that?'

'Do you take me for a fool? What are you going to do about it?'

'I'm not going back, if that's what you mean. I'm not going through all that . . . you can tell Sergeant McEvoy . . . I don't care what the police do to me . . . I don't care what you say . . . Sam! Do you hear me?' He sat immobile staring ahead. Suddenly he wasn't listening to her. He turned and she saw to her surprise that there were tears in his eyes. 'We want you, your place is with us, with the boys, with me. Oh, I know we haven't spoken to each other properly for years . . . there was always something between us. John . . . all that.' His voice was hoarse.

'Conor says he wants to be a farmer, like you. And he also wants to be a soldier, like you . . .'

'And Rory tells me that he wants to be a schoolteacher . . . like Pat Quinn, he told me, just like Pat Quinn.' Sam looked at Belle not disguising his hurt now. 'The man's a womaniser, it's well known. But he seems like a good teacher, I'll not begrudge him that.'

There now, Belle thought, I am divided. My life is cut in two. Sam has taken away Conor, and Pat will take away Rory. I only wanted the best for my boys. I cannot choose Pat, and how can I go back to Sam? Both ways I will be involved in all this killing . . . I cannot escape it.

'Belle!' Sam leaned towards her, grasping her head, tangling his fingers in her hair and pulling her to him, seeking her lips with his own in a surge of feelings that he had been bottling up for days, ever since he had tried to make her respond to him that night she came home. 'I need you,' he insisted, kissing her hard, savagely, demanding, his tongue seeking between her teeth. She's different, he thought, she wants me now, for the first time I know it, for years she's been keeping some part of herself hidden from me. Now it's different. I can feel it. Every part of her. His hands sought her body and grasped it savagely, reassuring him of its contours. She felt herself respond with an impatient hunger that startled her. 'Belle,' he muttered, 'you do feel it, you do want me, I know it.' She could feel his fingers seeking roughly, aggressively. Pat had been gentle. As if he sensed this, Sam's hands slowed to a soft teasing. 'You want me! Say it!'

'Yes, yes, yes,' she murmured at last, her fingers seeking him.

Eventually he drew back and stared at her boldly. 'I'm right. We are right . . . you and I,' he said with satisfaction. He started the car.

'Sam?' Belle asked, puzzled. 'We're going the wrong way . . .'

'Something I have to do . . . at the House . . .' He grinned at her.

'What did you forget?'

'I'm just remembering,' he said, running his hand up her thigh.

'Sam? Have you been up all night?'

He gave her a triumphant look. 'I'm not tired. Come on, woman, there are things I want to do with you.' The car sped up the road.

'About the –' she started.

'The House? It's a good solid house. It's time the new generation took it over.' He turned to her, winking. 'We might get you a new kitchen.'

'No . . . be serious . . . I wanted to talk about the job . . . at the school . . . I'm not going back there,' she said.

'You're not?' He looked at her joyfully. 'Well, if you want a job, then, the answer is the orchard. Would you not like to take it over? They could be your trees, couldn't they? You know a lot about them, from John and all . . . the orchard has always been special, hasn't it?'

Belle looked at him with a new understanding. Her beloved Sam. John was dead, today, she was sure of it, she could scatter his ashes in the orchard, lose those precious fugitive moments amidst his trees. And she would put all that madness with Pat behind her.

Pat's small holdall was heavy on her feet. She lifted it on to her lap. Something childlike in her made her slide the zip open. There were some assorted socks, a knobbly tweed sweater. She put in her hand and curled her fingers into the sweater. There was something cold, hard, metallic, unyielding, wrapped inside it. She knew at once what it was. The Armalite. From last night. The butt neatly folded. Neatly packed. No wonder the bag had felt heavy on her feet.

She felt Sam's keen eyes on her, and helplessly shook her head.